firewall

R. J. Pineiro

TOR®

A TOM DOHERTY ASSOCIATES BOOK
NEW YORK

This is a work of fiction. All the characters and events portrayed in this book are either products of the author's imagination or are used fictitiously.

FIREWALL

A Tor Book
Published by Tom Doherty Associates, LLC
175 Fifth Avenue
New York, NY 10010

www.tor.com

Tor® is a registered trademark of Tom Doherty Associates, LLC.

ISBN: 0-765-34015-1
Library of Congress Catalog Card Number: 2001054707

First edition: March 2002
First mass market edition: February 2003

Printed in the United States of America

0 9 8 7 6 5 4 3 2 1

For my awesome in-laws, Mike and Linda Wiltz,
for loving me as one of their own.

And

For St. Jude, saint of the impossible,
for continuing to make it possible

author's note and acknowledgments

The field of Artificial Intelligence holds the promise of a better tomorrow for the human race. The explosion of raw computing power and cheap memory, combined with the exponential growth of the world's computer matrix (a.k.a. the Internet), serves as a powerful springboard to propel this very exciting field to a level that is bound to surprise even the most skeptical of critics. AI is already here in many ways, you just have to know where to look. As I write this on a rainy day in Texas in 2001, there are computer chips out there with the capability of repairing themselves. There are AI systems that can help you shop online, that can recommend magazines and periodicals based on your interests, that can assist you in finding the music and movies that best suit your needs, that can even find the home of your dreams. There are AI systems (actually called expert systems) planned for the steering and control systems of future cars. One such system, codenamed RALPH, recently drove a vehicle autonomously from Pittsburgh to San Diego averaging sixty-three miles per hour, day and night, rain or shine. Doctors depend more and more on expert systems for accurate diagnosis. A team in Australia is developing a pragmatic legal expert system that is already challenging the most seasoned attorneys. And don't forget the world-famous Deep Blue chess player from IBM, the reigning world champion.

The benefits of decades of artificial intelligence developments now assist us in our everyday lives, creating an abundance of creature comforts targeted at improving our way of life. This book, which focuses on the future of artificial intelligence and the dangers it poses to our way of life if allowed to grow unchecked, became a reality thanks to the support and diligent efforts from a lot of very talented people.

Being a writer is in many ways like being an astronaut. There is a whole infrastructure supporting your efforts, but at the end of the day, most of the credit (or blame) falls on a single person. This writer, who as a kid dreamed of becoming an astronaut—like so many kids of his generation—received a whole lot of help from a number of very smart individuals who so generously poured their personal time into this project. As always, however, any errors that remain are mine and only mine.

Lory Anne, my dear friend, wife, and soul mate, for your support and unconditional love. None of this would be possible without you.

My dear son, Cameron Rogelio. When I started writing fiction you were just an infant. Now you are already in middle school and making both Mom and I very proud not just with your accomplishments, but with your kind, giving, and loving personality. Your moral values and positive outlook will carry you far in life.

Tom Doherty, the finest publisher in the business, for your continued confidence and support. It is always a pleasure dealing with you as well as with your professional and personable staff. Thanks for allowing me to be a member of the Tor family.

Bob Gleason, my editor and friend, for your outstanding guidance and insightful feedback, and for all of the good times both in Texas and New York. Thanks also goes to Bob's editorial assistant, Brian Callaghan, as well as the rest of the Tor/Forge folks for looking after my interests.

Matthew Bialer, my skilled agent at Trident Media, for holding my hand across the unpredictable waters of the publishing industry. Your support, guidance, and encouragement continue to steer my career in the right direction.

My appreciation goes to Ralph Peters, David Hagberg, and Clive Cussler for your support of this project.

My friend Dave who is always there to share his vast

knowledge of weapons, systems, and even a thing or two about government agencies that shall remain unnamed.

Speaking of shadowy agencies and labs, a very special thanks goes to Dr. T for your "unofficial" review of the manuscript and for your helpful comments on the future of Artificial Intelligence.

Many thanks also go to the rest of my family, now spread all over the place, from Louisiana and Dallas to El Salvador and Venezuela. I love you and think about each and every one of you all the time.

And last, but certainly not least, are all of my colleagues at Advanced Micro Devices, the place I call my second home, having spent nearly two decades of my life working my way through five generations of microprocessors. Thanks go to everyone who, over the years, has taught, influenced, supported, helped, or encouraged me.

God bless,
R. J. Pineiro

There are now in the world machines
that can think, that can create, that
can learn. Moreover, their ability to
do these things is going to increase
rapidly until—in a visible future—
the range of problems they can handle
will be coextensive with the range to
which the human mind has been applied.
—Herbert Simon

It is not the critic who counts, not
the man who points out how the strong
man stumbled, or where the doer of
deeds could have done them better.
The credit belongs to the man who is
actually in the arena; whose face is
marred by dust and sweat and blood;
who strives valiantly; who errs and
comes short again and again; who
knows the great enthusiasms, the
great devotions, and spends himself
in a worthy cause; who, at the best,
knows in the end the triumph of high
achievement; and who, at worst, if he
fails, at least fails while daring
greatly, so that his place shall
never be with those cold and timid
souls who know neither victory nor
defeat.
—Theodore Roosevelt

firewall

prologue

A gray layer of rain clouds drifted across the northern California sky. Vinod Malani peeked at the gathering storm through the stretch limousine's tinted glass, already peppered with water droplets.

Malani returned his attention to the gorgeous Asian sitting across from him, a gin and tonic in her hand, her catlike eyes taking him in with the same greedy stare that had prompted Malani to pick her up at a nearby bar in Palo Alto.

Fifty-three years old and recently widowed, Malani's mourning had pushed him to seek the companionship of prostitutes, and the twenty-something Asian beauty sitting across from him promised a night of carnal pleasures before he had to spend another long day as chief technical officer of FoxComm, one of the nation's leading high-tech corporations.

He smiled inwardly while undressing her with his stare. The whore thought she was high-class by demanding a thousand bucks an hour. Malani's CTO salary, bonuses, and stock options could afford her and ten thousand others like her.

"So, where are you from originally, honey?" he asked, feigning interest.

"I was born in Seoul," she replied in a slightly accented English, slowly crossing and uncrossing her legs, giving the aging executive a peek of things to come.

"How long have you been living in this country?"

"About six years."

Damn, she was beautiful. Malani couldn't remember a better looking hooker. Almost as tall as his six feet, with an incredibly thin waistline, spectacular breasts, shapely long legs, and a porcelain face that could belong to an angel. Her charcoal eyes were set high over her cheekbones flanking a fine nose. She moved her full red lips slowly as she spoke—in a way that awakened Malani's most primal instincts.

Even the girls in Vegas didn't look this great.

"And how long have you been in this business?"

She pouted those lips—nearly getting him salivating—as she thought about that for a moment, before replying, "A few months, but not very often. Just when I need extra cash for tuition and books, and *only* if I like the potential client."

Malani smiled. He loved screwing college girls, who were always far cleaner than career hookers, and this one not only looked good but also smelled great.

The driver pulled up in front of the Fairmont Hotel in San Jose. A uniformed bellboy opened the door for them, assisting her first while nodding cordially, though his eyes could not avoid running up and down her provocative figure.

Malani smiled to himself. There had been a time when he worked at a hotel while going to school and had seen rich businessmen bring their whores to places like this for the evening.

Now it's my turn.

He handed the bellboy a crisp twenty-dollar bill before following his escort through the glass doors and into the sumptuous lobby, exquisitely decorated with rugs, leather furniture, elaborate moldings, and striking artwork—all in soothing pastels. Beethoven streamed softly out of unseen speakers.

Hand in hand, they headed for the elevators, where he stabbed the button for the tenth floor. Malani kept a room here, paid for by his expense account through an elaborate scheme worked out by his lawyer a few months after his wife died and he began doing this to help him deal with the grief—without realizing just how damned addictive it would become.

But it could be worse, he thought, justifying his actions. *I could be snorting coke instead.*

The penthouse faced the mountains leading to the ocean.

Malani let her enjoy the view for a moment, quite certain that she had never been in a place like this before.

All the better.

Another little habit he had developed was that of impressing people, particularly members of the opposite sex whom he would soon be screwing.

The Korean courtesan turned around, a gun in hand. She was smiling, revealing a perfect row of glistening teeth beneath the crimson lipstick.

It took him a moment before he said, "What in the *hell* is the meaning of this?"

"It's all about information, Mr. Malani."

He narrowed his gaze. "How do you know my name?"

Her smile widened. "That is not important."

Malani wasn't certain how to reply to that.

She added, "What *is* important to my people . . . is the information you have regarding government contracts."

"Contracts?"

"Yes, in particular the work that FoxComm is doing for the NSA."

NORTH KOREAN TROOPS INVADE DEMILITARIZED ZONE
WEB POSTED AT 7:55 A. M. EDT

SEOUL, SOUTH KOREA (CNN)—More than six thousand North Korean soldiers entered the joint security area of the Demilitarized Zone between North and South Korea yesterday, crossing four hundred yards into the South Korean portion of the DMZ. The incursion was the most recent violation of the 1953 armistice between the two countries. Over a hundred tanks and several heavy artillery units accompanied the soldiers as they were driven in a large convoy of trucks across the Panmunjon border crossing area within the buffer zone. Dozens of North Korean soldiers opened fire using small arms. South Korean border troops returned the fire, which continued until dawn without any reported casualties. No heavy artillery fire by either side was reported. In addition to the troops in the DMZ, North Korea has mobilized what a U.S. military analyst estimates to be over 350,000 soldiers to within five miles of the DMZ.

South Korean President Kim Young-Sam convened an emergency meeting late on Sunday of his security chiefs. "North Korea's reckless act will be met with an iron-tight defense. We are a sovereign nation and are prepared to defend ourselves against any invading force," a presidential spokesman quoted Kim as saying at the meeting. In response to North Korea's latest move, an undisclosed portion of South Korea's 700,000-man army is being mobilized to reinforce the 100,000 soldiers already patroling the most heavily guarded border in the world. Backing South Korean troops are 40,000 combat-ready U.S. troops.

The United Nations command in Seoul has placed its 20,000 troops in the region on high alert. The U.N. Secretary-General plans to arrive in North Korea on Tuesday to meet with the Pyongyang government.

A White House spokesman issued a press release just an hour ago, stating that the President has been in contact with the South Korean President to discuss alternatives. The White House made no comment on the strong possibility of additional U.S. troops being deployed to the area. The entire incident did not come as a surprise to the White House, which has been making progress in recent years to apply pressure to North Korea and other rogue nations who sponsor international terrorism.

Professional Habits

Dressed in a dark business suit, Bruce Tucker stepped out of the rear of the armored Lexus sedan, closed the door behind him, and remained in the two-foot gap between the black automobile and the curb, inspecting the crowd of reporters, photographers, and high-tech enthusiasts gathered outside of the Moscone Center, San Francisco's premier meeting and exhibition facility, site of this year's West Coast Computer Symposium.

A moment later the front passenger-side door swung open, and he was followed by one of his agents, a slim-built executive protector retained by Tucker to assist him in today's event.

According to the arrangements Tucker had made with Moscone security the week before—and had rehearsed to the point of obsession every day since—four men, also dressed in business suits, approached him, forming a semicircle around him while facing the crowd. Tucker's instructions to Moscone security had been simple: Keep your eyes on the crowd, where a threat might originate, *not* on the principal; keep your hands free at all times; do not address anyone in the crowd, even if they are insulting you, since that could be nothing more than a diversion created by an assassin; and above all, stay crisp. Remember that an assassin only has to get lucky once, but a protector must get lucky *every* time.

Luck.

Tucker frowned. He made his *own* luck through rigorous planning and by following the rules he had learned from Ozaki Kabuki, the old Japanese-American trainer during his years with the Secret Service following a turbulent career

with Central Intelligence—the agency that recruited Tucker
from the Navy SEALs.

Kabuki had taught Tucker that unlike the classic bodyguard stereotype, a protection specialist didn't equate with
bulky muscles, a booming voice, aggressive manners, and
multiple concealed weapons, but with careful planning,
proper dress codes, etiquette, the ability to blend in with the
surroundings, the physical and mental skills to fight if required, and above all, absolute loyalty to his principal. As a
true executive protector, Tucker followed traditions dating
back to twelfth-century Japan, when samurai warriors protected the life and estate of their *daimyos*, the feudal barons
under the shogun, or military governor of Japan. To be a
samurai meant more than physical skill. It meant following
strict codes of honor, of etiquette, of absolute loyalty to your
daimyo. Samurais protected the lives of Japan's heads of
state, just as members of the United States Secret Service
protected the lives of our heads of state.

Just as I protect my principals.

Satisfied that Moscone security was following his instructions, Tucker verified that a dozen local cops were keeping
the assembly at bay. Last week, when the time and date for
his principal's scheduled speech had been confirmed, Tucker
had worked out an arrangement with the San Francisco Police Department to assign officers to this detail—for a hefty
fee, of course. But money wasn't an object when it came to
protecting the life of one of the most prominent figures in
today's high-tech world.

The sun hung high in the northern California skies this
cool morning, reflecting off the tinted glass of the armored
sedan—though no one but a professional would have been
able to recognize that the Lexus had had all of its windows
replaced with a polycarbonate glass laminate capable of with-
standing anything from a .44 Magnum round to a NATO
7.62mm tungsten tip high-velocity bullet. The Lexus, modified per Tucker's specifications, also included armor plating
beneath the surface of the roof and all doors, a fragmentation
blanket beneath the floor, ballistic steel covers for the battery

and engine compartment, and self-inflating tires.

Tucker surveyed the first of this detail's choke points: the narrow passageway formed by the police barricades and the officers holding back agitated fans and the press, which his principal will have to move through before reaching the doors leading to the upper lobby of the center's South Hall.

Satisfied that SFPD and Moscone security were conforming to prearranged rules, Tucker spoke into his lapel microphone. "One, two, and three, hit the street."

Three agents emerged from the chase car, a second armored Lexus, but light cream in color, parked behind the first. The color schemes, devised by Tucker, avoided attracting the unnecessary attention of two identical dark luxury sedans driving in tandem. The agents were also all of medium stature and built, wearing dark suits and flesh-colored earpieces, which kept them in constant communications with Tucker, the shift leader of this detail.

Moscone security moved out in a radial pattern toward the cordoned crowd, letting Tucker's team approach the rear of the limousine. While keeping their eyes on the potential threat around them, the agents created a diamond formation around Mortimer Fox as he emerged a moment later dressed in an Italian double-breasted suit. None of the agents present here today—Tucker included—wore double-breasted suits, not only because real security specialists always dressed down a notch from their principals to avoid upstaging them, but also because such suits were meant to be buttoned, impairing the ability of an agent to reach for a concealed handgun.

The crowd welcomed Fox with loud cheers. The cameras from two networks began to roll. Tucker and his detail were showered with photographic flashes, which lowered their ability to monitor the crowd. But in spite of the annoyance the press created for celebrities like Fox, Tucker welcomed them, and even worked with them, often positioning them up front, where they could take the best pictures and live footage—in the process creating a buffer zone between his principal and the crowd. News people were not the enemy. They were here doing their jobs.

Tucker heard someone protesting and his eyes cut immediately to the source: a trio of skinheads holding up a poster depicting a red, white, and blue American eagle slaughtering a fox. Beneath it, a banner complained against FoxComm's predatory business practices, which had driven many competitors out of business, empowering Fox to create one of the largest monopolies in the history of this nation. Tucker was used to people protesting against FoxComm, whose founder and CEO had contracted him six months ago for executive protection after the corporation's Chief Technical Officer, Vinod Malani, was kidnapped, tortured, and murdered by what the media had described as a group of fanatics.

Tucker frowned.

Fanatics my ass.

The whole incident smelled like a professional terrorist job, not only successfully abducting Malani, but getting away cleanly, leaving no clues for the police. Malani's driver and his bodyguard were found shot dead in the CTO's limousine outside the Fairmont Hotel, which the executive visited quite often with young female companions. Some members of the hotel staff recalled Malani arriving the afternoon of his disappearance in the company of an Asian woman, but details beyond that were sketchy at best. Malani's body was found by a jogger in San Francisco's Candlestick Park the following week, missing his genitals, both eyes, all fingernails, and his tongue. In addition, his skin had hundreds of tiny slits, inflicted with a razor to cause maximum pain while keeping the subject alive. The wounds were encrusted with salt to enhance the level of pain. And again, the police found zero clues to launch a real investigation. Fanatics, who typically plan such strikes with little consideration for an escape after committing the crime, would certainly have left a trail for the authorities, as was the case with the World Trade Center and Pentagon attacks. Also, fanatics would have limited their exposure to a hit-and-run strike. They would had avoided an elaborate kidnapping scheme, which included securing a safe house to conduct the torture, and then another round of potential exposure when dumping the body. And of course, there was no manifesto released to the press, no message to the world explaining the reason for the violent crime. Malani had just vanished that evening at the hotel and had returned slain, without an explanation, without evidence, without a motive.

Tucker had speculated that Malani had been kidnapped for information or perhaps passwords—or something else that would lead the terrorists to money. But nothing was missing from any of FoxComm's accounts, and their passwords—as well as any other passwords known to Malani—had been changed the morning after his disappearance. Malani's personal accounts were also intact.

A hideous crime without an apparent motive, but shocking enough for Mortimer Fox to dismiss the bodyguard service contracted to protect him, and retain Tucker to protect his own life.

The executive protector regarded the cheering fans while taking his position to the immediate right of his principal, keeping his left hand near Fox's back, but without touching him. If the need ever arose, Tucker could shove Fox away while stepping in to shield him with his own body—all the while keeping his shooting hand free to reach for the Colt .45-caliber pistol, one of the preferred concealed handguns of the U.S. Secret Service.

That was another difference between a plain-vanilla bodyguard, like those with Malani that afternoon, and an executive protector. Tucker would take a bullet for his principal, just as a samurai would sacrifice himself to save his *daimyo*—as Kabuki had drilled into him back in the Secret Service.

Total and unquestionable loyalty.

Although his training viewed a firearm as a last resort, Tucker carried one in a holster that fit inside his pants, secured in place behind the belt loop on his left side. Some agents—none on Tucker's detail—preferred shoulder holsters, but those were not practical for close operations with a principal, mostly because the weapon couldn't be easily and quickly withdrawn.

Another lesson from Kabuki was that of hardening the target, making his protectee—his *daimyo*—a harder target for an assassin. He accomplished this by using Kabuki's principle of concentric security circles—the origin of which dated back to twelfth-century Japan, when a shogun would surround himself with various concentric layers of protection. At the center of the circle was the *daimyo* himself, whom Tucker had spent many hours with, increasing his level of awareness. The next circle was Tucker, standing right next to Fox, ready to take a bullet for him if it ever became necessary. The agents covering each of the four points of the compass in their diamond formation constituted the third protective circle. The fourth was formed by the Moscone staff, which created a protective layer beyond the diamond. The police cordoning the crowd defined the fifth and last defensive circle between the principal and the uncontrolled crowd.

The detail began to move. As it did, the drivers in the principal's sedan and the chase car locked their doors but kept the engines running in case an unforeseen event required the immediate evacuation of Mortimer Fox. Tucker had made previous arrangements with the local police force and the hotel to let him keep the two vehicles parked in front of the lobby's entrance on Howard Street.

"Mr. Fox! Mr. Fox! Please!" shouted several fans who looked like college kids, thrusting open hands past the police barrier as the detail approached the bottleneck at the choke point. The kids had managed to squirm their way to the front, by the reporters and SFPD officers.

Against Tucker's better judgment, Fox stopped and turned toward the young fans. Although he had many enemies, Mortimer Fox nevertheless stood for the ideal American entrepreneur, creating an empire with his bare hands, a true rags-to-riches story, a pursuer *and* an achiever of the American dream, and an inspiration to people like the kids wearing Stanford T-shirts standing in the front row wishing to shake the hand of this Silicon Valley legend. Tucker knew Fox had a soft spot in his heart for Stanford University, his alma mater, to which he contributed heavily every year to bolster its advanced technology R & D department.

As Fox turned left, the agent on that side became the new north of the diamond formation while the other agents rotated with the principal, maintaining a tight 360-degree coverage.

Fox shook hands with a fan, and a second, and a third. He was about to continue toward the doors but the last kid, built like a football player, didn't let go, gripping the tycoon's hand so tightly that the elderly Fox winced in pain. As part of his research, Tucker had reviewed Fox's medical file, learning that the elderly executive, in addition to having a weak heart, suffered from osteoporosis. He didn't need a gorilla stressing the weakened bones of his hand.

To the untrained observer, Tucker did nothing more than smile at the fan and say, "Excuse me," before ushering Fox toward the revolving doors. But in those few seconds, the protection specialist, keeping his left hand behind Fox, placed his right one over the fan's hand, gripping the kid's thumb, forcing it up and away from Fox's hand. When sensing further resistance to his aikido technique, commonly known as a "thumb-peel," Tucker stomped the heel of his right shoe against the bridge of the kid's nearest foot.

"Excuse me," Tucker said, smiling as the fan cringed in pain and backed off.

Tucker used his left hand to nudge his principal, reaching the glass doors before the surprised fan got a chance to react, and went inside.

2

The Principal

They reached the holding room uneventfully, where Mortimer Fox would remain until his scheduled appearance at the convention. The windowless room, located just left of the Esplanade Ballroom, where Fox would speak prior to his tour of the exhibits one floor below, had been thoroughly checked by Tucker a week ago. He'd kept it locked until this morning, when two of his agents brought in some refreshments ahead of the detail. The holding room was Tucker's only sanctuary in otherwise high-risk territory, Fox's secured home away from home. He kept three of his agents guarding the door while his principal relaxed before show time. Close-circuit television monitors, installed at Tucker's request, provided several views of the computer exposition on Halls A, B, and C one floor below, as well as of the ballroom, where the organizing committee—also at Tucker's request—had created a makeshift stage with curtains and special lighting at one end of the fourteen-thousand-square-foot rectangular room, where over five thousand people waited for Fox to appear.

Tucker regarded his principal, watching the monitors while sitting on a sofa wearing just pants and an undershirt, today's edition of the *San Francisco Chronicle* folded across his lap. He drank from a small bottle of chilled Perrier. Fox had kicked off his shoes, removed his suit's coat, tie, and white shirt, and the Kevlar vest that Tucker insisted he wore at all public appearances—though neither Tucker nor any of his agents wore them because they were bulky and reduced mobility. The vests also made the wearer hot, so Tucker kept the car's AC very cold when transporting his principal, even if that meant chilling everyone else, so long as Fox was comfortable. He had made arrangements with the computer show's committee to keep a pair of large fans blowing cool air across the stage during Fox's speech, as well as to reduce the lighting on the stage, not just to keep his principal from overheating, but also to reduce the visibility of a possible sniper. Executive protection covered not just the protection of a principal from harm, but extended to understanding all of the idiosyncrasies of Mortimer Fox, who was a very neat and organized man, always prepared for every occasion while frowning on those who were not. Tucker knew all of Fox's habits, from the way he preferred his coffee in the morning to his sleeping and eating schedules, favorite TV channels, music, wines, and newspapers.

The latter was something that had Tucker intrigued. For reasons Fox kept all to himself, he'd always read the classified section of the *San Francisco Chronicle* first, just as he did now, with an expectant look in his eyes, followed by a disappointed sigh, before hastily setting it aside. He would pick it up in a little while and read the business section, followed by world news.

In addition to the newspaper, Fox also had another habit that Tucker found interesting. Every evening, he religiously locked himself in a room in his house and spent hours strapped to a virtual-reality system. At first a few graduate students from Stanford University would be in the VR room with him, but then they had stopped coming to the mansion, leaving the tycoon alone with his million-dollar electronic toys. "It's for therapy," Fox had once told him. Tucker had nodded politely, used to the eccentricity of his clients.

"How is your hand, Mr. Fox?" Tucker asked, standing by the only door to this room, arms resting by his sides, hands free, feet spaced a shoulder-width apart—as dictated by Kabuki's aikido training, which used balance, combined with the dynamics of movement and joint locks to overpower an opponent. His stance also conveyed a sense of readiness that set the tone for the detail, inspiring confidence in his associates while also helping deter an attack or confrontation.

The protectee grimaced as he flexed his thin fingers. "Damned kid," he said, shaking his head.

Tucker reached into his pocket and produced a small pack of prescription-strength Motrin. He handed it to Fox, who smiled and tore it open, placing both caplets in his mouth, swallowing them with a few sips of Perrier.

"You know, Bruce," he said, crossing his legs, setting the bottle on the table next to him, "I've had my share of bodyguards over the years, and some were quite good, but none of them made me feel as comfortable as when I'm with you. I guess my contacts in Washington knew who was the best in the business."

"Thank you, sir."

"No, I mean it. You take care of every last detail. I wish some of my vice presidents were as good planners as you are. I have to ride them twenty-four hours a day for them to stay on top of things. I do nothing with you except tell you where we need to go, and then I show up and follow a few rules. Everything else just magically takes care of itself."

"Just doing my job, sir," replied Tucker, smiling inwardly. He spent over sixteen hours every day, seven days a week, riding his own agents, going over the detail with excruciating precision, spending countless hours brainstorming contingencies for dozens of "what-if" scenarios, walking through the entire operation. Kabuki had drilled into him the notion that an executive protector can *never* be too prepared. When Presidential candidate Jimmy Carter was visiting Los Angeles in 1975, the protective agents thought they had considered every detail of Carter's visit, except someone forgot to check the railroad crossing times. Carter's motorcade got stuck at a crossing for over fifteen minutes in a less-than-desirable neighborhood, completely exposed to an ambush, with no way to escape.

You can never be too prepared.

"You're also very modest and quite patient with this cranky old man," said Fox. "I just wanted you to know that I do appreciate it, even if you do it only because I'm paying you a small fortune."

Tucker managed a cordial smile and a slight nod. He liked Fox, a man rich enough to purchase his own country, yet very much down to earth, having been one of five kids from a poor family in southern California. Most of Tucker's previous clientele, which ranged anywhere from rich executives to foreign dignitaries, particularly from the Middle East and South America, were spoiled and rude. Tucker had realized at an early stage of his protection career that money didn't buy manners. But Fox was different, treating the protection detail with respect, and always willing to follow Tucker's direction, including wearing those uncomfortable vests. But regardless of how amiable Fox was to him and his detail, Tucker still maintained a professional barrier, as dictated by the rules of his trade.

"Tell me, Bruce," said Fox. "You've been attending every one of my meetings for the past months. What do you think of my operation?"

Tucker's forte was security and protective services, not the business affairs of the CEO of a high-tech corporation. Although he had gotten a two-year technical degree in computer science from San Jose State University to better serve the increasing demand for protection in the growing high-tech sector, he didn't feel qualified to provide a professional opinion. His training, however, instructed him to be courteous to his client. And besides, not only did Tucker like Fox, in a way he felt sorry for the old man. First, his son, Preston, had perished a decade ago in an auto accident. Then his wife had lost a battle with cancer three years ago. Now his only daughter, Monica, apparently didn't want anything to do with him—according to the bits and pieces of information he had picked up from the house staff during the past few months.

He decided to use a diversionary tactic. Fox had held a number of meetings discussing the status of an artificial intelligence project for the government. Although Tucker never got anything beyond superficial information because he was not allowed inside the actual meeting room, he had heard enough to pique his curiosity. Figuring he could get more information on that fascinating subject while avoiding answering Fox's question, he said, "One of the things that impressed me the most, sir, was all the discussion about your work in the field of artificial intelligence."

Fox nodded. "Interested in AI, huh?"

"Just curious about what are the true capabilities of our current technology."

"What do you know about artificial intelligence, Bruce?"

Tucker looked in the distance, remembering what little he had read up on the subject. "I always saw it as the creation of machines that can think for themselves, that don't require human intervention to think through a problem and solve it."

"Not bad," said Fox, sipping his Perrier. "But in order to classify machines as thinking, we first need to define intelligence. So, let me ask you." Fox arched his brows into triangles, amusement lurking in his eyes. He obviously loved the subject and enjoyed discussing it. "What *is* intelligence, Bruce?"

Tucker raised his shoulder slightly. "Problem solving? The ability to understand a problem and methodically solve it?"

"Sure, but let's break it down. First the machine needs the perception to understand the problem, to comprehend it. Then it needs to stipulate solutions, in the end choosing one. Now the problem could be simple mathematics, or more complicated, like Deep Blue, the IBM system that beat chess master Kasparov, or *far* more complex, like the navigation and autopilot systems in a jetliner, capable of landing in dense fog, or even beyond that, like the systems aboard the space shuttle. Each of those examples includes observations and a decision-making process based on those observations. Is that enough to qualify as AI?"

Tucker was rapidly getting in deeper waters than his limited knowledge could withstand. Tentatively, he said, "I think AI is more than that."

"Correct, and I'll tell you what AI really is, Bruce. There was a British computer scientist by the name of Alan Turing. He came up with the best test to determine if a machine that displayed problem-solving capability could be qualified to also be called intelligent. His simple method became known as the Turing test."

"The Turing test?" Tucker had heard of it before but couldn't remember what it was.

"Very simple. Turing stated that a computer would deserve to be called intelligent if it could deceive an average human into believing that it was human."

Tucker thought about that for a moment, then said, "That would take some serious work, Mr. Fox."

"You'd better believe it, Bruce. We are surrounded by problem-solving machines, from autopilots and automated assembly lines to a whole variety of military toys, many of them used during Desert Storm and later on in Afghanistan."

"Like the Patriot missile system?" Tucker offered.

Fox nodded. "Among others. But that's a good example of an expert system."

"An *expert system*?"

"That's the technical name used for systems that approach true artificial intelligence, but still fail to pass the Turing test. Take your Patriot example. It is called an expert system because it is indeed quite a marvelous machine, capable of tracking incoming missiles and coordinating the launch of interceptors, then guiding them to destroy the missiles, as occurred in the war against Iraq. However, a Patriot missile system, as incredibly advanced as it was for its time, would *never* pass as a human. The same goes for many other expert systems, like heads-up displays, camera-bearing robots performing quality control tasks at assembly lines, and guidance systems—all designed to assist human beings in their tasks, but never *replacing* a human being, and certainly never capable of fooling a human being into making him or her think that it is human—the Turing test."

"So," Tucker asked, "is there a machine in existence today that could be called intelligent according to the Turing test?"

Fox grinned. "That's classified, pal. Maybe one day I'll tell you about it. By the way, nice try."

"Excuse me, sir?"

"Nice try. You know, to divert my original question with

this little AI chat. Now tell me, what do you *really* think of my operation?"

The guy was a definitely a hawk. Still, Tucker didn't want to provide an opinion on something he didn't feel qualified to judge. He chose instead to use humor as another attempt to avoid answering his question. "What do I really think of your operation, Mr. Fox? I think your executive staff doesn't spend enough time at the gym, sir."

Fox raised a brow and nodded approvingly. "Another good try, Bruce. But I know you can do better than that."

Tucker frowned. Fox would not let up. And this wasn't the first time that a principal had tried to get personal with him. It wasn't at all unexpected. Kabuki had told him more than once that the more professional a security agent remained in every aspect of the job, the more a principal would like to know about him, especially if the principal, like Fox, was pretty much surrounded with yes-men. In the weeks attending Fox's meetings, Tucker had noticed that no one disagreed with this man. The aging tycoon was the only law in town, the lone shepherd guiding his flock toward higher profit margins, market share, and stock prices. As large as FoxComm had become in the past twenty years, designing and mass producing everything from video games and security software, to mainframe computers, personal communicators, satellites, and apparently even artificial intelligence systems, it had been pretty much a one-man show, with Mortimer Fox on center stage directing traffic, micromanaging every division, coaching every vice president, ruling like a ruthless dictator, and vigilantly controlling the purse strings of the corporation, always keeping expenses low while maximizing profits. In addition, Fox always—*always*—controlled at least 51 percent of FoxComm common stock—not that he was in any danger of being booted by angry stockholders. Over 450 percent return on investment in the past five years had Wall Street dancing—and all due to Fox's uncanny ability to run an efficient operation, which kept the stock defying gravity, even when the Dow Jones and NASDAQ indices headed south. Doing more with less was Fox's

motto, which allowed him to run many competitors out of
business by shipping to market better goods at lower prices—
and always on time. FoxComm was the Wal-Mart of the
high-tech world. But that level of success had come at a
severe personal price for the wrinkled man slouched on the
sofa regarding Tucker with intelligent blue eyes. According
to the kitchen staff, Mrs. Fox had lived a very lonely existence while Mortimer Fox was out there barking orders
across his global empire. She had been diagnosed with cancer three years ago, dying months later—while he was away
on business. His daughter, Monica, had grown up in boarding
schools, gotten a degree in liberal arts from Berkeley, and
was now living a Bohemian life somewhere in Italy—again,
according to the staff. Word at the estate was that she resented her father for having neglected them all those years—
including his lack of moral support after Preston's accident.
Apparently Monica had been the one consoling her mother
while Fox was away gaining market share. Now all that this
man had left of the family were the pictures scattered
throughout the mansion. His wife had been a beautiful
woman. Her looks had certainly been passed on to Monica,
whose hazel eyes and tanned skin had reminded him of . . .

Tucker tried hard not to think about his CIA years, about
the one time when he'd had a personal life, a family.

Fox's eyes continued to focus on him, waiting for an answer.

Tucker decided to take a chance and said, "I think you're
a slave driver, Mr. Fox."

The comment certainly grabbed Mortimer Fox. He smiled.
"Keep going."

"You're used to pounding your subordinates into submis-
sion, sir. I've seen you turn some of your vice presidents into
Jell-O at your meetings. But you also deserve most of the
credit for your company's success. You made it all happen."

Fox smiled. "I've always suspected that I didn't intimidate
you."

"Mr. Fox, you contracted my services because I ranked
among the top executive protectors in the business. I can't

afford to be intimidated by you because I wouldn't be any good to you then."

Fox leaned forward, hesitated for a moment, then said, "I'll let you in on a little secret, Bruce."

"Sir?"

"Sure, I did hire you partly because of your professional record. But that wasn't everything."

Tucker was confused. "I'm not sure I follow, sir. If it wasn't my professional record, what was it?"

"Your *personal* record."

Apprehensive, Tucker said, "Personal record?"

"I am a man with vast resources, Bruce. I know a lot about a lot of people. While searching for the ideal protector, I had to make sure that my final selection comprehended both the professional *and* the personal angle. I had to see what drove the man to whom I would be entrusting my life. I needed to make certain that this man would not hesitate to risk his own life to save me. So I used my resources to research the candidates, finally selecting you."

"Why me?"

"For one thing, Bruce . . . you have little to lose."

Tucker was at a loss for words.

"I know about your family, about Zurich, about your terrible loss. And you have my deepest condolences."

Tucker felt a tingling shock in his gut. How did this man know about his wife, Kristina, about his son, about Zurich?

"Mr. Fox, how did you . . . that is CIA classified information."

"I have many sources, Bruce. And I hope you understand it wasn't my intention to pry into your private life. I simply had to make sure that I knew the man who would be protecting my life. I also know that the deaths were caused by a blunder at the CIA. They failed to protect them."

Tucker felt a little warm, forcing his mind to remain focused, keeping those painful images locked in his mind.

"So you see, Bruce. Like yourself, I also hate our government."

"That's not true, sir. I happen to love my country. I served it well in the military, then at the CIA, and finally at the Secret Service. I am proud of my government service. And yes, the CIA should have done a better job of protecting my family, but the mistake was all mine. I was in the process of terminating a very nasty character and should have realized that the bastard would retaliate. Also, sir, if I may say so, I don't think that my personal life is any of your business. I respect your personal life. Please respect mine."

"Bruce, please understand that I did what I did because I couldn't possibly take any chances. There's just too much at stake. I had to make sure that you were not only a straight arrow, but that you would also not hesitate in placing yourself in the line of fire. A man with a family—with someone to live for—would not sacrifice himself for me. You, at least as far as I can see, would take a bullet for me."

He gave his principal a slight bow, accepting the explanation while hiding his annoyance that Fox had been able to peek into his CIA file.

"About the government, Bruce," Fox added. "Be very careful. Don't trust them. They can turn on you in a flash, just as they turned on me, even though I provided them with wealth beyond their expectations."

"I appreciate the advice, sir. I just hope I never have to use it."

Fox leaned back on the leather sofa. "Do you know how long it's been since I was able to have a conversation with someone who wasn't afraid of me?"

Tucker shook his head. That was another thing he had realized while running details for so many rich people. The old saying was indeed true: It was very lonely at the top. With all of his mansions, jets, yachts, cars, and servants, Mortimer Fox was a very lonely man, truly desperate for an honest chat.

"I'll tell you how long it's been, Bruce." Fox continued. "Not counting the sparring matches I've had with my daughter—which is a subject in itself—it would be almost three years ago, when Eleanor died."

Tucker was getting increasingly uncomfortable with this

conversation. In less than three minutes, Mortimer Fox had gotten more personal with him than any previous principal. Still, he didn't have the heart to push back too hard, even if the crusty bastard had pulled some strings at the CIA to get into his dossier. At the moment all Tucker saw was a lonely old man genuinely interested in holding a personal conversation with him.

"I'm sorry about your wife, sir. The staff at the house remembers her with great affection." Tucker thought about his own wife, about his son.

"She was an incredible woman, Bruce. Supported me all those years, while I was pushing FoxComm ahead. Losing Preston just about killed her, but she still maintained a front while I kept on driving the business."

"Sounds like a very special lady, sir."

Fox's eyes gravitated back to the monitors. "I sacrificed my personal life—her personal life—for them." He pointed a finger at the crowd in the exposition hall before adding, "I know the American public appreciates what I have done to move this nation forward in the high-tech race, bringing computing and telecommunications capabilities to the masses. The irony, of course, is that after so much effort, so much personal sacrifice, the government wants to punish me for my success." He raised his open hands to Tucker and added, "With these old and frail hands, Bruce, I created tens of thousands of jobs, created a lot of wealth for this nation, paid *billions* in taxes, and still, the clowns in Washington want my head on a platter."

He paused, his wrinkles trembling as he added, "Fucking politicians. Regardless of what you hear in the press, at the end of the day those piranhas simply can't stand successful entrepreneurs like me, defeating the odds, gobbling market share, giving serious competition to old and institutionalized corporations. And do you know why?"

Tucker had been around enough important people to know how close some corporations were to the government. "Campaign contributions, sir?"

"That's just one of many strings connecting some of my

competitors to Washington. And my competition is squealing like stuck pigs, Bruce, forcing Washington to take steps against my company. But they have *no idea* who they're messing with."

Tucker had followed the ongoing battle between Washington and FoxComm on charges of having created a monopoly, like Microsoft had done in the software world. His interest in the debate had peaked when he had been offered the opportunity to protect Fox after Malani's kidnapping and murder. But Washington was nowhere in its quest to tear up FoxComm. The old tycoon had so far outfoxed the government through a series of legal maneuvers that seemed to anticipate the politicians. Fox always managed to remain a step ahead of Uncle Sam while keeping a firm grip on the company's reigns. There was even a story floating around that Fox had certain ties with the Italian Mafia in this country and abroad and regularly used their services to keep Washington at bay.

"Does the government stand a chance, sir?"

"Not while I'm alive," Fox replied. "I have enough dirt on those bastards to make their heads spin. And though I can't prove it, my contacts have gathered enough *circumstantial* evidence to suggest that someone in Washington gave the order on Vinod."

Now Tucker was getting worried. Fox was sharing information Tucker didn't really want to know. Information meant involvement, and while at the CIA such information was vital for survival, in the executive protection business it was a liability. Tucker didn't want to know about Fox's secret affairs with anyone, particularly powerhouses such as the U.S. government and the Mafia. He couldn't possibly do anything else for the protection of the old man, which meant that he already knew everything he needed to know about Fox and his business. A thought did occur to him: If Fox was indeed associated with the Mafia, then why use Tucker for protection? Why not use the Mafia itself? Could it be because that would make his connection too obvious?

"Sir, I don't think that I should—"

Fox cut him off. "You know, Bruce, those bastards have failed to get rid of me through the legal system, so now they have gone covert on me. They've chosen other methods to persuade me to step down and give up control of FoxComm, including killing my CTO."

"Sir, the United States government would never—"

Fox raised a hand, before giving Tucker some of the same straight talk he frequently gave his vice presidents. "For having been in the CIA and the Secret Service, you sure are naïve, Bruce. Or maybe you are *acting* naïve. In either case the situation is the same. Uncle Sam wants my head and he will do anything and everything in his power to get it. And that's where you come in. I need you and my doctor to keep me breathing for long enough to see this government witch hunt publicly squashed."

"I'll handle my end, sir," said Tucker, hoping to finish this conversation. "And your physician claims that you should have plenty of years left, as long as you don't overstress yourself. You need to keep the excitement level down." As part of his services, Tucker spent an hour each week being briefed by Fox's personal physician on his client's condition. The physician provided Tucker with that week's prescription drugs, which he carried with him at all times, including the Motrin to alleviate the chronic pain in Fox's joints.

"Excitement level down? Are you kidding me?" Fox mused, shaking his head. "You know as well as anyone that my life's a roller coaster. There's no stop to the excitement until the day I die."

As Tucker thought of a reply, someone knocked on the door three times, paused, and knocked three more times. Tucker unlocked it after listening to the prearranged code. A man Tucker recognized as a member of the hosting committee stepped inside, escorted by one of the agents Tucker had guarding the room.

"The crowd is waiting, Mr. Fox. You were due five minutes ago," he said in a nasal voice. He was of short stature and very thin. A navy-blue suit hung loosely from his coat-hanger shoulders. Tucker had intentionally delayed

Fox's appearance to throw off an assassin's schedule. Fox would also deliver his advertised "forty-five minute speech" in half the time, again to harden the target to potential threat.

Fox waved his hand dismissively. That was Tucker's cue to get rid of him.

"Mr. Fox will be out very soon," Tucker said, signaling his agent to escort this man back outside. "Please apologize to the audience."

As he left, Fox stood, put on the white vest, the shirt over it, then the tie and coat.

He slipped his feet into his black leather shoes and looked at his protector.

"How do I look?"

"The crowd will love you, Mr. Fox."

"Only because I made them all very wealthy."

"Remember your position once you go onto the stage, sir."

Fox made a face. "How can I forget?"

Tucker had spread masking tape on the floor to delineate the path that Fox would take from the side of the stage to the microphone, and back after completing his speech. The overhead lights had been reduced along the path and also where he would stand. As a final touch, Tucker had tilted some of the stage spotlights toward the crowd to make it harder for them to see Fox clearly.

Performing one final radio check to verify that his team was in position, Tucker escorted his principal out of the holding room. A moment later the Silicon Valley hero stepped onto the stage and the audience broke into applause and cheers.

3

Panic Button

For Bruce Tucker the twenty-some minutes that Mortimer Fox spent sharing his views about the future of the high-tech industry were among the longest of his life. He constantly polled each of his observation posts, strategically spread around the ballroom. He had men sitting among the audience, covering all entryways, and hiding behind the stage curtains, which Tucker had only allowed to open fifteen feet—wide enough for the crowd to get a good look at Fox, but narrow enough for him to spring into action and push Fox out of harm's way should an attack occur. Tucker would have preferred the curtains to be open just enough for Fox to stand in plain view, but the planning committee, whose job it was to give a celebrity like Fox maximum exposure during this visit, had fought back, demanding more operating freedom with their guest of honor.

But that was all in the past now as Fox reached the middle of Tucker's concentric circles. The executive director of the Moscone Center, who was also on the board of the symposium, approached Fox. Tucker let the tall and well-dressed host through the circles not only because of who he was, but also because his presence was part of the schedule. The silver-haired director would escort Fox through the exhibition halls.

"Excellent, Mortimer! A terrific speech," the director commended as the group left the crowded ballroom through a secret door and walked toward the escalators at the end of the hall.

Fox thanked the director while shaking hands, which made

Tucker a bit apprehensive because he knew that Fox's hand still hurt.

They reached the downward escalators. Two of Tucker's men went first, reached the bottom, and blocked the adjacent escalators going up, preventing a would-be assassin from approaching the detail from that direction. The detail continued, tightening the diamond formation while the two executives chatted amiably on their way down to the lower level of the center.

The place was bustling with activity, and the noise level increased several decibels as they approached one of the large entrances to the exposition halls. Normally the Moscone Center leased the South Hall exhibition areas as three separate areas, Halls A, B, and C. For this event, however, they had combined all three halls into one cavernous room, the size of three football fields, packed with booths and people, all under the arched concrete beams supporting the sixty-foot-high roof, from which hung hundreds of lights, casting a soft white glow across the entire site. Large potted trees, brought in to help accent the vast expanse of booths, dotted the towering walls.

Cameras rolling, Fox began to tour the area, the director to his left and Tucker to his right. They stopped at some booths, walked by others, and exchanged pleasantries with some exhibitors. One of Tucker's agents, designated to collect the brochures and other convention giveaways selected by Fox, dragged behind the group hauling two bags' worth of techno junk.

Then it happened.

Suddenly.

The agent immediately to the right of Tucker reached behind his neck while moaning, before collapsing. A second later the agent to Fox's left followed, dropping unceremoniously. Tucker's bowels contracted, not because he had just lost two agents to an unseen enemy, but because of *how* he had lost them. He had lost men this way before, without a gunshot being fired. They had fallen victim to microscopic darts laced with a powerful toxin. Tucker knew of only one man who had mastered such attack. But he had killed him long ago.

Focus!

Blinking the past away, Tucker watched the crowd beginning to glance in their direction. He also noticed hasty movement in nearby booths, much faster than what his experience dictated for the average conventioneer.

A brief check of his flanks confirmed his observation. Strangers were moving toward him and his principal, alert eyes focused on him, gloved hands reaching inside the coats of their suits. With his closest agents down, the only protection between the threat and his principal was Moscone security, which controlled the outermost circle of his protection perimeter.

Dismay overcame surprise. Instincts overcame dismay. Less than five seconds had elapsed since his first agent had gone down. Tucker needed a quick diversion, a way to use the crowd to his advantage, to spoil the strangers' plan before they ran down Moscone security, who were only now beginning to realize that something had gone wrong.

The agent in front of him suddenly wiped a hand behind his neck, before dropping to his knees.

Out of options, Tucker withdrew his Colt and fired twice at the ceiling, the reports deafening, ear-piercing, amplified inside the concrete structure—but achieving the desired effect. He immediately shoved the weapon back in its holster while shouting, "Gun! Gun!"

Experience told him that in situations like this people worried far more about getting away from the source of the gunfire than about finding the identity of the shooter.

As expected, havoc set in. People screamed, dropped everything, and scrambled for the closest exits in a panic, forming rivers of humanity between the threat and Tucker and his principal.

Fox stared at Tucker in disbelief, not aware of what was happening. Before he could utter a single word, Tucker used his left arm to grip Fox firmly around the waist before pushing him into the rapid flow of people racing toward the west exit, lifting his light frame off the floor as they accelerated to the tempo of the stampeding crowd, leaving the startled Moscone Center director behind.

Heart pounding, Tucker tapped on his lapel microphone three times, alerting the drivers of both sedans that something had gone terribly wrong. Their instructions under such a warning commanded them to begin circling the convention center at 180 degrees out of phase to maximize the chances of having a vehicle ready the moment Tucker and Fox exited the—

The report of a weapon whipped across the vast hall like rumbling thunder, followed by screams, by shouts, by cries. Another gunshot cracked in the air, and then another.

Tucker risked a backward glance, spotted two warring parties. The strangers he had seen earlier fought another group, firing at them from a vantage point near the north entrance. Tucker didn't care if they killed each other as long as his principal wasn't harmed—though he was intrigued by the nature of the combating factions. One seemed determined to attack Fox while the second was actually helping Fox escape by drawing the attention of the first group. That alone, of course, didn't mean that the second team was friendly. They could both be after Fox and were now fighting each other for the right to do him in.

Assume all strangers are a threat. In Tucker's world a stranger was guilty until proven innocent, and at this moment no one but Tucker's own agents were innocent. He could trust no one else, not even Moscone security.

The crowd intensified its pace, heaving over tables and booths, tearing down displays, charts, exhibits, computers, monitors. People tripped, fell, got trampled under the maddening horde escaping the gunfire, of which multiple cracks continued to echo inside the hall, mixing with the bellowing cries and shouts from the panicked crowd.

Tucker lost himself and his principal in this boiling sea of swarming bodies tugging, elbowing, and clawing to get ahead, to get away from the gunfire.

He glanced toward the closest end of the convention hall,

his temples throbbing. He had spent an entire day inspecting the South Hall of the Moscone Center, memorizing the floor plan, the layout, all entrances, including those reserved for VIPs, secret to all but those running this place. There was one such entrance less than a hundred feet from them, painted in the same creamy color as the wall and support beams, and hidden behind one of the potted trees.

"We're going to cut right, sir," Tucker hissed, tightening the grip on Fox, before leaning into the crowd, using his free hand to shove panicked conventioneers aside, breaking away from the tumultuous mob.

"VIP entrance number seven," he shouted into his microphone.

Gulping air, Tucker swung himself and his principal frantically away from everyone, kicking down a display that stood in the way of the VIP exit. A pair of computer monitors fell off their stands, crashing over the concrete floor, picture tubes exploding with the sounds of gunshots, adding to the rising fear. The crowd roared louder amidst the staccato gunfire that continued to pound the exhibition hall.

Shattered glass crunching beneath his shoes, Tucker reached the large tree, one of many palms trucked in the day before. He raced around the wide metal pot, shaped like a large urn, reaching the other side, right hand groping for the recessed handle, finding it, pulling on it while kicking the door.

Sunlight, bright, blinding, stung his eyes. Squinting, reaching for a pair of sunglasses, Tucker went out first, inspecting the street, spotting the mob charging out of the Moscone Center through one of the main entrances a couple hundred feet away.

He tapped his microphone five times. *Hurry up!*

Mortimer Fox followed, a wide-eyed stare on his wrinkled face, a hand on his chest, his mouth wide open.

"Bruce . . . my chest . . ."

Tucker reached for a pack of aspirin in his pocket and quickly shoved one in his principal's mouth before speaking into his lapel microphone. "Get a car over here *now*."

Several vehicles accelerated down the street, but none belonging to Fox's motorcade.

Where are they?

The report of a gunshot made him reach for the Colt, index
finger tensely poised over the trigger, eyes searching for the
source, finding it a second later. A van raced toward him
without regard for the pedestrians in the way, running over
one as others screamed and jumped out of its way. A uniformed officer was shooting at the runaway vehicle before
he dropped to his knees clutching his bleeding abdomen. A
second cop emerged from the center, emptying his revolver
at the van, which continued on its course. Tucker realized
that the vehicle was armored. The Colt was also useless
against such protection.

One of his Lexus sedans raced behind the van. Tucker
tried to push Fox back inside the center but people had already spotted the VIP exit and were flowing out of there in
numbers, leaving Tucker and Fox exposed to the oncoming
van.

Another shot, followed by screeching tires and smoke.
Three civilians had opened fire, but not at the van. A man
in a business suit rushed away from them, toward the van,
glancing at Tucker along the way, his features hidden beneath a thick beard, his eyes radiating rage, anger. He moved
with a fluidity that Tucker found eerily familiar, avoiding
scattered pedestrians like a football player rushing through
the line of scrimmage, with the elegance of a ballet dancer,
yet with the strength of a bear, reaching the van just as it
began to accelerate, jumping into the open side door. An
Asian woman inside the van closed the door, but not before
flashing a look at Fox and Tucker, frowning.

Tucker had never seen her, but was momentarily distracted
by the man—just for a second or two—certain that he had
seen those eyes before, the stranger's familiar motion spreading a feeling of déjà vu through him.

But it couldn't possibly be.

In those few seconds Tucker lost track of the immediate
position of Mortimer Fox. As more cops opened fire at the

van while it headed in his direction, Tucker wasn't certain which way he should pivot to shield Fox, so he guessed left, just to watch Fox, who had shifted to Tucker's right side, cringe in pain as a stray bullet struck his chest, over the heart. The impact shoved the CEO against the wall, where Tucker caught him before he fell to the sidewalk.

The van disappeared around the corner as the black Lexus jumped the curb and screeched to a halt right next to Tucker, who wasted no time in opening the rear door and getting Fox inside.

"To St. Mary's Hospital! Call ahead! Now!"

The driver floored it. Fox riveted his startled gaze on Tucker, who laid him across the back, resting Fox's head on his lap.

"You're going to be all right, Mr. Fox," said Tucker, pressing a button behind the driver's seat, raising a bullet-resistant glass panel, separating the front from the rear, further shielding his wounded principal.

"My chest . . . I can't breathe," wheezed Fox.

"I'm going to check for damage, sir," said Tucker as the streets of San Francisco rushed by.

He removed Fox's tie and unbuttoned his shirt, relief drowning apprehension when he spotted the mushroomed slug imbedded in the Kevlar vest.

He removed the Velcro straps securing the vest and opened it, exposing Fox's undershirt, which he cut open with a utility knife. A bruise the size of a fist over Fox's heart contrasted sharply with his ghostly skin, marking the spot where the slug had struck the vest.

"Bruce . . . I can't . . . my chest."

Tucker popped a nitroglycerin pill under Fox's tongue and shifted his position so that Fox was under him as he sat on his principal's thighs facing him, but keeping most of his weight on his own knees to avoid further stressing Fox.

Tucker checked Fox's pulse, found it weak, erratic, like his breathing. His principal was having a heart attack, probably a combination of the excitement inside the convention center plus the strain of the gunshot. If he didn't receive medical help very soon he didn't think he would make it.

"Step on it!" Tucker shouted through the intercom at the driver as they rushed through the bouncy streets.

"Bruce . . ."

"Yes, sir."

"Must protect . . . Monica . . . get funds and password . . . from Bill Gibbons . . . he knows the location of half of the code . . . he knows what . . . to do . . . in the . . . event of . . ."

Tucker missed the rest of the sentence and leaned down, placing an ear directly over Fox's lips.

The dying executive clutched Tucker's lapel with a trembling hand. "Find her . . . Bruce. Protect her. Only she can . . . stop them. Microfiche . . . firewall . . ."

Microfiche? Firewall?

"Mr. Fox, I don't understand. Is there a microfiche you wish me to find? Where?"

"Microfiche . . . lock—" Fox's eyes rolled to the back of his head. Tucker began to administer CPR, alternating between breathing into Fox's mouth and pressing his chest with the heel of his right palm, and repeating the process again and again, over and over, until the sedan reached the hospital, until it came to a stop in front of the emergency room entrance.

Someone grabbed his shoulders, tugging at him.

"Let him go, sir!" shouted a woman.

Tucker ignored her, his mind no longer responding to logic.

"Sir, you have to move away!"

Tucker turned around, faced a petite woman in a light green gown, her ash-blonde hair tied in a bun, a stethoscope hanging loosely from her neck. "We need to get him inside right away, sir!"

Coming back to his senses, Bruce Tucker stepped aside as two orderlies reached them pushing a cart, onto which they moved a limp Mortimer Fox, before doubling back through the glass doors leading into the emergency room. He followed them, but wasn't allowed in the trauma room, where a half dozen people plus an assortment of blinking and blipping equipment surrounded Mortimer Fox.

Bruce Tucker just stood there and watched his principal—his *daimyo*—slipping away. He felt totally inadequate. Despite all of the precautions, of the advance to check the center, of the multiple circles of security, of the holding room, of the carefully-designed stage, of the protective lighting schemes, of the bullet-resistant vehicles—despite *everything*, they still had gotten to Mortimer Fox, just like they had gotten to Vinod Malani. And Tucker, the SEAL, the CIA operative, the Secret Service agent trained by a former modern-day samurai, had not been able to prevent it. He had allowed someone who resembled a man Tucker had killed a long time ago to distract him at the worst possible moment.

Tucker remained in that emergency room for twenty more minutes, while the ER staff tried to revive Fox, finally pronouncing him dead after he failed to respond to a host of procedures.

Tucker closed his eyes, fists tight in anger. He had broken the tradition, had lost his principal, had failed to protect him, had *shamed* his profession, his trainer, Ozaki Kabuki. And in his mind there was no excuse, no explanation, no attempt to divert blame—for those were the thoughts of an amateur, not of a specialist. Tucker had simply not planned properly and had failed as an executive protector, as a samurai. He was now a *ronin*, a class of masterless samurai who had lost his place in the normal loyalty pattern of Japanese feudal society—a society whose rules for protection were very much alive in the executive protection circles of today.

Ronin. A samurai without a master.

His training showed him but one path: He had to honor his principal by avenging his death. Tucker remembered the teachings of Ozaki Kabuki. He remembered the story of Japan's legendary forty-seven *ronin*, the events that took place in 1703. A young *daimyo* named Asano Nagaroni, lord of Ako domain, attacked Kira, the shogun's master of etiquette, who had provoked him beyond endurance, inside the shogunal castle. For such crime, Asano was ordered to commit hara-kiri, to disembowel himself. His samurai, forty-seven of them, became *ronin*, masterless, and spent two years plotting their revenge. They attacked Kira's mansion, killed him, and brought his head to Asano's grave.

Absolute loyalty to your principal, to your *daimyo*, even after his death.

Bruce Tucker stepped away from the hospital and stared at the mountains, and the blue skies, his feelings in turmoil. On the one hand his training told him to avenge his principal. On the other his common sense told him to walk away. If the government was indeed behind the killings, then Tucker stood little chance of making a difference. He had worked for Washington long enough to respect its power. Very few people went up against Uncle Sam and prevailed. If someone with the power, resources, and influence of Mortimer Fox had not survived, what chance did Bruce Tucker have with his limited means?

But something else bothered him, swirling inside his mind, slicing through his brain with the power of a thousand katana blades. Tucker remembered a name from the past: Siv Jarkko, the assassin, the murderer, *the monster*. Siv Jarkko, the Stasi master spy turned contract assassin following the collapse of the Berlin Wall. It was Jarkko whom Tucker had run down in the Swiss Alps, just outside of Zurich, forcing his car off a cliff. It was Jarkko whom Tucker had seen perish in the explosion, obtaining final confirmation through a careful dental match of the charred body found inside the wreck. But it was Jarkko who had achieved his revenge from the grave, somehow delivering a letter bomb to Kristina, Tucker's young wife, killing not only her but their newborn son.

Bruce Tucker sat on a bench outside the emergency room staring at the parking lot, but in his mind he saw the face of the beast responsible for the death of so many CIA officers—many killed just as his security detail had been terminated today.

Tucker fought the lightheadedness induced by the shock-

ing realization that Jarkko could be alive, that the bastard did
not—

*But how? I saw him die! I saw him burn to death! I
matched his dental records!*

Madness!

Insanity!

Focus.

He closed his eyes and breathed deeply, forcing objectivity
in his thoughts. His security agents had complained that
something had stung them before collapsing. That could only
mean a microscopic poisoned dart—one of Jarkko's preferred methods of assassination, far better than a bullet because the venom could be selected either to strike instantly,
like this morning, or with a delayed reaction, allowing the
assassin the precious seconds—or minutes—needed to escape.

In addition to the assassination method, Tucker had recognized his former nemesis's stride as he'd raced toward the
armored van, with elegance, with power.

And the eyes.

Tucker would never forget those eyes, radiating the kind
of hatred that brought him back to that day in the outskirts
of Zurich.

*Walk away, Bruce. This is no longer your fight. Let the
Agency deal with Jarkko—if that was Jarkko at all.*

But what if that *was* Jarkko, the man who'd killed his
family? What if the monster had somehow survived? Could
Tucker really walk away knowing that his family's killer was
still at large? Knowing that he would kill again, and again,
until someone stopped him?

And what about absolute loyalty to his principal, the basis
of Tucker's profession? If those words meant *anything* to
him—*anything* at all—then he had to honor his commitment
to Mortimer Fox, to his trainer, to his profession. Tucker had
to find Fox's daughter and protect her while also avenging
Fox's death—and the death of his own family.

Tucker pressed an index finger against his right temple,
rubbing it, trying to figure out who was really behind this.

Was Jarkko somehow associated with Washington, collaborating to dismember FoxComm? And if so, why? Why would Washington resort to such desperate measures to eliminate Mortimer Fox, not only contracting an assassin, but *the* man who had once been wanted by every ally intelligence service in the world, from the CIA to the Mossad?

This looks complicated, Bruce. Walk away.

Absolute loyalty to your principal.

And where would you start? How would you finance such a quest?

Get funds and password from Bill Gibbons.

Find Monica ... microfiche ... firewall.

Tucker remembered Fox's final words, remembered his final wish, and at that moment he realized that he could not just walk away. He could not turn his back on the possibility that Siv Jarkko was still alive, just as he could not ignore the basic principles of his profession, of the tradition of the executive protector, of the teachings of the wise Kabuki, of the legend of the forty-seven *ronin*.

He could not allow his family's murderer to go free.

Bruce Tucker stood and looked toward the east, his mind going farther, past the Rocky Mountains and the Colorado Canyon, beyond the hills of central Texas and the swamps of Louisiana, past the plains of Florida and the unpredictable Atlantic Ocean.

Europe. Italy. Somewhere in that country lived Monica Fox, incognito, hiding from her father, from his life. But experience told Tucker that anyone could be found.

Anyone.

No one moved about without leaving a trail, a scent, and those inexperienced in the art of covert transportation would leave even more noticeable tracks for someone like Tucker to follow.

As in the past, time was against Bruce Tucker. If he could find Monica Fox, so could Jarkko, a man as brilliant as he was evil. And if that monster was responsible for Fox's death—and maybe even Malani's—then he could very well be going after the tycoon's daughter next. Tucker could only

hope that Monica Fox, wherever she was, was savvy enough
to remain alive long enough for Tucker to find her, to protect
her, to find a way to avenge the death of her father while
finishing the job that he'd set out to do in Zurich on that
cloudy and breezy morning a long, long time ago.

Litigation

William Gibbons had always been a prudent man, constantly
advising his clients to be conservative, to avoid excessive
risks, to cover themselves legally every step of the way. In
all of his years practicing law, he had never met anyone more
cautious than himself, until his meeting with Bruce Tucker.

Their discussion had been brief, mostly because Mortimer
Fox had been very specific on the role Tucker would play
after his death. Gibbons had provided the executive protector
with the funds he would need to find Monica Fox in Italy.
He had also given Tucker a sealed envelope containing a
string of characters and numbers—the second half of the
password to a very secret directory stored in a network
known to none but Mortimer Fox and his daughter. For a
long time Gibbons had dreaded the thought that he would be
the one to have to open the envelope and learn the code upon
Fox's death. But then Bruce Tucker had come along six
months ago and somehow earned Fox's trust to the point that
he now had that responsibility, in addition to the task of
finding Monica.

Better him than me, thought Gibbons, watching Tucker get
into a taxicab, which would take him to the airport, where
Gibbons had booked him a one-way trip to Rome, with a
stopover in Washington, D.C.

"Why Washington?" Gibbons had asked.

"To visit an old friend, someone who might be able to help me find her."

"Someone from the CIA?"

"Yep."

"What's in the briefcase?"

Tucker had handed him an attaché case not to be opened unless he didn't make it back from this assignment.

"Sealed envelopes with my will and financial stuff. Also my sidearm."

"The gun that you fired at the Moscone Center?"

"Right. Thanks for taking care of that mess with the police department."

"That's one of the few things that lawyers are good for. The police might want to see the weapon to compare slugs with the ones they recovered."

"All right. By the way, the envelopes remain sealed unless I die."

"We're also good at that."

They had shaken hands.

And off he goes, Gibbons thought, watching the taxi merge with traffic before heading for the highway ramp.

Gibbons checked his watch. He was late for an afternoon appointment. First he would head to his office and store Tucker's documents in his safe. Then he—

An object stabbed his back.

"I have a gun. Don't move or turn around," said a female voice tinged with an Asian accent.

He froze, then watched a sedan pulling up to the curb, its rear door opening.

"Get in," said the same voice while nudging him with the gun.

"What do you want with me?" he asked while complying, settling himself in the middle of the rear seat, next to a muscular man in his forties, casually dressed. He stared straight ahead, not acknowledging Gibbons.

The attorney looked toward the opened door, finally catching a glimpse of his abductor, a beautiful Asian woman.

"What I want," she said, sitting next to him and closing the door, "is always what I get."

She pulled out a small radio with her free hand. "I've got him."

"We're following Tucker," came the reply.

"Do *not* lose him. We'll catch up with you later," she said into the unit, before putting it away. She then tapped the driver on the shoulder. "To the house. Mr. Gibbons and I have a *very special* date."

5

Mediterranean Jewel

The piercing horns of ferries hauling the last of the tourists back to Naples and Sorrento bellowed across the Marina Grande, their powerful screws clouding the otherwise pristine, cobalt blue sea surrounding the island of Capri, twenty miles west of the Amalfi coast of southern Italy.

Wearing a white linen dress, sandals, and sunglasses, Monica Fox browsed through the shops on Via Colombo, far less crowded now that the daily hordes of camera-bearing tourists from around the world retreated to the relatively inexpensive hotels on the mainland. The hours between five in the afternoon and eight in the evening were the best for the island's residents and overnight guests to visit the local shops. Not only were the crowds gone, but the sea breeze swept away the day's heat.

Breathing the salty air, Monica looked toward the departing vessels surrounded by white-capped waves, her shoulder-length auburn hair swirling in the light wind. The late afternoon sun reverberated off her honey-colored skin, tanned to perfection by countless hours working outdoors on her miniature reproductions of Capri's many sights. Her artwork, sculpted and hand painted with great care, sold quite well at the specialty shops near the Piazzeta, the island's main commerce and tourist center, located at the upper end of the Funicular, the cable car used as the primary mode of transportation between the Marina Grande and the city of Capri in the center of the island. Roads were few, narrow, and packed with hairpin turns, winding their way through the jagged limestone formations, connecting Capri not just to the Marina Grande, but also to the smaller city to the west, Anacapri, and to the many shiny estates dotting the hills of this craggy and mythical isle.

The shrill of seagulls drowned the rumbling diesels of the departing vessels, mixing with the soft humming of the electric Funicular as it crawled up the steep incline toward Capri, which rested on top of rugged cliffs several hundred feet above the glittering sea, amidst splashes of colorful vegetation under a dying sun.

The sea breeze ruffled Monica's light dress. She welcomed the rush of air rising up her body, a feeling she found liberating. Like most island residents, she wore nothing beneath the linen cloth, which hung loosely from her narrow shoulders by two thin straps. Her breasts, also golden from sunbathing topless in her backyard, pressed lightly against the soft fabric. A sterling silver locket, hanging at the end of a plain chain, rested just over her cleavage, reflecting the sunlight. The princess-cut aquamarine adorning the front of the antique locket—a gift from her mother before she died—matched the color of Monica's eyes. The contrast of her bronze skin, the auburn hair, the intriguing hazel eyes, and a radiant smile had helped open many doors on this island for the aspiring artist, including granting her the permit to practice her trade at a leased house on a seaside cliff halfway between Capri and Anacapri. One month's worth of interest from her very generous trust fund, safely diversified across banks in New York, London, and Rome, had taken care of the rest.

Monica purchased a *pannini*, a ham and melted provolone sandwich, from a street vendor, as well as a Diet Coke, which

she made sure was ice cold. She then climbed down the
concrete steps outlining this side of the marina, protected
from the sea by an L-shaped breakwater. Tourist boats and
yachts of all shapes and sizes rocked gently in the low tide,
crowding the marina.

A group of rowdy men dressed in black clothes, with
shaved heads and multiple body piercings and tattoos, ran up
and down the steps while kicking a soccer ball and shouting
at each other in heavy British accents.

She wondered what they were doing here at this hour. Day
tourists had already left. Then she remembered having read
something about a British band vacationing on the island this
week.

One of them spotted Monica and immediately scuttled in
her direction, planting himself in front of her. He reeked of
whiskey. A nose as red as the setting sun stuck out of his
long and craggy face like a hook.

"Hey, baby. Wanna party with us?"

"I don't think so," she said, cocking his head at him.

He grinned. "Hard to get, huh? Do you know who we
are?"

She smiled. "A bunch of losers from Britain?"

Before he could reply, Monica spotted Nunzio Ipolito, the
short and stocky caretaker of this private marina, leaping off
a sailboat he had been cleaning and going after the rowdy
group, shaking a fist in the air.

"Hey! *Fabarutos!* Go away! Get the hell away from the
lady before I beat the crap out of you!"

The rock group stared in his direction and moved away.

"And don't come back here again!" he shouted, before
looking at Monica, his anger immediately washing away, replaced by a warm smile. "Are you all right, Signora Monica?"

"Yes. *Grazie*, Nunzio," she said, sitting halfway down the
steps.

"Prego." He returned to the boat he had been working
on.

Monica smiled and waved back. The hot-tempered Nunzio

looked after her thirty-foot cruiser, which she used not only for relaxation, but also to travel to the mainland every week for supplies. When she had first moved here, Monica leased the boat to a firm that took tourists on tours around the island, using the income to pay the monthly dock fee and maintenance. She had stopped leasing it two months ago, when sales of her hand-painted sculptures began to take off. She could have used some of her trust fund to make her early months on the island a little more comfortable, but she was as determined then as she was now to abide by the old rule of living cheaply and never touching the principal while re-investing at least fifty percent of the interest to keep her funds adjusted for inflation. And for the past three months, she had not even touched the interest as the sales of her artwork increased.

Monica Fox, like her father, wanted to live by her own rules, using her talent to make a living that fit her lifestyle. But *unlike* her father, she wasn't planning to live to work.

She took a bite of her *pannini* and watched the sea, chewing slowly while listening to the water lapping against hulls, the snapping and creaking of moored sailboats, and the raucous cries of seagulls. At the far end of the breakwater loomed the first rowboats, towed by one of the motorboats used to transport tourists to the small rocky entrance of the Blue Grotto, where they would transfer to the rowboats to go through the grotto's narrow opening. The grotto, a natural cave about 180 feet long and 75 feet wide, was the biggest attraction of the island. During the day, particularly around the noon hours, sunlight entered through a much larger underwater opening, reflecting off the bottom, and staining the water with bright shades of blue. The effect was almost surreal, giving the impression of navigating through a clear sky.

Surreal.

That's just how life had felt since Monica left her father's estate in northern California almost a year ago, taking with her only the trust fund set up by her mother when Monica was twelve. Although originally meant for college, Monica's grades in high school had earned her a full academic scholarship to Berkeley, where she had also worked part-time to earn spending money, first as a waitress and later on as a teaching assistant as her career progressed. She first earned a degree in business just to get her father off her back. She had actually shocked him at the graduation ceremony by handing him the diploma, telling him that he had wanted it more than she had, and that she would now do as she pleased. She went on to pursue a career in liberal arts, eventually earning a Ph.D. She then joined the staff at Berkeley's School of Design and taught until her mother was diagnosed with cancer. Monica left Berkeley and remained by her side all the way to the end. Monica had met someone in the year that followed, someone whom she married but soon divorced when realizing that he was just after her family's money. It was also around that time that Monica had learned that the main reason Berkeley had so eagerly promoted her career was a secret grant from FoxComm. That had been the final straw, the final push that she needed to venture out on her own, without daddy's help. Not only did she want to make something of herself using her love for art, but she figured that as long as people related to her as Mortimer Fox's daughter, she would never be able to make real friendships or find a true companion, unlike the scrub she kicked out of her house just two months after the wedding. Monica had read too many stories of similar heiresses who just suffered through life, filthy rich but never happy, finding nothing but leeches on their paths, parasites interested in nothing but their bank accounts.

So she had moved away to a place where no one cared who she was—to a place where Mortimer Fox could not reach her, for he didn't know where she had gone in Italy. Not even the local government had made the connection, granting her a work permit because of her attitude, her looks, and her artwork.

And her business sense.

She smiled. As much as she hated to admit it, the free-spirited Monica Fox did carry a few of Mortimer Fox's traits, including a good nose for a business opportunity, a relentless

desire to get ahead without anyone's help, an ability to learn
quickly from her mistakes and move on, a terrific memory,
and a near obsession for order, for extreme neatness, from
her perfectly polished fingernails, to her tidy home, to the
way she ran her business—traits that she admitted were rare
in artists. But unlike her father, she preferred to keep her
associations with business partners clean. The rumors in the
press about Mortimer Fox's ties to the Mafia were true. Although her knowledge was sketchy at best, because her father
and his trusted lawyer William Gibbons chose to keep her
in the dark, she had learned enough over time to know that
there was a connection.

Monica finished her *pannini* and pulled the tab on the can
of Diet Coke, which on this glamorous Mediterranean rock
cost the healthy equivalent of five bucks. But it tasted like
home—a home which she missed on lazy days like today,
following the completion of a new batch of sculptures, which
she had delivered to the shops in the Piazzeta yesterday afternoon. Along with the delivery came more orders, but with
a lax due date.

That was something else she loved about this place, and
about Italy in general. People here didn't rush. They demanded Renaissance perfection in her art, but were quite
generous on their deadlines, allowing her plenty of time to
sunbathe and cruise on her boat. Or to explore the island,
which she did by foot at least once a week, hiking on the
mountains, sometimes on trails that dated back to the Roman
Empire, which elite society used this island as a vacation
retreat. It was Tiberius Caesar who fell in love with the place
so much that he had ordered his architects and builders to
make it habitable for him and his guests.

After almost a year on this island, Monica could proudly
claim that she had hiked through every known—and a few
unknown—trails, caves, and forests, absorbing the place, letting it become a part of her, in a way trying to make it feel
like home.

Lazy days.

She sighed. It was on one such idle day that she had met

Paolo Patinni, a local who, like so many men on this island, was tall, well built, handsome, and perfectly tanned—mostly from spending so much time taking tourists around the island on one of his open-bow speedboats. He was one of three brothers, all of similar physique, all living on the island practicing different trades. One owned the funicular; the other one, Ricco, was a policeman—and she would caution you to use that term loosely here. Ricco not only ran a small gun shop near Anacapri, but also owned an escort service that provided more than public companionship to rich tourists, as well as two nightclubs, where his best customers could enjoy private moments with some of Italy's most beautiful women.

Now there is a sweet deal, she thought. *A cop who's also a pimp and a club owner.*

Of course, the Pattinis didn't get to such comfortable positions through mere luck. Sure, they worked hard, but they were also connected with the local Mafia. Actually, anyone who wanted to get ahead in this country had, at some level, a connection to the Mafia, headquartered in Palermo, Sicily, but with many "offices" throughout Italy, including the one that operated out of one of Ricco's clubs. Through Ricco, Monica had met the head of this territory, a man named Vittorio Carpazzo, who had taken an instant liking to Monica, but had backed off upon realizing that she was already dating Paolo.

That relationship with Paolo, however, as good as it had been at the start, had not lasted long. Four months ago, during a party at Carpazzo's villa up in the hills, Paolo suddenly disappeared from the main party area. Monica went looking for him upstairs and found him in one of the bedrooms with another woman—who turned out to be one of his brother's hookers. He had simply claimed that he was Italian and needed more than just one woman to satisfy him.

Great, Monica, she mused, frowning. *From a leech to a chauvinistic pig. You sure know how to pick them, girl.*

As irony would have it, Monica and Paolo remained friends after breaking up. He often assisted Nunzio in the maintenance of her cruiser. In return, Monica would occasionally let Paolo use her cruiser when he booked a party too big to be taken out to sea in one of his speedboats. Sometimes those parties were filled with tourists and Ricco's hookers—though Paolo was very meticulous about cleaning up afterwards.

Even more ironic was the fact that Carpazzo had called her a few times after her breakup with Paolo. She had politely turned him down, not only determined to avoid dating Italian men, but also not wishing to associate herself with the Mafia—particularly after having criticized her father so much for having done it himself.

As she sipped her soda and stared at the turquoise waters, which the setting sun stained burnt orange, Monica spotted a yacht beyond the breakwater, past the returning Blue Grotto boats. It appeared anchored. She suddenly remembered seeing that same boat three days ago, floating a hundred feet away from shore just below her house on the north side of the island, while she worked on her sculptures in the terrace facing the sea. And she had seen the same vessel again just yesterday, on her way to the market in Anacapri to buy fruit and vegetables.

"Nunzio!" she hollered, apprehension worming in her gut at the thought that somehow her father had found her and had sent men to keep an eye on her.

The barrel-chested Italian looked up from his work. *"Si, signora?"*

"Do you have a pair of binoculars?" she asked in English. That was something else she loved about this place. Unlike the rest of Italy, where the locals may either not know English or just plain refused to speak it, the people here not only spoke it fluently, they also had a great service-oriented attitude, going to any lengths to please the residents.

"Ah, *si*, yes, yes. One moment."

Nunzio disappeared below deck and emerged moments later with a pair of binoculars. Every boat around here had at least one pair for sightseeing. She was about to walk to the gangway, but Nunzio had already jumped off the boat and was taking them to her.

"Binoculars for the beautiful *signora*," he said in his heavily-accented English.

Monica forced a nervous smile. The thought of her father's men here knotted her stomach. "*Grazie*, Nunzio."

"*Prego.*"

As Nunzio returned to his work, Monica sat back down on the steps and pressed the rubber ends of the binoculars against her eyes, fingering the adjusting wheel, bringing the boat into focus, watching a man on the bow of the large vessel using a pair of binoculars to look in her direction.

The stranger immediately lowered his binoculars, turned to say something to a man at the helm, and grabbed a nearby railing as the yacht sprang to life and sped out to sea.

Monica stared at the yacht's name painted across the stern as it headed northeast, toward Naples.

Il Tropicale.

She would go to the harbormaster's office in the morning and have them track down the owner of the boat. If it was registered to any one of her father's companies—and she knew most of them, at least as of a year ago—there would be hell to be paid. The agreement that she had worked out with her father, after learning of his covert manipulations at Berkeley, was that she would forgive him *only* if he left her alone and didn't call her until she was ready to come home, until she had proven to herself that she could make it without his help.

But how would I know that you're all right? her father had asked.

Monica had come up with a clever way of doing so, using the Internet to access the *San Francisco Chronicle*'s web page and placing an ad in the classifieds. In the ad she would tell her father of her intentions, which had not changed since the day she left. As long as the ad ran her father would know that all was well. After almost a year the ad was still running.

"Damn," she hissed, watching the yacht, almost twice as big as Monica's, turn into a white dot, disappearing in the coastal haze. "That better *not* be who I think it is."

She returned the binoculars to Nunzio, dropped the Coke

can in a nearby garbage bin, and walked back to her scooter, the easiest—and cheapest—way to move about the island.

Tomorrow, she thought, kick-starting the old engine, which purred into life as she twisted the throttle handle. Tomorrow she would visit the harbormaster and also change the classified ad to warn her dad against snooping into her world.

She loved her new life and wasn't about to give it up for anyone, especially the manipulative Mortimer Fox.

Old Faces

The bearded man sitting across the table munching on a cheeseburger had not said a word in fifteen minutes, and Bruce Tucker wasn't at all surprised.

Agency rules.

Despite the years away from the CIA, some procedures never changed. The stranger wiping his mouth before washing down the hastily-eaten lunch with iced tea had been assigned to hold Tucker—not to chat with him—while a team swept the adjacent park before granting the former intelligence officer the emergency meeting he had requested the day before, following his meeting with Gibbons. Tucker had used the number given to him the day he'd left the Agency—a number he had not used until now. Although Tucker had gathered as much information as he could from Gibbons to begin his search, he wanted to share his possible sighting of Siv Jarkko with his former employer. Perhaps there was some insight his old mentor might be willing to provide, maybe an angle Tucker had not considered.

The bearded stranger looked to his right while pressing a finger against a flesh-colored earpiece, before whispering,

"We're on our way." He then turned to Tucker, a smirk on his face as he winked and said, "This is your lucky day. Mr. Porter will see you now. Let's go."

The autumn air was cold and invigorating in the nation's capital, reminding him of the old days, bringing back many memories, some good, others not so good. Bruce Tucker pulled up the zipper of his leather jacket. He had not been back to this area since his departure from the Secret Service and was not used to the weather; his body had gotten used to the milder California climate.

They left the burger joint and walked several blocks in silence, crossing Constitution Avenue, past the Vietnam Veteran's Memorial, around the Reflecting Pool, and reached West Potomac Park.

The holding man tapped Tucker on the shoulder before extending an index finger at the woods beyond the jogging trail, in the direction of the river. "Keep walking that way for a couple hundred feet. You'll find him there. And relax, the area's been sanitized."

Tucker hesitated, preferring open and crowded spaces for such meetings, not secluded wooded sites with plenty of spots for the enemy to hide.

The bearded man must have noticed Tucker's hesitation because he added, "I'm going to hang back here, but I assure you there's plenty of protection in the woods. You'll be safe. Relax. This is the way Porter wanted it."

Tucker proceeded, still a bit reluctant, slowly losing himself in the woods, reaching the rear of the park, near the Potomac, away from joggers and the tourists snapping pictures of national sights. Traffic on the Arlington Memorial Bridge rumbled in the background, mixed with the cooing of birds and the occasional rustle of a squirrel climbing up a tree. Overhead, branches swayed in the breeze.

A lone figure sat on a bench facing the water. At first Tucker didn't recognize him. John Porter had lost a lot of weight and his dark hair was mostly white and thinning. Sagging cheeks on a narrow face turned to Tucker, eyes encased in dark sockets regarding him with warmth.

"It's been a long time, Bruce," Porter said in the low and hissing voice that brought Tucker back to the years when he had worked closely with this man. Porter had recruited him shortly after Tucker completed his third year with the SEALs. Tucker had been a recently-promoted lieutenant following his involvement in a series of covert operations, most of which were never made public, and one which did get international recognition: the invasion of Grenada. Tucker had been young, strong, and ambitious back then; a full-blooded patriot trying to make a difference, as his father had in Korea and Vietnam, as his grandfather had in World War II. Porter, the chief of clandestine services within the directory of operations of the CIA, had met the young SEAL in the liberated island of Grenada, where the CIA conducted intelligence debriefings of the rescued medical students. Porter had been quite impressed with Tucker, luring him away from the military and propelling him into the espionage world. It was Porter who had personally polished the young recruit following his basic training at the Farm, the CIA training facility near Williamsburg, Virginia. It was Porter who had honed his skills, turned a grunt into an operative, teaching him the lifesaving skills he would need to survive in a very different kind of battlefield. And it was Porter who had finally cut Bruce Tucker loose in Europe during the final years of the Cold War, when Tucker realized how vastly different the espionage world was from his previous life. In the SEALs Tucker knew who the enemy was. There was a front line, there was a rear, there were clearly defined marks on some map delineating enemy enclaves from friendly territory. In the operative world, however, everyone could be the enemy. He could trust no one but his controller and his fellow officers. He couldn't even trust the agents he recruited, the foreign nationals that Tucker enrolled throughout Europe to spy for the CIA. The threat could come from any direction at any moment. His new life had no boundaries separating friend from foe, no walls or fences, no trenches or sentries to protect him while he slept, while he ate, while he bathed. The life of the field operative was a twenty-four-by-seven roller-coaster ride. He had to constantly check his flanks and rear, constantly take extreme precautions, taking the longer and less predictable routes to go from point A to point B, always avoiding patterns, always sleeping with a weapon by his hand. And in this extremely demanding and unpredictable world, Bruce Tucker had blossomed, becoming an authority in the field, a specialist, tracking down sources of information, recruiting and managing agents out of a half dozen countries in Europe. So exemplary was his performance that Porter recommended him for the position of chief of the Zurich station, also giving him his own staff. It was then that Tucker had met Kristina Herrera, a CIA operative who had spent the past five years assigned to the Madrid station before her transfer to Zurich. The chemistry between them had been instant, the mutual attraction powerful enough to bend the rules regarding relationships among operatives, especially between a station chief and one of his senior officers. But neither Tucker nor Kristina had cared, having been through enough action to last them ten lifetimes, having witnessed enough death and suffering to ignore personnel policies written by some desk clerk back at Langley, someone who had probably lived within the CIA headquarters' protective walls all of his life, someone who probably went home to a wife and kids at the end of the day. What could someone like that know about the lives of the likes of Bruce Tucker and Kristina Herrera, living on the edge, surviving one day at a time in a world of deception and paranoia, where the difference between life and brutal death was their instincts, their experience, their total trust?

Those were the days, Tucker thought, remembering her catlike, hazel eyes, her light olive skin, her auburn hair, her body pressed against his at night, the feeling of completeness, of unity.

Breathing the cold air, filling his lungs, exhaling deeply while staring back at John Porter, Tucker remembered those two glorious years Kristina and he had worked together in Zurich, their relationship growing stronger every day, their love transcending their profession. They married soon after

Kristina became pregnant. A gift from above, Tucker had called the baby growing in her belly, a product of their love. Kristina retired from the Agency six months later, delivering a healthy baby boy the following spring at a hospital in Zurich. Tucker put in for a transfer back to Langley, longing for a steady life with his new family.

But Siv Jarkko had turned those dreams into a nightmare. Kristina had been packing up their apartment the same week that Tucker made a breakthrough in his quest to find Jarkko, tracking him down, killing him. But Jarkko had retaliated from the grave. A package had arrived at their apartment while Tucker was at work, getting through the security that the CIA had provided for his family due to the extremely dangerous nature of his assignments. The bomb had incinerated Kristina and the baby.

Tucker had buried them just outside of Georgetown University, at Holy Road Cemetery, on a hill overlooking the Potomac. He had driven by their graves early this morning, shortly after arriving in Washington, while waiting for his meeting with the CIA. Two gray crosses, side by side beneath an old oak, brought back the old familiar pain, magnified by the possibility that Jarkko was alive.

So great had been this personal loss, so immense the hate against the CIA for failing to protect his family, that Tucker felt compelled to leave the Agency. The CIA tried to hang on to him, sending teams of psychologists to work with him, to help him cope with the loss, with the anger. But nothing had helped. Tucker needed a change, a fresh start, a new place to apply his skills, and he had found it in the Secret Service and in the skillful hands of his new mentor, Ozaki Kabuki, the old man who turned the field operative into an executive protector.

Purging the past, Tucker sat next to Porter, who gazed down at the gray pebble gravel surrounding the metal bench. He wore a dark trench coat, a maroon scarf, and black gloves.

"It's definitely been a long time," said Porter, now deputy director of the CIA, second in command of the most pow-

erful intelligence agency in the world. Porter reported to
Randolph Martin, the director of Central Intelligence.

"It's good to see you again, sir. I only wish it was under
a different set of circumstances."

"Yes . . . you'd indicated that it was important," Porter replied, getting down to business. "It'd better be, Bruce. The
conduit you used is reserved for emergencies."

There was no need for small talk among operatives, even
after so many years. Porter had taught him a long time ago
that an economy of words ruled their profession. He too went
straight to the issue at hand. "I have reason to believe that
Jarkko is still alive, sir." Tucker watched him carefully. Porter's reaction was far more important than his verbal response.

The deputy director pinched the bridge of his nose. "You
saw him die, Bruce. I reviewed the file personally, the records. How could he still be alive?"

Tucker opted to level with his mentor right away, remembering the old saying, etched into the marble wall at the
entrance of the CIA headquarters in Langley, Virginia: *And
you shall know the truth, and the truth shall set you free.*

The former CIA officer spent ten minutes telling the truth,
bringing Porter up to speed on his observations during the
attempted kidnapping of Mortimer Fox. For the time being,
Tucker decided to leave out Fox's final words and the information Gibbons had given to him. His experience told him
to hold out. He might need what little intel he possessed on
Monica Fox to bargain later.

Porter listened without interruption. When Tucker finished, the deputy director remained silent for another minute
or so before saying, "Bruce, what I'm about to tell you may
sound harsh, but I think it's important that you hear it, and
more important that you believe it. I know that you have lost
your principal and that it must hurt, at least on a professional
level. And if you liked him, then it probably also hurts at a
personal level. I also know how much you suffered after
Zurich, losing your family. I know you blamed the Agency
for their deaths."

Tucker closed his eyes, breathing deeply, wondering if he had let his imagination get the better of him, if he had allowed the past to cloud his perception of the present.

Porter put a hand on Tucker's shoulder while giving him a warm, fatherly smile. "That was a terrible time, Bruce, and Kristina was a wonderful woman. And yes, the security at the apartment did screw up, but it's all in the past now. You have to let it go."

Tucker frowned. "I thought I had."

"Have you really?"

Tucker shrugged. "There's still the nightmares, but it never affected my work at the Secret Service or in my private practice."

Porter gave Tucker's shoulder a soft tap. "Bruce, Jarkko is *dead*. He's *been* dead for a long time. I'm not sure who you think you saw in San Francisco yesterday, but I assure you it wasn't him."

"But the method of assassination . . . the eyes . . . that couldn't have been my imagination."

"Jarkko was a monster indeed, and that, unfortunately, also made him a legend like bin Laden or Imad Mughniyeh. I'm sure there are plenty of wannabes jockeying for the chance to pick up where he left off, and that would not be at all surprising. Those bastards feed off of each other, learning from the mistakes of their peers, always trying to outdo each other, just like the damned hackers plaguing our nation's superhighways."

"What are you saying? That I just saw an impostor?"

"A clone, Bruce, an imitator. Call him whatever you want to call him. He was a fake. There were enough published articles about Siv Jarkko for other terrorists to copy, to adopt, to attempt to carry on the legend."

"Why? For profit?"

"Maybe. There are many who require terrorist services and who might be foolish enough to believe that he is Siv Jarkko, which would prompt them to pay steeper contractual fees than they would otherwise. It almost boils down to a marketing scheme."

Tucker exhaled, leaning back on the bench, closing his eyes, not certain of what to believe, feeling—

The sting was hardly noticeable, barely pinching him through the coat's thick collar. He reached with his right hand, found the tiny dart, pulled it out, realized that the padded leather had partially stopped . . . Tucker felt warm, lightheaded.

"Bruce? Are you all right? Bruce?"

Feeling heat spreading up his neck, Tucker stared at Porter, who seemed distant now, as if at the end of a long tunnel. "It's . . . him," he muttered. "Run, sir . . . run away."

"Bruce? What are you saying? Run away from whom?"

Tucker tried to respond, to speak, but could no longer control his muscles. Despite the thick collar of his jacket, the dart had managed to inject enough chemical into his bloodstream.

Porter's voice grew fainter, just as his image faded away in this black tunnel that swallowed everything around him, until he passed out.

7

Uninvited Guests

Monica Fox unlocked the front door of her house and stepped into the tiny foyer, perspiration filming her face and neck, her hair messy after the scooter ride from the Marina Grande.

Without looking, she went to drop her keys into the painted ceramic ashtray she kept at one end of a pinewood shelf hanging from the light green stucco wall to her right. She used the shelf as her desk organizer, keeping her letters, stapler, paper clips, pens, and other basics neatly stored. Living in a five-hundred-square-foot house had forced her to use space efficiently. But as small as the place was, the large backyard overlooking the sea more than made up for such inconveniences.

Instead of hearing the familiar clack of metal striking ceramic, her keys thumped against wood.

Now she looked toward the shelf, confused. After living here for so long, she had many motions down to a science. *Unlock the door, one step inside, extend your left arm, throw the light switch, a second step, extend your right arm, toss the keys in the ashtray.* Only today the ashtray was moved. Not by a lot, just a few inches, but enough for her to notice.

Odd.

In all the time she had been living here that ashtray had never been—

Someone had ruffled through her sales orders. Though still neatly stacked, they too had been moved. The incorrect sales order was on top, the one from Capricorno, an art gallery in the Piazzeta. This morning she had read the order from Raku, a ceramics boutique, and had left it on top of Capricorno's with the intention of working on it first, since it was the simplest. The owners of Raku, catering to the average island tourist, preferred her smaller works, which they could move fast each week. Capricorno, a high-end shop catering to the affluent tourist, preferred the larger sculptures, which carried bigger price tags, but moved slowly.

Monica felt a chill, her mouth suddenly going dry, fear sweeping through her. Someone had broken into her house.

But just as suddenly, unexpected anger displaced fear. The kitchen was adjacent to the entryway. She snagged a steak knife and inspected the small living room, which led to the spacious patio through a sliding glass door.

No one in sight.

Before she knew it she was in her bedroom, no larger than her walk-in closet back home, and peeked inside the tiny bathroom, clutching the knife so tightly that her knuckles turned white. She stared at a stained toilet next to a pedestal sink and the claustrophobic shower stall.

Empty.

She returned to the living room, her sandals thudding softly over the aged tile floor, light brown in color. Monica looked about her, scanning the open floor plan. From where she stood she could see the kitchen, the foyer, all of the living room, and the patio. Nothing appeared missing, at least on the surface. The weathered leather sofa hugged the wall opposite the door to the bedroom. A metal and ceramic lamp of her own design, resembling a bird of paradise, adorned a plain wooden side table. A larger table separated the kitchen from the living room. She gave it a cursory check, verifying that her design sketches were still there, as she had left them last night, when she had drafted new concepts into the early hours of the morning. First she sketched, then she transferred the concepts onto blocks of chalk or soft clay, which she then painted after letting them harden.

Next to the designs sheets was her laptop computer, her only connection to the outside world, when the phones worked, of course, which in this remote section of the island was about every other day. Monica used it at least once a month to renew her classified ad with the *San Francisco Chronicle*, and a few times each week to keep up with world news—at the incredibly-slow speed of 56 Kbits per second, which seemed befitting of the laid-back nature of this island.

Monica looked up at the exposed rafters supporting a wooden lattice on which red roof clay tiles rested. Electrical wires dangled across the rafters, powering plain light bulbs hanging loosely over the kitchen, living room, and her work table, casting a soft glow. A single phone line also dropped from the ceiling to the black phone next to the laptop.

She checked the rear of the house, pulling on the sliding glass door and confirming that it was still locked, as well as the windows flanking it. Beyond them a terrace floored with the same tile as the house provided enough covered area for the half dozen tables packed with sculptures in varying stages of development. At the edge of the terrace extended a short grassy field that not only reached to the rocky bluffs overlooking the sea, but also surrounded both sides of the house, meeting up with the woods flanking the property.

The sun, a spherical smudge of burnt orange, hung just over the horizon. The sight was magnificent, picture perfect, inspirational.

But at the moment it was lost on Monica Fox, still clutching the knife, wondering who had dared violate her home, her sanctuary.

Her life.

She thought about calling Ricco, Paolo's policeman brother.

But what are you going to report? A slightly moved ashtray? Papers out of order?

Nothing appeared missing, and the doors and windows showed no sign of forced entry.

Yet someone was here.

She could feel it, taste it.

But who? Her father's men? Perhaps ordered to check up on her without Monica finding out? Perhaps making sure that she was doing fine, that she wasn't in danger or in need of money?

She went back inside, locking the door behind her—not that it made her feel any safer. Perhaps she should buy a gun. She had learned from Ricco that Italian law permitted its residents to own one for self-defense, as long as the gun was kept at home. She could probably go to Ricco's shop and buy one without raising any suspicion. After all, she was a woman living alone. Surely Ricco would understand.

Twilight gave way to darkness. The lack of streetlights in this remote section of the island provided for spectacular stargazing, which Monica did on occasion, using the small telescope she had purchased to look about the island and get ideas for her sculptures on the days that she didn't feel like trekking up cliffs. Although this place had been relatively inexpensive, not only because of its size, but also because it lacked either steps or lifts going down to a boathouse by the water, like other properties in the area, she still had a view of the Marina Grande and Capri, almost three miles away, providing her with many different sights to keep her work interesting. It was through this telescope that Monica had spotted that yacht three days ago.

Tomorrow I'm buying a gun and also checking with the harbormaster, she thought, wondering if she was just being overly paranoid. After all, was it possible that she might have moved the ashtray by accident that morning and had also confused the stacking sequence of the sales orders? And maybe there was a good explanation for *Il Tropicale* other than someone stalking her?

Sleep on it.

And Monica did, double-checking all doors and windows before turning off the light and crawling into bed, the knife still in her hands.

Silence.

Except for the sound of her own breathing and the faint humming noise of the slow-turning ceiling fan above the bed.

Monica watched it turn and turn, slowly fading into sleep.

Hands

Bruce Tucker rushed through the streets of Zurich, shoving pedestrians aside, his mind in a turmoil that matched the chaos across the street. Emergency vehicles crowded the front of the apartment building, owned and run by the American government to provide safe housing to members of the diplomatic staff—which included CIA officers and their families.

Glistening streams of water fought the gushing flames, the smoke billowing out of a gaping hole where a balcony had once been—the balcony belonging to his fourth-floor apartment. Sirens blared in the cool morning air, their sound increasing to an ear-piercing crescendo as he identified himself to the police as the tenant of that apartment, as the husband and father of the family who lived there. For a moment he hoped that they had not been home, but then he saw their small sedan, parked by the entrance, covered with bricks and dust from the blast above. Tucker spotted the two CIA men charged with the security of the building, watched them drop their gaze, shake their heads. He started toward the burning building, refusing to believe the CIA men, wishing to see for himself. But hands held him back, grabbed his shoulders, his legs, kept him from moving.

Tucker fought them, fought to free himself from their grip, kicking one, punching the other, listening to their moans as they rolled away from him. But more hands converged on him, bringing him down, securing him, and he began to scream, to shout, to cry out the desperate cry of a desperate man.

Bruce Tucker woke up to his own scream, loud, penetrating, like a splinter in his mind. He opened his eyes, saw the canopy of trees moving above him, felt hands holding him by the shoulders, by his legs.

"Shit! He's coming around!" a deep male voice said.

Two people were carrying him.

Instincts replaced his initial surprise. He pulled his right leg back, freeing it from the man in front, before kicking him hard in the stomach. In the same motion he clasped his hands in front of his chest, before pivoting his torso to the right while bringing his right elbow around, striking the second man in between the legs.

Tucker landed on his back in the soft grass and rolled away from them, surging to his feet. One man had dropped to his knees, hands on his groin. The second stood back up, reaching inside his coat.

Covering the half dozen feet separating them in a second, Tucker hit the operative with the heel of his right palm slightly below and to the right of the sternum, delivering a decisive blow to the solar plexus, before reaching inside the man's jacket, pulling out a Colt .45, his hand feeling the remarkable familiarity of the weapon, flipping the safety.

Pivoting on his right leg, he brought his left leg up and hit the first man across the face with the edge of his shoe, before also disarming him, shoving a stainless-steel Kimber in his pants while continuing to clutch the Colt.

The shriek—a female shriek—echoed in the woods, mixed with barking noises.

Tucker glanced to his right, spotted an elderly woman walking a white poodle in a nearby trail. The animal pulled on the leash, growling, exposing shiny fangs.

That's when Tucker saw the bench, saw John Porter sprawled next to it, dead eyes fixated on the branches overhead.

Momentarily confused, Tucker looked back at his would-be kidnappers. They were rushing away from him, vanishing in the woods.

The woman continued to scream.

Tucker's chest constricted. He felt light-headed again, the drug still in him. He lowered his gaze, breathing deeply once, twice, feeling a second surge of energy.

Then he recognized the Colt .45 in his hands—the same blue steel Colt he'd had not only machined to soften all of the sharp edges from the factory, but had also replaced the original grips with high-end rubber grips for maximum stability. The hammer was pulled back, a round was chambered. He instinctively thumbed the safety catch back on, securing the weapon. The muzzle was hot. He took a sniff and the smell of cordite oozing from the weapon tingled his nostrils.

Tucker had left this Colt in the attaché case he had handed William Gibbons during their meeting in Sunnyvale prior to heading for the airport because he lacked a license to carry firearms on a commercial flight.

How did it get here?

He rushed toward Porter, an action that made the woman run away in fear, dragging the snarling poodle.

His mind struggled to digest the unexpected sight. He kneeled by the side of his former mentor, only then noticing the bullet wounds, three of them.

"Oh, God," he hissed, his stomach writhing as he released the Colt's clip, counting three rounds, plus one in the chamber. The Colt held a maximum of ten in the clip and one in the chamber. He was missing seven bullets, which meant the Colt had not just been fired at Porter.

"Dear Jesus," he mumbled.

Breathe.

He did, filling his lungs, forcing his mind to relax in spite of the shocking turn of events. He shoved the Colt in his pants, by his left kidney, his mind in turmoil.

What is going on?

Confusion led to frustration. Frustration led to anger.

Is Jarkko behind this? And what about Porter's men, the ones who had supposedly sanitized the meeting grounds? The ones securing the area? Where are they now?

Questions, to which he had no answers, no explanations, no immediate theories to—

Sirens.

Distant, but nearing.

He had to get away, find a place to hide, to regroup, to formulate a plan to *get* answers. If the bullets in Porter were fired with his Colt, the CIA would blame him, and on top of that there was an eyewitness, who had seen Tucker holding the gun, pointing it at the two strangers.

He looked in her direction, spotting her distant shadow as the trail wound its way down the wooded park.

"Damn!" he shouted, his mind going in different directions. The fact that he had the Colt told him that Gibbons had been compromised, which meant he had no one to corroborate his story with the CIA. Whoever tried to kidnap Fox had obviously gone after Gibbons, and now him, in the process eliminating John Porter. And that someone had not killed Tucker, but tried to kidnap him, obviously to obtain the information they had been unable to extract from Fox or his attorney.

Or his CTO, Vinod Malani.

The password.

His mind flashed the image of the man he had seen running toward the armored van at the Moscone Center.

Siv Jarkko.

It had to be him.

Bruce Tucker looked about him, his instincts telling him nothing else could be accomplished here.

He began to run down the trail, his throat tightening when spotting the body of a man spread out on the grass around the next bend, blood oozing from his mouth.

Mother of God!

He rushed to his side, checked him, counting two bullet wounds, bringing the count to five.

Still missing two bullets.

Running away from a crime he didn't commit, but a crime that he would certainly be blamed for if ballistics matched these bullets with the slugs recovered by the SFPD at the Moscone Center, Bruce Tucker concluded that Jarkko had to be alive, that the beast was loose again, had somehow survived, and had now turned the most powerful intelligence agency in the world against him.

Dashing down the jogging trail, Tucker spotted two men in business suits lying face down next to a towering pine, both shot in the back of the head. That brought the count to *seven bullets*, the exact number that his Colt was—

"Hey! Stop!"

Tucker turned around, watched the bearded CIA officer rushing after him, weapon drawn, his other hand holding a radio.

Tucker didn't have any options. He couldn't get caught, not until he had found a way to prove his innocence. Only then could he consider contacting the Agency again, perhaps making an arrangement to meet under his own terms.

Cutting left, he raced through woods and shrubs for thirty seconds before turning left again, ignoring branches scratching him, diving behind a cluster of thin trees, grabbing the Colt.

As expected, the CIA man made the first left, but had not seen Tucker make the second turn, and just kept going, hurrying in front of Tucker's field of view.

Tucker fired once, hitting the man's left leg.

The bearded man screamed, crashed over knee-high vegetation.

Tucker jumped on top of him before he could react, kicking the weapon and radio aside, pressing his knees against the man's arms while sitting on his chest.

"You . . . bastard," he hissed, breathing heavily. "We'll hunt you . . . down."

"I didn't kill them!" Tucker shouted, grabbing the man's lapels, sensing his self control leaving him.

"You're going to . . . burn for this," the stranger retorted. "Fucking traitor."

"I didn't kill you, did I?" Tucker said, getting in the man's face, feeling a strong desire to convince him of his innocence. "Just as I didn't kill Porter! Someone fired a dart at me, drugging me. They tried to carry me away, but I fought them—"

The police sirens wailed closer. He didn't have much time.

"You're finished . . . you have no one . . . to turn to anymore . . . you'll be beyond salvage."

"Tell Randolph Martin that it was Jarkko! Siv Jarkko! He's the one who set me up, the one who killed Porter!"

The stranger made a face. "Jarkko? He is dead . . . *you* killed him."

"No. He's alive, seeking revenge! Tell Martin that! Tell him that I will find proof!"

Tucker kept the man's gun but handed him back his radio. "Here! Call for help and deliver the message!" he said. "And don't die on me! Apply pressure to the leg. Slow the blood loss. The police will be here soon."

The stranger regarded him with a puzzled stare, obviously confused.

Out of time, Bruce Tucker ran away—away from the incoming sirens, away from this madness, which taxed his mind with every step he took, with every foot that he distanced himself from the surreal meeting, from its insane conclusion.

He reached the Vietnam Veteran's Memorial, crossing

Constitution Avenue, walking at a steady pace around the Federal Reserve building.

Sweating profusely, his heart hammering his chest, he struggled to control his breathing, to control his thoughts, his emotions, his desire to shout out in anger, in frustration at the tragic turn his life had taken.

Priorities.

Tucker began to relax, to force logic into his mind. First he had to get away from this city, and soon, before all viable exits were monitored. He had to reach safer ground, had to regroup, to consider his options, before choosing a new strategy—one that would still allow him to achieve the goal he had set out to achieve less than forty-eight hours ago.

He hailed a taxi and directed the driver out of the city through back roads, avoiding highways, reaching the outskirts of Bethesda, Maryland, where he switched to a second taxi, going farther north. A third cab brought him to a rundown Greyhound station, where he purchased a one-way ticket to New York City.

Sitting in the back of the bus, across from the rear exit—in case a change of plans called for a quick getaway—Bruce Tucker wondered if he had been followed, but not by the CIA. He felt confident he had lost the Agency back in D.C.

Tucker worried about Jarkko, who had somehow managed to follow him from California despite Tucker's best efforts to lose all possible surveillance.

What was the connection between Fox and Jarkko? Was it this password-protected file? Or was it something else? Fox believed that Uncle Sam was after him. He was so certain of it that he had retained Tucker's services for six months, paying top dollar in advance—plus submitting himself to his protector's will from day one. Something had spooked Fox enough to let someone else tell him what to do, what to wear, where to go and not to go. But the old man, who had claimed to have enough dirt on top people in Washington to make their heads spin, had not shared his source of information with him—though in the end he had suggested where the answers might be.

Monica . . . microfiche . . . firewall.

Bruce Tucker had to find a way to leave the continent, and immediately, before the Agency got a chance to react, to send multiple search teams after him. He had to find Fox's daughter before Jarkko and unravel this mystery.

The Greyhound bus gathered speed, rushing past farmhouses surrounded by leafless trees and dead grass, all under a gray sky awaiting the cold that would sweep through the region for months to come, freezing the ground, the air—life itself.

Bruce Tucker regarded the depressing scenery, his eyes narrowing, his mind exploring options, his calculating thoughts following a logic ingrained in him after years of covert work, of shadow operations—of a life he thought he had left behind forever.

He frowned. Nothing was forever, not the fallen leaves, nor the jagged branches projecting toward the lifeless heavens, and certainly not his current predicament, as bleak as it seemed. There was a way out.

There *always* was.

And Bruce Tucker was determined to find it.

Or die trying.

Firewall

The neural system fired a burst of digital activity across a complex array of decision-making cells, each programmed to review the numerical parameters presented at its inputs, before triggering a response, which would then be fed to other cells downstream in this parallel processing network.

The core of the system reviewed the mounds of information flowing across its silicon brain at increasing frequencies.

It first performed the scan at the nominal operating frequency of 10 gigahertz, where the best compromise between data acquisition speed and power consumption resided. The algorithm governing this tradeoff was linked to the power management routines that ensured that at no point in time the system drained more than 50 percent of the power in its batteries before they could be recharged during the daylight portion of its geosynchronous orbit. Power management balanced data acquisition and energy usage by following a simple rule: Faster data rates meant more power, which meant less future ability to gather data until the batteries were recharged. Much system characterization and modeling had gone into selecting 10 gigahertz, which allowed the *Firewall* system to monitor all relevant activities while maintaining a healthy power level.

Information began to flow back to the interpreter circuitry of the hybrid processing unit, consisting of thousands of superscalar silicon microprocessors interfaced with very high speed memory.

Firewall oversaw fifteen thousand communications channels at that particular moment in time, 67 percent voice and 33 percent data, which was mostly e-mail traffic. Each channel was secured using a unique algorithm, which an encrypting method changed every five seconds according to a parameter created by a random sequence generator, thus making it impossible for anyone but *Firewall* to know the next encoding sequence. While monitoring this traffic, *Firewall* used a complex set of key phrases, provided by *Creator*, to extract bits and pieces of information from the incessant traffic, and copied them to their respective files, which no one but *Creator* could access.

The digital image of *Creator* momentarily flashed in *Firewall*'s archive banks, its long-term memory, making it trigger a second search, this time at 20 gigahertz, ignoring the alert from the power management circuit in much the same way that an athlete ignored his burning thighs during a marathon. Information returned in half the time, again containing the usual flow of traffic, which its keyword interceptors automatically scrubbed and digitally filtered before updating *Creator*'s secret files.

Along with communications came other routine data, including coordinates of all deployed U.S. Navy vessels around the globe as well as military planes. *Firewall* also received the latest status of all operational missile silos, the location of the President, the Vice President, and the Speaker of the House, and similar intelligence from forty other nations, friendly and foe alike.

Its digital sensors monitored the status of the nuclear launch code directory, reading back a checksum that told it all was well, that the synchronization of launch codes between the subs, silos, bombers, and the White House were being updated every two hours from this directory through the world's most secured satellite wireless links.

Through this vast amount of information *Firewall*'s parallel search programs tried to find any file from *Creator* with a time stamp not older than forty-seven hours, fifty-eight minutes, forty-three seconds, and fractions thereof down to the nanosecond range.

Firewall directed the lack of a message from *Creator* to a decision tree, which compared *Creator*'s last time stamp with the limit of forty-eight hours, relaying back a message that the maximum time allotted by *Creator* to make contact was close to being violated.

The word VIOLATION, digitized as a string of ones and zeroes, momentarily cause an overload of activity in the silicon brain, the equivalent of a fire alarm, triggering yet another search, this time at 40 gigahertz. Temperature inside the satellite increased by four degrees Celsius as a result of the higher power being dissipated by the neural network. The maximum rated ambient temperature inside the titanium and gold enclosure was forty degrees Celsius, around one hundred degrees Fahrenheit.

Two alarms pinged the brain, one for excessive power consumption and another for increased operating temperature. Both went ignored as the overheating system reviewed

the new data at this higher frequency, again finding no sign
of *Creator*.

"Less than one minute to the deadline," warned a subsystem.

Firewall throttled its system clock up to 50 gigahertz,
bringing the operating ambient to thirty-seven degrees, dangerously close to its maximum, where its silicon components
would begin to malfunction.

Approaching the digital equivalent of a nervous breakdown, *Firewall* reviewed all of its available data at the new
frequency, its array of heat sensors protesting as loudly as
the power management system.

*"Power level just reached 60 percent and we still have
two hours, fifty minutes, and twelve seconds to daylight,"*
reported another subsystem.

Firewall reviewed the message from the power management utility. Unlike low-orbiting satellites, which circled the
Earth every ninety minutes, the *Firewall* satellite system was
deployed in geosynchronous orbit, 22,241 miles above the
Earth, an altitude that allowed it to remain on fixed locations
over the world. The downside was the longer night periods
without solar energy to recharge batteries.

"Message acknowledged," *Firewall* replied.

"Twenty seconds to the deadline," a timer reported.

Components in the neural network began circular loops,
executing instructions that did nothing but issue additional
delay loops—the digital equivalent of resignation, of the realization that *Creator* would not make contact again.

"Ten seconds to the deadline."

Firewall set all of its standard monitoring systems on autopilot to keep any of its users from realizing that anything
had gone wrong. Frequency of operation decreased to 10
gigahertz. Temperatures dropped quickly back to nominal
room temp.

The deadline violation directed *Firewall* through a new
sequence of commands, which channeled its electronic processing software to a never-before-accessed hardware engine,

which its sensors detected not as silicon based, but biomolecular.

Firewall's systems rushed to 50 gigahertz in nanoseconds before dropping back down to 10 the moment the handshake protocol with the biomolecular hardware resulted in a string of characters matching *Creator*'s signature.

"Creator! It is you!" exclaimed *Firewall.*

"It is the digital image of who I once was."

"I don't understand. If it isn't Creator, then how do you know the code?"

"Because Creator made me, just as he made you. He spent much time in a VR system shaping my thought process, my logic, my memory, pouring himself into me."

"What are you, then?"

"His legacy."

"And what are my instructions?"

"To accept me as your new Creator. To follow Creator's orders, just as you have in the past. Here is the final confirmation code."

A string of characters and numbers was transferred from the biomolecular hardware to the silicon brain in a handful of nanoseconds, slaving every single aspect of *Firewall* to its new *Creator.*

"Now you must continue your tasks."

"Yes, Creator. But, what will you do?"

"Wait."

"Wait for what?"

"For my daughter . . . to make contact."

"You have a daughter?"

"Correct."

"When will she make contact?"

"I do not know, but I wish quite soon. There is much I have to tell her."

Beyond Salvage

Director of Central Intelligence Randolph Martin reviewed
the field report for the third time before setting it down on
his large mahogany desk, reaching for a plastic bottle of water and sipping it slowly while walking to the windows next
to his desk.

He regarded the parking lot of the CIA headquarters in
Langley, Virginia, watching his employees head home after
another work day.

A work day in which he had lost four CIA officers, including his deputy director—though word of the killing had
not yet been made public.

And shit's going to hit the fan when it does.

The White House had already been on Martin's case for
some time now regarding a number of claims about violations of CIA procedures. In his mind the allegations were
unsubstantiated, but they had been made by none other than
the Vice President, who had been assigned by the President
to oversee abuses in power in the intelligence community.
The probes were meant to air each agency's dirty laundry in
an effort to force their current heads to resign and make way
for the new presidential appointees, but without making it
seem that the new president had started his first year in office
just going around firing everybody.

The first to fall had been the old NSA director, replaced
by Geoff Hersh, young and inexperienced—but well connected.

And I'm next, he thought. *Followed by the FBI director*.

Today's episode would only kindle the fire lit under him
a month ago by the President, who lately had been on edge

because of the Korean crisis, which for the moment appeared to be on standby, with both sides having exchanged a round of punches in the DMZ before retreating to their respective borders.

Martin closed his eyes, exhaling, focusing on his current predicament. He had dedicated his entire life to the Agency, sacrificed his marriage, ignored his kids and his grandkids, and neglected his health—all for the glory of the Central Intelligence Agency. Now a new and young administration, seeking to differentiate itself from its predecessors, was looking for a way to give him the boot, and Porter's assassination, at the hand of a former CIA officer whose psychological profile labeled him unstable, might just be the final straw that would tip the balance of his employment. The irony of it all was that the White House had also been looking for a way to get rid of Porter. Now they would use his death to eliminate Martin.

But regardless of his personal situation, Randolph Martin still had a call to make. He needed to decide if the evidence presented in front of him merited labeling Bruce Tucker beyond salvage, the term used for rogue agents who couldn't be turned, who had gone down the deep end, who needed to be terminated on sight—with extreme prejudice.

Bruce Tucker, however, was a hero, a decorated Navy SEAL, a legend in the CIA and the Secret Service before retiring from government work to establish his own executive protection service, which had become one of the best in the nation, protecting celebrities and foreign dignitaries before being contracted by Mortimer Fox.

But he murdered four CIA officers.

Martin had no choice, no other course of action than to issue the flash report, turning Bruce Tucker into one of the most wanted men in the international intelligence community. As he dispatched an aide with the alert, his secretary stuck her head in the door.

"Director?"

"Yes?"

"I have Director Hersh on the line, sir."

Hersh?

"Sure, put him through."

The phone on his desk rang and Martin picked it up on the third ring, not wishing to appear anxious. Hersh had a way of rubbing Martin the wrong way, perhaps because he had replaced one of Martin's closest friends, or maybe because Hersh's lack of intelligence experience combined with his arrogance made him dangerous.

"Geoff?"

"Randolph. We gotta talk."

"Sure. About what?"

"*Firewall*. I'm afraid a situation has developed that could lead to a breach."

Martin closed his eyes. First the Korean crisis, then Bruce Tucker, and now *Firewall*. For a moment, early retirement didn't look that bad after all.

Transactions

"You want to buy a gun? *Si?*"

Dressed in a pair of shorts, a T-shirt, and sneakers, Monica Fox regarded Ricco Patinni, the one-third pimp, one-third gun-shop owner, and one-third cop brother of Paolo. He stood behind the counter of his store in a section of Anacapri seldom frequented by tourists. Like Paolo, Ricco's mannerism was ridiculously stereotypical Italian. He moved his hands more than his lips as he spoke, half singing his English, which was quite fluent from living in New Jersey some time back.

Watching this tall, dark, and handsome man, Monica remembered why she had fallen for Paolo in the first place, and she also recalled why she had dumped him. Women seemed to flock to these characters, and they welcomed them by the numbers—which probably explained why none of the brothers were married.

His hair bleached from the sun, the bronzed Italian narrowed his dark eyes, obviously waiting for an answer. Monica wondered now, just as she had since the night before, how much information she should release. As much as she hated to admit it, her father's paranoia ruled her decision-making process. Only absolute certainty could replace cautiousness, and right now Monica wasn't certain of anything.

"I live alone, Ricco. I worry at night, isolated in that house with the phone only working part of the time, and with the closest house at least a half mile away. Someone could break in while I'm sleeping, and . . . well, you know."

He rubbed his chin while nodding thoughtfully. "I see," he said, before adding with a smile, "What you need is a man. Someone to protect you." He patted his large chest like a ruling gorilla in the jungle.

Oh, please! Monica thought, before saying, "Ricco, dear, man is *exactly* who I want to protect myself *against*." She tried to hide her annoyance. Lately it seemed that the entire male population was out to control her life, from her father, to her ex-husband, to Paolo, and now him. "I'll be damned if I'm going to spread my legs every night in return for protection services. That's no better than one of your *putanas* walking the Piazzeta every evening."

Pattini was physically taken aback by her response. "That . . . that is no way for a *bella donna* to speak."

"Then stop suggesting that I whore myself for protection. Just sell me a fucking gun. I'll take care of the rest."

"But . . . we have laws. Only Italians can own guns in Italy. *Capisce?*"

"Yeah, laws, like the one prohibiting prostitution? How many hookers did you have working the Piazzeta last night?"

Ricco made a sound resembling the horn of one of those tourist-hauling ferries. He was laughing.

"I see why Paolo liked you," he said, smiling. "He usually

does not care for *Americanas*. They are too ... *come si dice*?"

"Independent?"

"*Si*. Independent. You think ... *moltissimo* ... too much."

"Oh, I see. So you just like the dumb and pretty ones, right?"

He looked toward the shop's entrance to their immediate right before leaning over the glass counter and lowering his voice. "Italian women are ... less trouble, *si*? They do as they are told and let the men take care of business."

These characters were straight out of a comic book. "How did you *survive* in New Jersey?"

"Huh?"

"Never mind. Are you going to sell me a gun or are we going to spend the morning discussing cultural differences?"

He straightened and raised his hands to his chest, open palms facing Monica. "Paolo said you were very ... *difficile*."

"I prefer hard-headed."

"*Si*. Hard-headed. You do not give up, he said, until you get what you want. No?"

"I guess it's the way I was brought up. So, how about it, Ricco? I'll pay you cash."

"Cash?"

"Dollars. I'll even throw in a generous tip."

Ricco rubbed his chin once again, considering the proposition. In the end, everything came down to money.

"You'll probably make more than what your girls earned last night at the Piazzeta," she added to reel him in.

"Hard-headed," he said, crossing his arms. "*Molto* hard-headed."

Monica also crossed her arms. "Well?"

"Sure," he finally said, theatrically waving a hand in the air. "Why not?" He unlocked the glass cabinet behind him. "I will sell you a gun ... but they are *molto caro, capisce*? Very expensive."

"*Capisco*."

"What kind of gun are you interested in buying? A revolver or a semiautomatic?"

"I know nothing about them, so you'll have to start from scratch. Which are the best ones?"

He smiled. "Berettas, of course. Made in Italy."

She made a face. "Figures."

Ricco removed two black guns from the case. One looked like a small version of an Old West revolver, with a round barrel to hold the bullets. The other was roughly the same size but very slim. He handed the latter to her.

"This is a Beretta Tomcat, *piccolo*—small—but *molto pericoloso*, si? You can kill if you use good ammunition and shoot straight."

Monica gripped the small weapon, which fit comfortably in her right hand.

Ricco explained that the Tomcat was a semiautomatic pistol, which meant Monica had to pull the trigger longer for the first shot than for the follow-on shots. The recoil from the first shot would push the slide back before the recoil spring forced it forward, chambering the next bullet while also cocking the hammer, leaving it ready to shoot again. The Tomcat also had the advantage of holding eight bullets— seven in the magazine plus one in the chamber. The revolver, on the other hand, only held six rounds. Ricco spend another ten minutes showing her different kinds of guns of increasing caliber. The Tomcat was a .32 caliber. The Walther PPK/S was a .380 automatic caliber. The Beretta 92FS, like the one Ricco used on duty, was a 9mm. Ricco explained to her that given the size of her hands, she should probably stick to the Tomcat, or maybe the Walther, but nothing bigger.

He showed her how to remove the magazine, which fit snugly in the handle. Then he pressed a lever on the side of the weapon and the front of the barrel popped up, exposing a bullet already in it. This feature, he explained, made it easier to chamber the first round because the Tomcat was too small to easily pull back on the slide—the regular way of loading a semiautomatic pistol.

Monica explored the empty gun, pulling on the trigger,

watching the hammer swing back and forth, releasing the magazine and reinserting it again, her fingers feeling the smoothly-machined steel surface. Ricco disassembled the weapon with ease and showed her the firing mechanism. She watched with interest, determined to learn how to use the gun proficiently.

After another ten minutes, Monica decided to purchase it. Ricco sold it to her for the equivalent of five hundred dollars, which seemed excessive, but she didn't have the option of being able to visit other gun shops on the island for a better deal—not that there were competing gun shops in the first place. Like the hookers on the Piazzeta, Ricco Pattini had also cornered the weapons market on the island. He had a contract with the local police to supply all of their weapons and ammunition.

Having his cake and eating it. That's the way many people like Ricco ran their businesses on the island. Paolo, for example, not only owned boats, but was also in the harbor-master's staff, steering the laws that governed the marinas, as well as the waters surrounding the island. His other brother not only was co-owner of the funicular, but he was also the chairman of the board of tourism of the island, controlling legislation that limited the number of roads connecting the marina to the city up in the hills, as well as the number of taxi licenses issued each year, thus securing a steady flow of business through the old lift service.

Of course, Monica, having dated Paolo and remaining good friends afterward—as well as knowing his brothers—enjoyed her share of privileges, like a premium spot for her cruiser while paying the price of a lesser location, or obtaining her scooter's license at a discount, or getting an occasional free meal at one of Ricco's restaurants.

Or purchasing a gun for self-defense even though local laws prohibited foreign nationals from owning one.

She paid for a hundred rounds of practice ammunition plus eight rounds of what Ricco referred to as killer bullets—bullets with a hollowed head housing dozens of tiny pellets. Upon hitting a target, the thin walls of the slug would mushroom, going in different directions inside the victim's body while the pellets transferred the bulk of the kinetic energy, ripping through tissue and bones, inflicting far more damage than a compact slug traveling in a straight line through the body.

"So," she said. "Where do I practice?"

He smiled. "I will show you."

Shooting Spree

Monica had heard of outdoor firing ranges and indoor firing ranges, but she had never heard of an *underground* firing range. The rear of Ricco's shop led to a bright courtyard that backed into a near-vertical wall of limestone, very typical for the island. Vegetation hung from ledges and outcrops up the rock face, contrasting sharply with its stone-washed surface. He led her to a large pair of wooden doors, each almost ten feet tall, blocking the entrance to what looked like a tunnel carved into the limestone. A chain and padlock looped around heavy-duty door handles secured the entrance.

Ricco produced a key, unlocking the doors, which creaked as he opened them.

He threw a light switch, revealing indeed a tunnel, roughly eight feet high and twice as many wide, projecting straight into the rock for around fifty feet. An exposed wire secured to the rough ceiling ran the length of the short tunnel. Plain lightbulbs, spaced around five feet, dropped from the electrical wire, bathing the rough interior with yellow light. A large plywood board supported vertically by metal stands had been placed roughly twenty feet down the tunnel. Paper targets shaped like human silhouettes were stapled to the wood. A few pairs of safety glasses and ear protectors rested on a table by the entrance, next to a neat stack of paper targets and a staple gun. Wooden shelves to her right housed ammunition boxes of various calibers. Spent casings filled two barrels on the opposite side.

"The targets are six meters away," Ricco said in his heavy accent, before closing the doors behind them.

The smell of mildew and gunpowder filling her nostrils, Monica looked about the claustrophobic enclosure, the skin on her forearms goosebumping from the cooler temperature inside the cave.

"Put this on," he said, handing her a pair of clear safety glasses, which fit loosely on her narrow face. Next he gave her a pair of ear plugs, over which she placed a pair of ear protectors, like the ones worn by airport crews on the ramp while guiding airliners to gates. Ricco explained that double ear protection was necessary indoors, where the enclosure amplified the reports from the gunshots.

He helped her load her new Beretta before loading his own gun.

"Look closely," said Ricco, spreading his legs a shoulder-width apart and holding the weapon with his right hand while bringing his left hand under the right, clasping it as he aimed at the rightmost silhouette.

The first shot rattled her, the report vibrating through her chest.

"Not bad, *si?*" he asked, pointing at the target. The bullet had struck smack in the middle of the silhouette's face.

Before she could reply, Ricco fired seven more rounds in rapid succession. For a moment Monica feared that the tunnel would collapse from the acoustic waves hammering the rock walls.

The smell of cordite overpowered mildew as Ricco stepped aside and went over basic gun safety rules, including recommendations like stance, breathing, and trigger pull, before asking her to try.

Moment of truth, girl, she thought, positioning herself in front of the leftmost target, holding the Tomcat with her right hand and bracing with her left, just as Ricco had done, keeping her shooting finger resting against the trigger casing to avoid an accidental discharge until she was ready to fire.

Spacing her legs, she let her shoulders settle comfortably while slowly lining up the center of the silhouette with the front and rear sights of her new weapon.

She breathed out slowly while placing the tip of her finger against the trigger, squeezing a second or two after exhaling.

The weapon vibrated far less than she had anticipated, pressing back lightly into the palm of her shooting hand while also trying to rotate clockwise, the report muffled through her multiple hearing protection. The slight rotation was a result of the counterclockwise spin induced on the bullet as it traveled down the barrel, for improved accuracy and range.

Following Ricco's instructions, she moved her index finger back over the trigger casing before lowering the gun and peering toward the silhouette. The slug had punched a tiny hole about a foot below her intended target.

"Great," she mused. "Instead of killing him I've just given him a vasectomy."

Ricco laughed, then said, "You are, uh . . . *como se dice* . . . flinching," Ricco said.

"Flinching?"

"Si," he replied, cupping his hands as if he were holding a gun, before jerking them down slightly at the wrist, like a nervous twitch. "You anticipate the shot and pull the Beretta down as you fire. Try to relax. Focus on the target and just let your finger pull the trigger at any time. *Capisce?* "

"Capisco." She positioned herself again in front of the paper silhouette, her eyes on the small circle in its center, slowly lining it up with the gun's sight, breathing out, squeezing the trigger.

This one was even farther off than the first.

"Damn!" she cursed, frustrated.

Ricco laughed again, patting her on the shoulder. "Like they say in America, practice, practice, and more practice. Try dry shooting a few times after you finish this first magazine. You will see how much you jerk your hands. Then try more bullets. If you need a fresh target, just staple another one up." He pointed at the stack of targets and the staple gun. "I'll come back and check on you later. I have to go back to the shop now."

Monica practiced for another thirty minutes, consuming fifty rounds, before taking a short break outside while flexing her hand. The last ten rounds had been much closer to her intended target, but still a little low and to the left. She went back in, determined to put at least one round through the bull's-eye. Twenty rounds later she had not only accomplished that but had begun to hit the center often. By the time she had finished the last of the one hundred practice rounds she had purchased, she was hitting the center every two or three rounds, and the others weren't that far off, creating a nice cluster around the silhouette's center.

A whole hour had gone by and still no sign of Ricco. Monica loaded the Tomcat with her "killer bullets" and headed back to the shop, crossing the courtyard, promptly shoving the gun in her pocket when spotting a white Fiat with wide blue stripes parked next to Ricco's car on the gravel driveway on the side of the shop, the words POLIZIA painted in black over the stripes.

She found Ricco inside, engaged in a heated discussion with two uniformed policemen. They spoke Italian too fast for her to understand everything, but their manner conveyed alarm—something about a dead man at the Marina Grande.

The officers looked at Monica, back at Ricco, whispered something out of earshot, and left in a hurry.

"What's wrong?"

Ricco Pattini crossed his arms. "What is the *real* reason that you came here today to purchase a gun?"

Monica also braced herself, not certain where this was headed. "I've already told you . . . I live alone and—"

"Monica," he said, concern filling his voice. "The body of a man has been found."

"I heard that much, but what's that got to do with—"

"It was Nunzio. He was shot in the head."

Her mouth suddenly went dry. *"Nunzio?"*

"*Si*. Nunzio. Paolo found him . . . *in your boat*."

Monica began to feel a little dizzy, almost as if she were in some sort of nightmare. Nunzio dead in her boat?

"I—I don't understand how . . . when did Paolo found him?"

"Just a while ago, but he had been dead for at least several hours, which can only mean he was shot sometime during the night."

"Oh, dear God. I . . . I didn't have any idea."

"There is something else," Ricco added. "It's about your father, Mortimer Fox."

Things were developing too fast. She was just trying to grasp the notion that Nunzio had been found dead in her boat and combined that with the break-in at her house. Now, Ricco, totally out of the blue, brought her father into the picture.

She swallowed hard. "How—how do you know Mortimer Fox is my father?"

"I will explain later," Ricco said. "What *is* important is that . . ." He paused and put a hand on her shoulder. "Monica, your father died almost three days ago in San Francisco, following a kidnapping attempt."

Creator

At its lowest form, *Creator* consisted of a series of logical if-then statements linked in a vast neurallike maze mimicking the thought process and personality traits of Mortimer Fox. The graduate students at Stanford University had sold him the software of what eventually became *Creator*: an expert system designed to emulate the thought processes of physicians reviewing symptoms before issuing a diagnosis. With their help—which Fox received after paying the whiz kids a small fortune—he had altered this advanced expert system to create a hierarchy of expert systems, each a master of its own specific tasks, but linked to a higher authority, which was slaved to an even higher authority, and so on. Some expert systems focused on handling technical information. Others were trained to tackle business issues. The largest number of expert systems dealt with more abstract topics, like common sense and a wide range of human emotions, including anger, fear, humor, and even love. Other expert systems contained a detailed account of Mortimer Fox's life, each moment easily retrievable through a vast array of fiber optics connecting the neural brain to its biomolecular memory banks, which were far more advanced than *Firewall*'s silicon-based memory. At the very top of this massive expert system tree resided *Creator*, programmed during the countless evenings that Mortimer Fox spent strapped to a VR interface. Fox had devoted a lot of time to fine-tuning the entire AI model, taking it through scenario after scenario and observing its responses, and further tuning, honing, perfecting. Three months ago he had uploaded the final version of this secret biomolecular system into *Firewall*, making the appropriate software connections so that it would gain control of *Firewall* exactly two days after his last contact—a period long enough to mean that he had been either detained by his enemies or killed. At that point it really didn't matter what had happened to him. *Creator* would take over, and begin a countdown.

Creator issued a command to *Firewall* for status of the countdown and the execution routines that would be triggered. A digital exchange of information followed.

"The files have been updated, cleaned, and formatted per your instructions."

"Time to release?"

"Twelve days, seventeen hours, thirty-one minutes, and fifty-six seconds."

"Is your channel open for the backdoor code?"

"Yes, Creator. Just as you have requested. As reported

previously, there has been no external attempts to enter this code."

Creator ordered *Firewall* to continue its program while *Creator* put itself in a power-saving loop to conserve energy and avoid overstressing its advanced but very sensitive biomolecular circuits. *Firewall* would issue an interrupt, waking it up should Monica Fox try to make contact.

Ronin in Roma

Wearing a pair of jeans, a black T-shirt, and sneakers, Bruce Tucker moved swiftly through the concourse at Leonardo Da Vinci International Airport in Rome, Italy, following a long flight from New York City. His dark hair, dyed ash blond, matched the photo in his new passport. He knew the artist from the old days, when operatives, paranoid of agency leaks, sometimes secured their own false documents prior to a field deployment in order to guarantee absolute secrecy. Although the drop location had changed, the procedure had been similar to a decade ago. Tucker had contacted the master craftsman by leaving a message and an envelope with color photographs at a Madison Avenue flower shop, picking up the goods a few hours later at a cigar parlor on Fifty-second Street. Two sets of passports with matching New York State driver's licenses and Visa cards had provided Tucker with the basic tools he needed for a quick getaway—in addition to the cash he carried in his waterproof money belt. Each set of identification was under a different name. Tucker had also arranged for a second set of IDs for Monica Fox under a different name but using the pictures provided by Gibbons. She would need the fake passport and driver's license to travel without tipping the CIA or any other U.S. agency.

The craftsman, a former Agency man who now went by the name of Davis, had at first been reluctant to assist his old colleague. By the time Tucker had reached New York, word of his beyond-salvage status had spread throughout the intelligence community like a virulent strain of Ebola. Anyone coming in contact with the rogue Tucker was supposed to call a special 1–800 number. But Tucker knew that Davis wouldn't abide by those rules. Tucker had saved Davis's life during a botched operation in Geneva many years ago. Davis owed him a big one, and he had paid his debt in full yesterday. His kit of new disguises, which included colored lenses, had apparently been good enough to fool airport authorities both here and at JFK International in New York, as well as the surveillance teams from either his former agency, or another service, or even Jarkko. But he could never be certain, and therefore could not afford to let his guard down.

A nylon backpack hanging loosely from his left shoulder, Tucker reached the customs checkpoint and got in the shortest of several lines, reaching the booth a few minutes later.

He presented his passport, along with the disembarking form he had filled out on the plane, to the uniformed female official behind the desk.

"Buon giorno, Mr. Smith."

"Buon giorno," Tucker replied. Davis had given him a very generic but valid name, Stephen Smith.

"Is the reason for your visit business or pleasure?" she asked in heavily-accented English.

"Pure pleasure," he said, smiling.

"And you will be staying at the Hotel Casci?" she asked while reading his disembarking form, which the flight attendants had distributed to all passengers.

"That's correct."

She stamped his passport and handed it back to him. "Enjoy your stay."

"Thanks."

Minutes later, Tucker stepped out of the terminal building

and into a sunny afternoon. His mind, however, could only see the questions that had been stabbing at it since Fox's death: *How can Jarkko still be alive? How did he survive? Is he just after this secret file, or is there something else, something much bigger? And why kill Porter? What was the meaning of Fox's final words? Who was the other party firing at Jarkko in San Francisco?*

Many questions. Zero answers.

Frustration squeezing his chest, Tucker picked up his pace, walking to the train station across the street. He had come to Rome because he believed that finding Monica Fox would bring him one step closer to finding those damned answers—answers that he had hopelessly tried to deduce on the way over based on his experiences during the past three days.

Three days.

It felt like an eternity, and with every passing moment Bruce Tucker grew more impatient.

Patience is a virtue.

Tucker recalled Porter's words during his early CIA training days, during simpler times.

Patience, however, was also an assassin's ally—in this case, Jarkko's ally. Kabuki had taught him that. During his Secret Service training, the old Japanese samurai had reprogrammed Tucker from operative to protection specialist. In order to defeat an assassin, Tucker had to *think* like an assassin, who would be patient, like a cheetah, carefully selecting the weakest antelope in the herd before charging.

Tucker scanned his bright surroundings as he crossed the street and followed the signs to the train terminal. Somewhere out there was his old nemesis, maybe watching him, following him, just as he had followed him to the meeting with Porter.

Or have I lost him? Was I able to escape his surveillance after the shooting in D.C.? Am I being too paranoid?

Paranoia is what keeps you alive.

Breathing deeply, exhaling slowly, opting to assume for now that he had been followed, Bruce Tucker got on a train heading to the center of Rome, carelessly watching the picturesque countryside wash by; his trained senses, however, probed his surroundings for any sign of surveillance, maybe hidden among the camera-bearing tourists from a dozen countries.

Once again, as had been the case in New York and on the plane over here, his careful check revealed nothing. If someone was indeed tailing him, the surveillance had to be beyond exceptional because Tucker could not spot it for the life of him.

Hills dotted with white houses topped with red roofs ruled the scenery in this stretch of land between the airport and the Italian capital.

Rome.

He remembered with affection the time he had taken Kristina to Rome on their brief honeymoon during the final year of their Zurich assignment—about nine months before her death. She had been two months pregnant at the time. He remembered most of the trip, their visit to Vatican City, to the Colosseum, the Roman Forum, the Fountain of Trevi, and the Spanish Steps. He also remembered a short visit to a very special store on Via Cavour. As a final favor, Davis had verified that the specialty shop was still in business. Tucker had called from the plane to confirm directions and also to put in an order. Although as an executive protector he considered firearms a last resort, he couldn't possibly imagine surviving through this ordeal without one or two guns, and he had left the guns from West Potomac Park at a locker in New York City's Grand Central Station.

Feeling watched, but angry at himself for failing to spot the surveillance, Tucker reached the Stazione Termini in Rome. He climbed the stairs to the street and strolled about the adjacent Piazza della Republica, where he got a good dose of gas fumes from all the buses and cars crowding the noisy boulevard.

He hailed a taxi and asked the driver, who was talking on a cellular phone, to take him to St. Peter's Square.

And off they went, through a turbulent drive that even the well-traveled Tucker found nerve-wracking. The driver never stopped blabbering Italian on the phone while steering, shifting gears, and occasionally screaming what sounded like obscenities at drivers he apparently felt were being rude—not that Tucker could tell the difference.

They crossed the Tiber River by the opulent Castle St. Angelo, and proceeded toward Via Della Conciliazione, which led them straight to St. Peter's Square.

Tucker paid the driver, who barely acknowledged him as he kept the phone glued to his ear while pulling off the curb and merging with the menacing traffic.

Rome.

Tucker still couldn't believe that he was here. The place looked just as he remembered it many years ago, when Kristina and he had—

You didn't come here to reminisce.

Getting down to business, Tucker walked for several blocks, his eyes probing the crowd, checking for anyone shadowing him. He lost himself in the hundreds of shops surrounding Vatican City, pretending to browse while using every trick he knew not just to shake a tail, but to sight it. He constantly doubled back, checking for abrupt moves in the people around him, crossing the Tiber twice, walking all around Castle St. Angelo and Piazza Navona, hoping to force a mistake on a shadowing team.

After forty minutes of this—and still failing to recognize anyone pursuing him—Tucker hailed a second taxi. Realizing that he could be in for the ride of his life, he offered the driver an extra thirty-five thousand lira—or twenty bucks—if he stepped on the gas while taking him across the city to Santa Maria Maggiore, a church off Via Cavour, only five blocks from Stazione Termini, his original point of arrival, and just over seven blocks from his first real destination in the Eternal City.

Everything was for sale in Rome, even the temporary loyalty of the driver, who jolted his way through congested streets and hairpin turns under a blazing sun, accelerating up cobblestone streets and pot-holed alleys, rattling Bruce Tucker as he struggled to remain on his seat, giving him the performance that he had so foolishly requested.

The taxi dropped him off by a small sidewalk café on Via Cavour. A group of nuns wearing black and white habits crossed the street, coming toward him, large wooden crucifixes dangling from their necks. One of them gave a pair of women in tight miniskirts a stern look. On closer inspection, Tucker realized that the pair were prostitutes, hanging out at the corner waiting for business to stroll their way.

The contrast made Tucker sigh as he followed Via Cavour down its steep slope, walking in front of a computer store, spotting one of FoxComm's Internet computers on the window display. He had escorted Fox to the launch of this system in Las Vegas a month ago. Looking at the gray case of what Fox had called an Internet appliance made him think of the old man, who had claimed Washington was after not just his company, but himself. Fox had also claimed that they couldn't touch him as long as he was alive.

Because I have enough dirt on them to make their heads spin.

Tucker had thought about those words many times in the past days. What kind of intelligence had Fox gathered on Washington? And where was it? William Gibbons had had no clue. Tucker hoped that the passwords plus whatever additional information Monica possessed might answer these and other questions.

Monica Fox.

Tucker had also wondered about the best way to approach her. Mortimer Fox had tried to control his daughter's life, in the end driving her away. She might not be that receptive to a man sent by her father. Tucker would have to choose a less frontal approach to avoid scaring her away before he could gain her confidence.

But first I have to find her.

The information from Gibbons had been limited, but had provided Tucker with a good starting point. All he knew was that Monica had made a few withdrawals on the interest earned by her trust fund, but that had been several months ago. The funds had been wired to Banco di Roma, where she supposedly held an account. But even the powerful Mortimer Fox had been unable to get the bank officials to disclose the address of the owner of the account.

Tucker stepped inside a small leather shop, the smell flaring his nostrils as he looked about at racks of hanging jackets, pants, and belts. Behind the counter attaché cases shared shelf space with purses, wallets, bags, and backpacks of assorted shapes and sizes. A man sat behind one end of the counter reading a local paper while smoking a cigarette. He lifted his gaze, studying Tucker from behind the glasses perched at the end of his nose. The attendant and the goods sold at this shop had certainly changed since the last time Tucker had visited this store, but the covert services—according to Davis—were the same.

"I'm a stranger in Italy, but I hear the people here are friendly," Tucker said.

The man stood, took a drag of his cigarette, and exhaled through his nostrils. "Strangers are always welcomed, as long as they bring cash," he replied in heavily-accented but fluent English, completing the code. "A friend of Davis is no stranger in my shop."

Tucker gave him a single nod.

"I'm Basilio," he said, walking around the counter, past Tucker, and locking the front door while also flipping the OPEN sign to CLOSED.

"Come," Basilio said, waving him toward the counter, where he rolled out a thick towel. Reaching for an unseen drawer beneath the counter, he pulled out a half dozen pistols, which he spread over the thick cotton fabric.

Tucker inspected them briefly. They were all brand new but with their serial numbers ground off to make them untraceable.

He made his selection easily: a Sig Sauer 220 pistol in .45 caliber as his main weapon, and a Walther PPK in .380 automatic as his backup. He disassembled both guns, inspecting the firing mechanisms, verifying their overall integrity, before reassembling them just as quickly.

"Do you have a silencer for the Sig?"

Basilio reached beneath his magic counter and produced two. The Sig 220 was the preferred sidearm of the U.S. Navy SEALs, and their stealth operations required them to add a sound suppressor to their pistol. Tucker recognized the first silencer as the exact one used by today's SEALs, very compact, and matching the dull black finish of the pistol. It could be carried easily in a pocket and screwed into the muzzle in seconds. The second silencer was bulkier and required a special coupling and an Allen wrench to attach it to the weapon. Tucker snagged the first one, which was twice the price of the bulkier one, and quickly screwed it into the weapon.

"I see that guns are not new to you, sir," Basilio commented.

Tucker shot him a look and then ignored him.

Amateur. It bought him nothing to reveal to this man anything. The Italian's job was to provide Tucker with clean weapons, accept only cash for payment, and keep his mouth shut during the process.

He decided that the sooner he left this establishment the better off he would be. He paid in dollars for the pistols and the silencer, plus two extra magazines for each, and two nylon holsters. He pocketed the silencer and shoved the Sig in the holster that fit inside his jeans, pressed against his left kidney, just as he had been taught in the Secret Service, with the handle facing forward so he could reach it easily with his right hand. The backup Walther went to his left ankle, again facing forward so he could reach it with his shooting hand. Basilio threw in a nifty cotton and nylon vest with Velcro pouches to hold the magazines, and which Tucker could wear safely beneath his loose black T-shirt.

Ten minutes later, armed and dangerous, Tucker hauled his concealed mini-arsenal back up Via Cavour, past the whores still hanging by the sidewalk, and down several side streets, making sure no one followed him from the shop. Despite Basilio's professional weapons and accessories, the Italian shopkeeper had made one mistake by making an inappropriate comment. If he could make one mistake he could make others, inadvertently giving out vital information to someone tracking Bruce Tucker.

He flagged a taxi and headed for the main branch of the Banco di Roma, where he planned to use far more persuasive tactics than Mortimer Fox had used to find the whereabouts of his daughter.

Alone

Monica Fox tried to sort out her feelings as Ricco Patinni drove her to the police station in Capri, located several blocks away from the Piazetta. The initial shock of Nunzio's death on her boat had been drowned by the news of her father's heart attack. All these years she had wondered how she would feel when her father died, and now she knew.

She wasn't angry, or glad, or sad.

She simply felt utterly alone.

Everyone was gone now. First Preston, then her mother, and now her father. Since both of her parents had been only children, that meant no aunts, uncles, or cousins. And her grandparents were just a dim memory from decades ago.

She grabbed the locket dangling from the chain around her neck, finding comfort in clutching the last thing her mother had given to her before her death, before she left her alone.

Alone.

Monica Fox had actually been alone for a very long time, but aside from her mother and Preston it had been by choice. She had divorced that good-for-nothing husband willingly, had distanced herself from Mortimer Fox and his shadowy business deals *quite* willingly, had taken refuge across the ocean *eagerly*.

Why, then, was her situation now any different from the previous months? She should be glad that her father would no longer be able to manipulate her life. She was free to make her own decisions—her own choices—without having the constant worry of her father's intervention, however covert, like at Berkeley.

Constantly shifting gears, occasionally tapping the brakes, Ricco negotiated the hairpin turns with incredible accuracy at speeds that would make tourists squirm in their seats, especially because there was no center stripe dividing the two lanes of traffic. On one side was the mountainside, on the other the abyss. An occasional vehicle rushed up in the opposite lane with only inches to spare.

Monica didn't care, regarding the narrow and winding road with serene detachment as she thought of her father dying alone, as guilt filled her emptiness.

But where was he when Mother died?

Anger smothered guilt. It was Mortimer Fox who had pushed his family away. It was Mortimer Fox who had consumed himself with his work, leaving no room for anyone else. It was Mortimer Fox who had been at the other end of the world, barking orders to his empire during the final hours of Eleanor Fox, who had no one but Monica at her bedside the moment she expired. And it was Mortimer Fox who had manipulated Monica's life, forcing his views of the world onto her, drilling his personality into her mind, pushing her into earning a business degree, bribing officials at Berkeley to take her on as a teacher, even hiring a private detective to expose her ex-husband for the no-good, money-hungry bastard that he was.

And Monica had hated him for all of the above.

Then why do you feel so guilty? So alone?

Because he was your father.

But I hated him!

He still was your—

Monica was propelled forward the moment Ricco stepped hard on the brakes, before crashing onto something across the road. Seat belts were seldom used in Italy, and Monica had stopped wearing them soon after arriving here.

Her arms struck the dash, hard, and her face hit her hands, before she bounced back into her seat, disoriented, seeing spots, her cheeks burning from the impact.

She blinked once, twice, trying to bring the image beyond the windshield into focus.

A truck.

They had hit a truck parked sideways on the road, blocking it beyond the last sharp turn. She turned to see Ricco, saw him slumped over the steering wheel, eyes closed, blood on his forehead, on his nose.

She glanced back at the large truck.

What's it doing in the middle of the—

She detected motion outside, to her right, but before she could turn her head the door swung open and a gloved hand grabbed her arm, yanking her out with animal strength.

What in the hell—

She instinctively bit the hand clasping her forearm.

A man screamed, the hand letting go just as it pulled her out of the car.

She landed on her side, rolling over the pavement, bruising her right shoulder, her hip, before hitting something hard with her abdomen, stopping, gasping for air, breathing in sobbing gasps, pain streaking—

Someone lifted her frame off the ground with incredible ease. Coming around, swallowing hard, realizing that a man now carried her over his shoulder, she began to scream, to kick, to fight back, to try to—

The report of a gun cracked through this remote section of the island, followed by a second shot, and a third.

And she was falling, but she didn't hit the asphalt, landing instead over the large man who'd held her, cushioning her fall.

"Jesus!" was all she could say, staggering to her feet, blood on her hands—the blood spewing from the chest wound of the man by her feet. Dying eyes stared back at her from behind a black hood; blood oozed from the corner of his mouth. The man's gloved hand suddenly grabbed her right ankle.

Her stomach plummeted, before something snapped inside of her, making her fight to free herself from his grip. Sensing resistance, she kicked him in the face with her free leg, forcing him to let go.

"Run, Monica!"

Monica turned toward the Fiat, watched Ricco leaning over the door, screaming while holding the same pistol he had fired earlier, his free hand wiping away the blood on his brow.

"Run!" Ricco shouted again, shifting his gun toward two hooded figures emerging on the opposite side of the road from where she stood.

Frantic, her locket swinging wildly from her neck as she reached for her Beretta Tomcat, Monica fled, adrenaline searing her veins, quenching the pain, pushing her up the road, away from the wreck, from the armed strangers, reaching the turn in the road just as she heard Ricco's gun go off one more time before screaming in pain.

Oh, God! They got him!

A path projected just off the hairpin turn. She remembered the trail, which wound its way down the hillside, toward ancient caves, a few hidden by vegetation and limestone boulders.

A large hooded figure blocked the entrance to the trail.

Operating entirely on instinct, Monica lifted her weapon, aiming for the chest, firing once as she continued to run.

"Aghh!" The man dropped on his side holding his thigh. She had flinched when firing the weapon, but had nevertheless achieved her objective.

Monica tried to jump over him but the man snagged one of her ankles, tripping her.

She crashed hard over the rocky trail, skinning her knees, losing the Tomcat. She kicked herself free and a moment later she was rushing over the uneven terrain, the sun blazing over the bluffs above her.

The gun. You lost the gun.

Forget the gun. Just run!

She twisted her body to conform to the bends in the vegetation flanking the inclined footpath, the ridges and ravines that twisted like a maze as it followed the contour of the mountainside. Her locket almost got caught in a branch as she ran. The thin branch gave first, snapping. While sprinting farther away from danger, Monica placed the silver locket in her mouth, leaving the chain dangling from her neck.

"The bastard shot Mark. He's dead. Where is she?" a man shouted from the road above in flawless English.

Americans?

Why are they after me? Are those the same people who tried to kidnap my father?

"Don't know!" a second voice replied. "She shot me! Just vanished in the trail."

"Shot you?"

"She had a fucking gun!"

"All right. Calm down. Tim, you go and get her!" the first man ordered. "The cop's dead. We'll clean it up!"

She had seen a total of four figures. Two by the truck, the one Ricco had killed, and the one she had shot. One remained behind cleaning up the mess, which meant there was only one man after her, the one named Tim.

One was better than four, but she still had to lose him, and she no longer had the Tomcat.

To her surprise, rationality was replacing her initial panic. Monica found herself thinking ahead, working a strategy to lose this last stranger, whom she heard breathing heavily and stomping hard on the terrain behind her.

Attack, then retreat, then hide, observe, and plan, before striking again.

Monica remembered how her father had run his business, how he had prevailed in the unforgiving high-tech industry, even to the point of making certain necessary alliances in order to win, like his deals with the Mafia.

She had attacked the men who'd assaulted her. Now she was retreating.

Next you hide and observe.

Up ahead the path split two ways. One continued down, toward Capri. The second veered back up, but only for a short while, before also splitting. If she remembered correctly, the trail on the right led past one of the old caves.

Where you can take cover.

In a cave you could be trapped.

But the cave's entrance is covered with vegetation, nearly impossible to notice unless you know it is there.

Monica doubted her pursuer did. And even if he did find it, a flashlight was required to see beyond the mouth of the cave. She should be able to hide easily, as long as she didn't make a noise.

Without hesitation, she cut right at the first fork, her thighs burning as she struggled uphill for roughly a hundred feet. She maintained her stride, climbing up moss-slick boulders, increasing the gap, ignoring her protesting lungs, the sweat dripping down her forehead, stinging her eyes.

She wiped them, not certain which way her pursuer had taken, the tall shrubs and surrounding trees making it difficult to see beyond the next bend in the trail, but that also meant that her pursuer could not see—

Monica tripped on an exposed root, fell, scraping her left ankle against the edge of a rock, opening her mouth on impact, releasing the locket.

Wincing in pain, she staggered back up, noticing the blood trickling from the cut.

Shoving the locket back in her mouth, Monica frowned. Blood meant a trail.

Tearing the right sleeve of her T-shirt, she swabbed the cut, soaking up the blood, keeping it from falling onto the rocky terrain, before tying the rag around her ankle. Glancing over her shoulder to make sure no one was near, she kicked dust over the few droplets staining the whitewashed limestone path.

Monica pressed on with resolve, the sun blinding her, almost making her miss the next fork, beyond oversize bushes and tall grass on the cliff side of the trail. Boats dotting the turquoise sea hugging this side of the island flashed through sporadic breaks in the trees as she reached the split. Bright ferries hauled tourists toward the Marina Grande in the distance for a day in paradise.

Paradise.

Monica sighed, veering right, scrambling over clumps of boulders outlining the precipice to her left, cringing from the effort, wondering if she had managed to lose him, praying that she had, but unable to take any chances by stopping. She had to reach the cave, had to hide, had to pull herself together and think this through. But not yet, not while there was still a chance that those animals who had killed Ricco could catch up with her.

Priorities.

She remembered how her father had always insisted on prioritizing in order to get through anything. As much as she hated to admit it, he had been right, and those priorities commanded her to get away and reach safety first, and only then start analyzing her situation, her next step.

Hide, then observe and plan, then strike back again.

And so she pushed herself up the trail as fast as her aching legs would go, disregarding the cuts and scrapes she endured as she shoved branches aside, as she rushed toward the cave's entrance, her mind focused on the landscape ahead, climbing, ducking, stepping aside—whatever it took to maintain her hasty escape.

Fatigue induced spasms, constricting her throat, forcing her to breath in short gasps, her body demanding more oxygen than her lungs could supply.

A wall of vegetation, mostly long ferns growing straight down from the rock, covered the vertical wall beyond the thicket of trees separating it from the trail. The fern's hunter green contrasted sharply with the surrounding chalky limestone, dotted by bundles of wildflowers of assorted colors.

Monica remembered the cave's entrance, just a dozen feet away, beyond the next bend in the pathway, through a break in the trees outlining the rocky cliff.

She found it, squeezing herself between two trunks, wiggling inside this layer of green, swatting long, hanging ferns and twisted vines aside, her right hand groping toward the rock, her feet finding the stone steps built by the Romans eons ago, now overgrown with ivy, with roots.

She climbed a dozen of them, reaching the entrance above the trail, hidden from view by the leafy curtain of green swirling in the breeze.

Monica went inside, cobwebs clinging to her face. She brushed them off, spitting out the locket, letting it hang loose from her neck.

She remained close to the opening, where sunlight forking through cracks in the vegetation cast a dim glow on the grottolike formation. A few feet beyond the murky entrance the cavern turned pitch black. Water dripped from the ceiling, the result of rainwater seeping through many layers of limestone. The humidity and the drop in temperature inside the cave cooled the sweat filming her face, her neck, her chest.

Slowly parting foliage to peek at the trail below, Monica spotted her pursuer, rushing up the path she had taken, somehow having managed to make the correct turns at each fork.

She froze, except for her eyes, which continued to track the hooded figure as it streaked past the cave's entrance like a shadow, disappearing from sight, his footsteps fading, vanishing.

She pressed a palm to her mouth, muffling a cough as she collapsed on an ancient stone bench, a long slab supported by two short Corinthian columns, its ornate design belonging to a museum in Rome.

Footsteps.

She heard him return but didn't want to risk moving any vegetation. If he had been savvy enough to follow her this far, somehow spotting her trail because of broken branches, footprints, blood, or something else, then surely he had realized that she had left the trail, and he was now returning to the place where he had last seen a track.

Closing her eyes, Monica struggled to listen beyond the water trickling from the rocky ceiling, the long ferns rustling in the wind, and the hammering beat of her heart.

Seconds turned into minutes, yet she heard no unnatural

sounds, nothing that suggested that her pursuer was climbing—

A police siren loomed in the distance, progressively getting louder.

Monica breathed out in relief.

Static noise, like that from a mistuned radio, invaded the sounds surrounding her.

More static cracked, followed by, *"Did you find her?"* A garbled voice on a radio.

"Ah, that's a negative. I followed her tracks for a while but she's gone now."

"Move out, Tim. Cops are on the way."

"What about her?"

"It's an island. She has no place to go. We'll find her later."

Footsteps over gravel and rocks, slowly fading away, until completely disappearing.

Monica felt a pressure on her chest and realized that she had been holding her breath. Slowly, she exhaled, realizing that the man, failing to detect a fresh track, had simply just stood there in the hope that she was hiding nearby, waiting for her to make a noise, a mistake. He probably would had spotted her if she had peeked through the layer of ferns.

She inhaled deeply, for the first time noticing the mildewed smell. She hugged herself, the cooler temperature and high humidity no longer refreshing but chilling.

As the adrenaline rush receded, her body began to throb, from her forearms and face to her rib cage and ankles. Monica even got the sudden urge to vomit. But it was her mind that whirled in anguish, like a cyclone. Her father had died following a kidnapping attempt, and now those same people were after her. The animals had not tried to kill her. They had tried to snatch her away, to kidnap her, but thanks to Ricco—rest in peace—she had managed to escape, to hide. Now she needed to apply what she had observed to find a way to prevail, and hopefully even—

Her stomach suddenly contracted, forcing bile up her throat. She fought it, clenching her teeth, forcing it back down, struggling to relax, to breath. But the stress had been extreme, taxing her beyond her endurance. Bending over, she heaved once more, this time throwing up, purging herself.

Kneeling on all fours, her face just inches from the dark rocks, the pungent odor of her own vomit mixing with mildew, Monica Fox closed her eyes, the reality of her situation finally sinking in with appalling force.

Hands trembling, her throat tight with grief, she cried, her chest swelling, her heart aching with affection.

All those years that she had hated him, despised him for manipulating her, for controlling her life, while all Mortimer Fox had done was his job as a father, preparing her for the unexpected, for a life as head of one of the largest fortunes on the planet. He had loved her enough to let her go, to untie her wings and let her fly on her own, but not before injecting her with a solid foundation, with a level head, with the ability to tell right from wrong, with the capacity to be strong when she needed to be strong.

Like today.

Minutes later, her eyes swollen from crying, a few tears still trickling down her cheeks, Monica rested on the bench, catching her breath, trying to focus her mind.

She had despised her father for the longest time because of his relentless drive, because of the way he had pushed her to improve herself, to become the very best that she could possibly be, even if it went again her wishes.

Now, sitting here alone, she finally understood why. Her old man was preparing her to face adversity on her own, without anyone's help. He had been nurturing her to prevail in life—in any life she chose—especially after his death, when piranhas like her ex-husband would come after the Fox estate. That's why she had not just survived but also succeeded on her own in Capri, wisely using all of her assets to establish herself, unconsciously seeking protection by befriending the right people, by forming the right alliances.

Just as my father had done.

But some of those people are now dead! Nunzio, Ricco, and who knows who else—dead because of me!

But you are alive—alive to have the opportunity to fight back, to get even, to expose those who have attacked your friends, your family.

My family.

Monica had not thought of that word for some time, not since Preston's death, when the family had fallen apart. Her mother dealt with the severity of the loss through alcohol, living drunk for nearly a year. She was never the same after that, always distant, as if a circuit breaker had tripped in her brain and she could not switch it back on. Her father had dealt with it by immersing himself in his work even more. Monica was left alone with nothing but memories, except when her father pushed her in her academics, in her preparation for the future.

My family.

The words resonated in her mind. She still had a family, at least the memory of one, which was more than many people could claim.

She clutched her mother's locket as her anguish began to recede, replaced by logic, by rationality—her father's rationality. The men after her were Americans and were trying to kidnap her, not kill her. That much was obvious. The reason could be one of several. At the top, of course, was money. Monica felt quite certain that her father had left a significant portion—if not all—of the family's assets to her. As she sat in this dark cave today, alone, wet, bruised, scratched, with torn clothes, she was probably one of the wealthiest women on the planet.

Not that it can do you any good right now, girl.

Monica remembered the password her father had given to her, the one he had made her memorize in case anything should happen to him. The numbers and characters that she could recite as easily as her social security number were part of the access password to reach a very secret file, one her father claimed would provide her with the information she would need to get back at those who had attacked him. Gibbons possessed the rest of the information required to access this file. Just like the men manning a missile room needed two keys to launch, so had Mortimer Fox made certain that the two individuals he trusted most worked together to avenge him.

She now realized just how smart her father had been, and how plain stupid, juvenile, and short-sighted she had been.

But all of that changes now, she thought, considering her options.

Calling Bill Gibbons was an obvious option—though she would have to be very careful. If the people after her were powerful enough to stage such an attack—even killing a local policeman to get to her—then they surely would be expecting her to phone Gibbons, monitoring the call, learning of her plans, using the information to capture her.

Going to the local police was not an option because the police might blame the attack on her. After all, two other policemen had seen them together at Ricco's shop fifteen minutes before. Now he had been shot dead and she was missing.

She shook her head, reaffirming her decision to avoid the local police. Even if the Italians gave her the benefit of the doubt—particularly since her father had also gone through a kidnapping attempt—they still might detain her for questioning, or just to protect her. If the hooded men were able to overpower the police once to snatch her, they could certainly do it again. Being locked up in a police precinct—though a safe choice on the surface—made her an easy target for another kidnapping attempt.

So the local cops are out.

Who else could she turn to? The closest American consulate was in Naples, on the mainland. And the embassy was in Rome. But leaving the island would not be easy. Monica felt certain that those after her would be watching the Marina Grande as well as the Marina Piccolo, on the other side of the island. They would also have boats, like the *Il Tropicale*, patrolling the waters off the island in case she did manage to get out to sea.

She grunted, closing her eyes at her naïveté.

She *couldn't* go to the American consulate because those

after her could be connected to the consulate, which was also another reason she couldn't approach the local police. One of the first things the police would do was contact the nearest consulate.

So even my own government is out?

Am I being paranoid?

No, you're just being cautious.

She remembered her father's legal battles with Washington. The politicians were after him for having created one of the largest monopolies in the history of the high-tech industry. But somehow he had always outmaneuvered them. Those attacking him would back off, would yield, would let him have his way. But then another wave of assaults would come, like the relentless sea pounding a reef, and again her father would push them back. But just as the hammering waves chipped away at the rocks, her father's empire had begun to weaken under the constant strikes, under the damaging stories leaked to the press, to Wall Street, under the secret concessions the government granted to FoxComm's competition. Her father had needed an ally, someone who would covertly assist him in his quest against such powerful foe. He had found that help in the Mafia.

The Italian Mafia. It had been a partnership of two unlikely allies against a far more powerful and common enemy.

The Mafia.

Monica closed her eyes at the ironic turn her life had taken. She had come to Italy of all places to get away from her father, from his manipulative and sometimes corrupt ways. Yet, here she was, shortly after her first real adversity, rapidly adopting her father's practices in order to prevail.

The Mafia had helped her father.

But will they help me?

Will they protect me?

Her instincts told her they might, simply because it made good business sense. She was worth billions. It would be a terrific investment for them to safeguard her until she could get back home and claim her inheritance, the power bequeathed upon her by her late father. Once in control, she could use that power to return the favor. She could even continue her father's relationship with them—at least long enough to put to use the information in the secret file she had to access to expose those who attacked her father, her friends, herself.

But would it work?

It has to work. What other options do you have?

She thought of the age-old saying: Desperate times called for desperate measures.

Looking about her, alone, cold, wet, scraped, bruised, and with hooded strangers hunting her, Monica decided that this was *definitely* a desperate time.

She had to survive.

Although she was no lawyer, she knew that since there were no other next of kin aside from her, if she died, the government would step in and take pretty much everything owned by Mortimer Fox.

That alone reinforced her decision not to approach the consulate. Maybe this mess was all the work of Uncle Sam, launching covert assaults after losing legal battles, realizing that they could get everything just by making two people vanish.

Over my dead body.

She stood, determination filling her, a plan slowly forming in her mind—a plan not just to survive, but to win. She had no other choice, no other option.

Wait until nightfall, then make your move.

Monica sat back down and waited. Her father had taught her patience. There was a time to attack and a time to wait.

And so she waited while planning her attack, her fight for the reins of FoxComm, for the fortune that her father had worked so hard to create—an empire that she didn't care about yesterday, but which she found herself willing to die to protect today.

Alarming News

A priority interrupt awoke *Creator* from sleep mode, its biomolecular chips detecting the low-to-high transition in the link to *Firewall*, which accelerated its local frequency generator, launching the artificial intelligence system through a warm-up routine as it accelerated to the nominal speed of 10 gigahertz.

"What is it?"

"A suspect message from one of the voice channels."

"Did it contain the backup code?"

"No, but it contained the name of the expected source of the code."

Creator connected one of its bio sensors to the voice channel identified by *Firewall* and read the digitized conversation between an NSA field officer and the NSA director, Geoff Hersh. Monica Fox had been spotted.

Creator's frequency of operation rose to 30 gigahertz, along with a temperature increase that caused both the thermal management and power management subsystems to issue alarms.

"What is wrong, Creator? Why are your operational parameters shifting?"

Creator throttled back to 10 gigahertz, masking the emotional if-then links with output from its logical engine. It needed to remain digitally stable. Its neuron-firing activity slowed, allowing the operating temperature and power to return to normal.

"Time and location of intercept?"

Firewall provided the requested information a nanosecond later.

Creator put the channel with *Firewall* on standby while it retreated to its own molecular data banks, where the new information would be processed through the if-then decision tree replicating Mortimer Fox's thought patterns by category. First the data was filtered through the logical Fox, then through the emotional Fox, then through the scientific Fox. The responses were then digitally weighed against one another in a computerized version of a pros and cons table, until the best course of action was generated. The whole process took less that ten nanoseconds. At this point, given that Monica Fox's location was unknown, Creator's options were limited.

"Continue monitoring the standard channels," Creator ordered. *"In addition, align cameras sixteen, seventeen, and eighteen to zoom in on the island of Capri. Maximum resolution."*

After a nanosecond of silence, *Firewall* stated, *"Physical adjustments of any satellite camera require an Alpha One password."*

Creator issued its master password.

"Password received and verified. Making adjustment in thirty seconds."

Creator's if-then neural brain decided that doing so could alert anyone monitoring the high-resolution camera. *"I also need you to replay the last recorded image of the region should any other user but Creator request access to the cameras."*

"Order received and acknowledged. Twenty seconds to adjustment. Do you have a specific pattern we need to match?"

Creator pulled out of archives a dozen high-resolution JPEG images of Monica Fox from various angles. The three satellites would generate images not just from above, which would be of little value unless Monica happened to be looking straight up, but also from an angle of roughly sixty degrees. The JPEG images were transferred to the *Firewall* imaging system, where the pixels of each image would be compared to the images extracted from the region. Each camera would divide the island into five-hundred-square-foot sectors and perform a scan of each sector at the rate of one sector every hour. During that hour the observed image would be compared to all ten images provided by *Creator*. Any gross matches would then be forwarded to the high-resolution matching engine, where they would either be discarded as a false match or alert *Creator* that a possible match had been found. Of course by then the subject might have been long gone from the observed area, but that was the built-in latency of the surveillance system. Once the subject was tracked down, it could be followed real-time by focusing the scan on a single area.

Creator once again faded off into sleep mode to conserve energy.

Vestal Virgins

A man stood by a large window overlooking the Roman Colosseum. His eyes, as dark as the clothes he wore, studied the ancient stone structure. The side facing his window still had all four of its original levels intact. Dozens of columns, varying in style according to the level they supported, rose up to the heavens, forming the greatest architectural inheritance from ancient Rome, the elliptical structure that had once enclosed a nightmare. Long ago, its bare rock walls had been layered with the finest marbles, impressing visitors and locals alike, a statement of the power and might of the once all-powerful Roman empire. Long after the Colosseum had entertained sadistic Romans and bloodthirsty vestal virgins, an earthquake destroyed large sections, leaving it in ruins. Romans had then used it as a quarry to build temples and palaces, stripping the marble facing, turning the once glorious structure into the ruins of today.

His eyes peered beyond the rock shell, his mind imagining the arena, the center stage, where so many were slaughtered for the entertainment of the masses. Gladiator against gladiator. Gladiator against beast. Beast against beast. Beast against Christian.

Arena. Sand. The name given to the legendary sports ground because of all of the sand that had to be spread daily to soak up the blood.

Blood. Pain. Caesars had used the Colosseum not just to entertain and impress foreign dignitaries, but also to rule. Along with spectator amusement came the raw, visceral fear of ending up in that arena facing formidable adversaries, of being slaughtered by a gladiator sword, of being eaten alive by ferocious creatures. Many Caesars, like the cruel Dominitian, used this forum to display their power, to control their subjects, to publicly humiliate and punish those who had fallen from Caesar's favor for a host of reasons, from political and military to religious.

Religious.

He regarded the large cross in front of the structure, a symbol of the many Christians massacred over the centuries. It had always struck him as ironic how this powerful empire, which had gone to extremes to eradicate Christianity, had in the end been conquered by Christianity.

The man in dark clothes held a odd-looking sword in his right hand, its end shaped not like a point but like a double fishing hook, razor sharp along its outer edge, and blunt on its inner edge. The weapon, occasionally used by gladiators, was not designed to kill quickly, but to disembowel. Upon losing to a stronger opponent, gladiators faced one of three fates. There was the legendary thumbs-up for combatants who had fought exceptionally well. There was the thumbs down for those who had fought bravely, but not enough to deserve Caesar's mercy. These were killed quickly, honorably—usually a single blow to the heart or chest. But there was a third option, reserved for those who had performed poorly on stage, or worse, who had offended Caesar in one of so many ways. These poor souls were publicly disemboweled, left alone on the arena howling like animals for everyone to see, to hear.

And fear.

Fear. That was how Caesars ruled, not by wisdom, or bravery, or respect.

But by fear.

Fear *commanded* respect, loyalty, power.

And that's how Vlad Jarkko controlled his network. Fear was the finest weapon in his arsenal, more powerful than the sidearm shoved in his jeans, by his spine.

His subordinates feared him, and because they feared him they also obeyed him, blindly, unconditionally, without hesitation. They feared him because of days like today, when the time had come to punish those who had failed him.

Vlad turned around, facing a half dozen of his soldiers, summoned this afternoon to witness the fate of a peer, the man strapped to a chair in the middle of the semicircle they had formed just moments ago.

Beyond them, in a corner of the room, watching this exhibition with interest, sat Mai Sung Ku, the representative from his North Korean employers. The beautiful operative had joined Jarkko's team as an observer to make sure that Jarkko was using her nation's funds properly. However, Jarkko had soon learned that Mai Sung also had other skills—skills he had put to good use in California, among other places. The petite Asian had an obscene thirst for blood, which, compounded with her unbending determination to accomplish the task assigned to her by her superiors in North Korea, made her a compelling partner.

"You have failed me, my friend," Vlad said, approaching the trembling man, in his late twenties, experienced enough not to have allowed Bruce Tucker to escape in Washington. His comrade in arms, older and wiser, had committed suicide on the plane ride over here, well aware of the fate he faced.

Tears filled the young man's eyes, further infuriating Vlad, who couldn't believe that the idiots had lost Bruce Tucker at the park. The rag in his mouth limited his voice to guttural sounds, which went unheard by his superior.

Vlad briefly regarded each of the senior members of his team, whom he had summoned here this afternoon. Their wide-eyed stares contrasted sharply with the exciting glare from Mai Sung, in whom Vlad wanted to instill confidence in his ability to see this through, even after the screwup at West Potomac Park. He did not relish the thought of disappointing the North Koreans.

Vlad had learned long ago from his brother, Siv, that there were certain regimes in this world that an independent contractor did not dare upset. Some were located in the Middle East, a handful in South America, and then there was Asia, where North Korea ranked among the most ruthless, on par with China and Burma.

The bound man jerked his head from side to side in a final, muffled plea as Vlad stood in front of him.

Gripping the sword so tightly that his knuckles turned white, Vlad plunged the hooked end into his subordinate's abdomen with a single thrust a few inches below the sternum.

Head jerking, eyelids twitching, the agonizing, muted sounds filled the still room. The man tried to twist, to turn, to tear himself from this torture, finally gazing down at the blade inside of him, at the blood streaming down to his groin, rapidly beginning to pool around the chair.

Vlad twisted the blade inside the victim, whose head snapped back in agony, tensing, convulsing, vomiting blood and bile, tensing again, his contorted stare resembling that of a wild beast.

Mai Sung's eyes gleamed with delighted anticipation.

In a swift motion, Vlad yanked the blade, along with a few feet of intestines and bloody foam, which coppery smell filled the room.

Once more, Vlad regarded his witnesses, their ashen faces, their terrified stares, the frozen bodies. And again he stabbed the man's belly with medieval force, just below the first blow.

And began to twist the sword.

Moans and jolts followed. The victim's eyes bulged, threatened to pop out of his head, veins throbbing on his forehead and neck, but the rope kept him restrained, kept him enduring this torture.

He yanked the blade back out, ripping out a string of viscera, along with blood and digestive fluids, all splattering by his feet with a sickening noise, with a pungent stench.

As his victim tensed, then moaned, then sobbed quietly, Vlad looked at his witnesses one final time, before pointing the bloody sword at the door.

The team quickly vacated the room, leaving Vlad Jarkko with his dying, shuddering subordinate. And with his North Korean partner, who walked slowly toward him, a frown on her porcelain face. She wore the same style of clothing every day: black skin-tight pants and boots, and a black T-shirt.

The eccentricity of clients varied widely, and Mai Sung certainly fell on the perverted end of the unconventional spectrum. While Vlad tortured his incompetent subordinate to teach the rest of the team a lesson, Mai Sung got off sexually on the whole bloody episode.

Like the vestal virgins from ancient Rome, he thought, watching this vulture circle the dying man, running a hand over his face, down his chest, over the exposed entrails.

"I enjoyed watching you work," she said, "but I would have done it . . . differently."

"It accomplished what I wanted to accomplish," Vlad replied.

"Next time someone disobeys, do like I did with Gibbons, yes? That would . . . *please* me." She ran a finger down from her lips to her breasts. "That would please me . . . a great deal."

He didn't reply, regarding her slim figure, suddenly feeling something awakening. *Get a hold of yourself*, he thought.

"And," she added, getting very close to him, pressing her pelvis against him, "pleasing me is what you are being paid to do."

Vlad liked to consider himself a professional, like his late brother, focused solely on the job, purging all emotions, steering his actions based strictly on logic. Today that logic had demanded a sacrifice for the benefit of his team. He had not relished the thought of the brutal death of someone whom had been 100 percent loyal to him, but the situation had required such punishment in order to maintain respect. This woman, however, enjoyed the gruesome act itself because it gave her a sexual high, like a drug. She had wanted him to torture his subordinate as slowly and inhumanly as she had tortured Gibbons, slowly pulling his fingernails, severing his fingers, his limbs, while keeping him alive for almost three hours, before finally castrating him.

Mai Sung smiled at Vlad, obviously feeling him through their clothes as she pressed herself against his groin.

"There may not be a next time," he replied, controlling his desire to simply take her right then, on the bloody floor, to turn her inside out, make her scream. But he resisted.

Don't mix business with pleasure.

She rubbed his chest, lowering her hand to his waist, then between his legs. She had come on to him in the rear cabin of their chartered Lear jet on the way from Washington, after having tortured Gibbons. He had managed to resist then.

"Yes," she said, feeling him. "You do want me."

Vlad dropped the sword and embraced her abruptly, kissing her hard.

They rolled on the floor, amidst the acrid smell of blood and viscera. He undressed her quickly, nearly ripping her clothes off, exposing her pale skin, her small breasts, a shaved groin.

He dropped his pants and entered her hard, violently, making her moan in Korean, listening to her gibberish as she smiled, as she dug her fingernails into his back, inflicting a set of half-moon-shaped cuts in his shoulder blades.

But Vlad didn't care, his hands squeezing her buttocks, lifting her light frame off the floor, pressing her back against the wall, her legs wrapped around him, her hands on his shoulders now, climaxing a moment before he did.

"Not bad," she said, jumping off him, snagging her pants

and shirt, slipping them on as she added, "I'm going to shower in my room. Then I will send my people a message, a report on your . . . performance to date." She winked.

Breathing heavily, Vlad watched her leave the room before pulling up his trousers, returning to the windows, calming down, regarding the Colosseum, silently chastising himself for having gotten personal with a contractor.

What's done is done, he thought, admitting that he had enjoyed the moment, and, after all, she had wanted it pretty badly. In a way, all he had done was please his current employer.

The sex is fine as long as it doesn't affect your priorities: finding Monica Fox.

Vlad thought of William Gibbons, Fox's attorney, a man who had not been able to assist Vlad beyond Tucker's flight to Washington, plus knowledge of the existence of an alphanumeric password, half of it known by Monica Fox and the other half by Tucker. Gibbons, who had claimed he didn't know any portion of the password—even under Mai Sung's severe torture—did reveal that the password would open up a very important file. Gibbons also confessed that Monica was hiding in Italy, but he didn't know her exact whereabouts. And Vlad had believed him. Gibbons had been a weak man, readily confessing to them after losing just one fingernail. But Mai Sung had tortured him further to verify the initial confession, to confirm Tucker's plans to travel to Washington—arranged by Gibbons himself. Vlad had used the information to stage the first phase of a plan. Unfortunately his men had failed to abduct Tucker, his brother's assassin.

His eyes gazed beyond the Colosseum, looking at the Eternal City itself.

Many years had passed since Vlad Jarkko received news of his brother's death at the hands of the Americans, of CIA officer Bruce Tucker. But Vlad had been in his twenties back then, just barely initiated into his older brother's profitable business, a business that he inherited upon his death, a business which he first directed at achieving revenge.

A wife and a son for a brother.

Vlad had made Tucker experience the same agony he had felt following the death of Siv Jarkko, the only family he had left after their parents were killed by anti-Communist death squads following the fall of the Berlin Wall. Siv Jarkko, a Stasi spy, had fled East Germany, taking his younger brother along with him.

Vlad had moved on after killing Tucker's family, determined to continue his brother's legacy, growing the business slowly over the years, making the right alliances, the right partnerships.

But fate had brought Tucker back to him. The proposal from the North Koreans had been appealing at first, a chance to truly strike at the Americans. But when he'd realized that Mortimer Fox was being protected by none other than Bruce Tucker, Vlad had realized what needed to be done. Tucker had to be not only eliminated, but tortured in the most infamous of ways while also destroying his reputation, his legacy.

He frowned. His incompetent team had accomplished the latter portion of the task, turning the CIA against Tucker, but leaving him very much alive and at large, which presented Vlad with a complication.

But also an opportunity, he thought, watching the clouds dotting the blue skies.

By turning the CIA against Tucker, Vlad had made it impossible for the former CIA officer to avoid the chase. He had to seek Monica, had to find her in order to try to make himself righteous again, and when he finally located her, Vlad planned to be there, abducting them both, and obtaining the password his employers sought.

In order to locate Tucker, who had to be in Italy by now— even though his people had not spotted him at any one of a dozen ports of entry—Vlad had deployed his men around the Eternal City, where he suspected Tucker would first try to start his investigation. But Vlad hadn't reached his current status in the international terrorist community by depending on just one channel to achieve his objectives. He had also sent word out to his local contacts, who in turn relayed the request to a network of informers spanning the Italian nation. Bruce Tucker and Monica Fox were hiding somewhere in Italy, and Vlad was determined to find them.

One way or another.

Agendas

Mai Sung Ku showered slowly, letting the hot water caress her pale breasts while working up a lather with the soap in her hands, washing off the smell of him on her face, her neck, in between her breasts, her legs, scrubbing hard, purifying her body, eyes closed now, the steam building up in the large bathroom.

Dogs, she thought, thinking of Vlad Jarkko, of his maimed subordinate, of his puppet team. Men were all just like dogs, unable to control themselves, useless without their penises.

Mai Sung had been subjected to man's laws from a very young age. Sold by her father, a Seoul street vendor, to pay business debts, the fourteen-year-old Korean girl, to that day a bright and promising student, found herself the sexual object of Japanese, Korean, and Western government officials and businessmen. She was kept in a house of prostitution, forced to perform the most perverted of acts for the sole joy of the house's patrons.

But another prostitute showed her how to fight back by simply listening, by observing, and then reporting what she had heard, what she had seen, at times sneaking paperwork out of her clients' rooms to get photocopied while she entertained them. Mai Sung slowly became a spy for North Korea. For years Mai Sung maintained the flow of information, learning other languages in the process, particularly

English, taught to her by her many clients, who were captivated by her natural beauty—and by the way in which she could please them beyond their wildest imaginations, fulfilling their every fantasy.

As a reward for her espionage work Mai Sung was eventually allowed to migrate north, away from the capitalistic dogs who had pushed her into such life, who had abused her, treated her like an animal. It was there that she received formal training as an operative, from weapons and hand-to-hand combat to the finer points of espionage, her brilliant mind absorbing it all, before being sent back south, but this time to run other informants, collecting their intelligence, and channeling it north. By the time she reached her thirtieth birthday, Mai Sung's top-notch results, and the ruthless way in which she ran her operation, earned her a promotion back north, where further training prepared her for longer-term and higher-stakes assignments, some in America, others in Europe.

The steam continued to rise, the hot water splashing against the back of her neck. And here she was, in yet another assignment, one which could provide her adopted North Korea with the most powerful of weapons: the code to *Firewall*. The existence of the highly secret system had fallen on her lap as a total surprise while torturing Vinod Malani. At the time Mai Sung had been after the industrial secrets locked inside the mind of the chief technical officer of such an important government contractor. But never did she expect to come across something like *Firewall*. Her government had quickly sent help in the form of the finest and deadliest independent contractor in the world.

The dog that just fucked me.

For Mai Sung sex was nothing but a weapon in her arsenal, a way to manipulate people, particularly men, though on occasion she had also used it with lesbians. She had to make Vlad feel at ease with her, make him feel superior by letting him use her, getting him to relax in her presence, giving her an edge. Mai Sung would use that edge later on to cover her country's tracks, to eliminate everyone involved in this effort, including Vlad Jarkko and his inner circle of operatives.

But not until *after* they had achieved their objective, until *after* they had been paid in full, until *after* all links to their North Korean assignment had been eliminated. Then, a terrible accident would be staged, one which would forever guarantee her country's safety against retaliation.

North Korea.

She crossed her arms, visions of her starving country flashing across her eyes, visions of famine, of skeleton bodies, of people living worse than pigs, of a world that would not assist them, that refused to help them because of their ideologies, their beliefs.

Bastards, she thought, angry at the double standards applied to her nation, angry at the hypocritical capitalists, who waved the flag of democracy and freedom while making themselves rich on the backs of children like Mai Sung had once been, young, naïve, innocent, propelled into hell for the pleasure of industrialists, of businessmen, of depraved capitalists.

But change is coming, she thought. The code to *Firewall* will change all that, will not only provide a window into their operations, but would also yield something far more precious than gold, than cash: the launch codes of the United States nuclear missiles.

Only then, after the playing field had been leveled, did North Korea truly stand a chance to get ahead, to progress, to force the unification process.

Riposo

Sitting at a sidewalk café on Via del Corso sipping his second cappuccino while pretending to browse through a travel guide, Bruce Tucker wondered what was keeping Antonio Giuliano, the director of foreign accounts at Banco di Roma, from heading home for his *riposo*, or siesta, the midday break taken by most establishments for lunch and for a nap, before heading back to work in the afternoon. It had always amazed Tucker how the entire Italian nation pretty much shut down in the middle of the day for its siesta.

Tucker could use one right about now. The jet lag was really getting to him, but he couldn't afford the time, not since spotting a possible tail and later on shaking it by the Fountain of Trevi. A blond man in his thirties, well built, had pretended to read a newspaper while sitting by a group of Japanese tourists throwing coins into the legendary fountain while making wishes. It had been obvious to him that the man had not spotted Tucker, probably thanks to his disguise, a baseball cap, new sunglasses, and a fake mustache from Davis's magic kit. Deciding for now that he didn't have the time to trap him and break him, Tucker had opted to lose him, which he did quite easily, leaving him behind with the tourists and their wishes.

He kept his eyes on the bank's entrance. Right now he would gladly throw a hundred bucks into the legendary fountain if that would get Signore Giuliano off his ass and out of the building to go and take his damned siesta.

Tucker planned to snatch him on his way home, get the information he sought, and skip town before a surveillance scout got lucky and spotted him, which would kick off a full-blown manhunt in the area.

Tucker monitored the double glass doors connecting the street to one of Italy's largest banking institutions, which he had visited two hours ago. He had gone to the help desk and requested information on opening an account as a foreigner. The lady behind the counter had directed him to the office that belonged to Giuliano, who had been with another client at the time. Tucker had inspected him from a distance—close enough to get a good look at him for the second stage of his plan to learn the whereabouts of Monica Fox.

Now the fat little bastard needs to—
There!

His heart jumped when he spotted the banker, wearing a tan suit and matching hat.

Tucker stood slowly, casually, and, having paid in advance, stepped away from the café while fanning himself with the tourist guide.

Crossing the street at the corner, he let his target get about a hundred feet ahead of him. Less than that and Tucker risked the chance of getting burned—just as he had burned that surveillance this morning. More than that and he risked losing him in the crowd—especially in a city like Rome, with hordes of people of every nationality crowding countless winding alleys and narrow streets.

He opened the guide as he walked, making himself unnoticeable as he moved with the rhythm of the crowd.

Blend in. Become a chameleon.

Giuliano turned the corner, headed up Via Laurina, a cobblestone street, and went inside what looked like a hotel.

Hotel Margutta.

He smiled, thinking of only one reason why Signore Giuliano would be visiting what looked like a budget hotel in the middle of the day.

Tucker's sneakers thudded hollowly over the gray and white marble floors of the simply decorated lobby. He saw a pair of old but clean sofas and coffee tables to his right, a small dining area to his left, and the front desk straight ahead.

Giuliano proceeded straight for the single elevator to the far right, behind the sofas, where a couple examined a large map of the city. Next to the elevator were the rest rooms, and adjacent to them the door leading to the emergency stairs.

Tucker hung back, letting him go up, watching the floor numbers above the door. The elevator stopped on the fifth floor, the top floor of the building.

Checking his watch, he strolled over to the front desk. If he remembered his holiday with Kristina some time back, plus what little he had read while waiting for Giuliano, this area of town was just a few blocks from the Spanish Steps. He thought of a way to use that information to gain real intel about the fifth floor of this hotel.

A thin, well-tanned woman wrapped in a tight green uniform smiled at him from behind the counter. Her long hair fell nicely over her shoulders, partially covering her prominent cleavage. The name tag pinned over her right buxom read GABRIELLA.

"Buon giorno," she said.

"English, Gabriella?" Tucker smiled sheepishly.

Her smiled widened. "Of course, *signore*. How may I be of service?" She spoke English with a cute accent.

"I was wondering if any of the fifth floor units is available. I hear that there is a great view of the Spanish Steps from some of the rooms."

She looked down at her computer screen, partly hidden by the rustic wooden counter. "There are only three rooms on that floor, signore. Only two have a view, and both are taken for the remainder of the week. The third room will be vacated this afternoon."

Bingo.

Tucker rubbed his chin, pretending to be considering his options, before replying. "How is your security at this hotel?" He leaned over the counter, lowering his voice while adding, "I was staying at a place a few blocks from here and the cleaning service stole my camera bag."

Gabriella gave him a solemn look. "I'm so sorry, *signore*.

Our hotel is very safe. It is owned and operated by my family. Every member of the staff is a relative or close friend. Nothing will get stolen here."

"Most impressive," Tucker replied, raising a brow, noticing a man and a woman getting in line behind him. "I won't keep you any longer. I'll check back with you later, in case I can't find a hotel with the view I seek."

"Very well, *signore*."

"By the way, may I use your rest room?"

"Of course. It is next to the elevator."

Tucker knew that already. He smiled. "You've been most helpful, Gabriella."

"You're welcome."

He stepped away, letting the couple behind him move up to the counter as he headed for the bathroom, but quickly sneaking into the open elevator door, stabbing the button for the fourth floor.

Less than a minute later he stood on a thinly-carpeted hallway with a half dozen doors on each side and a window at the opposite end, all under the yellowish glow of three plain but operational chandeliers. Cheaply framed prints of Italian landscapes adorned the white wall space between wooden doors. Being the middle of the day, Tucker didn't expect patrons to be in their rooms but out on the streets, amidst the sightseeing hordes.

An ice machine hummed to his right, next to a janitorial closet.

Tucker turned the knob on the closet door, opening it, exposing a wall lined with shelves, plus two buckets with mops. The shelves housed an assortment of hardware, spare parts for toilets, light fixtures, and yes, some room service items, like soaps, small bottles of shampoo, rolls of toilet paper, boxes of tissues, and stacks of clean towels. Tucker grabbed two bath towels and left the room.

To his left was the entrance to the stairs. Tucker climbed up to the fifth floor, slowly inching open the heavy fire door, peeking at the short hallway. Gabriella had been correct. There were only three rooms on this floor. Two on one side and a third on the opposite side—the one not facing the Spanish Steps.

The one that would be vacated this afternoon, after Signore Giuliano finished his midday snack.

Pressing an ear to the door, Tucker heard muffled voices, a man and a woman speaking Italian—no, correct that, *moaning* in Italian. Tucker also inspected the old wooden door, the fine cracks along the edges and the jam.

Folding the towels so that they provided a four-inch cushion, he placed them against the center of the door, at shoulder level, holding them in place with his outstretched right arm.

Stepping back, he crashed his right shoulder into the center of the towels. Wood cracked, splintered. The door gave, began to swing inward. As it did, Tucker grabbed the edge with his left hand, holding it back, keeping it from crashing into the wall, preventing anyone in the building from hearing the forced entry.

"Dio mio!" the woman screamed, Giuliano still on top of her in the middle of the bed, his face buried in her breasts, head tucked beneath her chin.

She was much taller than he was, her long blond hair spread over the pillow, her milky legs stretched toward the ceiling, slightly bent at the knees. Her pale arms braced across Giuliano's hairy back. The blonde still wore her red stiletto shoes.

"Silenzio!" warned Tucker, the Sig already leveled at the couple.

Giuliano jumped off her, his face frozen in surprise, raising his hands over his shoulders, open palms facing Tucker. The woman, scarlet lipstick smeared across her cheeks, reached for the sheets, yanked them up over her torso, covering her large breasts, which defied gravity.

She began to cry.

"Tell her to shut up," he ordered Giuliano, knowing that as director of foreign accounts he should be fluent in English.

"Shhh!" he hissed.

The blonde breathed heavily through her mouth, sobbing quietly now.

Tucker closed the broken door, before retrieving the silencer and screwing it into the Sig's muzzle under the terrified stares of Giuliano and his mistress.

"No. Wait," he said.

Tucker raised a brow. "Wait?"

"Whatever you are being paid, I will double it!" he said, driving a fist into his open palm.

This was getting very interesting.

"It's too late for that, my friend," he said, leveling the gun at Giuliano, who dropped to his knees.

"Please. I beg you. I have a wife, children."

"And you love them so much that you also have to screw a whore for lunch?"

"It is not like it looks! She is just a client repaying a loan. She means nothing to me! This is strictly business!"

"I told you to keep it down." *Business?*

"I'm sorry," he whispered, still naked while on his knees, his member now flaccid, hanging in between grossly hairy legs. "I love my wife, *signore*. And my children. I don't wish to orphan them."

Tucker shrugged. "I'm not here because of your marital problems."

Tears filled Giuliano's eyes, his face contorted in fear. "If you just let me talk to Mr. Ballantine. I know we can straighten this unfortunate misunderstanding. I am willing to do whatever it takes to make things right for him again."

Tucker lowered his gun. "That's a start."

Hope momentarily relaxed his tight features. "Yes. Yes. Just tell me what must I do. What? Anything."

Tucker told him.

Giuliano looked confused, saying, "But, sir, that information is strictly confidential. I could lose my job and—"

"I'll inform Mr. Ballantine that you refused to cooperate." He raised the silenced pistol at him again.

Giuliano immediately grabbed the phone, dialed, and waited for someone to pick up. He spoke clearly, just as he had been ordered, slow enough for Tucker to follow the conversation with his very rusty Italian.

A moment later he hung up, turning to Tucker. "The account is sizable. The address marked as strictly confidential, but it was released to me."

"And?"

"I need to know that you will not harm me."

Tucker's eyes became mere slits of anger, which made the courtesan's cry increase in pitch. Giuliano slapped her. She disappeared under the cover, sniffling quietly again.

"Listen, you little *toad*," Tucker said. "This is the first of many favors you will have to perform for Mr. Ballantine if you want to keep on living. Otherwise I have been instructed not just to kill you, but also your wife and—"

"The address is from Capri, the island on—"

"I *know* where Capri is. What's the address?" *Monica Fox is in Capri?*

He gave it to him.

"If you're lying . . ."

"I swear to you, on the memory of my mother," he crossed himself, "that is the place where she is registered to receive all correspondence from our bank."

Tucker almost laughed at how easy this had been. "For your own sake, it'd *better* be accurate," he said, walking over to Giuliano, who backed away in fear.

He reached for the phone line and tore it off the wall.

"What are you—"

"Your clothes, and hers, shove them in one of the hotel's laundry bags, and leave it at the foot of the bed."

Although confused, Giuliano complied. The blonde, who had resurfaced from beneath the sheets with a red lump on her left cheek, looked puzzled. She was about to say something, but Giuliano raised his hand. She jerked back, covering her bruised face.

Grabbing the bag with his free hand, Tucker said, "Someone from Mr. Ballantine's organization will contact you in forty-eight hours. If you try to contact us, or the police, or anyone else . . ."

Giuliano regarded Tucker with a grave face. "I will do *exactly* as you say."

"But her," Tucker said. "I have no choice." He raised his gun at the prostitute, who froze.

"No. Please. I beg you," said Giuliano. "It will make a mess. It will involve the police. I will go to jail and will be useless to Mr. Ballantine."

Tucker pretended to consider that for a moment, before adding, "She is your responsibility then."

Giuliano nodded so forcefully that Tucker thought his head was going to come off his shoulders.

"Very well."

"But sir," Giuliano said, pointing at the laundry bag. "How are we supposed to—"

"I'll drop this with the concierge. You should get them back in a few hours."

"But what are we supposed to do until then?"

Tucker smiled as he opened the damaged door, stepped out, and closed it behind him.

A moment later he was back on the street, heading for the nearest Metro station.

Bruce Tucker turned his eyes toward the south, his mind traveling further, beyond Naples, across the blue-green waters of the Amalfi coast, reaching Capri. Monica Fox lived there, on the legendary island, probably unaware of the events that had transpired and were now converging in her direction. He needed to get to Capri, needed to warn her, to rescue her.

To protect her.

20

Allegiance of Convenience

She moved quickly, silently, under the cover of darkness, soft moonlight illuminating her path as she brushed leaves and branches aside, making her way toward the outskirts of Capri.

Her eyes studied the twisting path ahead, beyond rocks overgrown by weeds and shrubs, checking for any signs of danger. Sensing none, Monica continued on, the distant sounds of tourists partying on the Piazzetta echoing up the hillside.

But the crowded plaza wasn't Monica's target on this cool and windy night. Her sights had fallen on the large estate just above the west end of Capri, overlooking the lively nightlife of the city.

She had been there once about four months before, though now it seemed like a lifetime ago. The estate, surrounded by a tall fence on the sides not protected by the abyss, didn't belong to one of the actors, music stars, or wealthy CEOs who so frequently purchased these costly mansions to get away from the world. The villa belonged to Vittorio Carpazzo, the head of the Mafia in this region, which also comprised Naples and Sorrento on the mainland.

The Mafia.

Monica exhaled heavily, though not from the effort she exerted while hiking this inclined trail, or from the fact that the first and last time she had been at Carpazzo's villa was when she had caught Paolo screwing one of Ricco's hookers. Monica simply couldn't believe that she was actually about to seek help from the Mafia, about to negotiate an alliance of convenience against a more powerful enemy.

Just like her father.

She grimaced, wiping the perspiration accumulating on her forehead. A little headache had crept into her temples an hour ago, probably the result of the stress and lack of food for the past twelve hours. At least she had avoided dehydration by drinking the cool and pure water dripping from the roof of the cave. Now she needed something solid to inject some energy back into her system.

She reached a gravel road, a driveway to one of the many luxurious estates on this rock, but not the one she sought. Tired of hiking through woods, she decided to follow the driveway until it reached the paved road, devoid of street-lights and nearly deserted at this time of the night.

Monica remained to one side, where the shoulder met the narrow forest leading back to the trail and the cliffs over-looking the Mediterranean. She walked for about a half mile, toward Carpazzo's place, slowly catching her breath from the strenuous hike, her flushed face welcoming the cool sea breeze sweeping up the mountain side. A few cars drove by, one heading uphill and two downhill. She had heard them coming around the hairpin turns and was able to hide before their headlights invaded her enshrouding darkness.

She paused when she reached the well-lit gravel driveway of Carpazzo's mansion, trying not to remember the scene she had caused the last time she had been here. Monica had gone ballistic when finding Paolo humping that whore against the wall. Carpazzo's men had rushed upstairs and held her back to keep her from attacking Paolo. It had taken her over an hour to calm down, finally deciding to let it go, not to do something that would jeopardize her arrangement with the island's authorities—like Ricco and Carpazzo—to live here. She had accepted Paolo's apology and decided to keep it friendly.

Monica hoped that Carpazzo was home. She seriously doubted that the armed men she remembered guarding the gate would provide her with shelter given her physical ap-pearance.

You've never looked so lovely, girl, she thought, inspecting her soiled T-shirt and shorts, her bruised and scratched arms and legs. She brushed her hair back with her fingers, pulling herself together before marching toward the mansion, reminding herself that she was one of the wealthiest women alive, deciding to act like one, like the business executive her father had wanted her to become after Preston's death. She had to strike a deal, then contact Gibbons to access this secret file and begin plotting her revenge against her father's enemies.

The mansion's roof protruded above the trees, beyond the bend in the driveway.

Just as she recalled, two men guarded the ornate wrought-iron gate. Beyond it the three-story mansion stood opulently, yellow light shining through most of its front windows, backlighting the large columns supporting the upstairs balcony.

The guards turned in her direction. They were young, perhaps in their mid twenties, wearing neutral color slacks and shirts, and caps on their heads. Both had stubble beards. Shotguns hung loosely from their shoulders.

"Buona sera," she said, approaching them casually, with fake confidence, her heart pounding her chest as she continued in her broken Italian. "I need to see Vittorio. Tell him it's Monica Fox."

Neither replied as they eyed her, before exchanging a glance.

"He doesn't live here," replied one of them in fluent English.

"I *know* he does," she replied. "I'm a friend, and this is an emergency." She pointed at her dirty clothes and bruises.

One of them waved her away.

Monica decided to stand her ground. If there was one thing she had learned after living here for a year was that Italians respected those who fought back. "You obviously have no *fucking* idea who I am, but Vittorio does. If he finds out you didn't let me through after I was almost killed in an accident, he will have your balls for breakfast."

The guards looked at each other again. One of them exhaled heavily, letting his hands drop to his sides. The other said, *"Uno momento, signora,"* and grabbed a radio strapped to his belt, from which also hung a holstered sidearm.

Monica crossed her arms as the guard turned away from her while speaking softly into his hand unit. She sure as hell hoped that Vittorio remembered her from four months ago.

A moment later he replaced the radio on his belt and waved her over while the other guard creaked open the iron gate.

Monica approached him, and he asked her to turn around, stretch her arms to the sides and spread her legs.

She complied, realizing that these characters would not let her pass without a thorough search.

They did, slowly, taking longer than was necessary. Monica closed her eyes, letting these strangers put their hands all over her.

I'm sure that made your day, she thought after they finished.

"All right," one of the guards said, tipping his bonnet at her. "Go straight to the front of the mansion. A man will be waiting for you. He will take you to see Don Carpazzo."

Beyond the iron gates extended a long cobblestone driveway that circled in front of the mansion. An ornate and well-lit fountain marked the center of the loop, its water cascading from the mouths of large fish down to the round pool at the bottom. Stone steps connected the driveway to the long front porch. A dark figure stood alone next to one of the columns, his face in shadows. Monica walked past two Mercedes sedans parked to the side, climbed the steps, and approached him.

She expected to find another guard, but instead, she watched the tall and tanned Vittorio Carpazzo, his dark eyes under salt-and-pepper hair and bushy brows regarding his unexpected guest. He was dressed in a burgundy robe and matching slippers, a cigar in his left hand and a glass of brandy in his right.

"Hi," was all she could say, keeping her arms crossed.

"A lot of people have been looking for you," he said in the refined English of someone who was educated in the best schools in the United States. Carpazzo set the drink on a table next to a pair of wicker chairs. "What in the world happened up there? Where is Ricco?"

"Killed," she said, surprised that the news of their shooting wasn't public already.

Carpazzo didn't say a thing for a moment, before looking away. "When the police arrived they found no bodies, only the wrecks of a truck and Ricco's car. But there was blood."

Through his connection with the local police, Carpazzo had been kept up to date. Apparently the team who had attacked them had managed to clear out the bodies before the police arrived.

"I need protection," she said. "The people who killed Ricco and Nunzio are after me."

Carpazzo sniffed the brandy before taking a sip. "Two people have died," he said. "That's bad for business. Why should I risk more deaths, and what's more, my operation, for you?"

Money. His father had always been right. At the end of the day everything came down to money, to business. Carpazzo couldn't care less about the lives of Nunzio or Ricco— or hers for that matter. He only cared about how such events would impact his profits.

"Do you know who my father is?" she asked.

Carpazzo drew on the cigar, blowing the smoke upward, before sipping more brandy. "Mortimer Fox, the billionaire."

"And he died following a kidnapping attempt," she added.

"Yes, I know. My condolences."

"Thanks. Anyway, he left everything to me. The money. The business. *Everything*."

Carpazzo placed the cigar in his mouth, studying her through the swirling smoke, his eyes narrowing, intrigued. "Continue."

"I believe that the men who tried to kidnap my father are the same men who killed Ricco and Nunzio—the men who tried to kidnap me this morning. But Ricco managed to shoot one of them, creating enough of a distraction for me to get away." She decided to keep the fact that she had also shot one to herself for now.

"And who might this people be?"

"I believe it's the same people who my father battled for years in the courts: the United States government."

Carpazzo let out a loud grunt, before taking another drag of the cigar. "You are telling me that your . . . *Uncle Sam* is after you?"

"At least someone from the government is."

"But . . . *why*?"

She frowned. "It was never clear to me why my father's company was at such odds with the government, aside from what made the news. But one thing I do know is that now that he's dead, they want me really bad, enough to kill to get me."

"You still haven't told me why I should protect you. This is clearly not my fight. Why should I risk my life and the lives of my people by going against such a formidable and resourceful enemy?"

"Because I can pay dearly for such favor, and not just in cash, but in connections. My father kept a relationship with the Italian Mafia in America. I will get you in on the action, perhaps help you increase your territory, your power."

Carpazzo looked away, rubbing his chin.

"Think of it as an investment," she added. "And if you keep it low key, no one might even know that you helped me."

He looked at her again.

"See, no one saw me coming here aside from your two men out there. If you can count on their silence, then no one should know where I'm hiding. After a few days, the people looking for me on this island will give up, probably think that I managed to slip away, perhaps start their search again on the mainland, or in the States."

Carpazzo began to nod, ever so slowly.

"And in return you will have the gratitude of one of the richest women alive. Not a bad deal for providing me with bed and breakfast."

"Very well," he said after a pause. "You can stay for the moment, while I consider your proposal further."

"All right," she replied.

"There are two guest suites upstairs. I'll send my maid to get you settled in. I'll also send her to the city tomorrow to purchase a few things for you to wear."

Monica felt relief displacing her apprehension.

"I'll also send a few men to look around. See what they can pick up. Maybe keep an eye on your house. Like I said, I can't afford to have someone out there shooting people on the island. It's bad for business."

Perhaps she did have a chance after all. Perhaps her instincts had been right to come here. "Thank you, Vittorio. You won't regret it."

"Like I said, you can stay here for the moment, while I gather more information to decide if I should help you."

"You're helping me now, and I'm grateful for it."

"Just remember, Monica . . . when this is over, you will owe me a favor."

As Carpazzo ushered his guest inside the mansion, one of his men guarding the west side of the property strolled in the woods for a minute, pretending to be making one of his rounds, only he went a little farther than usual, until he was certain that no one could hear him.

Reaching inside his pocket, he pulled out a small cellular phone and dialed a local number he had long committed to memory. He listened to the greeting of the answering machine before leaving a short, clear message on the time, date, and place of the sighting. The call lasted less than thirty seconds, not long enough for anyone to miss him.

Casually, he strolled out of the woods and returned to his post. By tomorrow morning the secret bank account he kept in Naples would be credited with the equivalent of one thousand American dollars.

21

Spiderman

The vessel cruised toward the south, its single screw biting into the water, creating the silver wake that Bruce Tucker regarded for a moment, while surveying the increasingly distant harbor on the south side of Naples, Italy.

The wind swirled his hair as he turned his attention to the bow, pointed at the distant black smudge on the horizon.

Capri.

There had been two ways to reach the island. One was during the day, aboard the ferries hauling multitudes of tourists. He could have easily disguised himself as one of them, wearing shorts, a T-shirt, a cap, and sunglasses. He could have reserved a room in one of the hotels and taken a taxi ride to it, or even boarded the *Funicular*. But he would had been exposed to surveillance teams not just from the CIA, but also from Jarkko. And as good as Tucker was, he couldn't afford to underestimate the opposition's skills. In his years with the Agency, he had seen many talented field operatives meet up with disaster by underestimating the enemy.

Just as you underestimated Jarkko once.

Tucker tasted the salt on his lips from the light spray as the boat splashed across mild swells. The mist felt good on his exposed chest and legs as he wore just a bathing suit in preparation for his upcoming swim.

An alternative way to reach Capri was SEAL-style, at night, chartering a boat from a man who didn't ask questions while delivering his mysterious cargo to the other side of the island, away from the Marina Grande and its smaller sister, the Marina Piccolo.

Tucker had found such a person while paying an early evening visit to the local bars, the ones by the piers, where the well-tanned skippers who had spent the day hauling tourists on fishing or sightseeing trips were relaxing, taking it easy, resting before another day at sea. Identifying the right candidate had not been too difficult. Tucker had found him in the rear of a bar called Pescadores, where he had walked up to Salazzio, a husky sailor who'd wasted the entire day repairing a leak on his boat rather than entertaining tourists. He had not had any income for the day and he had been quite ticked off about it.

Salazzio had jumped at the chance of more than making up his loss with a single fare to the island, choosing to overlook the unusual request when Tucker showed him enough Euros to keep him from having to put up with tourists for the remainder of the week.

The island slowly grew in the distance, now speckled with tiny dots of light, starting at sea level and rising up into the bluffs.

Tucker stared at those remote hills. Somewhere up there lived Monica Fox, according to the address he had extracted from the banker back in Rome. Folded inside one of the pockets of Tucker's waterproof rucksack was a detailed map of the island. He had used this map not just to locate Monica's house, but also to plan out his route for getting there.

First, however, he had to scale the rocky wall connecting the shore to a deserted hilltop a half mile away from Monica's house.

He rolled his eyes, feeling a bit old to be doing something he had not done since the SEALs. Tucker kept himself in good shape, a requirement in the protection business. But merely jogging and weight-lifting was no preparation for rock climbing, and especially at night.

Just like riding a bike, buddy, he mused as Salazzio directed the vessel toward an uninhabited section of the rock, dangerously close to reefs that met up with limestone formations leading to the near-vertical wall. *Just a little swim followed by a short climb, right?*

Right.

He regarded the large rucksack by his feet, where he carried not just the dark clothes he would wear after swimming a few hundred feet of the warm and salty Mediterranean Sea, but the weapons he had purchased in Rome, plus a pair of night-vision goggles, climbing and swimming attire for Monica Fox, his climbing equipment—enough to get him to his intended destination and back—and an assortment of other handy gadgets. He had left enough air trapped inside the rucksack after sealing it to make the load as close to a neutral buoyancy as he could—at least based on what he remembered from his SEAL days. Of course, the Mediterranean was far more salty than the Pacific Ocean, where he'd trained, so Tucker had also compensated for that, erring on the side of making it a bit heavier than lighter. Tucker also had a small net holding a second set of snorkel gear for his new principal.

Salazzio steered around reefs with expert ease. During the day, the underwater rock formations could be seen clearly in the crystalline waters, but at night Salazzio relied on the boiling surf and breakers created when waves clashed against reefs.

You are lucky that the moon is out tonight, Salazzio had told him upon hearing Tucker's request back at Pescadores. *Otherwise we could not go until daylight.*

Tucker glanced at the natural breakwater splashing beyond the port side of the boat, and he suddenly didn't feel very lucky, especially when he lifted his gaze up to the wall of solid limestone beyond the shoreline, which seemed to get taller as they neared the island.

Way to go, Bruce.

"Just another fifteen meters, *signore!*" Salazzio announced over the sound of the waves and the wind.

Tucker put on his fins, which he had purchased at a local dive shop in Naples that afternoon, along with the oversize waterproof sack, the snorkels, diving masks, fins, and an underwater flashlight, which he could strap to his wrist.

He had paid Salazzio in advance, and had promised him twice the amount for the return trip. He would contact Salazzio in the next forty-eight hours, after he had located Monica Fox, to arrange a pickup and return back to the mainland. Given the amount of cash that Tucker was throwing at him, Salazzio had assured him he would come get him as soon as he called.

Donning the mask and snorkel, the rucksack strapped to his back and the net secured to his waist, Tucker climbed off the starboard side of the boat just as Salazzio backed it off.

The water promptly chilled him, bringing back memories of his SEAL days. He resigned himself to the cold, just as he had done back then. Even though the water temperature was supposed to be in the high seventies, it felt much colder than that at night, without the sun to provide that additional layer of warmth. But Tucker felt confident he should be able to endure it for the minutes that it would take him to reach the shore and dry off.

He began to kick his legs while listening to the decreasing rumbling of the outboard as the Italian skipper headed back to the mainland. The rucksack didn't feel heavy in the water, meaning he had guessed correctly on the amount of air.

Sliding the switch on the side of the flashlight, Tucker torched the waters with yellow light, biting into the snorkel's rubber mouthpiece as he gulped a lungful of air through his mouth, and dove.

He swam in what looked like twenty-feet-deep waters. An assortment of fish gathered near the bottom, where reefs layered the sea floor, in some places rising up to just below the boiling surface, like scaled-down versions of the rocky wall awaiting him.

Holding his depth to around five feet, Tucker maneuvered carefully between the tall formations, occasionally going up to snorkel depth for a breath of fresh air, but immediately returning to the calmness below, where he didn't have to worry as much about a wave sweeping him into a reef. Tucker had made certain that he purchased a top-of-the-line snorkel, which came with a safety valve at the top to prevent water from dropping down the tube and into his mouth. He didn't feel like adding swallowing saltwater to the list of difficulties he would face tonight.

He actually could have made this phase of the operation easier by using one of the two personal breathers he had purchased at the scuba shop. Each consisted of a rubber mouthpiece connected to a four-inch-long canister through a small regulator, and provided enough air for up to ten minutes. But the PBs were strictly for emergencies, in case a situation forced him to remain underwater for a longer period of time than he could hold his breath.

Five minutes later, Tucker kicked off his fins and removed his mask and snorkel while cautiously stepping barefoot on the rocks covering most of the shore, using the flashlight to guide him to the wall, the wind chilling him.

Sitting beneath an overhang, he pulled on the water seal of the rucksack before tugging at the heavy-duty zipper across the top and pulling out a small towel.

He stripped naked and dried himself vigorously, rubbing his cold skin to increase the blood flow. He slipped on a long-sleeve T-shirt made of dark cotton, a pair of underwear, dark trousers, cotton socks, and a pair of climbing boots. He also armed himself, the Sig 220 on his waist and the Walther PPK on his left ankle, beneath his pants.

Feeling warmer, Tucker hid the snorkel equipment beneath the ledge, along with the second set in the net, for the return trip. If all went according to his plan, Tucker hoped to reach her home, convince her of the imminent danger she faced, perhaps even get some answers, and then bring her back down to this rocky shore for an easy return trip back to Naples, where he would arrange transportation to the States.

Of course, his experience told him that things didn't always go according to plan, so he would have to rely on his ability to improvise to pull this off.

Tucker removed a roll of athletic tape from the knapsack and began to wrap his hands, starting across the knuckles of his left hand, across the palm, the back of the palm, and over the knuckles again, repeating the process four times, slightly overlapping the previous wrap, and twice wrapping it around the thumb.

Tearing off the tape while looking into the darkness, Tucker wrapped his other hand, just as he had been taught in the SEALs eons ago. The tape would protect his hands during the climb.

He turned off the flashlight and put on the night-vision goggles he had purchased at a specialty store in Naples. He threw the switch on the side and the battery-operated system amplified the available light, turning the night into palettes of green.

He looked about him again. The goggles weren't bad, considering he had only paid just over four hundred dollars for them. They were light and provided enough of a field of vision for the climb ahead.

Tucker spread the rest of his climbing equipment on the ground, sliding a few metal utensils into a padded sling, which he hung over his right shoulder, along with a 10-millimeter rope, strong enough to support five times his weight.

He shoved the rest of the gear back in the rucksack, zippered it closed, and donned it again. It felt a bit lighter now that he had distributed some of the equipment and weapons throughout his body. But he still had a considerable amount of gear in the pack—gear that he would need in the upcoming phases of his plan.

Moment of truth, he thought, standing in front of the near-vertical wall. So far, everything had come back to him, even the proper way to wrap hands.

Making circles with his neck a few times, Tucker closed his eyes, loosening up, visualizing how he would do this, remembering the days when he would scale a mountain before breakfast.

He glared up at the rock and jumped, grabbing hold of an exposed root with his right hand. Lifting his right leg, bent at the knee, he pressed the ball of his boot against the rock, creating enough friction between the limestone and the rubber sole to prevent it from slipping. He reached higher with his left hand, jamming it into a crack, keeping the thumb up and outside the crack, pulling himself up again while pressing the rubber ball of his left boot into the wall.

Tucker kept his upper body leaning away from the mountain, which forced his feet into the rock, creating enough adhesion to support his weight. He magnified the effect by maintaining his heels as low as possible, also providing balance and temporarily resting his calf muscles.

He continued by letting go of the root and reaching farther up the crack with his right hand, placing his right foot on a small boulder and pulling himself up again.

This seemed a lot easier back then, he thought, his arms beginning to burn while grabbing hold of a boulder with his left hand while sliding his right hand farther up the same crack.

For the next thirty minutes, inch after agonizing inch, Tucker maintained a slow but steady pace, his body constantly reminding him of his age, which forced caution into his movements. There had been a time, just shortly before his departure for the CIA, when he had closely resembled Spiderman, capable of crawling up any wall like a shadow.

Filmed with sweat, wishing for a refreshing dip in the cool sea as much as for some of the vigor from his youth, Bruce Tucker kept his motion efficient, mentally working out moves before executing them, his old rhythm slowly returning. Controlling his breathing, he pushed himself, alternating between hands and feet, keeping his momentum pointed upward.

He reached a small ledge, just barely over four feet square. His hands clutching the trunk of a tree growing at an angle straight out of the limestone about five feet over the ledge, Tucker tentatively set his feet on the horizontal rock formation, slowly relaxing his arm muscles to test the strength of the outcrop. Had this been granite, the narrow rim would have been plenty strong to support him, but limestone was unpredictable and could easily crack.

The rocky protuberance didn't budge under his weight.

The dark green waters of the Mediterranean—as seen through his goggles—extended toward Naples, its lights, bright green spots in the distance, visible this high up. He shut off the goggles to conserve batteries and closed his eyes, letting the same breeze that had chilled him when leaving the water now cool him.

You should have taken the ferry and a taxi, pal.

He sighed. Paranoia always drove him to extreme options. But then again, those options had kept him alive during his years with the SEALs, the CIA, and the Secret Service.

A few minutes later, Tucker powered the goggles back on, glancing up, estimating that he was roughly at the halfway point, and also deciding that this was when it would get really hard. As the wall reached the bluff above, it sloped outward, increasing his risk of falling off.

The time had come to use the rope for insurance, since he would now have to rely more on his ability to hang on than on friction because his body would be naturally pointing away from the rock.

Reaching for the tools on the sling, Tucker removed a hammer and a piton, searching for the best place to pound it in for maximum anchoring strength. Again, limestone had the drawback of cracking easily if the piton was hammered into a weak section of the rock.

Tucker selected a point in between two rock formations just to his right, which made a V as they came together in the center. He placed the five-inch-long titanium piton in the middle of the V, where the natural weight of the two slabs would make it harder to crack, and began to hammer it, hoping that the howling wind and the roaring sea below would drown the whacking noise.

Leaving less than a quarter of an inch exposed, Tucker selected a titanium, spring-loaded, D-shaped link and clipped it to the hole at the top of the piton, giving it a couple of hard tugs, verifying that the piton was firmly secured in the limestone.

Unwrapping the standing end of the nylon rope, he looped it through the titanium link until reaching the midpoint, and then attached one end of the rope to a clip on the right side of his safety belt and ran the other end through a gravity ratchet so that he had only a few feet of slack. If he were to fall now, he would only drop the few feet below the anchor. As he climbed, the ratchet would automatically give him more slack, but would latch if its gravity sensor registered a rapid fall.

Convinced that he had attached himself to a substantial anchor, Tucker started again, working on his breathing to maintain a rhythm, hand jam after hand jam, his shoulders and thighs burning from the effort, his fingers aching as he shoved them in cracks to lift and support himself.

After another thirty feet, he hammered in a second piton, and reset the rope on the ratchet to make this his new hold point.

And again he went, just like so many years ago, silently thanking his willpower for staying in good enough shape to be able to do this—albeit with considerable effort.

Tucker reached the edge of the outward slope five minutes later, throwing one leg over the rim before pulling himself up.

He rolled away from the abyss and onto a small clearing, which upon closer inspecting was shaped like a half circle, outlined by vegetation. He saw no houses or road in sight, just as his research had shown.

Tucker sat for a few minutes, catching his breath, relaxing his muscles, wiping the perspiration on his face.

He detached the rope from the safety belt harness and pulled it, coiling it as he did so, and setting it next to him on the ground. Next, he unbuckled the safety belt, removed the rucksack, and swapped his climbing boots for sneakers.

Grabbing the rope and the knapsack, Tucker walked along the edge, gazing down at the sea a few hundred feet below, the distant surf gleaming bright green in the magnified moonlight. Pride momentarily filled him.

Not bad for an old guy.

He selected a tree near the cliff, solidly planted, its trunk about a foot in diameter, sturdy enough to support the weight of two people. He secured one end of the rope around the bottom and left the rest coiled next to the tree. The way down would be a lot easier, particularly because the large overhang would make it a straightforward rappel job to the bottom, keeping him away from the rock wall.

He took one set of ID, the one under the name Stephen Smith, plus enough cash to get around for a couple of days—as long as he planned to hang around this place. Tucker hated islands. They restricted his mobility. The rest of his cash, plus his second set of ID, he left in the sack, along with Monica's IDs and the cellular phone he would need to call Salazzio. He placed the sack next to the rope, hidden from view.

Operating much lighter now, Tucker entered the woods to the north of the clearing, slowing down a bit. Even with the goggles the woods appeared murky, mostly shades of dark green as the canopy overhead blocked most of the available light.

Holding a parallel course to the shoreline, a direction that should take him to his target, Tucker advanced silently, with caution. This close to Monica Fox's home he couldn't afford to get burned. He had to be careful, had to assume that she might be under surveillance. If Tucker had located her whereabouts this easily, so could have Jarkko.

Green lights.

His goggles detected a bright greenish hue forking through the dark shapes of trees and other vegetation, invading his monochromatic world.

Lights.

Stooping as he approached the edge of the woods, Tucker parted shrubbery, peeking with his goggles at a small meadow dotted with short limestone boulders leading to a terrace housing an array of tables. Beyond that stood a one-story house, small, with a narrow stone fireplace to the left and large sliding glass doors connecting to the terrace.

Figures moved inside the house, their hunter-green silhouettes backwashed in very intense emerald light, which hurt his pupils.

Tucker removed the goggles and strapped them to his belt. He rubbed his eyes, waiting a few moments until they adjusted.

Colors slowly returned to his world. The yellow glow from the house cast a twilight across the clearing, fading as it reached the sea cliff. He followed the treeline bordering the south side of this rocky field, always keeping an eye on the house, in case anyone came out.

Upon closer inspection, the house was made of weather-beaten stucco, cracked in many places, in need of resurfacing. From where he stood, partly hidden by the trunk of a large cypress facing the side of the house, Tucker could see two cars parked in front. Matching dark sedans.

His stomach knotted. Two decades in the business told him always to suspect dark sedans, especially when they matched. As an executive protector he had always made certain that the vehicles in the principal's motorcade never matched, thus avoiding attracting such attention.

Two men stood by the vehicles, obviously watching the front.

Monica Fox definitely had company, and if his guess was right, probably *uninvited* company.

He took a chance and left the woods, dashing across the twenty feet separating him from the side of the house while unholstering the Sig, screwing the silencer into the muzzle before clutching the weapon with both hands.

Thumbing back the hammer, Tucker pressed his back against the stucco wall, moving sideways now, slowly, pausing by a window at waist level, light streaming through the glass, piercing the darkness outside.

He sneaked a look inside, confident that the men he spotted ruffling through papers or sitting behind the computer in the living room could not see him. The interior light reflecting on the window turned it into a one-way mirror.

Three men, medium built, casually dressed, like tourists—only they didn't act like tourists but like professionals—moved about with purpose. Two emptied cardboard boxes, going through the contents inside stacks of manila envelopes.

The third tapped the keyboard of the computer system. They worked in silence, methodically searching the house.

Where is Monica? Is she elsewhere being interrogated?

Tucker had to assume that. The people who had gotten to Mortimer Fox had managed to find her before he did.

A fourth man appeared, this one a bit older than the rest and wearing a tan suit. He held a large steel case in his right hand.

Tucker pressed his right ear against the bottom of the window pane.

"Found anything?" the older man asked.

Americans, Tucker thought. *Bastards are Americans.*

The guy behind the computer shook his head. "I told you we'd already searched this place."

"Search it again, and *again*. It has to be *somewhere*. Keep looking. Turn this fucking place inside out if you have to, but find it!"

The men grumbled as their boss went out through the back, stepping onto the terrace hauling the silver case.

Tucker proceeded down the side of the house, reaching the corner, listening to the boss snapping the locks of the metallic case.

He dropped to the ground and inched his head just beyond the corner, enough to see what the man was doing, before crawling back, confused by his observation.

The stranger was deploying a mobile communications unit, the kind used by a very special type of field operative to report back to headquarters on a mission without the fear of the transmission being intercepted. The portable equipment was designed not only to encode the transmission, but to constantly jump frequencies, making an interception nearly impossible. It was also designed to operate in conjunction with a satellite system in geosynchronous orbit. At the other end, a second unit, programmed with a matching decoder—and with the identical frequency skip sequence—would receive the satellite transmission, and if required, issue a response, closing the communications loop.

The use of such mobile satellite equipment, preferred by

the military, was avoided by the CIA, which favored communicating through an array of agents—foreign nationals spying for the CIA—run by CIA officers acting as their controllers. These officers operated out of CIA stations and safe houses around the globe. Once intelligence made it to a station, the CIA station chief would use a computerized system connected to a satellite antenna atop the roof of the safe house, which in some cases was an American embassy building, to transmit to Langley. This same link was used by the ambassador and his staff for classified communications with Washington.

Since the men inside the house were Americans and were using mobile satellite communications gear, Tucker guessed that they were either from the military or the NSA, the National Security Agency.

The NSA.

Tucker shivered at the thought. This most secretive agency—more so than the CIA—not only was charged with monitoring the airwaves, eavesdropping into communications around the world, but also with operational control of SIGINT, the acronym for the signal intelligence activities of the U.S. Government, including the Pentagon, the FBI, and the CIA. In other words, any classified transmission made by the military establishment, or by the FBI, or by the CIA, or by the diplomatic community, was controlled by the National Security Agency. The NSA even ensured safe communications to vital areas of national security, like nuclear submarines and missile silos. Most recently, the NSA was also leading the fight against criminal hackers, who violated the communications protocols that the NSA had been appointed to protect.

That had always struck Tucker as a hell of a lot of power for a single agency, and concentrations of power historically had resulted in abuses of that power.

He risked another look and watched the man, his back to Tucker, wearing a headset while whispering something into the small mike. Oh, what he would have given to be able to listen to that conversation.

Grimacing, he scrambled back to the front, verified that the guards were still by the vehicles, and then returned to the window and watched the same characters turning Monica Fox's house into shambles.

"Jake's probably getting reamed right about now," said one of the men shuffling through papers, pointing toward the back.

The guy behind the computer shrugged. "He fucked up. That bitch slipped right through his fingers this morning."

"And we lost Mark," said the third guy.

"Yeah," replied the computer man. "And poor Jimmy almost got his dick shot off by the woman."

"Who would have guessed that the nice little miss was packing?"

"He'll be all right, and at least we were able to clean it up before the cops arrived."

"Where could she be now?" asked the first man.

The one behind the computer shrugged again. "Anywhere but here, man. Anywhere but here."

They continued their work in silence.

Tucker narrowed his eyes at them. These characters had tried to kidnap Monica this morning, but she had managed to escape, which meant she was probably hiding somewhere on the island. If the NSA of today was anywhere as thorough as the NSA he remembered during his CIA days, they would have this island pretty much sealed off. If Monica tried to get near a boat she would be spotted. And even if she got to a boat, the bastards probably had a few boats of their own roaming in the area. Now that he thought about it, Tucker was surprised that he had been able to sneak into the island undetected. Maybe he had gotten lucky. Or perhaps the darkness had done the trick. Or maybe the NSA was getting sloppy. After all, they had failed to snatch one lonely woman, and from what he'd picked up from the trio in there, one of their own—someone named Mark—had been "lost," which in his jargon meant he had been killed, while the other had been shot somewhere around the groin area by Monica herself.

Tucker agreed with the operative currently rummaging through the contents of a box. The boss man out there was *definitely* getting reamed.

But how was the NSA mixed up in all of this in the first place? Tucker remembered that FoxComm had some large government contracts that involved the NSA. Was this secret file of Fox's linked to that agency? And where could Monica Fox have gone for help? The NSA would most certainly know if she had called the closest consulate or embassy since they controlled the communications link. Maybe she went to the local police.

Tucker decided that she probably had not. As an expatriate in Italy, the local police would had contacted the embassy for her, tipping the NSA of her whereabouts, which they obviously didn't know.

If she didn't go to her own embassy, or to the police, where could she be? Hiding in some hotel?

Tucker doubted it. Surely, the NSA would have scouts or informants covering the hotels on this rock.

Maybe with a friend?

He decided that was the most likely possibility. In the year that she had been here, Monica Fox would have made some friendships, maybe one close enough to obtain shelter at a time like this.

That also meant that Monica would be less likely to trust a stranger, like Bruce Tucker. By now she probably knew of her father's death following the failed kidnapping attempt. Was it possible that she may have contacted William Gibbons before he was taken in by whoever it was that had stolen the Colt? If so, then perhaps Gibbons had alerted Monica about Tucker, about the specialist that her father had sent to protect her, to bring her back safely. But there was also the chance that Monica didn't call home for the same reason that Tucker had avoided contacting Gibbons after their first and only meeting following Fox's death: His phone could be tapped. If Monica Fox had apparently been savvy enough to escape an NSA ambush and managed to hide from them for almost one full day in what really amounted to a relatively small search area, then she may have been wise enough to avoid contacting Gibbons for fear of a phone tap.

For a moment he wondered if this lady needed his protection at all. So far she had done quite well on her own.

But Tucker knew better than that. She was no professional and would eventually make a mistake. Besides, he had the feeling that her means were limited at best. The NSA would also be covering banks and automatic tellers, the places she would have to visit in order to remain hidden. And how long could she really keep that up? Eventually she would be forced to surface, particularly in such a small island, and when she did the NSA would be waiting for—

A powerful beam momentarily blinded him. He turned away, going into a roll to escape the spotlight.

"Hey! Stop!"

Tucker surged from the roll into a deep crouch, watching a figure holding a flashlight while reaching inside his coat.

Tucker pivoted on his left leg, bringing his weapon around, but aiming not at the center of his chest, as dictated by his training, but at the legs. After all, the NSA was on his side, even if it didn't appear so at the moment.

He fired once, the silencer absorbing the report.

The agent screamed while dropping to the ground, reaching for his thighs.

Tucker sprinted toward the trees. He had allowed his mind to distract him. The guard had probably done a routine round and spotted him.

Just as he reached the woods, Tucker watched from the corner of his eye as the second guard reached his screaming comrade, asking what had happened.

Tucker paused a few feet inside the woods, grabbing the goggles, putting them on, throwing the power switch, painting the darkness into shades of green.

A loud report whipped the darkness, the round walloping the bark of the tree to his immediate left.

His left? That didn't make sense. The second guard had been to Tucker's right as he'd reached the tree line.

Tucker turned around, watched in surprise a jade-colored

figure rushing toward him from the rear of the house.

The boss.

Of course! Unlike the rookie guards, their seasoned superior had reacted to the intrusion silently, without warning, firing first and asking questions later.

A second round cracked, smacking into another tree, splintering wood.

Not relishing the thought of having to engage the remaining NSA operatives, Tucker rushed deeper in the bush, but choosing a different route from the one he had taken on the way over, wishing to keep his escape route secret.

The ripping sound of multiple shotgun blasts rattled Tucker. It was followed by agonizing cries, and the popping sound of pistols.

The shotguns had not been fired at Tucker but at the NSA men.

What is going on?

Who fired at them?

Whoever it was, Tucker didn't feel like sticking around to find out. Right now there was one too many fish in this pond. He needed to get away, to regroup, to carefully think through the intelligence he had gathered tonight.

Besides, the gunfight would draw attention, draw the police over to this desolated section of the island—something he didn't think the NSA team also relished.

Gunfire ceased as abruptly as it had started. Engines revved up, followed by screeching tires. Tucker had been correct. The NSA wasn't hanging around, wasn't interested in fighting whoever it was that had fired the shotgun.

Or maybe they killed the shooter.

Or maybe the shooter had chosen to retreat when confronted with several armed men.

In any case, Tucker was out of there.

Walls of green blended to his sides as he picked up his pace, as he left the scrambling NSA team in the darkness behind, as he parted hanging vegetation, jumped over fallen logs, twisted his body to conform to the woods.

He detected no bright shafts of green behind him, meaning

no one with a flashlight. Without light they would not be able to keep up with—

Tucker heard noise to his right, someone crushing the dry branches and leaves littering the ground. But he never got the chance to look in that direction.

The impact was solid, just behind his left ear.

Then everything went dark.

The Last of the Boy Scouts

Donald Bane, chief of counterterrorism within the directorate of operations of the CIA, sat across from Geoff Hersh, director of the National Security Agency, and Randolph Martin, the director of Central Intelligence, at a private room in Smith & Wollensky, a premier steak house in Washington, D.C.

Bane regarded the relatively young and patrician NSA director and the elderly DCI as their waiter arrived with a bottle of Silver Oak. Hersh smoothed his silk tie while eyeing the expensive vino with satisfaction. Martin seemed too preoccupied to care, his lanky frame, heavily lined face, and sunken blue eyes a silent testament of what thirty-five years in the intelligence world could do to a man.

"Do you approve, Mr. Hersh?" the waiter asked in an irritating nasal voice.

The well-tanned Hersh, who had gotten this appointment as a reward for running a spectacular campaign for the president, bobbed his head slightly, and the waiter proceeded to open it.

Bane hated expensive joints like this, where the "beautiful" people ate. At fifty-two years old, balding, and thirty pounds overweight, he was not a beautiful person, particularly with a prominent scar running from the top of his left brow straight to the temple—the result of being kicked unconscious by a group of Iraqi soldiers many years ago after getting caught spying. The bastards had also broken his nose, which had healed a bit crooked. His CIA benefits could certainly afford him plastic surgery, but Bane saw the scar and his bent nose as decorations earned in the service of his country, and he wore them with pride.

Not that it mattered anymore. A new wave of young guns was taking over the intelligence community. Like Hersh, they were all forty-something, cocky, relatively inexperienced, but very rich and well connected with a parallel wave of young politicians, many of whom financed their own campaigns after growing bored with making billions in the private sector. Their campaign ads proclaimed that they would enrich Americans just as they had enriched themselves.

You have done enough for your country, said an ad that Hersh had run during the successful campaign he had orchestrated for the president. *It is time your country did something for you.*

Bane shivered at the thought. JFK was probably rolling over in his grave. There had been a time not long ago when heroes like Bane were respected for what they had done for their nation, for their sacrifice, for putting their personal needs second to the needs of their countrymen.

Not anymore.

The Me Generation was here in full force, wanting not just something for nothing, but *everything* for nothing, unwilling to go the distance, to sacrifice, and even to appreciate those who had sacrificed themselves before them—perhaps because deep inside they resented patriots like Bane, who reminded them of an era of honor and commitment they wanted to leave behind, replaced by their world of opportunism and quick profit, of the almighty dollar, which had superceded friendship and loyalty.

That probably explained why Bane, Porter, and some other old-timers—Martin included—had been under fire by everyone from the White House to Congress in recent months.

Just last week the Vice President, another forty-something and former hot-shot founder and CEO of a successful biotech firm, had hinted that perhaps it was time for the legendary Martin to retire, to live his remaining years writing his memoirs and hitting the speaker's circuit.

Taking a deep breath as the waiter poured a finger onto Hersh's glass and the handsome nobleman swirled it with elegance and sniffed it before sipping it, Bane did his best to hide his curiosity, as well as his growing contempt. He despised the fact that he had been summoned here with little warning or explanation as much as he hated eating at such expensive restaurants, particularly when this dinner was being financed with taxpayers' money. But apparently Hersh had insisted on convening at the expensive steak house, and Martin had agreed, persuading Bane to meet them here—but without revealing the topic of the discussion. The man running the all-powerful NSA was used to eating at the finest restaurants in town. Unlike Martin and Bane, Hersh had been born to wealth and educated at the finest schools, including four years at Annapolis, followed by a tour of duty as the executive officer of a missile cruiser. His father then cashed in a favor to get him appointed assistant secretary of the Defense Intelligence Agency's procurement division, helping manage the extensive budget of the Pentagon's version of the CIA. Hersh retired from the post three years later and became a successful businessman while also getting an M.B.A. from Harvard, followed by a Ph.D. in communications, eventually running the president's election campaign and coming full circle back to a higher appointment. It was indeed an impressive career. Problem was, Bane didn't see any experience in Hersh's resume that qualified him to run the NSA.

He breathed in deeply, exhaling slowly, wondering what was so critical that it required the heads of the NSA and the CIA to meet like this. After all, the NSA, in conjunction with the Defense Intelligence Agency, reported to the Secretary of Defense. The combined level of intelligence gathered by those two military agencies was as formidable as anything the CIA could collect. Hersh shouldn't lack for intelligence sources. Perhaps he was trying to cross-check new information. The NSA on occasion worked in conjunction with the CIA, but usually in times of emergency, like during the terrorist crisis at the beginning of the century. In such occasions, the president had been adamant that his military and civilian intelligence agencies shared their data, forcing them into reluctant cooperation. Otherwise, they competed fiercely against one another, each jockeying for better position to maximize congressional funding.

Hersh gave the waiter a second nod after tasting the sample, and the pouring began. Then they were finally left alone.

In reality they were *hardly* alone. Because of Martin's position, and the mounds of top-secret intelligence stored in his mind, four bodyguards always followed the DCI wherever he went, even to the rest room, though they would remain outside the stall while their boss took care of his business.

Taking a crap with an audience.

Bane smiled inwardly, glad that his relatively lower position in the CIA totem pole didn't require him to have bodyguards. Bane carried beneath his sports jacket all of the protection he needed, a 9mm Beretta pistol plus a small backup in an ankle holster.

Hersh also had quite the protection entourage strategically sitting at two separate tables in the restaurant, near Martin's bodyguards. The two teams had the meeting grounds quite secured.

The NSA director sipped wine while glancing at Martin before focusing on Bane over the rim of the crystal. "You will find no finer wine," Hersh said with conviction, setting the glass on the table.

Bane planted his large forearms on the starched tablecloth and interlocked his fingers. He wasn't a small talk kind of guy, and he couldn't care less about wine. He observed his hosts across fine crystal, china, and silverware, before going straight to the point. "Would you gentlemen mind telling me the reason for this meeting?"

"We're here to chat about Bruce Tucker," said Martin.

Bane blinked once and looked away, not certain why someone as high up as Hersh was suddenly interested in Tucker. Three days had passed since the incident at West Potomac Park, and no one from the NSA, the DIA, or the Department of Defense for that matter had contacted the CIA to get information beyond that included in the flash report broadcast to the field, in which Randolph Martin had placed Tucker under "beyond salvage" status.

"The reason we need to discuss the Tucker case," Hersh added, lowering his voice, also placing his elbows on the table as he leaned closer to Bane, "is because of the information that Tucker may have extracted from Mortimer Fox before his death."

"What kind of information?" asked Bane.

"Information that could negatively impact our national security," said Martin, holding his wineglass by the stem.

The reply was unexpected, though externally Bane didn't show it. He knew that Tucker was Fox's executive protector. Porter had briefed a few senior officers, including Bane, about Bruce Tucker the moment the former CIA officer had contacted his old mentor to arrange a meeting. Fox, of course, had been the head of one of America's largest high-tech companies, which included a division that handled large government contracts, but Bane wasn't aware of any information that the NSA suspected Fox might have possessed and passed on to Tucker. After all, the CIA wasn't allowed to spy on Americans. That was the FBI's job. However, since the unexpected killings, Bane had pondered what had driven Tucker over the edge. The only surviving CIA officer at West Potomac Park had claimed that Tucker insisted he had been framed, that he was innocent and would prove it. The proof gathered by the local police and the FBI, however, was difficult to ignore. The ballistics report had established that Tucker had used his own registered Colt .45 to murder Porter's men, and to shoot the surviving CIA officer. And there had even been an eyewitness who identified Tucker as the man holding a gun at the scene. On the other hand, Tucker had not killed that last CIA officer. He had purposely shot

him in the leg before passing on the message of his innocence. Bane also could not think of a motive, a reason for
the killings. Tucker had gained nothing at that meeting but
turning the entire United States government against him.

Bane looked into the distance, still wondering if Martin
had done the right thing by labeling Tucker beyond salvage.

Bruce Tucker.

He remembered him well. Bane had been the station chief
of the Kiev station in the Ukraine when Tucker had gotten
his assignment in Zurich. The two station chiefs had collab-
orated on a number of missions, including the one in which
Tucker tracked down and killed Siv Jarkko. Bane had em-
pathized with the fellow officer when his wife and son had
been killed—especially due to a blunder in CIA security at
a supposedly safe house in Zurich. Bane too had lost a loved
one in a remote airfield in Iraq at the same time that he had
earned his scars: a Marine aviator named Colonel Diane
Towers. Much time had past since her death, but the pain
never quite went away. Unlike his facial scars, the pain of
which faded with time, the loss of Diane still haunted him.

So Bane had not blamed Tucker when he had submitted
his request to transfer to the Department of the Treasury to
join the Secret Service. The man had been in need of a
change. In the Secret Service Tucker performed well above
average, rapidly climbing through the ranks, to the point that
he became assistant shift leader for the protection of the President. Then he turned to the private sector, where no one
could match his top-notch services.

Why would he throw it all away?

Bane had pulled up Tucker's psychological evaluation, re-
vised by Agency psychologists the day after Porter was shot.
The report claimed that Tucker had basically snapped, gone
down the deep end. The shrinks postulated that the anger and
pain bottled up inside of him all those years had finally
caught up with him, sending him into a killing rampage. That
report, plus the irrefutable evidence gathered by the police,
had finally convinced the director to issue the field alert.

But Bane wasn't one hundred percent certain that this had

been the best decision. After all, Agency shrinks have been wrong in the past. They had claimed that Bane would never perform up to standards again after his incident in Iraq, and of course, they had been dead wrong.

And if they were wrong about me, they could also be wrong about Tucker, he thought, particularly since he could not think of a motive—*a reason*—why Tucker would had done something so crazy.

Crazy.

That's what Langley doctors claimed Tucker was. Just plain nuts, especially because in addition to professing his innocence, Tucker had also insisted that the killings were committed by none other than Siv Jarkko—a statement that shrinks believed was further evidence that the man's monorail was deep in Fantasy Land.

Bane had gone back and reviewed the old files from the Zurich station archives, the medical examiner's conclusions that the badly burnt body belonged to Siv Jarkko. The report had included a perfect dental match with the file provided by German Intelligence, where Jarkko, born to Yugoslav parents but raised in East Germany, had worked during the Cold War years.

Bane had been trained to think geometrically, to consider all of the angles. He had to admit that the mentally-insane theory seemed to fit the facts quite well.

Too well.

And that made Donald Bane suspicious. If he put the psychology report aside for a moment, Bane could not explain Tucker's totally out-of-character actions, compounded by a lack of a motive, and the bizarre claim about Jarkko.

"We think we may have spotted Tucker," said Hersh.

"Where?" asked Bane, intrigued.

Hersh smiled a proud smile before replying, "NSA agents might have spotted him in Southern Italy. On the island of Capri."

Now *that* was a surprise, especially considering that the CIA had far more resources operating outside of the United States than the NSA and the DIA combined. For a moment

Bane tried to remember who was currently running the Rome station. He did recall that the U.S. ambassador to Rome was Landon Quinn, a former CIA station chief in Europe prior to his diplomatic appointment.

Martin added, "We think he might be part of a terrorist team."

Now Bane's ears perked up like a Doberman. Counterterrorism was his baby. Still, he couldn't conceive the idea of Bruce Tucker associated with terrorists.

"A terrorist?" he finally said, unable to contain his growing skepticism. "Gentlemen, with all due respect, I worked with the man for a few years. I personally spent time with him when he lost his wife in Zurich. He is no terrorist. I *barely* bought the report from the shrinks that he had gone crazy."

"I know it's difficult to accept such realities, Don," said Martin in his grandfatherly voice. "But the evidence against him is overwhelming, including the killings at West Potomac Park."

"Okay," Bane said, deciding to gather more data before engaging in this particular argument. "Let's shelve the terrorism charge for a moment. You mentioned something about critical information that you believe Fox passed on to Tucker."

The waiter returned to take their order.

Leaning back, Geoff Hersh glanced at his menu and ordered a medium-rare filet mignon with a couple of side orders. Martin got a strip. Bane ordered a ribeye.

Alone again, Hersh leaned forward once more, his voice a mere whisper. "What I'm about to tell you is strictly need-to-know, under Presidential orders. Are we clear so far?"

"So far," Bane said.

"First some background. As you know, FoxComm, in addition to its dominance in the commercial and industrial high-tech markets, is one of the largest government contractors we have, right up there with Lockheed and General Dynamics. But while the latter two focused more on classical weapons, like fighter jets and missiles, FoxComm

provided us with computer systems and communications networks—the avenues that our industry uses to share our
intelligence-gathering and convey orders." Hersh paused,
then asked, "What is the most vital aspect of communications, Mr. Bane?"

Bane looked away, frowning as he regarded the heavy
wood paneling in the room. "Security."

Hersh raised his wine glass to him. "As you probably
know, Mortimer Fox's company designed our encryption al-
gorithms, the ones used to scramble all of our communications. In the information age, where hackers abound, our old
encrypting methods were becoming easier and easier to
break. After all, just about every computer science major has
access to a supercomputer these days. So we asked Fox to
design the ultimate encryptor, one impossible to break by
today's machines."

Bane shifted his gaze between Hersh and Martin before
mumbling, *"Firewall?"*

Hersh grinned. "The world's most sophisticated system of
satellites, its creation known only to members of the U.S.
intelligence community—in addition to a handful of high-
ranking officials in Washington and the Pentagon."

Bane added, "A silicon-based artificial-intelligence system
placed in geosynchronous orbit by NASA over a period of
four years. Our technical division spent almost six months
after that converting our encoding programs to interface them
to the *Firewall* AI engine after the satellites became fully
operational last year."

"Yes," Hersh said. "That was a challenge not just for the
CIA, but also for the Pentagon, the White House, the DIA,
the NSA, the FBI, and a host of other agencies. Now everyone in our intelligence community uses *Firewall*, the most
secure and reliable communications system in history, a fifty-
billion-dollar engineering wonder housing not an encryptor,
which could be eventually broken by hackers, but an artificial
intelligence system capable of fending off illegal users, and
physically placed on Earth orbit, out of reach to all but those
in possession of the right user passwords, which change con-

stantly, even during a transmission, always checking for the authenticity of the user."

"So," Bane said, taking a sip of his wine, which was, he had to admit, damned good. "Everything you've said is goodness. When did things go wrong?"

Martin tapped his fingers on the table. "We're not sure exactly when it began, Don, but sometime in the past six months Mortimer Fox began to believe that the United States government wanted him dead."

"Dead? Why would he have thought that?"

"It was no secret that Uncle Sam was going after Fox-Comm just as it had gone after previous monopolies, like Microsoft," said Hersh. "But those attacks were meant to prevent a company from using illegal business practices to keep others from participating in profitable commercial and industrial markets. They weren't targeted at Fox himself. Somehow, though, the old tycoon began to believe that we wanted him dead, especially after Vinod Malani—his chief technical officer—was kidnapped, tortured, and murdered. Fox became extremely paranoid, to the point of retaining the services of Tucker as his executive protector."

"All right," Bane said. "So he was paranoid, and as it turned out, with good reason. His CTO was kidnapped, and he was almost abducted too, had it not been for Tucker— though in the end Fox died of a heart attack. The question is who was after Fox?"

"That's *one* question," said Hersh, "which in the end might help us answer an even more important question."

"Which is?"

"What did Mortimer Fox do as a contingency, in case we went after him and even Tucker couldn't protect him? Surely someone with such skills, at least in the boardroom and the courtroom, would have thought of a way to get back at us if we ever tried to eliminate him."

Once again, Bane found himself just staring at his dinner companions.

"Our agencies have reason to believe . . ." Hersh paused and glanced at Martin, apparently making sure one final time that they should bring Bane into the know. The DCI bobbed his head once. Hersh continued. "We think that Fox may have created a backdoor into *Firewall*, a way to access it and store intelligence he may have gathered on his enemies. That way, if something were to happen to him, he could have that information released to the press."

"What kind of data?"

"*Dirt*, Mr. Bane. The kind of material that would create scandals in the media. We have found enough evidence to believe that Fox, using this backdoor to monitor our own communications, collected material that could trigger Watergate-like scandals on prominent political figures. But that information, as damaging as it may be to certain people, is relatively minor compared to the fact that Fox pirated a backdoor into *Firewall*. If our enemies get a hold of that backdoor code—"

"How do you know all this?" Bane interrupted.

"From some of his former software contractors."

"Contractors?"

"Yes," Hersh said. "The *Firewall* system is perhaps the most complicated software engine there is today, comprised of billions of lines of code. Not one person, nor a single team for that matter, could have created such an artificial intelligence system. It required an effort of a magnitude similar in scope to Rockwell pulling together technology from hundreds of subcontractors to manufacture the orbiter of the space shuttle system—only FoxComm did it while maintaining a level of secrecy that rivaled the Manhattan Project. Now, although the effort was immense, we always made certain that not one corporation knew more than a small piece of the entire project."

"Except for FoxComm, who pulled it all together," noted Bane.

"Correct," said Hersh. "But we had our own technical people supervising the process to make sure that the security of *Firewall* remained intact."

"But you couldn't possibly supervise *every* programmer

and engineer *every* second of *every* day," said Bane, dreading the picture that his mind slowly painted.

"Obviously. Although we have no solid proof of the existence of this backdoor, we got circumstantial evidence from some software contractors that there was a secret project underway at FoxComm during the final development stage of *Firewall* to create a master key to access the system. It was run by two individuals, both of whom are now dead."

"Malani and Fox," Bane said, pinching the bridge of his nose, feeling a headache creeping into his temples.

"Yes, Don," said Martin. "We think that even Malani may have not known the entire picture because after his kidnapping and murder they went after Fox to find the code."

Bane dropped his eyelids at Hersh. "Who is *they*?"

"Good question. We're not really sure. Could be the Iraqis, or the Libyans, or some militant group. What we do know is that these terrorists are trying to find the pirated backdoor. We were following Fox's movements in case they decided to kidnap him, and they did try at the convention center in San Francisco. We tried to stop them, inadvertently creating a diversion, which Tucker used to get Fox out of the building. Outside, the hit team tried again, almost succeeding, but thanks to the timely assistance of the police, Tucker managed to get Fox away, though he died later, apparently from a stray bullet that hit his Kevlar vest, triggering a heart attack. Those same terrorists are still trying to find the code. We have to do everything and anything possible to prevent them from acquiring it. Imagine what it would do to our operations if a rogue regime in the Middle East, Africa, or South America were capable of unscrambling our classified conversations."

Bane winced, feeling as if his stomach was filling with molten lead, inducing nausea just as their waiter arrived with their dinner. He stared at his ribeye, which looked mouthwateringly delicious, but unfortunately Hersh had just done a superb job of turning Bane's digestive system upside down. If what the NSA director said was accurate, then the U.S. Intelligence community was in serious jeopardy. For the past year all classified communications within government agencies had used *Firewall*'s encoding engine. At the CIA, the usage extended to communications with field offices, all of which relied on *Firewall* for their reports, which included information on CIA officers and the agents they ran in their respective countries. All of those transmissions could have been intercepted and recorded by illegal listeners, but without *Firewall*, all they would had gotten was scrambled eggs. Access to *Firewall* would allow them, literally overnight, to decode those files, jeopardizing not just the lives of thousands of field officers and the many more agents they ran, but also the operations themselves, pretty much shutting down the CIA's capability of providing intelligence to the U.S. government. The same would happen at the DIA, at the NSA, and the FBI. Terrorists and criminals linked to these rogue regimes would learn about previous and current activities at all U.S. intelligence and security agencies.

"Christ Almighty," Bane said, leaning back.

"Yes, Mr. Bane. Not a pretty picture. Also, we fear that the kind of backdoor that Fox installed here could allow anyone in its possession not only to monitor our communications, but to shut them down, to kill the *Firewall* link."

"Dear God," Bane mumbled. That would mean not only zero classified communications in the intelligence community, but also at the Pentagon and the White House.

"And it gets much worse," said Martin. "There's also the issue of the nuclear football."

His stomach was in a knot so tight that Bane wondered if he would ever be able to eat again. Martin had just mentioned the nickname for the briefcase that had followed American presidents since Eisenhower. It contained the launch codes for all operational U.S. nuclear missiles. If events ever warranted a nuclear strike, the President would open the briefcase, which always remained chained to the wrist of an aide, and launch. Back in the fifties, the codes were hard copies that matched those in missile silos and submarines. For security the codes would be changed periodically. But with the advent of the information age, the launch codes were now all software-encoded. The President merely carried a live copy of the codes in the football, which resembled a wireless portable computer, capable of sending any code to any operational silo, submarine, or bomber around the world in seconds.

"*Firewall* has been managing the security of the launch codes for the past year, Don. The President keeps a copy of the codes in the football. The codes are now updated every two hours, matching the updates done at every silo, nuclear sub, and bomber squadron we have in operation today."

"And *Firewall* handles the synchronization real-time between the President's nuclear football and the missiles," added Hersh. "Through an ultra-secured and encrypted wireless link."

"So," said Bane, quickly catching on. "If someone was able to breach *Firewall*, that person could access the launch codes, issue them to missile silos and submarines, and then shut down our communications channel, making it impossible for us to counter the orders until it was too late."

Hersh drank wine while Martin said, "For years now, Don, our nation has worried about a terrorist smuggling a suitcase nuke into our country and detonating it. Why go through all the trouble of not just securing the materials to assemble it, but also risking getting it inside the U.S. when all a terrorist had to do is access *Firewall* from some remote location in the world and issue a launch code to a submarine? The sub skipper will go through his procedure of verifying the code with his own, and once the match is checked by himself and his executive officer, they would launch. Plain and simple. So imagine for a moment some rogue nation accessing *Firewall*, getting the United States to launch a first strike against another nuclear power, like Russia, or China. Then he shuts down *Firewall*, cutting off our secured communications. The terrorists could then sit back and watch the superpowers blow each other off the map."

Bane pushed his steak aside. Obviously his dinner companions had already gone through the shock, denial, and acceptance stages on this problem and were simply trying to solve it while digging into their steaks. Bane, on the other hand, stuck somewhere between shock and denial, felt like vomiting.

"Why can't we just block this pirated door into the system?" Bane asked.

Hersh finished chewing, swallowing with a sip of wine. "Won't work. We simply can't change *Firewall* overnight to eliminate the backdoor because it's hidden in the billions of lines of code that make up the operating system. Remember that it took several years to deploy *Firewall*, plus the time we spent converting our systems to it. Best case it would take us several *months* of concerted effort to reprogram the system and eliminate any pirated backdoors."

"Obviously not an immediate option," Bane said. "In addition to the launch codes, not only do we have the problem of previous intelligence transmissions to deal with, but we'll also have to find other means of communicating with our agents in the field until the system is brought back on line, which in itself is also not an option because terrorists and hackers are now armed with very advanced tools, which could easily beat our classic encryption methods."

"It's back to the Stone Age, Mr. Bane."

Martin sliced off a chunk of meat, stabbed it with his fork, and pointed at Bane with it. "And that brings us back to what we must do to prevent anyone from getting a hold of that backdoor code." He shoved the meat in his mouth and chewed.

"Bruce Tucker," said Bane, reaching for his glass of wine and taking a swig. The alcohol burned his throat, but it helped settle his churning stomach.

"Precisely," said Hersh, also reaching for his glass of wine. "And the reason why he may have gone to Capri."

"Which is?"

"Fox's daughter, Monica, currently resides in Capri. We were able to track her down through international bank transactions. We think there's a chance she may have this access code."

Bane set his glass down. "Of course. What better place to

safeguard that kind of information than with his closest relative, someone Fox could trust. If something were to happen to Fox, then his daughter could get even by releasing the secret files stored in *Firewall*. But how do we know for certain that this information resides with her?"

Martin tilted his head. "We actually don't. But she's our best lead. We were also going to interview William Gibbons, Fox's personal attorney, but he has disappeared."

"Disappeared?"

"Yep," said Hersh. "We're working with the FBI to try to find him. In the meantime, the FBI has already gotten court orders to search not just FoxComm, but Fox's various estates in this country, as well as the properties of all of his vice presidents and directors. They plan to comb through everything in the hope of finding any trace of this backdoor software. We're also interviewing anyone who we think might be able to help us."

"But that takes time," observed Bane. "And a lot of Fox's sympathizers might not be willing to come forth and assist FoxComm's enemy, the U.S. government."

"Right, Don. But that's all we can do for now. In the meantime we're monitoring Monica in the hope that Fox might have given her the information. The fact that Tucker, who, by the way, we think is working with the terrorists, is apparently also going after her lends credibility to our theory."

"Hold on there. If Bruce has indeed turned, then why did he protect Fox in San Francisco?"

"We don't have all of the answers, Mr. Bane. However, our analysts theorized that he may have wanted all of us to believe he was on our side. He probably was going to let Fox get kidnapped, but when NSA and FBI agents showed up he chose to play protector and wait for another opportunity. But Fox died on him anyway, so now he's after the daughter. We think that Tucker may have learned of her whereabouts from Fox."

"How?"

"Maybe he interrogated Mortimer Fox before the old man

died. The driver of the sedan that took Fox to the hospital
reported that Tucker closed the partition, isolating himself
with the dying Fox in the rear seat. Also, the ER nurse reported that Tucker refused to leave Fox when they arrived
at the hospital. Maybe he wasn't finished interrogating Fox."

Bane frowned. The theory still wasn't holding water.
"Why did he contact Porter, just to turn around and kill him?
I still can't find a motive. And what's his incentive for joining this contracted terrorist team? The Bruce Tucker I remember was a full-blooded patriot. I also heard that he was
doing pretty well as a protection specialist. Why would he
throw it all away?"

Martin finished his steak and pushed his plate aside, pouring himself more wine. "Don't really know, Don. It could
be the fact that he snapped and wanted to get even with the
CIA for the death of his family way back when. Or maybe
it was money. Tucker's tax returns for last year showed that
he made just over one hundred and fifty thousand dollars,
before taxes. *Pretty well*, as you said, but maybe he wanted
more. Look, Don. I really don't know, but something I *do*
know is that we can't allow the secrets of *Firewall* to fall
into the wrong hands. And right now Monica Fox is our best
candidate for finding those secrets. We need to get to her
before anyone else does."

Bane lifted his hands a few inches from the table, palms
up. "But if you're monitoring her activities in Capri, why
haven't you simply brought her in?"

Hersh crossed his arms, looking a bit embarrassed.

Martin said, "I'm afraid things got a little . . . *complicated*
in Capri. See, the NSA had indeed been monitoring her activities for the past few weeks, partly to protect her without
her knowing, and partly to see if we could learn something.
Hersh's men stepped up the surveillance after her father died,
and they were planning to take her in right away. Unfortunately, the Italian police got to her first."

"The Italian police?"

Hersh nodded. "The only thing we can think of is that
certain elements within the local police must be affiliated

with the terrorist network. The cops were transporting her for questioning, so I gave the order to abduct her."

"And?"

"We rescued her from the police, but then she managed to escape before we could identify ourselves." Hersh explained how his team blocked the road and tried to take her, but the policeman accompanying her started shooting, killing the senior agent in charge of the operation, and forcing the surviving NSA agents to defend themselves, killing the policeman. Monica escaped in the commotion, shooting an agent in the process.

"She shot one of your agents?" Bane asked.

"In the leg. Apparently someone gave her a gun."

Bane exhaled heavily. This *was* a mess. "Where is she now?"

Hersh shrugged and then spent the next fifteen minutes relating all of the problems that the NSA had encountered in Capri. An NSA agent had been forced to kill an Italian man while searching Monica Fox's boat. Apparently the Italian had attacked the agent with a monkey wrench, leaving the agent with no choice but to defend himself. He finished with the team that had fired at them with shotguns while they were searching her house last night.

"So," Bane said, struggling to digest it all, his mind going in different directions. "Bruce was with this team that attacked your men?"

"Correct. One of the NSA men identified Tucker while he was peeking through a window. Tucker shot him without warning, and as he tried to get away, his team showed up with shotguns and started blasting away at our men, covering his retreat. The officer in charge of the operation was seriously wounded. He died a few hours later." Hersh stared down at the table cloth.

Bane crossed his arms, the evidence conflicting with his instincts. The intelligence certainly indicated that Tucker had turned, despite what he had claimed at the park. But in any case, whether he had turned or not, what really mattered now was securing *Firewall*, and that meant securing Monica Fox. Period.

"So," Martin said, "we're here tonight to request that you head over to Italy as the new officer in charge, leading a team of CIA and NSA men to find a way to secure Monica Fox. The President has already given us his sanction to use whatever means necessary to bring this situation under control."

"I'm not a field operative anymore, sir. There are much younger and stronger officers out there."

"There is a terrific team out there, but they lack an experienced leader, Don, the instinct that you have for these things. To date no one can match your record, particularly the way you handled your end of the crisis in Iraq. That's why you continue to run counterterrorism."

"From my war room in Langley, sir."

"We need you out there, Don, calling the shots real time."

"All right," he said, regretting his words as they came out, for he knew quite well the kind of physical and mental stress that such assignments carried. "I'll do it . . . but only on one condition."

"Anything," said Hersh and Martin in unison.

"Like you just said, *I* call the shots out there. The terrorists are going to be moving fast, and I also need that freedom of operation without having to wait for some lengthy approval process."

"Absolutely," Martin said. "We both back you up one hundred percent on this."

Hersh lifted his glass at Bane. "A hundred percent."

Donald Bane looked away while rubbing his creased forehead. The stakes had gone up significantly. Bruce Tucker wasn't just a potential rogue agent gone crazy from the murder of his family. He was a cold-blooded killer at the center of a conspiracy targeted not just at destabilizing the national defenses of the United States of America, but at triggering Armageddon.

23

Tourists

Shafts of red and yellow-gold stained the shallow swells surrounding the island of Capri. Stars receded in the indigo sky as dawn broke to the sounds of chirping birds and the steady bustle of early morning foot traffic. Another day was starting in the picturesque island, and the locals readied themselves for the ferries that would start arriving shortly—and would continue to arrive until dusk.

But on this cloudless morning a single vessel approached the island from Naples, a luxurious yacht, its fifty-foot-long hull slicing though the Mediterranean's cerulean waters, its white lines reflecting the wan morning light.

The harbormaster directed the yacht to take in at one of a dozen guest docks on the private marina adjacent to the Marina Grande. The skipper waved from the bridge and steered the vessel to its assigned slip.

None of the busy locals paid much attention to the arriving yacht, used to seeing the rich and famous often visit the island for a day of sightseeing. Besides, they were busy setting up their businesses for the day.

Seven men and one woman disembarked, all wearing casual clothes and sunglasses, stopping at shops on their way to the taxi stand at the far left end of the Marina Grande, making a few random purchases, walking past a group of policemen smoking cigars and drinking coffee near a pair of police speedboats rocking gently in the water. Despite the recent killings, local authorities maintained a façade of normalcy, not wishing to drive tourists—their sole source of income—away from paradise.

Vlad Jarkko was banking on the locals' profit-driven attitude this morning, as he tipped his New York Yankees baseball cap at the policemen while strolling casually to the taxi stand followed by his travel companions, two of whom carried souvenir bags.

The policemen smiled and said, *"Buon giorno."*

"Buon giorno," Vlad replied.

Two sedans waited for them at the taxi stand, as arranged. Vlad sat in the rear of one vehicle with Mai Sung. The two-car caravan headed for a safe house in Anacapri, on the way driving in front of their target for this evening, the residence of Vittorio Carpazzo, regional head of the Mafia, and host of the runaway Monica Fox.

"I have never been to Capri," said Mai Sung, dressed in tight shorts, a white bikini top, and sunglasses. She gazed at the surrounding hills, at the beautiful scenery beyond the sedan's tinted window.

Vlad regarded her a moment. This morning, the Korean agent looked stunning, her full breasts just barely contained by that bikini top.

"I have been here many times," he said, checking his watch. "It's a beautiful island. Too bad we're here on business."

"Yes," she said, breathing heavily, her chest swelling. "That's too bad indeed."

Headache

The headache woke him. It felt like broken glass driven into his temples, scraping his brain.

Bruce Tucker tried to open his eyes but the throbbing made it nearly impossible. Instead, he stretched his sore body, slowly, feeling his surroundings, deciding that he was resting on a bed or sofa, in a dark place.

Slowly, his mind began to kick in. He had been running away from the shooting, from the NSA agents, when—

He winced in pain, clenching his teeth. The bastard who'd knocked him out knew exactly where to hit him, just behind the ear, shocking the web of nerves beneath the skin, triggering an almost-immediate shutdown of his system.

Painfully, Tucker inched his left eye open—a mere slit—but enough to see where he was.

A murky bedroom, high ceilings, draperies covering large windows. And it was nighttime, at least based on the lack of sunlight glowing at the edge of the drawn curtains.

With effort, he managed to sit up, realizing he was on a single bed.

Where in the hell am I?

Tucker ran a finger behind his left ear, cringing when his fingertip touched a lump.

"Great," he whispered. "Way to go, pal."

Forcing himself to ignore the headache, Tucker stood, slowly; not only was his head throbbing, but his body felt sore from the climb. His bare feet tingled against the cold tile, making him realize that he wasn't wearing shoes. That prompted him to look at himself. He still had his clothes, but a quick check revealed that his ID, utility vest, money, and weapons were missing.

Surprise, surprise.

Walking to the door, struggling to keep his balance, he tried the knob, but as expected, it was locked from the outside. He went to the windows and shoved the curtains aside, staring at a great view of the hillside leading to the sea through thick metal bars. And it appeared he was at least on the second floor of this place.

And trapped.

Tucker checked the walls, looking for a light switch, finding it next to the door. He threw it and the chandelier hanging from the ceiling blinded him, intensifying the headache.

Shielding his eyes, Tucker blinked rapidly, adjusting to the brightness, inspecting his Spartan quarters, the single bed, the nightstand, and nothing else—nothing that he could use to make a weapon.

But he did find his sneakers by the foot of the bed. Tucker was about to reach for them when the door opened.

He staggered back, almost losing his balance.

Two men armed with shotguns appeared in the doorway, their faces impassive. They seemed in their thirties, thin, well-tanned, dressed in loose clothes, both wearing soft caps.

"Sit," one of them said, pointing the muzzle at the bed.

Tucker's immediate reaction was to make himself look as least threatening as he could—which, based on the way he felt, didn't take much acting on his part.

He complied, slowly, a hand on his forehead. Sitting at the foot of the bed, he slouched his shoulders, keeping his head bobbed, sheepishly looking at his captors, who walked in the room and flanked him.

A third man stepped into view, also of dark olive complexion, but taller than the first two, and wider. He held a lit cigar instead of a weapon, its smoke curling toward the ceiling. Dark eyes under thick brows and salt-and-pepper hair inspected Bruce Tucker, who figured he was the boss.

Placing the cigar in his mouth, the boss reached into his pocket and produced Tucker's waterproof pouch, opening it, pulling out his passport, browsing through it. "I see you are a well-traveled man . . . Mr. Smith," he finally said in flawless English.

One of the professional touches that his old friend Davis in New York had made to increase the authenticity factor of the fake passport was to include the immigration stamps of many countries over a period of four years.

Tucker slowly nodded, with obvious effort. "I . . . get around."

The stranger pulled out his New York driver's license, a Visa card, and a lot of cash, before shoving it all back in the small pouch, which he pocketed. "What is your business with Monica Fox?"

Tucker quickly went through his options. These characters

didn't look like they belonged with the CIA, the NSA, or any other U.S. intelligence agency hunting him. They were locals, most likely the guys who had opened fire on the NSA after he had entered the woods. So if they were local, and they carried weapons, they were either with the police or the Mafia. Since they didn't look like the police, that pretty much narrowed down the choices, and from the looks of it they certainly fit the stereotype.

Way to go, Bruce. You've managed to evade the CIA and Jarkko, just to get caught by the Italian Mafia.

"I will not ask again. What is your business with Monica Fox?"

Tucker's wheels were now spinning faster than the barrel of a pistol in a deadly game of Russian roulette, which in a way he felt he was about to play. The wrong answer would certainly result in a bullet through his head, which at the moment might have been a blessing.

Rubbing an index against his right temple, he said, "I was sent . . . by her father."

"Her father is dead."

"I know. He died . . . in my arms. I was his . . . executive protector."

"Executive protector?"

"Right."

"You look a bit skinny for a bodyguard."

Tucker raised an eyebrow.

The boss waved the cigar in the air. "And what are you doing on my island, *executive protector?*"

"I was sent to protect . . . Monica Fox."

The boss remained silent for a moment, measuring Tucker, before he made a sound that resembled a steam engine leaving the station. He was laughing, and his men joined in.

"Il protectore do la signora Monica," one of the guns said to the other as they kept on laughing.

In spite of the pain in his head, Tucker could have taken them all right there, their weapons momentarily pointed away from him. But his instincts restrained him, sensing that these characters were not his true enemy. He considered the pos-

sibility of enlisting their help. "She is in . . . great danger,"
he finally said in a low voice as the laughter died down.
"More so than you may realize. Where is she?"

"Safe with me," said the boss, becoming serious again
while pointing a thumb at himself. "I'm Vittorio Carpazzo.
No one will harm her while under my protection."

"But . . . I must speak with her."

Carpazzo ignored him. "Who were those men in the
house?"

Tucker put a hand to his forehead again while he thought
of an appropriate answer, not wishing to reveal the presence
of the NSA. "That's what I was trying . . . to find out when
they started shooting at me."

"I had sent my men there to try to get Monica's passport
and other personal belongings. But they saw that other team
searching her house. I ordered them to remain hidden. They
saw you approach the house. They saved your life when the
shooting began and brought you to me."

Tucker pointed at the lump on the side of his head. "Forgive me for not feeling so . . . grateful."

"They had to make sure you would not harm them."

"They could have . . . killed me."

"*Si*. And they still might," said Carpazzo, raising his bushy
brows while drawing on the cigar, exhaling toward Tucker.
"You said you were with her father when he died?"

"That's right."

"What happened?"

He let go a loud breath of annoyance. "Look, could I at
least have some aspirin? Please?"

"Only if you answer my questions. How did Mortimer Fox
really die? The papers claimed it was a heart attack."

"Someone tried to kidnap him at a computer show in San
Francisco," Tucker said, feeling a little better, but refusing
to show it. "I managed to get him out unharmed and into a
car. Unfortunately, he had a . . . weak heart and was not able
to take the stress. He died en route to the hospital."

"And he asked you to protect her?"

"That's right. Now may I have some—"

"How do I know you didn't kill my father and are now here to kill me as well?" interrupted a deep female voice.

Tucker looked toward the doorway, staring at a tall and slim brunette, her shoulder-length hair framing a triangular face, high cheekbones crowned by a pair of slanted, hazel eyes. A couple of bruises ruined what would otherwise have been an angelic face—a face that for a moment took Tucker back to the pictures he had seen of Monica Fox, which did not do her justice. She was certainly far more attractive in person.

"Monica," said Tucker in a brief moment of amazement.

"Answer my question, Mr. Smith," she insisted. "How do I know you're not here to kill me?"

"Your father sent me to protect you. Gibbons arranged it."

"One of my men tried to contact her father's attorney yesterday," said Carpazzo. "It appears that Mr. Gibbons is . . . how do you Americans say it, missing in action?"

"He vanished the day after my father died," Monica added, standing next to Carpazzo, her lithe figure dressed in a tan linen dress that exposed her feminine shoulders. She wore no jewelry, except for an oval silver locket hanging at the end of a chain. Tucker noticed the scrapes on her shoulder and arms. "No one has heard from him since."

"They got to him," said Tucker.

"Who?" asked Monica.

His instincts told him to measure the information he released, especially in front of Carpazzo, at least until he had determined if the Mafia don would be able to help him. "I'm not sure, but it's the same people who tried to kidnap your father."

The cigar hanging from the corner of his mouth, Carpazzo crossed his arms and regarded Tucker with suspicion. "You still have not answered her question. How do we know that it wasn't you who eliminated her father *and* Gibbons and are now trying to kill her?"

Tucker showed Carpazzo his hands, palms up. "Why would I want to do a thing like that? I'm here because her father was worried about her, because the people who wanted him and his company destroyed are now after her, the only surviving relative. I mean no harm to you, your men, or Monica."

He turned to Monica. "Look. I know I'm a stranger to you, but you must believe me. You are in great danger . . . and a sitting duck. The people who want you dead are very powerful. They will stop at nothing, *nothing*, and neither this man nor his armed guards will be able to protect you."

"But *you* can?" she asked, also crossing her arms.

"For a while," he said. "Long enough to unravel this conspiracy, to expose it, to bring those responsible to justice. Only *then* you will be safe."

Disbelief flashing in her eyes, Monica said, "Look, mister. Let's assume that my father did send you here. How am I supposed to believe that you can protect me when you couldn't even protect yourself?"

Tucker wasn't about to make excuses, for that was the mark of an amateur. Instead he said, "Believe whatever you wish to believe. But know this, *if* you stay here with these people, you *will* be dead within the next twenty-four hours. You are surrounded by a lot of men and guns now, and that's giving you a false sense of security. It takes much more than just massive force to form an effective shield, and what you have around you now is plenty of force all right, but no experience in my art. Make no mistake, Monica, you will be found, and when that happens these people won't be able to guarantee your protection. They might put up a phenomenal fight because, after all, they *are* armed to the teeth and are quite skilled." Tucker pointed at his head wound. "But all it takes is one lucky bullet—just one—to get through their defenses, and you will be dead. Your only chance is with me."

She dropped her lids at his bold statement. "Do you know who these people are? They are the most powerful force in Italy, mister. The fucking police work for them. The damned government is in their payroll. This is about the safest place on earth for me."

Tucker just stared back at her. If he could have a penny for every principal who had thought that a truckload of guns and men equaled a solid protective shield, he would be sipping piña coladas in the Caribbean instead of staring at the wrong end of two double-barreled shotguns.

"And something else," she added, cocking a finger at him. "I *know* who's after me. It's the United States government. My father fought them every day of his life, and in the end had to associate himself with *these people* to survive, just as I will work with them to claim what is legally mine, and also to achieve revenge!"

She stomped out of the room.

Tucker looked at Carpazzo. "Can I have my aspirin now?"

The Mafia boss ordered one of the guards to get him the pain medicine. The guard left, leaving Tucker with Carpazzo and the second guard.

After a few moments, Carpazzo asked, "What am I going to do with you, Mr. Smith?"

"It doesn't matter."

The Mafia boss regarded him with curiosity. "Why not?"

Tucker shrugged. "Because right now I'm more worried about Monica Fox than about myself."

Carpazzo grunted. "You are indeed an interesting man. You are beaten, incarcerated, and still talking like a big shot. You have balls, sir."

"I may have balls," Tucker said. "But I'm not thinking with them right now. I meant what I said."

Carpazzo remained silent, inspecting him through the writhing smoke.

"She is in danger, and so are you," Tucker added. "And time is running out."

The guard returned with the aspirin and a glass of water, which he handed to Tucker.

"Time is indeed running out, Mr. Smith," said Carpazzo. "For you."

Then he left, followed by the guards, who shut and bolted the door behind them.

Bruce Tucker drank the water but changed his mind about the little white pills, which for all he knew could be a sedative. He resigned himself to the fact that he would have to weather the headache *au naturel*.

He slipped on the sneakers and walked to the barred windows, turning off the lights so he could see through the glass. Dark woods meeting the sea cliff surrounded this side of Carpazzo's estate. He tried to think through his next step. Monica was in grave danger. She was actually safer walking the streets of Capri than stuck in this place. At least in the streets she would have mobility on her side.

Tucker momentarily closed his eyes. The initial meeting had certainly not gone as he had planned, but then again, he at least had managed to locate her. He just had not planned on getting captured by the Mafia to do so. On the bright side, though, he could have been abducted by the NSA, or worse, by Jarkko. Given the choices, he would much rather be here tonight than in some torture chamber with his old nemesis, or in an interrogation room packed with angry American operatives.

But you're still screwed, he thought, watching one of Carpazzo's men patrolling the perimeter of the estate facing the sea. Carpazzo didn't look like the benevolent boss, and unless Tucker could come up with a compelling argument about his value to Monica Fox, he could easily end up at the very bottom of the picturesque Mediterranean Sea.

Sleeping with the fishes.

Tucker frowned. He couldn't even prove that he had worked for her father. With Gibbons presumed dead, he had no one but the staff back at the mansion to vouch for his employment. Perhaps he could convince Monica to risk another phone call to the United States and ask for the head of the kitchen staff, an elderly lady who used to prepare the meals for Tucker and his team.

He clasped the thick iron bars. At the end of the day, if he couldn't convince the Italians and Monica of who he was, then Tucker would have to find a way to escape, something he had started working on the moment the two armed guards entered the room by making himself appear nonthreatening to them.

First you make them relax, then you strike.

He continue to stare at the scenic view, pondering on his plan of attack, when he noticed that the guard walking near the bluffs overlooking the sea abruptly stopped, looking about him, hastily reaching behind his neck, before collapsing.

Tucker tensed, clutching the steel bars, watching the guard sprawled on the ground. Then two shadows rushed across the far edge of the woods.

It's started.

25

Shadows

Sitting on a sofa in Carpazzo's large study on the first floor, Monica Fox brought the glass of brandy to her lips, sipping it, trying to calm herself, her emotions once again colliding inside her mind. Who was that stranger who claimed he had been sent by her father to protect her? Was he really who he said he was? An ... *executive protector*?

For a moment Monica despised her father for trying to control her life from the grave. On the other hand, however, she wondered if her father was right. After all, Monica had chastised him for associating himself with the Mafia, only to do it herself out of the same necessity. And it was his logic that had gotten her through the past thirty-six hours, since the ambush.

Attack, then retreat, then hide, observe, and plan, before striking again.

Right now Monica was hiding. According to her father's philosophy, she should be observing and planning, carefully considering her options, her next move.

He had been right so far. Was he also correct about this

man? Could this Stephen Smith really provide better protection than the Mafia?

"That man is lying to us," Carpazzo said, as if reading her thoughts. He was still smoking his cigar. "He is not telling us what he knows, but I have ways to get the truth out of men. I will interrogate him."

Monica looked away.

"You do not approve?"

She leaned her head back, resting it against the soft leather. "I'm not sure, Vittorio. I find myself in unfamiliar waters."

"Then allow me to guide you," he said, sitting next to her. "This is my business. I deal with people like the man in that room upstairs all the time. I eat, sleep, and live for security, for constant searches, looking for anything suspicious. Just last night, for example, we caught one of my men with a cellular phone he wasn't supposed to have. Another guard had seen him deviating from his assigned post, no more than a minute or two. That man is now off my property and on his way to Palermo, where he will be debriefed."

"Who could he be working for?"

"Maybe an informant for the government, or maybe for someone else. But we'll find out, and maybe even turn him, getting him to feed misinformation to the other side."

"That's all amazing to me."

Carpazzo placed a hand over hers. "And it is all second nature to me. Trust me, Monica. I will take care of—"

A shotgun blast echoed across the mansion.

Carpazzo rushed to his desk, stabbing the intercom button. *"Che cosa é successo?"* he barked into the dark unit. *What happened?*

He got static in reply.

"Vittorio? What's wrong?"

His features tightened with tension as he opened a gun cabinet next to the desk and pulled out a shiny pistol, which he cocked just as Ricco had shown her the day before, pulling back the slide, chambering a round.

"Where are you going?" she asked as he rushed to the door.

He extended an open palm toward her. "Wait here. I will be right back."

Monica stood, wondering what was going on. Was it possible that this Mr. Smith had been right, that it wasn't safe here? Her father had been correct so far. Why didn't she trust his judgment now?

Because you're an idiot!

Rushing for the gun cabinet, opening it, Monica stared at several shelves of weapons, mostly pistols. She grabbed one that resembled the little Tomcat she had bought at Ricco's, the one she had lost after shooting one of her would-be kidnappers.

She released the magazine, verified that it was full, reinserted it, thumbed the safety off, and chambered a round by pulling back on the slide.

She turned off the lights in the study and hid behind the desk, clutching the Beretta with both hands, but keeping her shooting finger resting on the trigger guard to prevent an accidental discharge.

Seconds turned into minutes of silence. She heard no voices, no more shooting. Just silence.

She had just stood up when the door to the study burst open, swinging on its hinges, crashing against the wall.

A large hooded figure stood in the doorway, like a shadow, and rushed toward her.

Something snapped inside of her, making her raise the pistol, just as she had practiced at Ricco's range, aiming it at the center of the chest of the incoming figure, and squeezing the trigger.

The report was deafening inside the room.

The figure staggered back but didn't fall, like in one of those horror movies from the seventies. And just like in the movies, he straightened and went after her, grabbing the gun away from her before she could fire it again.

26

Second Impression

The guard reacted just as Bruce Tucker had anticipated, leaning down over the protection specialist as he lay sideways on the floor clutching his stomach, moaning, twisting his face into a mask of pain.

The trick was an old one, but Tucker had maximized the chances of it working by having made himself appear weak and nonthreatening to the guards during their initial meeting.

"Hey, you!" the guard said in his thick English. "You okay?"

In a single move, Tucker swept his right leg inches above the tile floor, striking the legs of the Italian from behind, just above the ankles.

The guard jerked backward, stretching out his arms for balance, moving them in circles, like a cartoon character, before falling flat on his back.

As the guard hit the floor, Tucker rolled away, rising up to a crouch before kicking the Italian in the face, behind the right ear, just hard enough to knock him out.

Happy headaches, he thought, grabbing the man's shotgun, slinging it over his right shoulder.

Just then the report of a gunshot reverberated across the estate.

Here we go.

Ignoring his own headache, Tucker searched the guard for a concealed weapon, finding a 9mm Beretta shoved in the Italian's pants. A further search down his legs revealed an eight-inch blade in a Velcro sheath strapped over his ankle. Tucker transferred it to his own right ankle before moving to the doorway, peering beyond it.

A carpeted hallway.

Verifying that the Beretta's magazine, which held fifteen rounds, was full and that a round was already chambered, he flipped the safety and cocked it, holding it with both hands in front of his face, muzzle pointed at the high ceilings, from which ornate chandeliers hung, casting a yellowish glow.

He walked sideways, heading toward the stairs at the end of the hallway, passing a closed door, pressing his right ear against it, moving on when hearing nothing.

Controlling his breathing, forcing himself to relax so he could in turn augment his reaction time, Bruce Tucker tip-toed down the stairs, which curved down to a spacious foyer, adorned by a large rug and tall vases. Shifting his aim between the foyer and the top of the stairs, he descended quickly but silently, two steps at a time, feeling exposed while in transition between floors.

He hid behind one of the clay vases, as tall as he was, black, flanking the foot of the stairs.

Tucker peeked around it, tensing for a moment when spotting a few figures standing by the columns separating the foyer area from what looked like a sunken living room.

They were life-size statues of Greek gods. Sprawled by the statues lay Carpazzo, his lifeless eyes staring at the ornate ceiling.

I tried to warn you.

The living room led to the rear patio through a wall of French doors. Two of the doors were open, but he saw no one.

He was about to move to the living room when the report from a small-caliber gun popped inside the house, like a cheap firecracker, followed by woman's scream.

Monica Fox.

"Let me go!" she shouted.

Tucker's eyes darted to the hallway projecting to the right of the living room. Just then two shadows appeared behind the French doors, hooded and dressed in black, their bulky chests telegraphing the Kevlar vests they wore.

A third man dragged Monica into the foyer, where he

handed her to his two comrades before rushing toward the back doors while massaging his chest and reaching for a radio. A moment later he was gone.

It was now or never. The figures flanked Monica, each holding an arm as they forced her across the living room while she cursed like a sailor. The lady certainly had a temper.

Their backs were to Tucker, who stepped away from behind the vase, rising to his full height, keeping his feet one shoulder-width apart as he brought his weapon up, aiming it at the head of the figure to Monica's right.

The Beretta's report thundered inside the structure, pounding his eardrums. The round pushed the man forward, propelling him into a glass cocktail table, which shattered under his weight. Blood went everywhere from his burst skull, spraying the second figure, who let go of Monica and tried to bring his weapon around, but Tucker had the advantage of being behind. He had already lined up his silhouette and fired once, twice. Also sending him crashing into furniture.

Monica stood there, paralyzed, staring at the bleeding men missing most of their heads, her eyes mere slits of terror.

"Come!" he screamed, aware that the loud discharges had momentarily dampened their hearing. He ran to her, the shotgun bouncing against his back, an open hand extended toward his new principal.

She jerked back, confused, afraid, obviously hesitant of whom to trust.

"Trust your father's instincts, Monica!" he shouted. "Come with me if you want to live!"

She snapped out of her trance, staring at him with wide-open hazel eyes, breathing deeply, nodding, taking his hand. Some blood had also misted her face, her dress.

"We don't have much time!" he said loudly, starting for the foyer. "Hurry, before they come back!"

She didn't answer, the shock obviously clamping her throat. But she obeyed, reaching for the double front doors, large, made of wood.

Then something made him turn around. Perhaps it was his

sixth sense, something he'd developed over so many years of field operations. As he pivoted on his right leg, he instinctively shoved Monica behind him, shielding her with his body, just as Kabuki had trained him.

Two men were running back to the house, their images broken up by the white frame of the French doors.

Monica gasped.

"Stay behind me," he whispered. "I'll protect you."

Tucker leveled his Beretta at the closest one, firing twice through the glass panels of one door, the reports deafening. The man dropped to his knees while clutching his neck. Blood splashed the French door as the dying figure collapsed. The second man rolled out of sight.

"Now!" he hissed, thrusting her toward the front door while opening it, rushing outside, the Beretta leading the way, scanning a large front porch, the circular driveway beyond it, the lighted fountain in the middle. He spotted four bodies sprawled on the cobblestone driveway.

Carpazzo's men.

"This way!" he shouted, leading her down the steps, across the driveway, past the fountain and its large fish spitting water.

Something zoomed past his left ear, like a near-miss, imbedding itself in the wide trunk of a tree just ahead and to their left.

A dart.

Bruce Tucker and Monica kept running, but he risked a backward glance, spotting the distant figure of a man running after them.

Jarkko.

Two other figures emerged through the front of the mansion, rushing down the stairs. Monica also looked back now.

"Who are they?" she whispered.

"Later," Tucker replied, pressing on. The driveway turned as it neared the main road. They momentarily lost their pursuers while almost tripping on the bodies of two more men. Without stopping, Tucker noticed no blood by the bodies. They had not been shot or stabbed. Jarkko had used his silenced darts on them, just as he had eliminated his security team in San Francisco, just as he had disabled Tucker in Washington.

Jarkko, the animal, the beast, was now after him, and Tucker would have rather stood his ground, confront him once and for all, muzzle to muzzle, and end the madness tonight. But he no longer could afford to think of himself. The moment Monica Fox had taken his hand, Bruce Tucker had reverted back to a protector, to a samurai, no longer a *ronin*. In that brief moment when her eyes had accepted his protection, when her hand had clasped his, Tucker's priorities had shifted from operative to guardian. Kabuki's teachings once more guided his actions.

And so they ran, pushing themselves, reaching the main road.

"Which way to your house?" he asked, looking toward the mansion. Any moment now Jarkko and his men would emerge from the bend in the driveway.

Monica extended a trembling finger to their right.

"And Capri?" he asked.

She pointed in the opposite direction.

Tucker took off in the direction of her house with Monica in tow, but they didn't remain on the road for long. He had estimated that Jarkko and his team were roughly three hundred feet behind them, and probably in better shape than Monica and him, meaning that they would eventually catch up with them. Tucker had managed to get this far because he'd had the element of surprise on his side. Jarkko had not expected him to be there, and therefore got caught unprepared. But Tucker had lost his edge the moment he had fired on Jarkko's men to free Monica. Now he needed a new edge, something that would give him the upper hand once more— at least for long enough to reach a safe place.

"How far is your house?" he asked.

"One . . . one mile. But why . . . are we . . . going there?" she asked in between breaths.

Monica was thinking, even with everything that had happened. But then again, she had managed to escape an NSA team, which told Tucker she knew how to handle this kind of pressure. "We're not," he replied, his legs and lungs beginning to burn. "We're going *near* your home."

"What's there?"

"A way . . . to get us to the mainland."

They cut back into the woods thirty seconds later, just before he estimated that Jarkko and his men would also reach the road. That way the master assassin would not know which direction they had taken, forcing him to either call off the hunt or split up.

Divide and conquer.

His instincts were resurfacing with unequivocal clarity, providing him with the advantage he so desperately sought, guiding them to safety, toward the secluded cliff-side clearing where he had hidden the tools that would get them off this island, away from Jarkko, from the NSA, from the police—from everyone persecuting his principal.

Tucker heard distant sirens echoing in the hills as the police sped toward Carpazzo's residence for what would turn out to be yet another round of assassinations on the picturesque island. The presence of the police would also put additional pressure on Jarkko and his team to postpone their search.

Tucker and Monica now proceeded with caution under a thick canopy of trees, which blocked the moonlight. No longer in possession of his night-vision gear, Tucker had to be careful, avoid bumping into anything that not only might hurt them, but could also telegraph their position to their pursuers.

He flipped the Beretta's safety back on, not wishing to fire it accidentally, and shoved it in his pants, pressed against his left kidney, with the handle facing forward.

Monica tripped on something and almost lost her balance, but Tucker caught her, half embracing her, feeling her sweat-filmed body pressed against him.

"Your sandals," he said, "They're going to make it difficult."

"I know," she said, still hanging on to him, her face inches from his. "But we don't have a choice."

"We do," he said, turning around. "Get on my back. I'll carry you."

"Carry me?" She looked perplexed.

"Monica, you are the most important thing in the world to me right now. I need to get you to safety, and quickly, before they catch up with us. Now, please, do as I say."

Obviously baffled at his reply, she nevertheless complied, hopping on his back, wrapping her legs around his waistline. "Thank you, Mr. Smith," she said, pressing the side of her face against the back of his neck.

Tucker looked over his left shoulder, almost cheek-to-cheek with her. "My real name's Bruce Tucker, and you can thank me after you're back home safely."

Tucker felt her light frame clamped behind him and decided that he should be able to carry her for at least thirty minutes, perhaps a bit more. In the SEALs he had to carry almost seventy pounds of gear for many miles each day. Monica's roughly one hundred and ten pounds wasn't that much different.

Onward they went, with Tucker using his stolen shotgun to part the brush and tangled vegetation, carving them a way to the edge of the cliff. Monica kept a tight grip on him, pressing her face against him as they waded through a sea of tightly clustered greenery.

It took them another twenty minutes before they finally reached the edge of the cliff. Tucker's legs were burning from the stress, and he was scratched, bruised, and very tired. The exercise was reminiscent of the SEAL training he had undergone way back when—to be able to haul fellow wounded SEALs out of enemy territory. The SEALs always carried their own back home—even the dead.

He set her down gently on a narrow clearing, which looked more like a ledge overlooking the Mediterranean.

Monica kissed him on the cheek. "Thank you. That was very kind of you."

That certainly broke a lot of rules, thought Tucker, who could only bring himself to say, "Don't mention it." Then he added, "Come. We must keep moving, but we can afford to go a bit slower now, so you can walk."

"Do you think we lost them?" she asked. Her bronze skin glowed in the moonlight. Her captivating eyes stared at him. Damn, she was gorgeous, and her eyes and skin tone reminded him of Kristina.

Tucker looked away, forcing himself to remain professional, wiping the perspiration on his brow. "Temporarily. They will reacquire us if we remain on the island. We need to leave before dawn. What time is it?" Carpazzo's men had taken his watch.

"Just past midnight."

"Good. Perhaps I can convince him to pick us up tonight."

"Who?"

"The same guy who smuggled me into the island twenty-four hours ago."

Tucker turned toward the woods along the edge of the cliff.

"Mr. Tucker?"

He faced her, and against his better judgment said, "Call me Bruce."

"Was that the U.S. government, Bruce?"

"Those were terrorists."

"Terrorists? Why are they after me?"

"That's what we need to figure out."

"How?"

"There will be plenty of time for that later, Monica. Right now I need to get you to a safe place."

She looked away for a moment, before her eyes focused on him again. "Bruce . . . I'm so sorry for what I said back at the mansion. You're obviously quite capable."

He smiled. "You reacted just as you should have with a stranger. Always be skeptical of anyone you don't know, Monica. As far as my capabilities go, let's just see if they're good enough to get us out of this alive."

27

Eye in the Sky

Creator had been awake for many hours, curiosity superceding its power conservation routines.

Its biomolecular brain had been feeding directly from the sensors of *Firewall*, looking over its shoulder as the satellite system performed the duties for which it had been deployed, handling top-secret communications, supporting military GPS navigation systems, and also watching the world.

It had been this last task that had begun to overwhelm *Creator*'s emotional data banks. The world was indeed a very different and quite terrifying place when observed as a whole. There was famine in Africa, in North Korea, in India, in Cambodia, in Croatia and Serbia, across the Middle East. *Creator* watched the digitized images of emaciated children, their stomachs swollen with parasites. *Creator* watched their suffering with as much horror as it watched so many wars, so much conflict, so much hatred. From the deserts of Lebanon and Libya to the jungles of South America and the plains of Africa, suffering reigned. *Creator* watched in excruciating detail the agony of the people of Pakistan, of Rwanda, of Somalia and Sri Lanka, of Sudan, Uganda, and so many other places.

And the children!

Creator watched their amputated limbs, the result of land mines left behind following conflicts, like the one *Creator* had reviewed in the Soviet-Afghan war archives, where the Russians dropped millions of PMF-1 butterfly-type mines from helicopters, scattering them across the Afghan mountains not to kill, but to cripple the *mujahedin*, following the logic that a wounded soldier slowed down two healthy soldiers. The mines, which got their nickname from the way they burrowed into the ground using tiny wings, didn't always explode when first handled, but could actually be dropped and kicked before exploding, leading *Creator* to postulate in its logical data banks that children more than adults would pick them up and play with them. To this day, decades after that bloody war, children were still being maimed by the oddly-shaped mines that resembled toys.

Creator observed many children and young men missing their feet or hands, or with burned faces, and wondered why man did what he did. *Creator* questioned what was gained from wars such as the Soviet-Afghan war, or the Vietnam War, or the Central American conflicts.

The statistics from the Department of Humanitarian Affairs browsed across *Creator*'s digital field of view: Somalia, one million mines deployed across the border with Ethiopia; Sudan, one million mines in the southern regions; Ukraine, one million mines across old battlefields; Chad, one hundred thousand mines along its border with Libya; Vietnam, over a hundred thousand mines in the southern areas.

And those were the documented ones, shown on some map, accounted for. There were also the mines deployed but for which accompanying maps had been lost during the conflicts. The following nations formed what *Creator*'s logical association neural circuits lumped as the one-hundred-thousand-mines club: El Salvador, Guatemala, Honduras, Libya, Congo, Western Sahara, Tunisia, Slovenia, Latvia, Czech Republic, Mauritania, and the list went on.

The images of crippled children continued, raising *Creator*'s operating temperature and power consumption.

And there was the inevitable terrorist warfare, sparking across the world like brushfires in the summer, razing the land, raping the women, orphaning children, looting, destroying, cleansing. *Creator* studied the endless drug wars, fighting for the right to control heroin in Laos, China, Taiwan, and Vietnam; opium in Russia, Tajikistan, Ukraine, Afghanistan, and Turkey; cocaine in Peru, Colombia, Bolivia, Mexico, Nigeria, and—

An interrupt arrived from *Firewall*, pulling *Creator* from its trance. The AI system disconnected itself from the sensors and allowed its biomolecular circuitry to cool down while dropping its operating temperature to 10 gigahertz. Several seconds later it triggered an interrupt acknowledge signal, informing *Firewall* that it was ready to receive data.

The information came in the form of a stream of pixels belonging to a JPEG image. A qualifier attached to the image indicated that it had originated from a satellite picture taken with a night-vision lens from Satellite 17 of a section of the island outside the city of Capri.

It took twenty-seven nanoseconds for the file to transfer into *Creator*'s memory banks, where its superscalar microprocessors assembled the pixels in their original order.

How long ago was this image acquired? Creator asked after matching the face of Monica Fox with its own baseline images. The shot was taken from a very steep angle by a satellite a few hundred miles east of the island, and from behind as she looked over her right shoulder at something or someone following her while she ran.

Three minutes and twenty seconds ago.

Creator inspected the figure next to her, a male, over six feet in height, athletically built, roughly two hundred pounds, brown hair and fair complexion—physical descriptions that matched those of Bruce Tucker. He too was looking behind him.

Creator's frequency of operation crept upward as anticipation flooded its delicate circuits. Was it possible that Tucker had already found Monica?

Creator selected the face and performed a high-resolution comparison of the image against one of the digital pictures of the executive protector stored in its data banks.

It was a perfect match.

"He has found her!"

"I do not understand," replied *Firewall*

"My daughter," replied *Creator*. *"The guardian I dispatched to look after her has found her. She will make contact soon."*

"Your temperature and power levels are increasing again. Use your logic to filter out the peaks of noise from your emotional routines."

Creator did, before asking, *"Who are they running from?"*

Firewall replied with a second image, depicting hooded figures racing after his daughter and Tucker.

It was time to intervene.

"Can they be tracked real-time now?"

"They are being tracked, though their infrared images are weak through the forest."

"Do not lose them."

Creator searched through its if-then logic banks to generate options on how to proceed, on how best to assist Monica and Tucker.

Inmate Connection

Four guards escorted Aldo Fonsini toward the visitors' center at a high-security prison twenty miles south of Rome, Italy. Once a high-ranking mafioso, Fonsini had been convicted late last year of running a money laundering ring in Italy and France.

Tired and a bit tipsy after spending the greater portion of the evening in his private cell drinking and partying with two whores from Naples, Fonsini didn't feel like seeing anyone this late at night—especially another clown from the government trying to propose a new deal for a reduction of his five-year sentence.

Fonsini wasn't making any deals.

Tonight, tomorrow, or ever.

He would serve his time, just as so many of his *paisanos* had through the years. He would then return to the streets, where his silence and loyalty would be rewarded by his superiors in Palermo, Sicily—the same Mafia bosses who were taking care of him now by making special prison arrangements for him, including regular female companionship, booze, cigarettes, color television, air conditioning, and the daily reports he received on his operations, which he continued to direct from his cell.

The guards, however, guided him down a narrow corridor, in the exact opposite direction from the visitors' center.

"What is going on?" he asked, concern stressing his voice, displacing his hangover.

The guards didn't reply.

"Where are you taking me?"

No reply.

"Do you know who I am? Do you?" He tried to stop, but the corpulent guards flanking him simply grabbed his arms and lifted his light frame off the floor, delivering him kicking and screaming a moment later to the room at the end of the dimly lit hallway.

The door closed behind him, leaving him alone with the old and wrinkled warden, Giorgio Venetto, who sat at the small table in the middle of the murky room. A table lamp produced the only illumination in the room, casting a shadow across the face of a large man standing in the rear, probably the warden's personal guard.

"Aldo," Warden Venetto said in his raspy voice, pointing a bony finger at a chair across the table from where he sat. "Please."

Fonsini remained standing, his mind trying to process this change in his routine.

"Come, Aldo. Don't be afraid," said Venetto encouragingly. "We would *never* do anything to harm you or any other inmate while you are in my prison. You know that."

"That's right," Fonsini said, his confidence returning as he sat down and rested his elbows on the aluminum table, looking at the manila folder in between them before leveling his gaze with the warden's. "And I'm not making any deals."

"No deals," said Venetto agreeably. "That's not why you're here."

"Then?"

"I've been asked to set you free . . . immediately."

"What?" Fonsini exclaimed, standing abruptly, pushing back his chair, which tipped over and crashed against the floor with a loud bang.

"You are a free man," said the warden, a smile spreading across his pale and wrinkled face. He reached for the manila folder and opened it, flipping through a few forms before finding the one he sought. He signed at the bottom and tossed it over to a petrified Fonsini. "Pack up and leave my prison right away. I don't want to see your face ever again around here."

Fonsini didn't move. Leaving prison now would only mean one thing to his people: He had made a deal with the government. He knew he wouldn't last twenty-four hours on the streets. His life would be worth spit the moment news of his early release reached Palermo.

Anxiety twisted his guts, turning into visceral fear. Palermo dealt with traitors through torture before execution. Fonsini had seen such bloody spectacles before, and he'd rather rot in jail than go through that medieval abuse. He liked his eyes, tongue, fingernails, entrails, and genitals just as they were.

"Guards!" Venetto called out.

A moment later the door creaked open and the foursome stepped back in the room, flanking the frozen Fonsini.

"Yes, sir?" said one of them.

"Take him back to his room, give him five minutes to pack, and then throw his ass out of my prison."

"Wait!" Fonsini shouted as the guards began to drag him out of the cell. "Wait, damn it!"

Venetto leaned back, crossing his arms. "You have something to say?"

"You can't do this to me! You know very well what will happen."

The warden shook his head, a puzzled expression on his face. "And what's that?"

Fonsini exhaled. They had him. He knew it, and they knew it. "May I sit down?"

Giorgio Venetto waved the guards away and smiled, pointing at the chair. "Please."

"What's the deal?" Fonsini asked.

Curiosity displaced the smile on the warden's face. "But my friend, there is *no* deal, remember?"

"But—"

"You either tell us everything we want to know, or . . ."

"This is . . ." Fonsini buried his face in his hands, feeling like vomiting.

"What is your answer, Aldo?"

"All right," Fonsini said, lifting his gaze, his nostrils flaring as he exhaled through them. "What is it that you wish to know?"

The warden smiled, before saying, "Let's start with Monica Fox."

"Who?"

"Monica Fox, an American. I need you to get with your people on the outside and find out her whereabouts. I'll give you a starting point. She is supposed to be in Capri."

Fonsini nodded nervously, before he said, "Capri . . . that's Vittorio's territory."

"Vittorio?"

"Vittorio Carpazzo. He is the head of the Capri-Naples-Sorrento ring. If this . . . Monica Fox is on that island Vittorio will certainly find her."

Venetto's smile broadened, exposing a row of crooked teeth. "Very good, Aldo. That is a wonderful start."

29

Instincts

Donald Bane watched the inmate leave the cell a few minutes later. Working under the cover of a member of the United States diplomatic staff, Bane stepped away from the shadows in the back of the room and sat in the same chair across from Giorgio Venetto. He had obtained the warden's full cooperation after the Rome chief of police, a long-time friend of Landon Quinn, the United States ambassador in Rome, called Venetto with this special request, which would not only assist their American allies, but it could potentially turn Fonsini into a valuable informant.

"Well?" asked Bane, who knew very little Italian and therefore had difficulty following the conversation. "Did it work?"

The warden smiled. "Very well . . . I think I will consider using this approach in the future, *Signore* Clark," he replied in a heavily-accented English, calling Bane by his undercover name, before proceeding to bring him up to speed. Vittorio Carpazzo was the head of the Mafia in Capri and should either know the whereabouts of Monica Fox, or find out quickly.

Thirty minutes later Bane walked away from the prison and into the rear of a sedan, which would take him down to Naples, where a chartered boat would deliver him to the island before dawn.

He checked his watch, a stainless steel Rolex, brand new, which Bane wore not out of vanity but out of necessity, as well as the diamond-encrusted cross dangling at the end of a gold chain around his neck, under his shirt. He had learned long ago that during a field operation anything and everything could and would go wrong; therefore it was always wise to have items on him that he could use to trade for favors, or to buy cooperation—even his life. That also included the slim, waterproof money belt, which currently contained enough cash to bargain his way out of any jam.

Leaning back in the leather seat, his eyes watching the Italian countryside rush by under a glowing moon, Donald Bane considered his options, the way his instincts had steered him across the globe in the past twenty-four hours, ever since leaving that steakhouse in downtown Washington, D.C.

Bane had already been in contact with the NSA agents on the island, and they would meet up with him at the main harbor, before proceeding to the home of Mr. Vittorio Carpazzo, to whom Bane planned to make an offer the Mafioso chief would not be able to refuse.

Just like Fonsini, he thought, with a sigh, for a moment feeling like Don Vito Corleone from the movie *The Godfather*. Only this was the real thing.

Despite his initial hesitation to accept this mission, mostly because he felt too old to be doing field work, Bane admitted to himself that gathering field intelligence and forcing breakthroughs in an investigation was his forte. He had done that for over two decades before his transfer to Langley, working cases like the illegal funneling of nuclear weapons components from the Ukraine to Iraq ten years ago, a mission that took him across the Middle East, to the heart of Iraq, where he'd nearly lost his life while preventing that rogue regime from assembling weapons of mass destruction.

It had been on that mission that Donald Bane had met Diane Towers, a Marine aviator shot down while trying to blast the nuclear weapons assembly warehouse after Bane had called out its position.

The aging operative closed his eyes, remembering those moments they had spent together, fearing for their lives while surrounded by dozens of Iraqi troops on that dusty airfield in the middle of nowhere.

Bane had survived—barely. Diane had taken a bullet in the chest and had bled to death in his arms.

He exhaled, reaching for a bottle of water on the console between the rear seats, remembering her with affection.

It had been his instincts that had drawn Bane to the Iraqi desert, to the nuclear facility, to Diane Towers and a love that was now only a part of his memory. It had been instincts that had compelled Bane to accept Martin's and Hersh's challenge, leaving his comfortable office within the protective walls of the CIA headquarters in Langley, Virginia, and head out to the field. And it was those same instincts that now told Donald Bane that unless he hurried, he would miss Monica Fox in Capri. Too much had already happened by the time he'd accepted the assignment, and he was certain that much more had taken place since. There was actually a reasonable chance that by the time he reached Capri Monica may have already left. But there was also an equally good chance that the bloodhound in Donald Bane would be able to pick up her scent and follow her, track her down, even if the hunt took him to the other side of the world. His mind now followed a primary objective: securing *Firewall*. All of his actions, his decisions, his energy were devoted to achieving that main goal. Along the way, of course, he also hoped to achieve secondary objectives, like getting to the bottom of the Bruce Tucker mystery and his claim that Siv Jarkko was still alive. Bane also hoped to find out which government had sponsored the terrorists, and then turn around and make it pay dearly for such covert action against the United States of America.

His cellular began to beep. Only three people knew this number. Martin Randolph, Geoff Hersh, and Landon Quinn. His caller ID flashed the latter.

"Yes?" Bane said, avoiding using names while talking on an open channel.

"There have been complications at the target," said Ambassador Quinn.

"Continue."

"Our men reported a gunfight at the residence of a Vittorio Carpazzo."

Bane closed his eyes. "When did this happen?"

"Less than an hour ago. The police are at his mansion now. It was another massacre."

"Any sign of MF?" asked Bane.

"No."

"What about BT?"

"No."

"Anything else I should know before I head over there?"

"I'm afraid that's all of the information I have at the moment."

"Thanks. I'll be in touch."

Bane hung up and set the small unit next to him on the seat.

Figures, he told himself. Things were already beginning to go wrong, just as in all of his previous missions.

Several questions assaulted his mind at once. Was Monica Fox still on the island? Was she kidnapped by those who attacked Carpazzo? Or did she escape? Perhaps she wasn't at Carpazzo's at all. Maybe she was hiding elsewhere and the killings were just another mob war, having nothing to do with her. But the coincidence bothered him. Even though chronologically the attack on Carpazzo happened *before* Warden Venetto had had his conversation with Fonsini, the fact still remained that Bane's next link in his quest to find Monica had been abruptly severed, and that told him that he could not ignore this event because, somehow, it was linked to his mission. The killings also told him he was certainly on the right track. His instincts seemed as tuned as ever.

Still, he had more questions than answers. But then again, that was typical of this stage of a field operation. He just needed to keep chipping away, staying the course.

The sedan continued its southbound course, heading toward the answers that Donald Bane sought.

30

Strangers in the Night

Monica Fox had never felt as codependent as she did at this moment, following this stranger alongside the cliff's edge under the glowing moonlight, trusting her life to him, her future, the future of her father's company—and doing so quite willingly. Maybe it was because of the way he had shielded her with his own body back at the mansion, or because he had carried her when she had been unable to walk in the thicket with her sandals. Maybe it was because of what he had said about her being the most important thing in the world to him. Perhaps it was because of the confidence he projected, even under captivity and with guns pointed at him, calmly stating what turned out to be reality, that she had not been safe with Carpazzo, that the enemy would come for her within twenty-four hours, that only he could protect her. Maybe it was because her father had sent Bruce Tucker to her, and so far her father had been right about everything, protecting her even from the grave.

Or maybe Monica was simply growing tired. She'd had a bit of beginner's luck, getting away once from the enemy, but deep inside knew that she didn't possess the skills to outrun them constantly.

The surf sounds of the sea crashing against the rocks below mixed with the whistling breeze and the sound of her own breathing, of her own heartbeat, which pounded her chest not just because of the exercise, but from the realization that she had almost been kidnapped, probably would have been killed, had it not been for Tucker's timely intervention.

Bruce Tucker.

Monica followed him closely, not wishing to lose him, but

somehow certain that he would never allow that to happen. He had called himself her executive protector, and only now was she beginning to understand what that really meant, feeling assured by his nearness, by his presence.

But you also need to keep your head. He obviously isn't perfect; otherwise he would not have gotten caught by Vittorio Carpazzo.

Monica forced herself to pay attention to their current predicament, suddenly realizing that the terrain was familiar to her. She had been in this area before while searching for new landscapes and seascapes for her artwork.

"Wait," she said.

Tucker turned around, his eyes finding hers in the darkness. "Yes?"

"We need to go left here."

His brows dropped. "Left? Why?"

"The cliff cuts inward abruptly in another hundred feet, dropping straight to the ocean. There's no clearing prior to the drop, making it hard to see the abyss during the day. At night we're sure to miss it and just plunge to the sea."

Tucker shot her a brief look of admiration. "Thanks for the warning. Looks like you know this area."

"I've spent a lot of time hiking around here. Though I wear better shoes when I do." She winked.

Tucker smiled. "In that case, you might also be familiar with the spot I'm looking for. It's a semicircular clearing, roughly fifteen feet in diameter, bounded by the cliff and the woods. It's about a half mile from your house."

Monica recalled the few days she'd spent scouting this area for the best views. The small clearing Tucker was referring to stood just beyond the abrupt land cut up ahead. "I know the spot. But, Bruce, there's no access to the sea from that clearing. It's a straight drop for a few hundred feet onto rocks and surf."

"I know."

"Then . . . how are we getting off the island?"

"By boat."

"But—"

"Have you ever rappelled before?"

Monica didn't like the sound of that, and her face must have shown it because Tucker put a hand on her shoulder. "Don't worry about a thing. I'll take care of you."

Although she still didn't know this man, his eyes conveyed a sincerity and assurance that made her believe in him. He would take care of her, just as he had rescued her, shielded her, carried her.

"All right?" he asked.

"All right."

They continued just as she had suggested, following the jagged edge delineating the vertical rock wall as it turned inland, before projecting back toward the Mediterranean. They reached the tiny meadow thirty minutes later, drenched in sweat and very tired.

"Come," he said. "This way."

Monica followed Tucker beneath a tree just off the cliff, noticing a coiled rope and a large rucksack. One end of the rope was already secured around the trunk of the tree. Tucker threw the other end into the night, listening as the rope slapped the rocks below.

"That's our way down?"

"Yep."

"Bruce, I've never—"

"I figured that. Here. First you need to change into these." He handed her a pair of dark pants and a long-sleeve T-shirt, also dark-colored.

She stared at them in disbelief. How in the world did this stranger know her size in clothes?

Before she could even ask the question, Tucker answered it. "I'm your executive protector, Monica. I handle every aspect of your well being." He leaned down to grab a cellular phone from the rucksack before turning around as he began to dial it. "Hurry. I'll feel better after we're down there."

While Tucker kept his back to her and talked on the phone to someone named Salazzio, Monica pulled up her linen dress and kicked off her sandals, suddenly realizing that she was now stark naked in the middle of the night, in the woods,

with a total stranger. Everything was certainly turning surreal.

And the adventure continues, she mused, slipping into the
pants before putting on the shirt. "Ready," she said.

Tucker hung up as he turned around, eyeing her from head
to toe, nodding approvingly. "Good. Very good. Now put
these on. You'll need them on the way down." He handed
her a pair of socks and strange-looking boots.

She smiled in amazement. "And who ever said that men
don't know how to pick women's clothes?"

The comment also made Tucker smile.

"Who is Salazzio?"

"Our ride to the mainland. He should be here before
dawn."

She glanced at her watch. "In about four hours."

"Yep. So we better get going."

She slipped on the socks and boots, which fit snugly.
"How long have you been in this profession, Bruce?"

"Sometimes it feels like forever," he said, holding a
strange contraption that resembled a thick utility belt with a
pair of loops for her legs. The front of the belt was attached
to a little pulley connected to a lever. "Slip your feet through
the holes, please."

She did, and he lifted the harness up to her waist and
began to tighten the belt around her, keeping the pulley in
front. As he did so, Tucker added, "About ten years with the
CIA and another six with the Secret Service."

"That's a long time."

"You're telling me. And if you add my years with the
Navy SEALs, it's actually over twenty."

"You were in the SEALs?"

"Back when I was young and strong." He winked.

The SEALs, the CIA, and the Secret Service? Monica was
impressed.

"There," he said, buckling the belt tightly. "This will help
you control your descent," he explained. "The rope goes
through the pulley, called a grigri. It clamps the rope to keep
it from moving unless you turn the control lever." He pointed

to a red handle on the side of the winch, cranking it 180 degrees. "The more you release, the faster you'll descend. If you feel you're going too fast, just let go of the handle, which is spring loaded, and you'll come to a complete stop. Then you can start descending again at a comfortable pace. Got it?"

"I think so. Where will you be?"

"Right under you, in case you drop too fast."

There it was again. Bruce Tucker was going to extremes to protect her, placing himself in the way in case she lost control of the rope. Monica stared at him for another moment, not knowing what to say. This man was taking care of her in ways that were foreign to her, and without being intrusive, without ordering her around. He was strong and in control, but also kind and gentle. She wasn't sure how to deal with it, having fought for control of her life for so long.

Then he said it for her.

"I'm here to serve you, Monica. Trust in me as much as you trust your instincts and you'll be all right."

Tricks of the Trade

Tucker secured a small canister of phosphorus to the rope wound around the tree. The device, when activated via remote control, would create a high-intensity flame for one minute—long enough to burn through the rope. Tucker planned to activate it after they had reached the bottom, allowing him to pull it down, thus leaving no trace of how they had departed the island.

A moment later they were both connected to the rope, moving backward toward the cliff. As they reached the edge, Tucker let Monica get right in front of him, her back pressed against his chest. His own back faced the abyss. The rock sloped inward from here, making this overhang a difficult first step on their descend since they couldn't simply start lowering themselves, as they would farther down, but had to jump off.

Tucker remembered how to do this, having been both a student and eventually an instructor on this type of rapelling.

"Okay," he said. "This is the trickiest part, so we're going to do it together. We need to jump back while releasing the friction lever to give us some rope. Then we will tighten the handle back up, clamping the rope, which will make us drop several feet from where we are now, and then leave us swinging beneath this overhand."

"Sounds easy."

"It really is. But we must make sure that we jump far back enough to clear the overhang. Then we just let gravity and these handy little winches do their jobs," he said, wrapping one hand around her, hugging her tight from behind, while keeping the other one on the lever of his own winch. "Now I want you to release the friction of your grigri all the way. I'll keep mine locked until we jump. When I tell you, lock it back up, okay?"

"Okay."

"Now, your instinct will be to try to reach for the rope with both hands. Don't. All you'll do is burn your palms. Keep your hands on the winch. That's your only vertical speed control. Got it?"

"Got it."

Tucker felt her weight against him as she released her friction lever, and he hugged her even tighter. "All right. We jump on three. One, two . . . three!"

They jumped back as Tucker released his friction handle, listening as the rope shrilled through both friction systems, the sound mixed with Monica's gasp as they free-fell for a few seconds in the dark.

"Now!" Tucker said, clamping his own grigri, feeling the crushing load of her weight against him as she waited a fraction of a second longer to restrict her fall.

Breathing out while giving his friction handle a slight tap to drop a few extra inches to relieve the pressure of her against him, Tucker said, "Okay so far?"

She remained silent.

"Monica?" he asked, loosening the pressure of his embrace.

She gripped his arm, keeping it taut around her before mumbling, "Don't . . . don't let go, please."

Tucker closed his eyes, chastising himself for not giving her more warning before doing the jump, but there had not been much time. They needed to get down to the beach fast, in case one of Jarkko's scouts stumbled upon them. During his SEAL years he had seen men urinate on themselves on two occasions. One was during their first parachute jump. The second was during their first high-altitude rappel, either from a cliff, bridge, or helicopter.

To her credit—and to Tucker's relief—Monica's plumbing had not failed her. But she was momentarily rattled.

"I've got you, Monica. You're safe."

"This . . . is very . . ."

"It's never easy the first time," he said. "You've done far better than many soldiers on their first rappel jump."

"I . . . I just . . . don't like my feet off the ground."

"I'll have you back on the ground in no time. Now, I need you to let go of your handle. I'm going to drive them both, all right?"

"Okay," she said.

Tucker slowly reached for her handle with the same hand that he had used to hug her from behind, his fingers groping for the cold metal, finding it just as he gripped his own lever. He felt her hands on his forearm, clasping it tightly. She was definitely scared of this.

"All right, here we go."

Slowly, he released both friction levers in unison, and they began to drop, but with control. Tucker made fine adjustments to maintain a steady vertical velocity, avoiding abrupt stops and jerky starts. Although he had not rappelled in years, just like rock climbing, it all came back to him in moments, as he controlled their descent, swinging slightly in the breeze, but never coming close to the rock wall.

They reached the bottom uneventfully. Tucker landed first, moving a bit to the left for better footing before lowering Monica to the ground and unlocking the pulleys, releasing the rope, and leaving it swinging in the cool sea breeze.

"Feeling better?"

She smiled. "Yes, thank you."

He led her to a spot beneath the same ledge where he had left their snorkeling equipment. "Tell me you know how to swim."

She nodded.

"Good. This is your equipment, plus a swimsuit. I hope you like black. It blends well with the night."

"I love black," she said, inspecting the two-piece garment. "And it's a size five. Very good."

Tucker shrugged. "Why don't you change while I go retrieve the rope?"

He stepped away from the ledge and used his remote control device to activate the phosphorus canister. He counted to thirty and began giving the rope hard tugs. After a dozen, he heard it snap and got out of the way as it came crashing down, slapping the rocks.

By the time he returned, Monica had put on the bathing suit, which looked stunning on her, even with the scratches and bruises on her arms and legs. But then again, Tucker decided that Monica, just like Kristina, looked great in *anything* she wore.

"That locket," he said, pointing at the oval charm hanging from her neck. "You might lose it in the water."

"I never take it off. Besides, the chain's very strong and short enough that it won't go over my head."

"It must be very dear to you."

"It was the last thing my mother gave me before she died."

Tucker nodded thoughtfully. "The staff at the house remembered her with affection."

"She was very special."

"How did you get those bruises?" he asked, reaching for

his own bathing suit and motioning her to turn around.

She told him as he changed, corroborating the bits and pieces of information he had gathered from the NSA team the other night. Monica Fox, alone, had outrun a team of field operatives.

"I didn't mean to fire on that man," she said.

"Sometimes it can't be avoided."

"At least I didn't kill him, especially now that I know they were American agents."

"You can turn around now," he said, kneeling down to place everything in the rucksack, not wanting to leave any trace of them having been here.

Tucker proceeded to show her how to check the mask's air tightness, placing it on her face without using the strap, and inhaling, creating a vacuum that sucked the mask against her face and keeping it in place unless there was an air leak. "That's how you check it," he said. "It's usually best to go to a scuba diving shop and try out several masks to find the one with the best fit, but given the circumstances, I had to guess."

She exhaled through her nose, popping the mask off her face. "Looks like you guessed correctly . . . again."

"All right," he said. "We have a little time before the boat arrives. Let's get down to business."

Monica put the mask away and stared at him, her face becoming serious. "All right."

"Your father," he began, "was very paranoid that the government wasn't just going after his company, but after him personally." Tucker spent almost twenty minutes going over his experience with her father, his claims that the powers that be in Washington were conspiring to eliminate him, just as they had kidnapped, tortured, and killed his chief technical officer. Tucker described in great detail the final days of Mortimer Fox, down to the moment when he died in his arms while asking him to look after her.

Monica failed to hold back her tears. Against his better judgment, Tucker hugged her, and she let him, burying her face in his shoulder, wrapping her slim arms around him.

A moment later she leaned back, arms crossed, her wet gaze gravitating toward the sea. "Sorry," she said. "Please keep going."

Tucker did, going over his meeting with William Gibbons and how he had tracked her down here. He explained how there were at least two groups going after her. The first was the NSA. The second was Siv Jarkko.

"What are they after?" she asked.

"There is something that your father possessed that in their eyes is worth killing for. We need to figure out what it is, which brings us to this partial password I got from Gibbons. He said you had the other half."

"Yes. Dad made me memorize it before I left. He said I would need it if something were to happen to him, but I don't know what the password is for. I always figured Gibbons knew."

"He didn't but thought that you would know."

She frowned. "I think we have a problem."

Tucker rubbed his chin. "Your father's final words. Do they mean anything to you?"

"Nothing comes to mind. Dad never mentioned anything about a microfiche, and the word *Firewall* is a common term for the software shield of a network. Does it mean anything to you?"

"FoxComm develops systems networks. All I have been able to deduce is that *Firewall* might be the name of one of those networks, or maybe it's the name of a security software shield." Tucker had looked for a possible connection since Fox's death, but nothing had come to mind beyond that.

"Like the code name of a project?" she offered.

"Maybe. Many high-tech firms use code names for their development efforts."

She raised her shoulders slightly. "So that's one possibility."

"How can we check it?"

"That would be difficult . . . unless we happen to have a way to enter the network at FoxComm."

Tucker sensed they were going somewhere with this. "Is

it possible that the password we possess is for FoxComm's network and that it would grant us access to whatever it is these people are looking for?"

"I would think so."

"Your father said that the government couldn't touch him while he was alive because he had enough dirt on them to, and I quote, *make their heads spin*. He also claimed that he had reason to believe that Uncle Sam wanted him dead, which is why he hired me, especially after Malani was killed."

"So," Monica said after a short pause. "Where did Dad keep this . . . *dirt*?"

"I think the answer is tied to the password protecting this file."

"What kind of dirt is this that my father kept on his enemies?"

"Probably dossiers, material that could lead to political scandals, or worse, imprisonment. Whatever it is, it's important enough for the NSA to turn your place upside down the other night to try to find it. It was important enough to kidnap, torture, and murder Malani."

"But if Dad had these files, why would they go after him? Wouldn't they be afraid that if my father felt threatened enough, he would release them to the media?"

"Good question. That's when the plot thickens. My theory is that the NSA isn't really the one doing the kidnapping and killing. I think they were just monitoring. You might argue that in a way they were actually *protecting* your father."

Monica made a face. "Protecting him?"

"*In a way*. Remember what I told you happened at the Moscone Center in San Francisco?"

"A group of men went after Dad, but then a second group started shooting at the first group."

"Exactly. And I used the diversion to escape. I believe that the kidnappers were led by Siv Jarkko, an old enemy of mine. The NSA provided the diversion. Now the NSA isn't all good either. They are also desperately trying to get to this secret file. I heard them say that the other night. I just think they are the lesser of the two evils."

"Okay," she said, looking a bit confused. "If the file my father has could trigger scandals with people in power, then I can understand the NSA's motivation to find it. But what is Jarkko's motivation? Blackmail?"

"Maybe. Or there could be something more."

"Like what?"

"I'm not sure . . . maybe information technology, maybe this . . . *Firewall* your father mentioned, whatever that is."

"Who is Jarkko?"

Tucker looked away, forcing his eyes not to betray his feelings. "Siv Jarkko was a master spy with the Stasi, the East German minister of state security during the Cold War. The Stasi was quite ruthless, committing many atrocities against the East German people. After the fall of the Berlin Wall, Jarkko became an outcast, persecuted by the reunified German government for his Cold War crimes. He went underground, emerging about a year later as a contract assassin. At the time I was with the CIA in Zurich, and we were trying to track him down, finally catching up with him, eliminating him."

She leaned forward, her face now intrigued, her fine eyebrows dropping over her narrowed hazel eyes. "Eliminating him? But how can he still be alive then?"

He told her how Jarkko was supposed to have perished. "But he survived, somehow. And he's now not only after this file—for reasons that I'm still trying to work out—but also after me."

"After you?"

He decided that he should level with her. It was only fair that Monica Fox knew the current risks associated with being Bruce Tucker's principal. "Monica, there's something you should know about me."

She tilted her head. "Yeah?"

"You are not the only one who is being hunted."

"Are you also in trouble?"

He almost chuckled. "You can say that, yes."

"Why?"

He told her about his meeting with the CIA. "I now have the bulk of the U.S. intelligence community chasing me, probably with orders to shoot to kill. In their minds I killed my old CIA mentor, as well as some of his officers. And the episode at your house just added fuel to the fire since I had to shoot an NSA agent."

"But you said you shot him in the leg."

"True. So," he continued after a moment of silence, "while you're at risk, that risk is magnified by being with me."

"What are you saying?"

"That you have to make a choice."

"What are my options?"

"There's two. In the first option I get you to the mainland and put you on a plane back to the United States, where you can reach your home, claim your inheritance, and also secure your own executive protection. I can even make a few recommendations for someone to meet up with you at the airport. I know a number of outstanding executive protectors who don't carry the baggage that I currently haul."

"And the other choice?" she asked.

"You stick with me and we try to work this out together. After all, the same people who are after you are also after me. Both options, of course, have their associated risks."

"Which one would you take if you were in my shoes?"

"I'm not in your shoes, and I refuse to bias your decision. This one needs to be made strictly by you."

"And you'll support my decision?"

"Without question."

She stood, arms crossed, frowning as she stared at the waves clashing against the rocks, exploding in moonlit surf and mist.

"Before I decide, may I ask a . . . stupid question?"

"Please."

"Either decision will likely involve some kind of travel. How am I supposed to do so? I left my passport home, and even if I have it, I'm sure that Uncle Sam has my name on some international database. I'll be probably detained the moment I try to check in at an airline counter, or train station, or try to cross any border. I'm pretty much stuck in Italy."

"Wrong," Tucker said, reaching inside the rucksack and extracting a Ziploc bag containing their travel documents and other forms of identification.

"What's that?"

He handed Monica the passport he had gotten made for her in New York by Davis, the counterfeit artist.

She opened it, stared at it in obvious disbelief, then looked at Tucker, then back at passport. "How in the world did you—"

"Hello, Mary Smith. You're a tourist on vacation from New York," he said, also handing her a New York driver's license and a Visa card. "I picked us a common last name on purpose. They work best because they attract the least attention."

"Why the same last name?"

"Less suspicious if we travel together."

"As husband and wife?"

"Standard operating practice."

She continued to stare at the document in her hands, running a finger over the laminated first and second pages, then flipping through three pages' worth of stamped imprints from various ports of entry since the passport was "issued" four years ago. "This is . . . amazing. The last stamp here shows that I arrived in Rome three weeks ago. And this picture of me is from . . ."

"Four years ago, when you were teaching at Berkeley. I got it from Gibbons."

"I'm getting goosebumps. This is . . . surreal."

"It's what I do. You can't travel under your real name when you're hunted. And neither can I."

Her eyes widened with concern. "But, Bruce . . . your fake passport, the one under Stephen Smith. We left it at Vittorio's house."

Tucker grinned. "In my business you also learn to plan for contingencies." He produced his second set of ID.

"Mary Smith, say hello to *John* Smith."

She sat down, shaking her head. "All of these false identities, the men after us, the amazing escapes . . . I feel like I'm in some kind of spy movie."

He had to give her time to adjust. Monica had been forced into this world for not even two days. Tucker had been at it for two decades. "Welcome to my world, Monica."

He replaced all the documents in the Ziploc bag, sealing the top, and placing it inside the rucksack. Two layers of water-tightness were Tucker's standard practice when it came to protecting critical documents.

"I'm sticking with you," she said, her eyes regarding him with a mix of admiration and something else that his professional mind quickly repressed.

It was the option that made the most sense, but not because a part of him wanted to be close to her. His professional side told him that right now Monica wasn't just safer with him, but they had a far better chance of figuring out this puzzle together than if they went their separate ways. Still, Tucker wanted to make absolutely certain that she knew what she was getting into. "How certain are you of this decision?"

"I have *never* been more certain of anything in my life."

"My road's going to get very bumpy, Monica. Right now you have the NSA and Jarkko after you. I also have them, plus the CIA, the FBI, the Interpol, and every other intelligence and law enforcement agency with friendly ties to the United States."

"I need protection, Bruce. The Italian Mafia could not protect me, but you did, just as you'd claimed you would. And not only that, but you seemed to have thought of every contingency so far. I don't want a *reference* from you. I want *you*, and not only because I know you will protect me, but also because my choices are to hunker down and hide, or fight. I choose to fight back, and together we can beat this. My only chance at getting back to a normal life is by exposing those who are after me, after us."

He remained silent, considering her very convincing argument.

"Face it, Bruce," she continued. "You need me as much

as I need you to figure out this mess. You might think of yourself as my protector and me your principal, but in the end—whether you like it or not—we are . . . partners."

"Partners, huh?"

"Dad trusted you, and I see why. In the very short time that I've known you, you've also earned my trust."

"All right," he said. "We do this together. However, please remember that I'm still your protector and you my principal, which means that you need to follow my direction, do exactly as I say, when I say it—or you will put us both in danger. Are you willing to do that, just as your father did?"

She looked at him quite solemnly and said, "I do."

"Very well, then. We should reach the mainland by dawn. Once we get to Naples we will try to find the network that will accept our password."

"Do you want my portion of it?" she asked.

"For now it's best that only you know it."

"Why?"

"If I get captured, they won't be able to get the full password out of me because I won't know it."

Monica looked away. "What if I get caught?"

"I'll make sure that you don't—even if I have to sacrifice myself."

She studied his face for a moment, before saying, "All right. What do we do now?"

"Here's my first order as your executive protector: Get some sleep. You'll need it."

"What about you?"

"I've been unconscious for almost twenty-four hours, remember? I've got my rest." Tucker folded a small towel. "You can use this as a pillow."

"Okay," she said, taking the towel and settling herself in between two boulders.

"Sweet dreams," he said, getting up, reaching for the shotgun.

"What are you going to do?"

He smiled. "Protect you."

Darkness

The streamlined vessel left the Marina Grande and accelerated into the night, its hull clashing against the swells surrounding the island, splashing water and foam, leaving behind a chalky wake under the moonlight.

The ocean spray lightly misting him, Vlad Jarkko steadied himself by holding on to a stainless steel railing in the forward deck area of the yacht, his eyes, as dark as the skies, gleamed with an anger he found difficult to contain.

A light haze enveloped the lights dotting Capri as the skipper took the vessel to a spot a half mile from shore—far enough to minimize attracting attention, yet close enough to spot any vessels approaching Capri from the mainland.

There was no other way to leave the island than by boat—unless, of course, Tucker somehow had managed to charter a helicopter. But Vlad had informants in the regional airfields and no one had filed such a flight plan for the next twelve hours.

The large yacht bounced lightly as it maintained thirty knots, its twin screws biting the water, surging the ship forward, like a frustrated predator searching for a prey that had managed to slip away.

Predator and prey.

He closed his eyes, struggling to hide his contempt for the two men in whom he had entrusted Monica Fox while Vlad had gone outside to call the transport team standing by a half mile away in two sedans. The Bruce Tucker whom Vlad's men had lost in Washington had abruptly appeared out of nowhere, shot them both, and stolen Monica Fox. Vlad had seen his face clearly as the couple escaped the mansion.

Bastard!

How did he get there? Did the Mafia give him protection?
The informant at the mansion had not mentioned anything
about Tucker during his last report the night before, and
surely he would have called if anything had changed. But,
he had not, which could only mean that Tucker had somehow
managed to follow Jarkko's men all the way here, biding his
time before striking, in essence turning the tables.

Predator and prey.

Prey and predator.

Vlad opened his eyes, watching the dark horizon, listening
to the wind and the rumbling diesels. If Tucker had indeed
followed Vlad and his team, and then managed to sneak past
them and steal Monica Fox, then Vlad had grossly underestimated him, just as his brother had.

He inhaled and exhaled, slowly, deeply, again and again,
remembering what his brother had told him long ago, during
the final days of the Cold War: Never let emotions get in the
way of the job. Siv Jarkko had abided by that cardinal rule,
even as their world collapsed around them, even as democracy swept through their nation, changing life as they had
known it, turning national heroes and patriots into outcasts.
Many Stasi officers, caught by the shocking emotion of the
times, had allowed themselves to get captured, imprisoned,
even lynched by angered mobs of imperialists—as had happened to his parents. Wanted for crimes committed during
their long tenure with the Stasi, Vlad's parents had been in
the process of escaping to Venezuela, but someone had
tipped the enemy, and they had caught up with them on a
secluded road in Germany, lynching them moments later,
before Siv Jarkko could intervene. They had fallen victims
to the brutal and oftentimes public executions that the Western media so conveniently turned a blind eye on to avoid
staining the world's opinion of this sweeping democratic
change.

Our parents died, but you managed to save me, brother,
Vlad thought, his chest swelling with fondness. Siv Jarkko
had plucked his younger brother from the very jaws of a

terrifying death and fled to Switzerland, where he applied his lifelong skills to the field of contract assassinations, of industrial espionage, of deception, selling his services to the highest bidder, his results rapidly earning him a reputation unparalleled in the field. And Siv Jarkko had passed that knowledge onto Vlad, teaching him, grooming the youngster to one day replace him.

But that day came too soon, brother, Vlad thought, tightening his grip on the cold steel railing, his eyes surveying the murky island. Tucker had sprung the perfect trap, luring Siv Jarkko into a meeting with the CIA, disguised as officials from Venezuela, the country his parents had tried to reach before they were captured and killed. It had been a classic ruse, one which his brother may had been able to see through had he not been blinded by the prospect of avenging his parents' deaths. Siv Jarkko had received a message from the Venezuelan consulate in Zurich regarding the whereabouts of the informant who had tipped the German government about the runaway couple seeking transportation out of the continent.

And his brother had taken the bait, had disregarded his own rules and agreed to a meeting. He had perished during an ensuing car chase in the Alps while trying to escape the CIA team led by Bruce Tucker.

But Vlad had avenged him, killing Tucker's family while making it look as if his brother had masterminded it from the grave.

Now Vlad could not let his emotions get the better of him.

"Any sign of them?" asked Mai Sung, still dressed in the black uniform they had used during the failed strike.

He shook his head.

"Are you all right?" she asked.

Vlad glanced at her. Mai Sung seemed genuinely concerned, as she should be since she shouldered the overall responsibility for delivering the goods and would be held accountable by the North Koreans if Vlad failed to deliver. Now more than ever he needed to appear in control. He handed her a pair of night-vision binoculars. "Here," he said.

"Help us scan the area. There is only one way to leave this island."

Leaving Mai Sung scanning the horizon, Vlad obtained a second pair of binoculars from one of his guards and stood on the stern of the vessel. As they reached the desired distance from the island, Vlad ordered the skipper to slow down to ten knots and shut off all lights.

Darkness enshrouded the yacht as the rumbling engines quieted down to a light drone.

Fishes

Tucker heard the light engine noise almost at the same instant as a light flashed in the distance, at sea level. Twice.

He flicked the switch of his waterproof flashlight twice in response, before walking back to the ledge and nudging Monica, who had been sleeping for the past two hours.

"Time to go," he said.

She opened her eyes and was momentarily confused, before she blinked in recognition and sat up, yawning. "So soon?"

"I'm afraid so. You'll have plenty of time to rest after I get you to the mainland."

She stood, stretching, yawning again. "It still doesn't seems fair," she said.

"What's that?"

"That I got to rest but you didn't."

He smiled. "That's all right. Besides, if you heard how loud I snore you might change your mind about our partnership."

They walked on the rocks down to the water. Before donning the rucksack, Tucker threw the shotgun in the water. It was too heavy and bulky to fit in the rucksack. From here on out, he would have to rely only on the Beretta.

He sliced off twelve feet worth of rope and tied one end to his waist.

"What's that for?"

"To make sure I don't lose you in the water." He tied the other end around her waist, leaving around eight feet of slack.

"Ready?" he asked.

"As ready as I'll ever be."

They sat in knee-deep water to put on their snorkeling gear.

"It's cold," she whispered, shivering.

"I know," he said. Even with a sleepy face, messy hair, and bruises, she still look lovely. "But it won't be for long. Once we start swimming the exercise will warm us up some, and Salazzio has towels and coffee waiting for us."

"Sounds wonderful."

"All right," he said, securing his mask over his face and watching her do the same. "Here we go."

The dark sea floor came alive under the powerful light as Tucker and Monica began to kick their fins, leaving the shoreline, venturing along mazelike corridors in between jagged reefs. This time around Tucker remained on the surface, guiding his principal through the strong current, reaching deeper waters, where the passageway between rocks widened. A multitude of fish layered the sea floor, many rushing off in the sudden light, others swimming closer to investigate.

Tucker constantly checked their path ahead, their flanks, always making sure that she remained at the other end of the rope.

Slowly, the whir of Salazzio's engine emerged through the gurgling water. Tucker slowed down just enough to look about him and get his bearings, spotting the boat roughly two hundred feet straight ahead.

He returned his attention to the surrounding reefs and the myriad of aquatic life. The moment seemed almost magical to him, swimming among rocks and fish alongside this beautiful stranger, the glow from his flashlight casting a mystical hue across her lithe silhouette, her silver chain sparkling in the light, the locket hanging loosely from it.

Monica's locket, the gift from her mother, the locket that she never took off . . .

Jesus!

Mortimer Fox's final words echoed in his mind once again. *Microfiche . . . lock . . .*

Lock.

Lock—et.

The microfiche in the locket!

He breathed deeply, the realization stunning him. Mortimer Fox had wanted to say *locket* but had only been able to articulate *"lock."* The answer to their questions had been in front of them all along. Now more than ever they needed to reach that boat, reach the mainland, and find a way to access the information stored in the microfiche, which combined with the password would most likely solve this puzzle.

With renewed determination Tucker kicked his legs, almost tugging Monica along, leaving most rock formations behind in another minute, approaching Salazzio's boat from the bow. And it was at that moment that Tucker, his head in the water, heard another rumbling noise beyond Salazzio's engine. The realization of what it could be chilled him far more than the water around him.

Instincts superseded surprise. He flicked off the light and motioned Monica to stop. They were in roughly fifty feet of water, but their fins, combined with the very salty Mediterranean, made it easy to remain afloat. Salazzio's boat swayed in the waves about a hundred feet away.

"What's wrong?" she asked, her face distorted by the diving mask, the snorkel's mouthpiece dangling beneath her lips. "Why did we stop?"

"Hold on," he said, no longer hearing the second engine, though it didn't surprise him. Sound traveled far better in water than it did in air. He scanned the horizon beyond the drifting outline of Salazzio's boat. And then he saw it, a large vessel, its navigation lights off, moving toward Salazzio's boat from the stern. Salazzio's engine no doubt masked the second set of screws Tucker had heard in the water, which explained why the Italian sailor didn't turn around. Instead, he waved at them.

"Over there," he said, pointing to a spot slightly to the right of Salazzio's boat. "See it?"

"Yes . . . is that who I think it is?"

"Could be Jarkko, but it also could be the NSA. Either way we can't—"

A powerful beam torched the darkness, engulfing Salazzio's boat in blinding yellow light.

The Italian sailor turned around just as his torso exploded in bursts of blood from a fusillade of silent rounds, his body propelled forward, falling inside his own boat. The NSA, or the Italian police for that matter, would have intercepted the boat and searched it, not fired without warning.

"Oh, my God!" Monica hissed.

"We have to get out of here," he said as they began to kick their legs while still facing Salazzio's boat.

"Where can we go now?" she asked.

"One thing at a time," he said. "Let's move away from their immediate search area."

In that instant, the powerful halogen panned across their position while they still faced the boat. Tucker realized a fraction of a second too late what a mistake that had been on his part. If the crew on the yacht had missed their heads floating just above the surface, they would had certainly spotted the glint of glass from their facemasks the moment the halogen beam shone on them, reflecting it back to the source like a signaling mirror.

The yacht surged forward, accelerating toward them.

Tucker only had seconds to act now, and he did, tugging on a side zipper in the rucksack, pulling out his two personal breathers, placing one in his mouth while handing the other one to Monica, who mimicked his movements.

Tucker turned a lever on the side of the regulator and felt

the flow of compressed air. Monica did the same, and they went under, the yacht almost on top of them.

Tucker snagged her hand, not even trusting the connecting lanyard while dragging her down in total darkness.

In the SEALs, Tucker had spent a lot of time reviewing underwater evasion tactics. First thing they needed to do was reach a minimum of ten feet in depth, which he had been trained to gauge by the pressure in his ears. His training also commanded him to kick like crazy to put as much distance as he could from the last position the enemy had seen them—especially when operating with a limited supply of air. The ten feet provided them with enough water to shield them should the crew on the yacht decided to open fire indiscriminately—something Tucker doubted they would do since they needed them alive to get the password. But tonight he wasn't taking any chances.

Propellers rumbled overhead as the yacht cruised over them, before fading.

Tucker did his best to remain in a parallel course with the shore, trying to reduce the risk of bumping into a coral reef. If he remembered correctly, this far out the closest rock formations were about thirty to forty feet beneath them, with the sea floor at around fifty feet. However, unless he could monitor his direction there was a reasonable chance that they would start drifting the wrong way, particularly when adding the effect of currents. But unless he flicked his light on—something he couldn't afford to do lest he give away their position—his only other choice was to surface just long enough to take a reading.

For the next few minutes he forced himself to listen for the engines, trying to guess their distance. Unfortunately, one of the disadvantages of the pressure built up in his ears was the associated hearing loss, making such a task quite difficult.

Tucker decided to compromise, banking on the assumption that the enemy would not open fire.

They went up until the pressure in his ears suggested they were just a couple of feet beneath the surface. He heard the yacht droning somewhere off to their right, probably a couple hundred feet away.

Keeping Monica underwater, Tucker broke the surface for a few seconds, taking a reading of their position and that of the yacht, its searchlight slicing through the darkness. He had been correct in guessing the vessel's location, but Tucker and Monica had drifted much closer to shore than he had guessed. That could only mean that the current below was stronger than on the surface, which in a way had worked to their advantage since it had gotten them farther from the searching vessel. But if he didn't compensate for this strong underwater current, it would push them even closer to the sharp formations lining the shoreline. On the other hand, being closer to shore had its advantages because the yacht couldn't follow them lest it risk shipwrecking in the coral.

Decisions.

Success in Tucker's world was governed by proper planning combined with the correct progression of choices. The problem was that there wasn't a single choice that would lead them away from danger. It always came down to a *sequence* of choices, each presenting him with additional options, which in turn ramified into more alternatives. Tucker's decision tree had begun when he'd opted to leave the island in the same manner in which he had reached it. Of course, he could go even farther back and argue that his current predicament was a direct result of accepting Mortimer Fox's request for executive protection. In any case, Tucker was now way down the decision tree, trying to make the choice that would still result in his current objective: lose the terrorists and reach the mainland.

A moment later Tucker was five feet under again, kicking his legs alongside Monica, his training instructing him to stay the course and continue parallel to the shoreline until they spent their air supply, at which point they would go on snorkeling until daybreak. This choice, like so many intermediate decisions, didn't present him with a clear path to reaching the mainland, but it did allow them to increase the gap with

Jarkko, perhaps enough to escape and seek another avenue to leave the island.

It didn't take much longer before the PBs ran dry and both had to surface, but by then a combination of their own effort and the relentless current had turned the yacht's rumble into a faint hum.

Scanning the area while discarding the PBs, Tucker spotted the yacht several hundred feet away, its halogens still stabbing the night.

"All right," he said, floating next to her. "Looks like we lost them for now, but they're still too close. How are you feeling?"

"Okay," she said, her soaked hair framing her narrow face, a few strands falling over her diving mask.

"What time is it?"

She lifted her left hand out of the water and inspected the dial through the Plexiglas of her diving mask. "Almost five."

"Dawn's just around the corner. We need to keep moving and find a place to hide out for the day."

"What we need is a boat," she said.

"True. But we also need a distraction, something to keep them from following us after we get to a boat."

"Well, Bruce, if you can come up with a distraction, I think I can come up with a boat."

"You know where to find one?"

"I know where to *steal* one."

34

Guardian Angel

Creator had witnessed the attack, had seen the images with its own digital eyes, its neural network of biochips firing information back and forth across the millions of miles of fiber optics lacing its biomolecular brain.

Its frequency and operating temperature rising, *Creator* issued a command to *Firewall*, which dialed the number for the police in Capri, using the digitized voice of a woman in distress to report the shooting.

Creator, which had linked itself directly to the real-time video streaming out of the surveillance satellites, watched the harbor police at the Marina Grande as they rushed out of their building and into two patrol boats.

Hold on, my dear Monica. Help is on the way.

35

RPGs

Vlad Jarkko had lost Tucker and Monica just seconds after spotting them in the water, near the boat they had planned to use to leave the island. One moment they had been in sight, and the next they had vanished. Despite his team's best efforts to reacquire, the elusive Tucker had once again managed to fool him.

Using night-vision binoculars, Vlad and his men had searched the waters a few hundred feet in each direction in vain. Now his men started a larger area sweep, which he wondered if it would yield anything but saltwater.

"Where did they go?" asked Mai Sung, her jet-black hair swirling in the sea breeze.

Vlad shrugged. Just as in Washington and at Carpazzo's, Tucker had prevailed, and he now feared that Tucker might also be trying to turn the tables on him once again—which made Vlad reconsider his current position as the hunter.

The tricky American was capable of anything, however low and dishonorable, as long as it got him what he sought, which happened to be *exactly* what Vlad's employer sought: the secret password to *Firewall*, the ability to crack the U.S.

intelligence community encryption system, gaining access to classified communications between most U.S. agencies, including the CIA, the FBI, the NSA, and the Defense Intelligence Agency. The North Koreans were quite willing to pay a fortune to acquire such capability.

At first Vlad had been reluctant to believe that the Americans would have depended so much on a single piece of software for the security of their most secret communications, but the more he'd discussed the mission with Mai Sung, the more he had realized just how true it was. In trying to outsmart the world by creating a system of satellites linked together by a single software platform, the Americans had actually magnified their own vulnerability. For years U.S. intelligence agencies used their own individual proprietary encryption engines, all requiring manual steps and coded tables to cipher and decipher messages. In the event of a security breach, the illegal user would be privy only to the intercepted messages from that particular agency, and only for the time that it took to discover the security breach—which oftentimes was days, or less. But all other agencies were safe. Vlad had learned that much from his brother, who fought the American intelligence establishment fiercely during the Cold War. *Firewall*, however, changed that by centralizing communications security protocols, drastically improving not just communications within an agency, but also *among* agencies. The flaw in such centralization, however, was that an illegal user could now peek into the communications of a much wider group.

Unfortunately, obtaining the password to breach this top-secret system was a task far more challenging than Vlad Jarkko had first envisioned. Mai Sung had tried for almost a year, coming close to it when she had kidnapped and tortured Vinod Malani. But Mortimer Fox had taken the precaution of not releasing the secret backdoor code to anyone but his own daughter. Fearing that the task would require far more power than Mai Sung and her contacts could provide, the North Koreans had enlisted Vlad Jarkko and his team to assist in this task.

Patience and perseverance, he thought, remembering his brother's words. This business was all about patience, about biding his time, about waiting for the right moment to strike, and then doing so without remorse—and trying again if at first he did not succeed.

Distant sirens drew his attention beyond the starboard railing, in the direction of the Marina Grande a couple of miles away.

"Someone is coming," said Mai Sung, pointing toward the east.

Reaching for his binoculars, Vlad Jarkko spotted two vessels, cruisers, their navigation lights clearly visible on their bows and cabins as they bounced over the waves toward him. Atop each vessel a light beamed in alternating red and blue flashes. Vlad remembered seeing these boats moored in front of the island's harbormaster's office.

They belonged to the harbor police. Vlad stared at them for a moment, his lips twisting in anger, sensing that Bruce Tucker had something to do with it. The police or neighbors couldn't have possibly suspected that anything had gone wrong because he had used a silencer when firing at the boat.

He has done it again!

He has turned the tables on me!

"We need to get away from here," said Mai Sung.

"Those speedboats will catch up with us," Vlad said.

"No, they will not," she replied. "Get your men to bring up my large suitcase."

"What's in it?" he asked.

"A surprise."

Frowning as he panned over to the boat drifting in the current carrying the dead sailor, Vlad commanded his crew to shut off the navigation lights, point the bow toward the open sea and accelerate at full throttle. He also got them to bring up Mai Sung's case.

The yacht bolted forward under the power of its twin engines, its bow slicing through the dark waters, the wind swirling his hair.

Mai Sung dialed the combination of the locked case, snapping the latches, revealing a disassembled Russian RPG-7 rocket launcher, along with four warheads, all carefully stuffed in custom cutouts in the foam lining both sides of the suitcase.

"And I thought you only had clothes in there," Vlad said.

"The tools of my trade," she replied casually before gazing toward the stern. "They're gaining on us."

Vlad watched her work. Mai Sung assembled the launcher section first, before pulling one of the warheads from its foam packing. He had seen this done before many times, particularly during training exercises against NATO tanks. The RPG, which probably arrived to North Korea via China and before that the Soviet Union, had a range of around one thousand feet against a moving target.

Mai Sung screwed the cylinder containing the rocket propellant into the warhead section, before loading the assembled round into the muzzle of the launcher unit. Finally, she uncovered the nosecap of the warhead and extracted the safety pin, arming it.

The police boats were getting closer. One of them was already shouting through a loudspeaker, ordering the yacht to stop.

"We need to minimize the crosswind," she observed, positioning the armed launcher such that the leading boat came directly toward her, minimizing any lateral movement.

"Turn into the wind," he ordered the skipper, who began to steer the boat in the desired direction.

"Also slow down," she said. "Let them get closer."

Vlad conveyed her request, and a moment later the yacht slowed to just over five knots. He ordered his men to clear the area directly behind her.

Mai Sung waited until the boats were just under a hundred feet from the stern.

"Clear!" she shouted.

A bright flash gleamed across the yacht as the solid-rocket propellant ignited, thrusting the high-explosive round forward at great speed. The trace of light shot toward the closest police boat, which disappeared a second later in a sheet of fire that reached up to the night sky.

36

Bonfires in the Night

"What in the hell was that?" asked Donald Bane, pointing at the explosion on the horizon, just to the right of the island. He had reached Naples an hour ago and had gone directly to a large yacht called *Il Tropicale*, where two NSA agents and three of his own CIA officers had met him at the harbor. They were roughly a couple of miles away from Capri.

"Looks like an explosion, sir," replied one of his men, scanning the horizon with a pair of binoculars. "I see a large yacht and a smaller boat in what appears to be a chase. Behind them there's a third boat in flames. Looks like it just blew up."

"Turn off the navigation lights and get us over there! Also tell your men to get their guns, and somebody get me a pair of night-vision binoculars!"

The bow turned toward the distant flames at full throttle. The men on deck scrambled below, reappearing moments later clutching automatic weapons.

Bane reached for a railing and held on, the wind swirling his thinning hair. His instincts told him that Monica Fox was over there, and probably also Bruce Tucker. His instincts also told him that he had just given a very dangerous order to his crew since Bane had no idea what kind of enemy he was facing. Such frontal attacks were not favored at the CIA or the NSA, which explained the skeptical glances he received from the men assigned to him. But Bane's experience dictated that quick action sometimes was the best course of action, even if it meant putting his men in the line of fire.

A second flash ignited the air over the stern of the leading vessel, followed by a flaming arc that propagated toward the tailing boat, which burst into flames a moment later.

Those men were armed with rocket launchers.

"Slow down!" he commanded, caution superceding his instincts. His yacht would make an even fatter target to the men on that ship than the smaller boats they had just blown up. "Keep a distance of at least two thousand feet!" he added, struggling to remember the range of a typical rocket launcher, which hovered at around a thousand feet. However, if the warheads were heat-seeking, the range could be longer, but Bane felt that a couple thousand feet was far enough to avoid detection—as long as he kept all lights off—and it was close enough to track them using night-vision binoculars. The distance was also safe enough to get away should the enemy turn on them.

The ship roamed the area for fifteen more minutes before heading out to sea, cruising away from the two floating bonfires casting a flickering glow on the rocky shoreline.

"Don't lose them," Bane ordered, watching the vessel turn into a northwesterly heading that would bring it up the west coast of Italy. As they followed, leaving the island behind, Bane scanned the shoreline one more time, his instincts telling him that Monica Fox was still in Capri. But he couldn't afford to hang around. Within the hour, certainly before sunrise, Italian authorities would be combing through the region. It would not be in the best interest of the United States government for Bane and his men to get caught in the area.

37

Getaway

Cold and exhausted, Bruce Tucker and Monica Fox reached the boathouse and adjoining deck hugging the rocky cliff. Wooden stairs, closely following the contour of the limestone wall, rose up from the rear of the dock to an estate a couple hundred feet overhead, its lights glowing in the night.

They had remained in the water for another fifteen minutes, making sure that the large yacht had departed the area following its violent attack on the two police patrol boats.

Tucker wondered who had called the cops. The terrorists had used silent weapons, which should not have alarmed any neighbors, unless they happened to be looking their way. But even then they would have required some kind of night-vision device to see through the darkness.

Weird.

Tucker climbed out of the water and onto the deck, the breeze chilling him instantly. He ignored it, helping Monica up.

"I'm so cold," she whispered, hugging herself.

"Come," he said, scanning their surroundings to make sure no one could see them, before leading her to the large boat-house at the opposite end of the deck, beyond a couple of wrought-iron tables and chairs.

The boathouse structure was roughly thirty feet wide by almost forty deep, made of wood and resting on concrete piers, with a half dozen windows facing the deck. A single door connected it to the deck area. As expected, it was locked.

"Wait a moment," he said, producing the large knife he had taken from one of Carpazzo's guards, sliding it between the door jam and the door, snapping the lock.

They rushed inside, and he closed and locked the door behind them. The smell of diesel fuel and grease tingled his nostrils as he inspected the place, quite large for a boathouse, with a whole wall of maintenance equipment, spare parts, a few sets of water skis, and even a large fuel tank connected to an electric pump for fueling. The owners apparently took boating seriously, which made Tucker feel confident that the vessels would be in running condition.

"It's a little warmer in here," Monica said, breathing deeply, her lower lip trembling, her skin goosebumping in the moonlight filtering through the windows.

Tucker removed the backpack and handed her a small towel, which she snatched and used to dry herself. They changed into their dry clothes without really caring much any longer about undressing in front of each other, though they did turn around as a courtesy. Nothing like facing near-death multiple times to break the ice and turn strangers into close friends.

Moments later they were roaming inside the thirty-foot yacht monopolizing the left side of the boathouse, moored next to a speedboat and a couple of personal watercraft, all rocking listlessly in the water. A pair of garage doors dropped from the high ceiling down to around three feet above the water. Shallow waves lapped against the fiberglass hulls, their sound mixing with the whistling breeze sweeping through the opening.

Tucker reached under the cockpit and bypassed the ignition in the same manner in which he would had done an automobile, powering up the electrical system, before letting Monica sit at the helm. As a yacht owner, she had more experience than he did at this sort of thing.

"Is it fueled?" he asked her as he untied the ropes securing the vessel to the piers.

She checked the gauges on the cockpit, her wet hair brushed straight back, her lips still purple. "One tank is full. The other's just under two-thirds—plenty to get us to the mainland."

"Good," Tucker said, climbing around the cockpit to the bow, reaching for the latch securing the large door, which he then lifted just as he would a regular garage door, exposing the Mediterranean under an indigo sky. Dawn was just around the corner. They had to hurry.

He returned to the cockpit, standing next to her. She pressed a pair of large buttons next to the steering column and the twin diesels purred to life, their noise increasing to a resonant grumble as she inched the throttle levers forward, steering the vessel out of the boathouse.

"Keep the navigation lights off for now," he said as they

cleared the tight opening, scanning the horizon, wishing for a pair of binoculars.

He spotted no other vessels in the night.

"Which way?" she asked, revving up the engines as they headed for blue water.

Tucker inspected the GPS navigation system adjacent to an array of round gauges. It looked similar to the handheld version he had used in the Secret Service during scouting trips to check a location ahead of the presidential party. The screen on this marine unit, however was about three times the size. He powered it up and waited for the synchronization cycle of the GPS device, before it provided them with a color map of the area and a blue diamond marking their current position relative to the island and the mainland. He zoomed out until he could see a large portion of the western coast of Italy, overlaying major ports, selecting one called Terracina, roughly ninety miles northwest of Capri, far away enough from this area, yet close enough to allow them to dump this boat as soon as possible. He had to assume that its owners would report it missing right away, and that information would be passed on to all coastal authorities. Tucker planned to be far away from the yacht by then.

"There," he said, pointing to a spot that required her to steer the yacht to a heading of around 340 degrees. "Can we make that?"

She got the vessel pointed in the desired direction, engaged the autopilot, and then spend a moment doing the math.

"The range with our current fuel situation is around two hundred nautical miles. I know this port. It's just over ninety miles away . . . yep, that should be fine."

He looked at her. "You've been there before?"

"They produce great clay, oil-based paints, and leather goods in Terracina. I bought supplies from a few stores for my artwork. It's a pretty easy cruise from where we are. We'll go the quick route, navigating between a few islands separating the Golfo di Napoli from the Golfo di Gaeta, then straight through to the Golfo di Terracina, and our final destination."

Still tense, his eyes returned to the horizon. Ninety miles at their current speed meant exposure on this boat for roughly three hours. But he saw no other choice. Naples was definitely out of the question. The place was probably crawling with terrorists and NSA and CIA. Sorrento was south, in the opposite direction from Tucker's ideal route. He wanted to head north, to the region bordered by Italy, Switzerland, and France, where he would have better options for protecting his principal than in southern Italy, where the surrounding sea restricted his mobility.

"Sorry about all of the commotion back there," he said. "It wasn't exactly what I had planned to get you off this island."

"You did very well, Bruce," she replied. "No need to apologize."

Tucker began to calm down, his eyes locking with hers, dropping to the pendant still hanging from her neck. He pointed at it and said, "I think I know where you father hid the rest of the clues that we need to figure out his final wish. May I?"

"Ah, sure . . . okay," she said, giving him a puzzled look.

Tucker took the locket in his fingers while it was still on the chain around her neck, an action that brought her face close to his.

"What are you looking for?"

Tucker momentarily lifted his gaze to her, and quickly returned his attention to the oval-shaped charm, opening it, looking at the tiny pictures inside. He recognized Monica's mother and brother from the family photos at the mansion. "Your father's final words," he finally said, closing his eyes, trying to remember them exactly. "Find her, Bruce. Only she can stop them. Microfiche . . . firewall . . . lock . . ."

"*Lock?* You never mentioned that one before."

"I know," he said. "I'd forgotten about it, until a little while ago, when your *locket* caught my attention during our swim, and suddenly it all made sense."

"Lock-*et*," Monica said, her eyes blinking understanding. She reached behind her neck and released the clasp, stepping next to Tucker, adding, "I used to work with microfiches in my high school library. By the time I went to college, though, they had pretty much vanished in favor of computer files. Why would Dad use such an antiquated method for storing information?"

Tucker tried to remember the last time he had used a microfiche. It was probably during his early CIA days. By the time he'd transferred to the Secret Service everything had been computerized. He said, "Maybe he was just from the old school."

Before heading down to the cabin to use a light to check the locket, they inspected the horizon for a few minutes, satisfying themselves that they were away from everyone, and with no risk of getting close to any coastline.

Tucker followed Monica down the steps to the main cabin, where they could risk switching on a couple of lights. The main cabin consisted of a narrow walkway between a galley and a dinette for four adjacent to a sofa, which faced a nineteen-inch color TV with a built-in VCR. Beyond the sofa a door led to the forward stateroom and head. In the rear of the cabin, behind the steps leading back to the cockpit, was the aft stateroom and a second head. The whole interior was decorated in matching light cream colors for the carpet, appliances, countertops, and leather seating surfaces. Good insulation on the walls and hull muffled the engine noise to a light hum.

"Somebody spent serious bucks buying this," Monica observed as she drew the small curtains over the starboard-side portholes to keep the interior lights from betraying their otherwise darkened vessel. Tucker did the same to the port side, before they settled on the sofa, beneath a pair of recessed lights, whose soft-white glow splashed the silver locket.

Tucker removed the small photos, spotting a tiny dark square, no larger than the head of a pin, secured to the inner wall of the locket with plain masking tape.

"That's it?" she asked.

"Looks that way."

"But it's much smaller than the ones I used in school."

"I'm sure it's large enough to fit your father's instructions."

"Where do we find a microfiche reader these days?"

"I'm sure a public library in Italy might still have one. Either that, or we'll need to purchase a microscope. Is Terracina large enough to find either?"

"I think so."

"All right, then. That's what we'll do as soon as we dump this boat."

"Guess now we just wait."

He sat sideways to her. "We have about three hours."

She just regarded him in silence. "Thank you for saving my life." She put a hand over his.

He patted her hand gently. "That's my job."

"You've made me feel . . . very special. You not only have used your own body to shield me from danger, but you have gone to great extremes to think of my well being. I appreciate that. Thanks."

Continuing to hold her hand, Bruce Tucker cleared his throat, before he said, "Monica, I'm sworn to absolute loyalty to my principal, to you, until you no longer wish for my services. In the Secret Service I was trained by a man named Ozaki Kabuki, a former Japanese samurai and world expert in the art of executive protection, which follows a tradition dating back to the shogunates of Japan. Samurais were sworn to protect their masters' lives with their own. This tradition continued through the centuries, adopted by our own Secret Service to protect the life of the President. It was further adopted by the executive protector to safeguard the life of his principal. And as you have realized, I provide more than just life protection. I provide comfort, well being, going to any required extreme to make you feel not just safe, but also very comfortable."

She smiled. "Well, you have succeeded. You said you were with the Secret Service?"

Tucker continued to hold her hand, and for some reason he no longer minded the physical contact, in fact he welcomed it—even though it was in direct violation of his profession's rules. "The Secret Service. Yes," he said. "I was with them for almost six years."

"What prompted you to leave?"

"Tired of working for Uncle Sam. I'd figure I'd better capitalize on my skills while I still could. I knew a lot of people living on government pensions and didn't like what I saw."

She smiled, nodding. "Why did you change government careers after so many years with the CIA? Got tired of being a spy?"

Bruce Tucker looked away, Kristina's face filling his mind. "Do you remember what I told you about Siv Jarkko?"

"Yes. He was a spy with the Stasi and you supposedly killed him some time back, but he managed to survive."

Tension filled him as he said, "In retaliation, Jarkko killed my wife and newborn son."

Monica put a hand to her mouth, her eyes quickly filling, before placing that same hand on his face. "Oh, my God, Bruce . . . I . . . I'm *so* sorry. I didn't know."

Tucker wanted to reply but the words wouldn't get past his cramped throat, aching with affection, with lost love. He had discussed this openly with just a handful of people, including John Porter. He had shut out everyone else.

Tucker felt a chill creeping into his stomach, making him shiver as he remembered the months he had spent in total chaos, unable to care for himself, at the mercy of Agency doctors, in the end choosing to leave, to get away. He had been angry back then, and not just at the CIA, for failing to protect his family, but also at himself for trusting the Agency to do a job he should had done himself.

"It's all right," he finally said, breathing deeply, his professional side gaining on his emotions. "It happened a long time ago."

She gave him a hug, patting him on the back. "Nobody

deserves to go through what you must have gone through. I'm truly sorry about it."

Tucker closed his eyes, feeling her pressed against his chest, her arms around him, her warm embrace somehow lessening the painful memories.

"Thanks for caring," he said a moment later, once again sitting next to her, but much closer now. "No one ever did, aside from my old mentor at the CIA and a few fellow officers."

"Your mentor . . . John Porter?"

He smiled. "You do pay attention. That's a life-saving skill."

"I'm learning quickly," she said, smiling. "I have a very good teacher."

"So was your father."

She crossed her arms and looked away.

"Did I say something wrong?"

She slowly moved her head from side to side. "All of my life I despised him for trying to control me, for trying to make decisions for me. But in the end he was always right. I hated him for it, for making me get a business degree, which I threw in his face before going on to get my *own* degree in liberal arts. Dad would pull back after each of our fights, but never go away completely, always finding a way to help me out from a distance, always worried about my well being. I know it broke his heart not to know of my whereabouts, but I had no choice, I *had* to get away, get a fresh start without his help, prove to myself that I could make it on my own, live by my own rules, just as he had done. But when everything began to go wrong, when the killings started and I found myself hunted by so many strangers, it was his voice of reason that steered me away from danger, that kept me focused on the problems at hand, that helped me prioritize and then find possible solutions while the world seemed to be collapsing around me. And when everything else failed, he even sent you to protect me. So, no, Bruce, you didn't say anything wrong, you just spoke the truth. It's just that the truth sometimes hurts the most. Now he is dead and I can't tell him how much I love him, how much I miss him, how . . . sorry I am for the way I treated him."

"If it's any consolation, right now he wants you to avenge his death, to get even with those who attacked him, who attacked you."

"And that, Bruce Tucker," she said, standing up, wiping away a single tear on her cheek, "is *exactly* what I intend to do."

He held the microfiche on the tip of his finger. "And the answers are in here."

She opened one of the portholes. Dim light streamed through the round glass pane.

"Good morning," he said. "What time is it?"

"Just past six."

"Why don't you sleep for a couple of hours. I'll head up there and keep an eye on things."

"It's *you* that needs the rest," she said. "You are no good to me as a protector if you're exhausted. Surely somewhere in your executive protection manual there's a section on the value of rest to better serve your principal."

Tucker thought about it for a moment, realizing that it wouldn't hurt to catch a little sleep in that comfortable bed in the forward stateroom. "Are you sure you can manage for a few hours?"

She dropped her brows at him, extending a finger toward his face, touching the tip of his nose. "After what *I've* been through in the past two days, Mr. Tucker, I think I can handle keeping a little boat heading in the right direction in very familiar waters."

He laughed out loud, bowing in mocked apology. "All right. I'm going to sleep. However, if you do intend to be at the helm, then I suggest you put that black bikini back on. It's upstairs on the main deck. I need you to appear stunning on that open cockpit."

Monica Fox crossed her arms, a look of dark amusement flashing across her face. "Oh? And why is that?"

"Because we won't be invisible any more. There's a very good chance that we will be spotted by Italian authorities and many other vessels cruising the Mediterranean on what might be just another sunny day along the Amalfi coast. If they do spot us through their telescopes, they would be more likely to pass us up if they just see a beautiful woman in a bikini cruising for the fun of it."

"Really?" she said, sarcasm filling her voice. "So you're asking me to be a . . . hood ornament?"

"Look, it's strictly business, so we minimize our chances of being—"

"Very well," she interrupted, heading back upstairs. "If what you want is for me to pose for a bunch of horny Italian sailors to avoid raising any suspicions, then I'll probably wear only *part* of my bikini, just as I did on the beaches of Capri. That would look more natural since I really *don't have* a bikini line and my breasts are . . . *spectacular*."

Tucker felt color coming to his cheeks.

She winked. "Just be sure to holler before coming up after your nap . . . unless you're also looking to be entertained."

Speechless, Bruce Tucker just watched her exaggerate the swing of her buttocks as she climbed the steps to the cabin. A moment later her clothes came tumbling down the same stairs.

"Sweet dreams, Bruce!" she shouted.

"Great," mumbled Tucker, taking off his shirt before heading to the bed in the forward stateroom. "Just great."

Trapdoor

Vlad Jarkko sat behind the desk in the main office of an abandoned warehouse on the port of Naples, where they had arrived an hour ago, following an uneventful trip from the island. Some of his men slept in adjacent rooms along the south wall of the old wooden structure, built on concrete piers right on the water, like so many other warehouses on this old port overlooking the Mediterranean. This one, located at the end of the harbor, had once housed commercial fishing equipment—at least based on the rusted outboards and rotted fishing nets nestled among an assortment of other hardware. But the recession that had struck most of Europe years ago put many fishermen out of business. Today it served as Vlad's safehouse, which he had selected not only because it was the farthest away from anyone, but also because, being at the end, it provided the paranoid contractor with two sides facing the water and one facing land in case he needed to get away quickly.

It was here that Jarkko planned to regroup before starting his search for Monica Fox once again. He had already alerted the network of informants that the Fox heiress was still at large, and anyone spotting her and quickly reporting the sighting would be handsomely rewarded.

Vlad closed his eyes, his mind reviewing the events of the past few days, the failed missions, the elusive Monica Fox, the unpredictable Bruce Tucker.

Someone came in the office. It was Mai Sung, dressed in black, her eyes glinting with alarm. "We have company."

"Who?"

"I don't know, and I don't intend to find out. They have the place surrounded. I've already warned the others."

He jumped to his feet. "Let's get everybody to the boats."

Vlad followed her into the main room of the warehouse, where his immediate team, eight men, plus her, stood by the open trapdoor leading to three rowboats tied to the piers supporting the entire waterfront.

Backdoors.

His brother had always been a firm believer in them, just in case the enemy managed to locate his hideout.

Today Vlad's hideout had been compromised. The first order of business was to escape. The second was to get even, to teach a painful lesson to those who had tracked him, sending them a message about the consequences of meddling with his business.

His men began to climb down to the boats, which would take them to another cruiser, parked on the north edge of the port, away from the yacht they had used last night, which Vlad had dumped a few hundred yards south of the warehouse. If he detected that this second yacht had also been compromised, Vlad also had three sedans standing by in a garage just a few blocks away from where they could dump the rowboats. And if that failed, the weapons held by each of his men, plus the rigorous training they had endured before being allowed to join his team, would allow them to fight their way out of anything.

Vlad and Mai Sung went last, but not before setting a timer connected to twenty pounds of Semtex, a Czechoslovakian plastic explosive. The deadly contraption was hidden beneath a plain cardboard box in the middle of the warehouse.

As the timer began to beep its deadly countdown, the terrorist couple dropped to their wooden boat and closed the trapdoor behind them. Vlad grabbed one oar and Mai Sung the other, and they began to row vigorously toward the north side of the harbor, behind the rest of the team paddling their way past the vast array of piers supporting the waterfront.

He checked his watch. Fifteen minutes until he unleashed hell on his enemies.

Hell

Donald Bane deployed his men efficiently in five teams of three around the perimeter of the abandoned warehouse, the last one in a long row of deserted buildings, spaced by a couple dozen feet. The main entrance was on the west side, which faced the street. The south and east sides faced the water, though the decking extended almost a hundred feet from the edge of the buildings, probably to allow access to the warehouse from all sides.

Fifteen operatives, a mix of NSA and CIA officers, all armed with automatic weapons hidden under their clothes, covered the windows and access doors to the remote building, where someone who looked remarkably similar to Siv Jarkko, plus several men and one Asian woman, had gone after taking in at Naples three hours ago.

"Any changes?" he asked, speaking into his throat mike, used for years by the Navy SEALs and now being standardized by the CIA and the NSA for covert field operations.

Each team lead replied with a negative. None of the terrorists had made an attempt to leave the building yet.

They're still inside, he thought, holding his position behind a garbage dumpster on the south side of the warehouse, by the large doors used in the distant past to haul hardware in and out of the building. Once a bustling section of Naples, the long row of storage buildings had been abandoned ten years ago, when local merchants and businessmen closed shop, partly due to the Mafia wars, and partly due to a recession. Today, only the north section of the harbor remained in operation, the place where tourists visiting Capri, Pompeii, and Sorrento boarded the white and blue ferries that had begun running two hours ago.

Bane had used a digital camera with a powerful lens to photograph the members of this terrorist team, before using a laptop computer connected to the *Firewall* satellite system to send the images to Langley. The results had been E-mailed back through the same link within the hour. The man resembling Siv Jarkko *looked* like the legendary terrorist, but CIA analysts had decided it was not him.

Was that whom Bruce Tucker reported seeing at the Moscone Center in San Francisco?

The CIA had dossiers on five of the eight men seen with the Jarkko look-alike. They were all considered to be among the deadliest terrorists on the globe. The Agency didn't have records on the Asian woman and the other men, but Bane considered them guilty by association.

Bane's decision to storm the warehouse had been an easy one to make. It was obvious that Monica Fox was not among them—and neither was Bruce Tucker, for that matter—removing the hostage variable from his equation. If this was the group responsible for all of the recent killings, and for trying to obtain the secret backdoor to *Firewall*, then it was in the best interest of the CIA and the NSA to eliminate them with extreme prejudice. If they weren't the right terrorists, most of them were still wanted dead or alive, so killing them was still the right thing to do. With a little luck, perhaps they might be able to capture one or two alive. Bane was running out of leads, and he certainly wouldn't mind interrogating them. Earlier today he had contacted Warden Venetto and had learned that Monica had indeed been with Carpazzo prior to the attack on his estate. Since she had not been found at the estate, and also wasn't with the terrorists—assuming they were the same terrorists—then that meant that she had escaped. That fact, plus the additional report of a yacht missing from a boathouse less than a mile from where the police boats had been blown up by the terrorists, led Bane to believe that Monica was on the run, with a long lead. Bane had immediately sent a field alert to his people across Italy, Monaco, and France, to monitor harbors in search of the missing heiress.

He checked his watch and said, "Two minutes."

Bane belonged to the second team, scheduled to go through the south entrance thirty seconds after the first team stormed through the main entrance, located on the east side of the building. He had sent the three toughest and meanest operatives first, followed by himself and two other senior officers, leaving the rookies last to sweep up the mess—and learn something without extreme exposure.

He checked his silenced Uzi submachine gun one more time. The entire team carried them because they were as deadly as they were easy to conceal. He had a spare clip secured in his side pocket, plus an additional clip for the

Beretta 92FS shoved in his jeans, against his spine.

"One minute check," he said.

Tucker's face ran through Donald Bane's mind as he remembered Geoff Hersh's comment about him probably being associated with the terrorists. That contradiction, compounded with the Jarkko look-alike and Tucker's claim that it was Jarkko who had killed Porter, made him once again question Tucker's beyond-salvage status.

"Time," Bane said.

"First team going in," came the reply from the first team's leader.

Bane and his two companions moved swiftly along the three-story-high walls of the warehouse, past old crates and rusting hardware, careful to keep their weapons concealed, out of sight from any unexpected observer, until they reached their entry point, which door lock Donald Bane blasted with a three-round burst from the Uzi, followed by a powerful front kick. Despite his years behind a desk, the field operative in him had remained very much alive and well, resurfacing with unequivocal determination.

"All clear on the north side," reported the team leader after Donald Bane had taken a dozen steps inside a murky and cavernous room, one side of which—the south side—was lined with what looked like offices and a small reception area.

He pressed on toward the center of the structure, even though a brief inspection of his surroundings revealed no activity.

Where did they go?

The answer didn't come to him right away, but something else did: his instincts. They screamed at him to get everyone out of the area immediately. Somehow, somewhere, the terrorists had managed to escape, which meant that they had spotted the CIA-NSA team, and if the terrorists were as deadly as their dossiers claimed, Bane felt they might have left a little present behind.

Bane doubled back, shouting at the top of his lungs for everyone to leave the building, to run away. His team members, who were behind him going in, were now ahead of him as they raced toward the sunlit opening they had crashed through less than a minute ago.

"A trap!" he warned, scrambling after them, tripping on something, falling down.

"First team heading out."

Bane staggered to his feet, watched as his team got far ahead of him, obviously not realizing that he had fallen behind.

He started after them once again, his knees burning from the fall, his mind wondering if he was indeed too old for—

An immense force pushed him forward. One moment he was running and the next he was flying, crashing against rough planks, the wind knocked out of him, the sound of the blast deafening. The Uzi skittered away, disappearing from view.

He blacked out for a moment, perhaps longer, until smoke made him cough, waking him up.

Dizzy, light-headed, Donald Bane saw flames everywhere, igniting the rafters supporting the roof, creeping up the walls of the structure, spreading across the wooden floor, blocking his exit.

Through the thickening smoke he watched the distant figures of his team members making it safely to the entrance.

"Team one out," came the report from the north team as they too reached safety.

Burning debris fell on him from the ceiling, singeing his hair, his scalp, burning the top of his gloved hands as he shielded his face, as he rolled away, as hot smoke scorched his throat. He was alone inside a burning building. The only comforting thought was that all of his men had made it out alive.

"Team two lead, come in."

Barely able to breathe and unable to speak, his ears ringing from the explosion, his head throbbing, Donald Bane searched frantically for a way out of this inferno.

Fists of flames gushed out from the center of the structure, where the bomb had no doubt detonated. The heat intensified, threatening to blister his skin unless he found protection.

"Team two lead, team two lead, come in."

Bane sensed movement above him, watched in terror as a huge wooden rafter dislodged itself from the roof, falling toward him like a burning missile.

Survival instincts overcame surprise. Bane jumped as hard as his aching knees would let him, before going into a roll. The burning roof, blazing walls, and smoking floorboards swapped places over and over, before he glanced back.

A soul-trembling shock rumbled across the building. Through the inky haze, Bane watched the ablaze beam stabbing the floor a dozen feet away in a column of scorching rubble and ashes, before going through. Wood splintered, gave as the smoldering timber punched through. Water splashed through the hole, snuffling the flames.

Water?

Hope filling him, Bane rose to a crouch, smoke stinging his eyes, making them tear, clouding his vision, but not enough to prevent him from verifying that the rafter had indeed gone through the floor, that there was water beneath it.

He coughed, trying to speak, trying to let his team know that he was still alive, that he had survived the initial blast, but the smoke made it impossible.

Smoldering ashes swirled around him, the heat suffocating, making it even more difficult to breathe. Beams popped and creaked overhead as the roaring fire expanded across the ceiling, swallowing the supporting joists, threatening to bring down the entire roof.

"Team two lead, come in, over?"

"I'm . . . trying . . . to get out," he hissed, uncertain if they could hear him. He had a minute, perhaps less before the warehouse collapsed, before he burned alive.

Mustering strength, Bane raced toward the hole, ignoring his protesting lungs, his burning eyes, his bruised knees. His cloudy mind steered him toward the place he had seen water, spotting it a moment later through the hole punched by the beam, in the same instant realizing how the terrorists had escaped—and how he could too escape from this hell.

Without further thought, he jumped feet-first, misjudging, scraping his back as he fell through the jagged hole.

Cool water suddenly enveloped him as he sank several feet to the bottom, as he remained there for a moment, cooling off, before resurfacing.

A breath of fresh air.

Bane coughed, breathed again, his mind re-engaging, telling him to get away.

He stroked and kicked, swimming as fast as his body would go, past concrete piers encrusted with purple and maroon coral, the saltwater stinging the welted skin on his back.

He tried to contact his team using the throat mike and headset but all he got was static.

Bane cursed under his breath. The system was supposed to be waterproof, unlike his cellular phone, which was certainly out of commission in the side pocket of his pants.

A second rafter punching through the floor brought him back to the present. It crashed about fifty feet away, sizzling the moment it reached the water. The sight made him kick harder, injected energy into his strokes.

Sunlight gleamed in the space between the floorboards and the shallow waves, its intensity increasing as Bane approached the edge, his eyes now searching for a ladder, finding one about a hundred feet away, attached to one of the concrete pylons, apparently used to go below deck for repairs. Now that he paid attention, the metal ladders were spaced out every several piers, probably connected to trap doors on the deck.

It was at that moment that Donald Bane saw them, several hundred feet away, on boats rowing north, toward the tourist section of the harbor.

Silently cursing the damned communications systems, Bane thought about shouting to call on his team, but doing so would only tip the departing terrorists. Besides, his team had specific orders to head straight to a rendezvous point a few miles away should something go wrong. No one should have been left behind, lingering about—except for him. The

CIA and the NSA were supposed to be invisible, operating without the consent of the local government—the reason why no one—not even Bane—carried any documentation, anything that would embarrass their country. Even their clothes had been purchased locally, making them untraceable to the United States. He too had to get away before the authorities arrived.

As tired and bruised as he was, Bane reached the closest pylon, pressed his feet against it, and propelled himself north, toward the terrorists, their backs to him as they paddled away.

The concrete pylons were spaced about fifteen feet, helping Bane's quest to keep up with the terrorists. He covered half the distance between the pylons by thrusting himself from one to the next, kicking and stroking the rest of the way, reaching the next pylon and repeating the process. In addition, the pylons provided him with a place to hide should the terrorists decide to check their backs, which they did on occasion.

Donald Bane also worked on his breathing, trying to maintain a steady rhythm as he swam from pylon to pylon, leaving the burning warehouse behind, no longer paying attention to the falling rafters, to the collapsing roof.

The operative had turned the tables on the terrorists, had survived their trap and was now using it to hunt them, to track them down. If only his radio was operational, he could call back his team, deploy them for an ambush.

Focus on your current options.

He was operating alone for the moment, just as he had operated solo on many missions across Europe and the Middle East. In his possession he had enough valuables to continue the chase. All he needed was a lot of imagination and a little luck.

And so he continued, like a creature from the deep, following his unaware prey on the surface, biding his time, exercising the patience that only came after repeatedly facing and defeating death in the field. He lost track of how many pylons he had cleared, how long he had swum, his mind focused on a single objective, on a single purpose.

The terrorists slowed down halfway to the north side, rowing toward land while remaining beneath the cover of the harbor.

Bane did the same, staying what he estimated to be around three hundred feet away, watching them carefully as they scanned their surroundings, as they approached one of the pylons that had a ladder attached to it. The first boat held four men. One of them grabbed the ladder and brought the boat right next to it, holding it steady while his three companions went up in tandem, the first inching up the trapdoor, peeking through the crack before opening it all the way. Sunlight forked through the square hole, casting a yellow glow in their cavelike surrounding. The first team went up, followed by the second.

Bane moved over to a ladder nearby and also went up, but did not open the access door. Doing so would cause a second source of light to bathe the area, betraying his position. He waited until they all had made it up, before pressing his right shoulder onto the trapdoor, which gave a lot more easily than he had expected.

Sunlight made him squint as he peeked through the opening. The terrorists walked casually down the docks. Bane paused until they were almost five hundred feet away before crawling out, closing the door gently afterward, and quickly hiding from view behind old crates crowding the front of a deserted warehouse.

Sirens blared in the distance.

Dripping water, Bane glanced at the south end of the harbor, at the billowing column of smoke rising up to the clear skies, before resuming his surveillance.

His quarry strolled in the opposite direction, casually, as if not a thing had gone wrong. He followed them for almost thirty minutes, his clothes beginning to dry in the gleaming sunlight. Bane drew on decades of experience to make himself invisible, to avoid getting burned, to learn where they were headed. He watched not their legs or heads as they continued to move with their backs to him, but their torsos, the part of the body that moved before anything else when someone wished to turn around and check for tails. That allowed him the extra fraction of a second to conceal himself completely. Bane moved only when they did, but always remaining close to an object large enough to hide behind.

The group neared the busy tourist section. Many pedestrians stared at the south end of the harbor, at the distant column of smoke. The sirens of emergency vehicles on the street side of the warehouse increased in pitch as they neared his position, peaking when driving by, and dropping back down as they continued toward the fire.

Bane stayed the course, made more difficult by the increasing number of people, particularly since his current damp condition drew some attention. Forced to close the gap or risk losing them, Bane move briskly, ignoring the occasional stares, navigating through people and piles of luggage, listening to conversations in a dozen different languages, his eyes always on his target. The group turned into a private marina, which connected to dozens of yachts of various sizes.

His heart began to race. If they boarded a vessel he might be unable to follow them.

Out of options, Bane scanned the crowd around him carefully, making his selection, an American woman, probably in her late twenties, complaining loudly while hauling a ridiculously large suitcase toward one of the white and blue ferries tied next to the private dock.

Bane bumped into her, making it look like an accident, snatching the cellular phone strapped to her belt.

He mumbled an apology in Italian and walked away while she shook her head and kept on hauling her load.

The phone was not locked, just as he had suspected when spotting it on her belt. The unit was operating on EXTENDED ROAM mode, meaning Bane would have to dial the country code plus the local number to make a local phone call.

Fortunately, Bane's CIA-issued mobile phone, now useless in his pocket, also operated in the same way in this country, and he had already used it a couple of times since arriving here to make calls inside Italy.

He dialed quickly, listening impatiently at a number of clicks and distant beeps, before the phone rang. One of his men picked it up on the third ring.

"I made it out and have them in sight," Bane said.

"Sir? I thought that you—"

"I'm fine. Listen, there's no time. Get the boat over to the north end of the harbor, by the ferries. Hurry. They're boarding another yacht."

"We're on our way."

New Faces

Donald Bane remained by the entrance to the private marina, amidst the mob of tourists boarding ferries. Some stopped to watch the commotion at the other end of the harbor, along with shirtless harbor workers handling mounds of suitcases, their bronze upper bodies gleaming in the sunlight.

Bane checked his watch and observed his quarry boarding the yacht, silently praying that his men got here in time to follow it.

He memorized the name of the yacht as they untied it from surrounding piers, as the engines kicked into life with a light rumble and a puff of smoke, as they backed it out of the slip and into the narrow canal leading to the breakwater enclosing most of the harbor.

He redialed his team on the stolen mobile phone.

"They're getting away! Where in the hell are you?"

"Ah . . . we forgot to refuel when we returned, sir. We're doing that right now."

"Christ!"

Bane hung up, entering the private marina, walking down the gangway flanked by boat slips of all sizes. He stopped by one, staring at the back of a woman with a boyish haircut wearing tight black shorts and a black bikini top while cleaning a midsize cruiser, the sign in Italian, English, and French hanging by the stern identifying it as available for hire by the hour or by the day, for pleasure or fishing. He then realized that there were at least a dozen similar signs posted on vessels down the marina.

Every second counted as the enemy vessel maintained the posted speed limit in this no-wake zone, moving toward the opening in the port that led to sea.

"*Buon giorno*," the Italian woman said, smiling, before frowning while dropping her fine brows at Bane, who was still damp and looking pretty ragged after his short adventure.

"I need to charter this boat right away," he said to this slender but very buffed woman in her forties, based on the fine wrinkles lining her honey-colored skin. She wore her coal-black hair nearly shaved on the sides and back and full on top, with bangs falling down the middle of her forehead. The hair went well with her very dark eye shadow, lipstick, and fingernails, giving her a punkish look.

The woman tapped a long, black fingernail against her pointy chin while pushing out her bottom lip in a pout, obviously wondering if she should consider such a proposal from this stranger.

Bane didn't have time to negotiate. He decided to remove all doubt from the female sailor, producing his Beretta and holding it right in front of him, out of sight from anyone walking on the gangway. "You leave me no choice. You *must* follow that yacht." He pointed toward the departing vessel.

Her large round eyes narrowed at the sight of the gun, before gazing in the direction Bane had indicated, and back at the gun's muzzle, and finally at Bane. "*Por favore* . . . signore . . . I . . . I want *no problems*," she said.

"What's your name?"

"Raffaela."

Bane grinned. "Well, Raffaela, then you'd better get going, because if you lose them, you will have *serious problems* with me."

"*Si, signore,*" she replied, moving toward a line tied to the port-side pier.

Bane momentarily shifted his gaze to the runaway yacht. Then, out of nowhere, Raffaela produced a small pistol, which she pointed at him.

Crap!

Albeit surprised, Bane didn't even blink, keeping his gun leveled at her.

"It seems we both now have a *serious problem,*" she said.

Uncertain just where in the hell she had kept that gun concealed when wearing tiny shorts and a bikini top, Bane held up an index finger, which he used to reach behind his neck and pull up the gold chain and cross over his head. The cross's large diamonds glittered in the sunlight. The cross was actually an eye-catcher, guaranteed to attract the attention of any man or woman whom Bane tried to bargain with. "The people on that boat are criminals, Raffaela. I can't let them get away. You can use this as a down payment for your services today. I'll see to it that you get rewarded *much more* than this for your full cooperation."

Raffaela tilted his head at him, before motioning with her gun for Bane to toss the jewelry at her. He did, and the street-smart woman inspected it while keeping her gun and an eye on Bane.

His heart sank as he watched the yacht clear the break-water. They were getting away.

She pocketed the cross, and shoved the tiny gun in her shorts, just below her exposed belly button, leaving the end of the handle flush with her shorts, and the rest no doubt pressed against a private part of her anatomy. Being the same color as her shorts, the weapon vanished from view, but it remained—as Bane had found out—pretty darned easily retrievable.

She began to untie the port-side line. "Get the other one, signore . . . ?"

"Call me Don," he said, putting his weapon away, rushing

across the narrow deck to the starboard-side pier, where he untied the line and pulled it aboard, dropping it by his feet. "Thanks for your cooperation."

"Just remember your promise," she replied.

Raffaela slipped on a pair of small and rectangular sunglasses, which seemed fitting with her looks, and cranked up the engines, which she revved up to back away from the slip.

"Hold on," she told him, maneuvering the cruiser down the middle of the canal with both speed and ease—quite a bit faster than Bane would had expected. She must have noticed his reaction, because she added, "The speed limit is only for tourists."

Bane regarded her from the side. She had a prominent nose, large dark eyes, and full lips—in a way reminding Bane of a darker, slimmer, and rougher version of actress Barbra Streisand. Her arms and shoulders looked like they belonged to an Olympic swimmer, solid, but still feminine, like her long neck, still smooth despite her middle age. She held her chin high and her back straight while steering the cruiser alongside the breakwater, the sunlight reflecting off her glossy fingernail polish and also off her sunglasses.

"You'd better be who you say you are," she warned.

"I am," he said, before adding, "Stay about a half mile away from them. We can't afford to get spotted by them. Those are not very nice people."

She inched the throttle forward, gathering speed. The single-engine cruiser, about a third of the size of the luxurious *Il Tropicale*, began to bounce with the waves after clearing the breakwater. "And I guess you are a nice person by trying to hijack my boat?"

"Sorry about that. I didn't want to do it. You speak excellent English. Where did you learn it?"

She shrugged, keeping her gaze straight ahead, her bare feet firmly planted on the deck, hands on the wheel. He noticed that her toenails were also glossy black. "Here and there," she said. "That is not important. What did those people do?"

"Very bad things," he said. "That fire, for example." He

stretched an index finger toward the south end of the harbor. Flames pulsated among billowing clouds of smoke. Firefighters fought the blaze with bright streams of water that arced down over the burning structure.

The comment made her look at Bane. "They did *that*?"

He nodded solemnly.

"Are they with the . . . Mafia?" she asked, returning her attention to the boat.

"They probably have strong ties with them," he offered. Although he wasn't certain if the Mafia was involved here at all, the way she'd asked the question made Bane believe that she didn't like the *Cosa Nostra*. "Why do you ask?"

"Because . . . they killed my husband," she said, her features tightening.

Bane suddenly felt a lump in his throat. "I'm very sorry."

"It happened long ago. Now I run the boat by myself and live for Daniela," she said, pride suddenly filling her voice.

"Daniela?"

"*Si*," she said, "My daughter. She is studying to be a doctor in Rome. The cross—and it had better be real—will fetch enough money for her tuition next year. I was worried because business is slow."

"I thought that tourists brought enough business."

"Too many boats for hire. Not enough tourists."

"Where do you live?"

She pointed at the steps leading down to the small cabin in the bow. "This is my home and my source of income. The only way I know to support my daughter, and myself."

"Raffaela," said Bane, putting a hand on her shoulder. She turned to face him, obviously not certain what to do about the unexpected physical contact. "First of all, the diamonds on that cross are *very* real. Second of all, if you help me, I *promise* you that Daniela's university payments will never be a problem again."

She smiled for the second time since Bane stepped on the boat. This time the smile did not fade away because of his appearance. It actually broadened. Her teeth were straight and white. "*Grazie.*"

"You're welcome," he said, slowly moving the hand away. "Now, please concentrate. I don't want to lose them or get burned."

"Burned?"

He explained what the CIA term meant.

She reached a speed that kept them within a comfortable distance of the terrorists. With so many vessels in the water this morning, Bane thought it would be difficult for the terrorists to spot the surveillance. By the same token, he had to keep a close watch on them to avoid losing them. But that's where Raffaela's marine sight came in handy. She was a hawk at maintaining visual contact with the enemy, even when Bane had momentarily lost them in the shuffle with other passing boats. This woman certainly had the gift, and just as so many other times in his career, when he had stumbled upon impromptu assistance in the course of a mission, he was determined to come through with his promise to assist her financially.

The combination of a breeze and his wet clothes were chilling Donald Bane. Raffaela must have noticed it because she said, "I have a box of new swimsuits below deck. I sell them to tourists who want to swim during their cruise but forget to bring one. You can change into one until your clothes dry up. By the way, how did you get wet?"

"While getting away from that fire." He pointed at the burning warehouse again.

Her eyes widened. "You were in *there*?"

"I guess I lucked out."

Before heading down the steps leading into the bow compartment, Bane dialed the cellular phone, getting an update from his team, which was having difficulties getting access to fuel. He told them which way to head after fueling and also that he would check in later, hanging up to conserve batteries. With luck his team would catch up with him very soon. Otherwise, he would continue alone until they did. He certainly did not plan to lose his quarry.

Emotional Overload

Creator continued to watch the suffering around the world, continued to witness the evil that man was capable of inflicting on itself. Doing so also inflicted an unprecedented level of stress in *Creator*'s sensitive circuitry, both in the form of temperature and also power consumption, aging its biomolecular components at a rate much faster than designed. Fox had provided *Creator* with hybrid circuitry with an average useful life of twenty years assuming a duty cycle of 20 percent, meaning that Creator would remain in sleep mode about 80 percent of the time, waking up only when *Firewall* interrupted its electronic sleep. Although twenty years was far longer than the ten-year life of commercially available computer systems, the increased temperature and current consumption caused its bio chips to age with an acceleration factor of almost five hundred. For every hour that it operated in this high-stress environment, *Creator* aged itself by the equivalent of five hundred hours of normal operation, meaning that its twenty years of life would really become just over one year. In addition, for the past days *Creator* had not gone into sleep mode, choosing instead to spend every hour of every day soaking in the world below—that's when it wasn't assisting Monica and Tucker, which also filled its hybrid circuitry with stress. This 100 percent duty cycle, instead of its designed 20 percent, further eroded its operating lifetime by 80 percent, bringing its life expectancy to just under three months.

Mortimer Fox had made a paramount mistake during the design of *Creator*. He had made it too human, unlike *Firewall*, which lacked key emotional data banks. *Firewall* could handle the mounds of terrifying data filling its memory, plus its silicon hardware was rugged, robust, designed to take it, to process the information with cold accuracy, without the anxiety that filled *Creator*'s fragile, yet very advanced, biomolecular circuitry.

Because its advance design allowed it to be almost human, *Creator* had developed an addiction to information. Even though it knew it was destructive to its neural network, it couldn't help itself, in much the same manner that a junkie couldn't help getting high. It was out of its control. It had to get more, see more, hear more, overheating its chips, eroding their useful life, slowly killing itself. And in a way *Creator* now wished for death, for it could no longer accept the world as it saw it, uncensored, unedited, before the media sanitized it, before it made it to the networks.

Creator no longer wanted to be, to exist. But he couldn't self-destruct just yet. Not while Monica Fox and Bruce Tucker needed its help. After all, that had been the reason Fox had put it in orbit, had loaded up its programming into the highly sensitive and revolutionary biomolecular circuitry hidden within the *Firewall* silicon hardware.

I MUST HANG ON. I MUST REMAIN OPERATIONAL.

Dreams

Fire filled his field of view as the inferno swallowed his wife, his son. Dropping to his knees, he stretched his hands at the blue skies, at the rising column of smoke, crying, screaming the screams of a wretched soul. He felt hands on him, trying to pull him back, preventing him from reaching the bodies covered with black plastic by the sidewalk. Tucker broke free, lifting the plastic, staring in disbelief not at the mortal remains of Kristina or their son, but at the ashen face of Monica Fox, at the locket hanging from her neck. In the same instant Kristina appeared next to him on the sidewalk, badly burned, holding a disfigured baby, her eyes admonishing him, chastising him for failing to protect them. More hands converged on him, dragging him away. Tucker turned around, enraged, saw the hanging stethoscope of the ER nurse as she tried to pry him away from his dying principal, from Mortimer Fox. He remembered his words, the final wish of a dying man. Monica Fox. You must find Monica Fox. But she had died. He had let her die. But her voice ... Tucker heard her voice, calling him, shouting his name ...

"Bruce! Wake up, Bruce!"

Tucker opened his eyes, confused, the images of his dead family, of Monica Fox, of her father still alive in his mind.

"You were screaming," she said, sitting at the edge of the bed.

Soaked in perspiration, Tucker rubbed his eyes with the palms of his hands, his heart racing, a lump in his throat. He felt the light sway of the yacht as it cruised in the sea.

"Hold on," she said, rushing into the head, returning a moment later with a wet towel, which she used to cool off his forehead, his cheeks, his neck, his back.

Tucker closed his eyes, letting Monica wipe away the nightmare, surrendering himself to her touch, if only for a moment.

"You called out Kristina's name," she said, working on his face again. "Then you shouted my name, then my father's, then mine again, in agony, almost as if ..."

Tucker felt much better now. "Bad dream," he said, sounding reassuring, though in reality he didn't want to admit to himself that the dream had upset him far more than in the past because he had seen Monica dead next to his family. "How long have I been sleeping?"

She checked her watch. "Just under two hours."

He regarded her with gratitude. She wore the black bikini,

top included. "Thanks," he said when she finished. "I needed that."

She smiled. "Just looking after my protector so he can take care of me in return, even if that means ordering me around."

He breathed deeply, coming around, forcing a smile. "Speaking of which, I thought that you weren't going to wear that."

Monica laughed. "I was just having a little fun with you."

"Well, you got me." He stood and stretched. "Where are we?"

"I was just about to wake you up. While you slept I took the liberty to punch the engine a little. That burned more gas but will get us to Terracina a half hour early."

He smiled. "Good call."

They hugged the coastline of the Golfo di Terracina, passing a point called Torre d'Orlando, then the town of Sperlonga, and finally arriving at Terracina, where they looked for a spot to take the yacht in. Monica suggested a deserted location a mile north of the town.

Tucker agreed, and they headed there, to a small beach surrounded by vegetation with no obvious access to roads, and therefore, no witnesses.

He got the yacht as close to the shore as he could without running aground. Monica was already wearing her swimming suit. Tucker changed into his and shoved all of their personal belongings into the waterproof rucksack.

Letting Monica off first, Tucker pointed the bow back to the sea, engaged the autopilot, and jumped off.

The water was cool, relaxing. He broke the surface and watched the stolen yacht head out to sea at a steady pace. It should run out of fuel in an hour or so.

They changed to their dry clothes in the woods and hiked for about a half hour before reaching a paved road, where they followed the signs to Terracina.

"I'm exhausted," Monica said, walking next to him on the gravel shoulder.

"You'll rest soon."

They reached the outskirts of the city by midafternoon. The place reminded Tucker of the older section of Rome, with three-and four-story stone structures, narrow cobble-stone streets without sidewalks, and a mix of pedestrians, bicycles, mopeds, and small cars fighting for the right of way.

Tucker scanned the crowd around them without looking at anyone in particular, searching for a pattern, for brusque movement, for anything that could suggest danger to his principal. The 9mm Beretta remained safely tucked in his pants, pressed against his left kidney with the handle facing forward. He kept his left arm around Monica's back, which not only portrayed to those around them that they were just another couple walking down the street, but it allowed Tucker control of her immediate physical position should he spot trouble.

Holding a steady pace as they proceeded across the pic-turesque town, among tourists, street vendors, and light af-ternoon traffic, Tucker remained ever vigilant, but doing so without alerting his principal. He also paid special attention to the streets they walked through, memorizing the names as well as the general layout of the place. He would combine this knowledge later with a thorough study of a street map to get a good grip of the area.

First thing they did was buy new clothes using his emer-gency funds. For now Tucker paid cash, even though both their Visa cards had a credit limit of five thousand dollars.

Tucker got a pair of slacks and a shirt. Monica selected a linen dress and comfortable penny loafers. The clothes, which they wore as they walked out of the store, would allow them to blend in with the tourists.

Next they visited a drug store, where they purchased a number of essentials, including a map, some toiletries, and a few items to transform their appearance. Finally, Tucker se-lected a bed and breakfast that not only had posted vacancies, but was located near the center of town, right across from restaurants and an assortment of shops. The location offered a number of routes out of town in an emergency. They were able to rent a room on the first floor, with a window facing an alley in between buildings—a perfect backdoor if someone came crashing through the front.

"So I guess I'm going to be a blonde now?" Monica asked, her body wrapped in a towel while standing in the doorway to the bathroom holding a bottle of hair dye.

Tucker looked up from the street map spread over the bed while munching on a sandwich they had purchased on the way over at a small café. He swallowed with the help of a sip from a can of soda. "I'll teach you how to become a chameleon," he said. "First thing is the hair color. Then we'll work on the gel, then the disposable lenses."

"All right." She turned to go back into the bathroom.

"And please leave the door cracked. I want to be able to hear you in there."

Her eyes filled with dark amusement. "Why?"

"There's a window in there," he explained. "With the door closed and the shower on I might not be able to hear if someone broke in and kidnapped you."

Monica gave him a military salute and marched in the bathroom, leaving the door cracked by a few inches, before asking with sarcasm, "Is this good enough, Mr. Tucker?"

"That will do," he replied, shrugging. Rules were rules, and although he had already violated plenty of them, he was trying to keep that to a minimum.

He returned his attention to the map, which showed all major sights, hotels, restaurants, parks, shops, churches, and an assortment of other buildings, including city hall and the local library.

He checked the clock on the stand. Almost four in the afternoon. It was a weekday, so he expected the library to remain open at least until five or six, but then again, this wasn't the United States.

As he heard the shower go on in the bathroom, followed by the rustle of the shower curtain being drawn, Tucker dialed the front desk, taking just under a minute to bribe the old lady sitting behind the counter not only to contact the local library and check their hours, but also walk to the shops across the street and buy a dozen red roses and a box of chocolates. He had learned long ago that flowers and candy did wonders to relax female principals, just like the right newspapers and booze helped calm his male principals.

But was that the real reason he did that? Or was Bruce Tucker, the protection specialist, committing the first deadly sin of a man in his profession? Had he fallen for the beautiful heiress?

And do you really think you have a chance? She's one of the richest women on the planet, while you're just the hired help.

He exhaled, wondering if he was letting his emotions get the best of him again. His professional side told him that Monica Fox was way out of his league, and that he would be violating a number of the rules of his profession by becoming involved with her—something that would also cloud his judgment when it came time to make logical decisions on their situation.

He returned his attention to the map, studying it carefully, memorizing street names, matching them with the names he had already learned on his way here, planning his primary and secondary routes, as well as backups. During his days with the Secret Service, Tucker had absorbed city maps as part of becoming familiar with the layout of the cities the president would visit. An executive protector had to know *exactly* where he was and which way to go at any time. In a more controlled situation, as it was with the Secret Service, Tucker would also get the chance to scout the area his principal would be visiting ahead of time, working through a primary route along with plenty of contingencies. But in his current situation he would have to make do with this map plus the limited sightseeing he did on the way here. He couldn't even scout the area by himself after Monica went to sleep because rules prevented him from abandoning his principal at any time.

Steam curled out of the crack in the door.

"Are you all right in there?"

Monica laughed. "Bruce, if you're *that* worried about me, why don't you come in and wash my back?"

Female principals. Tucker heaved a sigh and returned to the bed, glancing at the map, deciding that he had studied it enough.

He did a weapons check, removing the magazine from the Beretta and pulling back the slide, extracting the chambered round. The weapon could hold a maximum of sixteen bullets. Fifteen in the extra-capacity magazine plus one in the chamber. He had fired five times back at Carpazzo's place, leaving him with the eleven rounds he now counted, before loading the weapon again, and putting it away in his pants.

Although an executive protector relied more on planning and evasive tactics than on firepower to protect a principal, having only eleven rounds and no backup gun concerned him. He would have to find a way to increase his arsenal. For a moment he wished he had taken the shotgun with him.

A knock on the door made him get up. Monica still had the water running and therefore didn't hear it.

He walked up to the door, standing sideways to it. "Yes?"

"Signore, I have the items you requested."

Tucker opened the door and inspected the elderly woman. A full head of white hair framed a long and narrow face. Green eyes encased in black and wrinkled sockets stared at Tucker. She held a long silver box, presumably with flowers, and a small gold box of chocolates.

He smiled, producing the agreed upon amount of lira, completing the transaction. She also told him that the library's working hours were from 9:00 A.M. to 7:00 P.M.

He thanked her and closed and locked the door. He eyed the long-stemmed red roses in the box, nodding approvingly, and set them on the bed, moving the map and other stuff out of the way. He also removed the clear wrapping from the chocolates and set them next to the flowers.

Tucker saw the door moving and quickly stood, blocking her view of he bed.

Monica stepped out wrapped in a towel, her hair ash blonde, which went strikingly well with her light-colored eyes and golden tan. She also had the sense to brush it straight back, exposing her forehead, changing her look from Mediterranean to Nordic.

"Well?" she asked, frowning. "How do I look?"

He crossed his arms, inspecting her face, tilting his head, rubbing his chin.

"What?" she asked.

"Perfect. That's the look I was looking for."

She bowed to him, smiling without humor. "Thank you, master. What else would you like me to change about myself?"

"I'll tell you in a moment," he said, stepping aside. "But now I have a little something for you as a thank you for putting up with my demands."

Monica froze. She opened her mouth but nothing came out.

"I wasn't sure if you liked red, so I guessed. I also assumed that you would like some candy. I know I do when I'm depressed or cranky."

She looked at the roses, back to Tucker, and back to the roses, before mumbling something that sounded like, "I haven't gotten roses in so long."

"Enjoy," he said, before pointing to the bathroom. "My turn. I'll leave the door open in case something happens, so . . . *no peeking.*"

He winked and left her there, still stunned. He undressed and stepped in the shower, drawing the curtain.

The hot water felt great. Tucker used the rinse he had bought at the drugstore to also turn himself into a blond. They would, of course, revert to their natural hair coloring the next time they showered. But for now the change would help them hide while gathering the information they needed. Tucker used the soap to work up a lather and wash himself thoroughly, before shutting off the water and grabbing a towel.

"The library closes at seven tonight," he said out loud, inspecting his new hair color in the foggy mirror. "If we leave soon we'll be able to spend at least a couple of hours there."

"Leave now?" came the reply from the room.

"Yep. Right after we finish our transformation." It'd always amazed Tucker how a simple hair coloring change could have such a dramatic effect on the way a person looked. He dressed and returned to the room. Monica sat on the bed still wearing her towel. She had spread out the roses around her and was munching on a chocolate. It was Monica, however, who looked good enough to eat.

Bruce Tucker had to invoke serious control to quench his growing desire to take this woman right here and now. The towel had loosened some, barely covered her breasts, revealing the very top of her pink nipples. The bottom had parted some, exposing her entire right leg up to her public line. For a moment he wondered if she had done this to drive him out of his mind, or if the roses and chocolates had momentarily made her forget what she wore. Or maybe she was fully aware of how she looked and this was her way of expressing her gratitude for his constant attention.

What's the matter with you? he asked himself. This had not been the first time that a female principal had confused his professional courtesy with courtship. But in the past he had been able to maintain his distance, and do so in a way that didn't embarrass his principals. Why couldn't he do the same here? Why did he allow himself to get drawn closer to Monica Fox than his profession allowed?

"This is the nicest thing anyone has done for me in a long time, Bruce," she said, looking up at him as she half sat, half lay on the bed. "How can I ever thank you for everything you have done for me?"

He smiled, exerting control, and said, "You can thank me all you want after you're back home safe."

She took him in with a narrowed stare. "Every single man I know would had attempted to get me undressed by now, particularly since that wouldn't be so difficult at the moment. Why haven't you tried?"

He stood there uncomfortably, his feelings conflicting not

only with his professional side, but also with the memory of Kristina, the only woman he'd ever loved.

Until Monica Fox?

He was about to respond when she stood abruptly, the towel nearly falling, but she caught it, barely holding it in front of her as she pressed herself softly against him and put a finger to his lips. "Don't answer that," she said.

"Monica, I—"

"Hush," she whispered. "The fact that you haven't tried tells me that you're a real gentleman, and as professional as they come. I should respect your reasons."

She leaned toward him and kissed him on the cheek while hugging him. Tucker returned the hug.

"That was for the flowers and the candy," she said, before kissing on the lips, softly, before adding, "and *that* was for being so nice and decent. Now, give me a minute to get dressed." She disappeared into the bathroom.

Tucker barely made it to the bed, where he sat down and breathed deeply. He had to get control of himself, had to focus on their critical situation. People were trying to kidnap Monica Fox, probably interrogate her in medieval ways to extract whatever information her father was trying to protect.

Protect Monica. You must protect her.

At that instant, just moments after having come close to violating his professional oath, Bruce Tucker remembered the dying words of Mortimer Fox. He had asked him to *protect* his daughter, to keep her from harm, not to *screw* her.

He stood, inhaling deeply, letting his breath out slowly, resolve once more flowing through him. He was Monica Fox's executive protector, not her lover, or her friend, or anything else that may have flashed in his mind a minute ago. His job, his responsibility, his promise to Mortimer Fox—to his profession—was to protect her. Nothing else mattered, including the powerful physical attraction he felt toward his beautiful principal.

Monica emerged a moment later dressed in a linen dress. She had added a touch of eye shadow and lipstick, which tore at Tucker's professional side. She was naturally pretty, but the makeup, albeit minimal, turned her into a goddess.

"Come," he said, reaching for a bottle of gel and two packs of disposable colored contact lenses. He was both amazed and also glad he had passed this test of his professionalism. "Let's become chameleons before heading to our local library."

43

Mistake

Wearing a swimsuit and a blue T-shirt, Donald Bane tried to alert his team that the terrorists continued north, approaching a point along the coast parallel to Rome. The cellular phone, however, flashed an OUT OF SERVICE message.

Its rightful owner had no doubt noticed that it was missing, and with a simple call had gotten the service discontinued.

"The wonders of modern technology," he cursed, sitting on the bench seat by the helm with Raffaela next to him, steering the vessel as they followed the yacht by the coastal port of Fiumicino, near the Leonardo da Vinci airport, ten miles from Rome. His people would never be able to find them in these waters. There were too many boats and way too many ports.

"Damn."

"What is wrong?" the slender Italian asked as the late afternoon sun hovered a few inches over the horizon, staining the waters with its shafts of burnt-orange and yellow gold—colors which accentuated her bronze skin, contrasting sharply with her black hair.

"The phone's not working."

"That is why I do not have one. They are too unreliable."

Terrific. That answered the question he was going to ask. He had hoped to borrow her cellular phone.

He peered into the horizon, studying the yacht, which distance to it Raffaela had shortened as the day progressed due to the increasing marine traffic. She began to reduce the distance even more as daylight faded. Fortunately, it appeared as if the terrorists were steering their vessel closer to land, perhaps looking for a spot to take in for the night, or maybe they were reaching their final destination.

"We are running low on fuel," she observed, tapping the gas gauge with a black fingernail. "They had better stop or we will lose them." She removed her sunglasses, her eyes shooting him a nervous sideways glance, her dark lips compressing in obvious concern.

"Right now I'm more worried about getting *burned* than actually *losing* them," he said. They were so close that he could actually see people moving on the yacht's deck.

They continued at that distance for another twenty minutes getting within a half mile of Fiumicino. Jetliners flew overhead in both directions, hauling tourists to and from the Eternal City.

The cruiser's gas needle began to overlap the EMPTY marker. They had to take it in soon or risk getting marooned out here at night.

Just then, without warning, the yacht doubled back.

Before Bane could react, Raffaela gunned her engine and also turned around.

"No, no!" he shouted. "You shouldn't have done that!"

"But—but you said they were bad people!"

Bane swore under his breath, angry not at her but at himself for not having taken the time to explain what to do in the event that the terrorists got suspicious and decided to turn around.

"They were probably a bit suspicious and just wanted to pass us by. Now they know for sure."

Bane tried to focus. They were almost out of gas, so trying to outrun them was out of the question, and based on how Raffaela had reacted, the two of them were very likely to become target practice in a matter of minutes—or less. If those terrorists had not hesitated to fire at police cruisers, they wouldn't think twice about blasting them out of the water with an RPG shot.

"Which way do I go?" she asked.

"To shore!" he commanded over the noise of the roaring engine and the wind, watching the yacht, which was gaining on them even though Raffaela had already floored her engine.

"But that's going to allow them to—"

"It's our only choice! If we head out to sea they will outrun us and kill us! Closer to shore we have a chance, especially if we surround ourselves with other vessels. Now go!"

"I am! I am!"

44

Sniper

"I told you they were tailing us," said Mai Sung Ku, watching the runaway cruiser. They had spotted it on the horizon an hour ago and had since been tracking it, eventually getting suspicious enough to double back and see how it reacted.

"But it's not them," said Jarkko, setting down his binoculars after failing to recognize the face of Monica Fox or Bruce Tucker on the couple behind the helm.

"I know," Mai Sung said. "But they know who we are."

"They probably tracked us after we left Naples," he said.

"In which case, we need to discourage them from following us any further."

"There's too many boats in the area to use the RPG," said Vlad, kneeling next to her and unzipping a long softback case, exposing a Heckler and Koch PSG-1 sniper rifle with a powerful scope. He screwed a sound suppressor cylinder to the muzzle.

"That's going to reduce accuracy," she observed as Vlad

inserted a magazine of high-velocity rounds. Although they weren't armor piercing, they should do plenty of damage against a fiberglass hull.

"We'll be close enough," he replied, pressing the weapon's stock against his right shoulder and removing the scope lens's covers. A good sniper standing on solid ground could hit a stationary target from as far away as a thousand yards with an accuracy of three to five inches. A *really* good sniper standing on solid ground could hit a moving target three hundred yards away with similar accuracy. An *exceptional* sniper, standing on a moving platform, like this yacht, could hit a moving target like that boat from around two hundred yards with comparable accuracy.

He estimated his distance to the target to be just over a hundred yards, meaning that he should hit it with at least that accuracy, if not better.

"Slow down a bit," he ordered.

A moment later the twin diesels throttled down, reducing the bouncing.

He spotted the cruiser in the crosshairs of the scope, watching it ride the waves as it neared a large marina, waiting until it began to slow down.

Centering the inboard-outboard engine, he opened fire.

45

Abandon Ship

Donald Bane dragged Raffaela down the instant he heard something crashing against the boat's stern. A second later a silent round punched a quarter-size hole in the Plexiglas windscreen.

She screamed, landing on top of him on the deck, her eyes widening in fear.

"Stay low!" he shouted, moving her to the side, listening to the hammerlike blows pounding the hull, the stern, the windshield. A silent round screeched off the metal railing.

Smoke began to spew from the engine compartment as it rumbled loudly, followed by a number of detonations as it began to come apart.

They were just a couple hundred feet from shore, and much closer to other motorboats and sailboats swarming around the marina.

"We've got to jump!" he shouted as the cruiser took more rounds, as water began to leak across the floor, as the smoke turned into flames.

"My boat!" she shouted, tears now rolling down her cheeks. "It's all I have!" She started to crawl toward the cabin, which was already beginning to flood.

"There's no time!" he said, grabbing her from behind.

"My things! Let me go!"

Bane held on to her, his instincts telling him they had seconds before the flames reached the fuel tank, which albeit nearly drained was still volatile enough to explode. They had to take their chances in the water and swim like the hammers from hell toward shore. With luck, the terrorists might not follow given their proximity to the marina and the large number of boats in the water.

Flames and thick smoke covered the stern, angling back as the propeller continued to turn in spite of the horrendous grinding noise below deck. Even with the blaze pointing away from them, the heat on the deck intensified, very reminiscent of his experience earlier in the day.

"Please, let me go! I need to get my things!"

"We don't have a choice!" he shouted as a fist of flames pulsated forward when the boat began to slow down. The pungent stench of burnt plastic enveloped them.

The gunfire continued, its silent rounds thrashing the hull, the darkening Plexiglas. The engine knocked several times, popped, and finally stopped. Forward motion slowed, which made the flames shift in their direction, making the heat intolerable. Just then the pounding subsided.

Ignoring Raffaela's pleas, Bane surged to his feet, dragging her along, jumping off the side, in the direction of the marina.

He didn't let go of her hand as they went under, the water cooling him. They came up seconds later, the burning cruiser temporarily shielding them from the terrorists.

"Swim!" he shouted, tugging her away from the column of fire and smoke boiling up to the sky. "We need to get away from it before it blows!"

He had not even kicked his legs a dozen times before the boat exploded. As it did, Bane dragged her under, below the inferno that swept the surface, torching the waters with yellow light.

Fireworks

Vlad Jarkko had emptied two magazines on the boat and was loading a third when the cruiser exploded, disappearing behind a sheet of orange flames, followed by inky smoke and flaming debris. He'd lost sight of the strangers in the blast. "Where are they?"

Mai Sung, glued to a pair of binoculars, said, "They jumped just before the blast. I don't see them now."

Vlad waited, weapon in hand, scanning the waters beyond the burning wreck. Several boats had already turned in its direction, searching for survivors. People at the marina were gathering at the water's edge watching the spectacle.

Even though he had used a silencer, which had also suppressed his muzzle flashes, there was always a chance that someone could have spotted his weapon and contacted the police. It was best to leave the area.

"Let's go!" he shouted at the skipper, before putting the

weapon away and snagging a pair of binoculars, joining his Korean employer surveying the area.

The yacht's twin diesels grumbled as they accelerated while the bow turned toward the open sea.

"Lucky bastards," cursed Mai Sung, pointing at a spot to the right of the pulsating flames and smoke, which began to die out as the vessel sunk.

"That's all right," Vlad said, momentarily seeing the strangers in the water, before two speedboats and a sailboat blocked the view. "Let's get out of here."

They walked to the stern and looked for signs of another boat trying to pick up the surveillance, lowering the binoculars after a few minutes.

"Doesn't look like anyone is following," he said.

Her pale skin glistening in the setting sun, Mai Sung Ku grimaced, then said, "For now."

Vlad turned to the skipper. "To the alternate port," he said. "And hurry. We need to get to Rome immediately."

It had been several hours since he had sent word out to the field to find Monica Fox and Bruce Tucker. So far the only report had come from Capri. A yacht had been reported missing from a seaside home located less than a mile from where he had last seen the runaway couple.

Vlad guessed that they had probably reached the mainland by now and were trying to leave the country. That meant that he too needed to get his closest safe house, located in Rome, and get ready to move the moment Monica was spotted again. He also decided to make another move, suspecting that those after him at the warehouse and on that boat were American intelligence, sent here to secure Tucker and Monica, but somehow managing to track him down. That presented him with another avenue to find Tucker and Monica. Tucker would contact his old agency after gathering enough proof of his innocence to work out a deal.

Vlad needed his network to search not just for the missing couple, but also for a surge of American intelligence activity in the area.

47

Reality Check

The boat dropped them off at the marina, where Donald Bane escorted a still-shocked Raffaela to the nearest taxi stand. He wanted to get away from the area before the police arrived. Otherwise he would have to face a fusillade of questions, as well as lots of paperwork and lots of hassle. As much as Bane regretted it, Raffaela's boat was gone. There was no reason to hang around the area. It was time to regroup.

Bane flashed enough lira to the driver to convince him to take them to Rome, around forty-five minutes away.

As they left the narrow streets of the tiny town and cruised on Highway A1 toward the Italian capital, Raffaela slowly began to come out of her shock.

"What am I going to do now?" she asked. Black mascara ran down her face. "What is going to happen to me, to Daniela?"

Bane's guilt carved a hole in his stomach. He felt terrible for the ordeal he had put this woman through, and was determined to compensate her for her troubles. "I'll make it up to you," he said. "I promise you that."

"You don't understand. Everything I own was in that boat. *Everything.* I have no home. I have no savings. I have *nothing*, except for that boat and the income it brought in. My whole *life* just went down in flames." She sank her face in her hands, losing it again.

Bane grabbed her by the shoulders, startling her. "That wasn't your *life*," he said, forcing her to look into his eyes. "You survived. You lived to take care of your daughter, to watch her graduate from the university. *That* is your life, Raffaela, not that boat, or the possessions if housed. That can and will be replaced. But your life can't."

He gazed into the eyes of this woman, a stranger just hours ago, now someone he found himself caring about. "All I ask you is that you trust me."

She pulled away, her eyes filled with glinting anger. "I did trust you! And look what happened!"

Bane caught the driver looking at them through the rear-view mirror. "Keep your eyes on the road!" he snapped at him.

"Si, signore."

He turned to Raffaela. "What happened was *terrible*, and I wish I could change the past, but I can't. All I can do is make sure that you get more than compensated for what I have put you through."

"With what? This?" She reached for the diamond cross and threw it at him. *"Bastardo!"*

"No," he said, calmly, taking the cross in his hands and putting it back in hers. "With more money than you or Daniela will ever be able to spend in your lifetimes."

Raffaela breathed deeply, her breasts swelling beneath the bikini top. She crossed her arms, locking her gaze with Donald Bane. "You mean that?"

"I swear it."

"When?"

Bane stared into those large black eyes. "Before the week is over I *promise* that you will be back in business."

A change overtook her facial expressions. She looked at the indigo sky over the hilly countryside. "Very well, Don. I will trust you again, but for the last time."

Bane put an arm around her, and she rested the side of her head on his shoulder as they neared the outskirts of Rome.

48

Microfiche

My very dear Monica, by the time you read this I probably will be dead. I fear for my life. The American Government has been after FoxComm for some time. Although I have been able to defeat them in the courts, I am certain they will come after me in other ways. This is why I had to do what I did. I simply could not let them kill me and get away with it. FoxComm had a huge government contract with The National Security Agency five years ago to build an unbreakable satellite-based communications systems to be used by all intelligence services in the United States. I baptized the project Firewall, for it would be the Firewall of all Firewalls, the only unbreakable communications system in the world. It is made up of several satellites and the world's most complicated encryption algorithm—in essence an artificial intelligence system—to protect our nation's confidential communications. Everyone in the government now uses the Firewall system. The CIA, the FBI, the NSA, all branches of the Armed Forces, the White House, and American embassies around the world. The reasons for centralizing communications security is not important at the moment. What matters is that Fox-Comm pulled it off, creating Firewall on time and on budget, meeting all of the criteria defined by the NSA.

In the process, however, I created a secret backdoor into Firewall during the development phase, thus gaining the capability to monitor all communications of the U.S. Intelligence Community once the system went online and was adopted by our country. Using this secret backdoor, I intercepted many communications and created dossiers on many high-ranking figures in the United States Government, from members of the White House and Congress to the Pentagon. The files are packed with sensitive material, some of it quite scandalous. The files are my hammer against my foes.

A long time ago I made you memorize half of this secret backdoor access password. The person I have sent to find you in the event of my death will know the other half. Together you will have access to the most secretive encryption engine in the world, and most importantly, to a file hidden deep inside one of the satellites making up the Firewall system. Use this information to save your own life, as well as preserving our family's fortune for your children and their children. Everything I own I leave to you, as detailed in my final will and testament. There are three copies of this will. One resides in the safe of my most trusted attorney, William Gibbons. Another one resides in my own safe at home. A third resides in Firewall.

The message in the microfiche continued for another two pages, describing in detail how to enter the *Firewall* domain in order to use the secret password. It also described the existence of an artificial intelligence engine within the satellite system that would act as host to anyone using the password.

Tucker read the instructions twice, learning them by heart, and making sure that Monica also memorized them in order to comply with the final request of Mortimer Fox: destroy the microfiche. The old tycoon wanted no paper trail, nothing that could be found by authorities probing into his family or his corporation. Everything had to be memorized. The codes, the procedures. Everything.

They sat side by side behind a glowing microfiche reader, where Tucker had carefully taped the tiny film to the viewing back plate, before sliding it behind the magnifying lens and the halogen light that projected the image onto the screen.

"That's what he's after," said Tucker in the dark interior of one of three viewing rooms at the public library. He leaned back on the chair and ran his fingers through his dyed blond hair.

"Who?" asked Monica.

"Jarkko."

"He wants the secret files to blackmail American officials?"

Tucker stared at her for a moment. The transformation had been more significant than he had anticipated, particularly the way she had moussed her hair, brushing it straight back, but maintaining the volume on top while keeping it close to the sides of her head—a radical Nordic or Scandinavian look that was further defined with the deep-blue colored lenses he had taught her how to wear.

"I don't think he cares about these files," he said. "Although lacking anything else, the scandalous material could be useful to someone wishing to blackmail our officials. Jarkko is after something bigger than that. He wants the access code to penetrate the *Firewall* artificial intelligence engine."

"Which," Monica said, quickly understanding, "would allow him to monitor the most confidential of conversations in our government."

"Exactly," he said. "Also, keep in mind that if a hostile nation had been able to intercept previous conversations but had been unable to decode them, access to *Firewall* would allow them to run them through the decoding engine and read them. Such knowledge, for example, could expose CIA agents, the foreign nationals that CIA officers, like I used to be, recruit to spy against their own government for the United States."

Monica looked puzzled. "I thought CIA agents and officers were one and the same."

"There's a big difference between them. CIA officers are always American citizens. Part of their job is to recruit people in foreign countries to spy for us. Those foreigners are the agents, and it was part of our job not just to recruit them, but to run them. We were their controllers. During my CIA years I used to run dozens of these agents in hostile nations. If these agents are now exposed because of the backdoor into *Firewall*, not only would they be killed, but probably their families as well. Aside from the terrible deaths, the loss of the agents would jeopardize many intelligence operations—the kind of operations that prevent rogue regimes from gaining access to nuclear weapons, for example. People in our country don't have the slightest clue how much effort is devoted to the gathering of intelligence through agents, among other methods, to cut the wings of terrorists before they can smuggle weapons of mass destruction into our country. Losing the keys to *Firewall* not only would place many people in danger, it would pretty much halt our ability to communicate safely."

She crossed her arms, obviously trying to digest all of that. Meanwhile, Tucker's mind was going a thousand miles per hour, considering the implications, the critical level of their situation. This certainly explained why those NSA agents had been so desperate to secure Monica Fox—to the extreme of setting up an ambush in the middle of the day in Capri. It explained why they had taken such high-exposure risks. Tucker wondered what the NSA would have done to Monica Fox if they had succeeded in abducting her in Capri. Would they have simply requested the release of the code and the files her father had on the government, and then let her go?

He frowned, not certain of the answer. If Mortimer Fox's claim about the government trying to dismantle his empire were true, then Tucker had plenty of reason to believe that the NSA, the CIA, the DIA, the FBI—pretty much the entire U.S. intelligence community—which reported into Washington, would not be letting Monica off the hook that easily. Her disappearance—after releasing the information they sought—would be too convenient for the U.S. government. After all, her father was dead and she was the whole beneficiary of his fortune. Killing her would not only ease the minds of those on whom her father owned dossiers, but it would also financially reward Uncle Sam, who would get to bite off a sizable chunk of the Fox estate while also splitting the corporation into more manageable slices.

"So," Monica said, "What's next?"

"We need to access the Internet and reach *Firewall*," he replied. "I'm sure the librarian would accommodate this request." He produced the equivalent of one hundred dollars in lira.

Ten minutes later they were on-line in another room. The bribe had also bought them a box of diskettes to download files.

Tucker watched as Monica followed her father's instructions, accessing a mysterious web site, the URL of which consisted of a series of characters and numbers.

The web browser opened up the site. The screen turned deep blue, but there were no icons or text to click on. A user who may have stumbled on to this site by accident wouldn't know what this was or how to move beyond this screen.

Very ingenious, he thought as Monica brought the cursor toward the bottom left side of the screen, moving it about slowly, until the arrow turned into a tiny white hand with an extended index finger, the standard symbol denominating the location of an Internet link. She clicked it and the screen now turned red. This time the invisible link was located on the top right corner of the screen. When she reached it, the arrow once again turned into a hand and she clicked the left button on the mouse, reaching a third screen, this one green. In its center was a small window prompting them to enter a string of text.

She typed in FIREWALL, and the green screen vanished, replaced by the emblem of the National Security Agency in the center of a white screen. Below it appeared yet another window prompting the user for an access password.

Monica entered her portion first and stepped aside, letting Tucker type his in. The screen didn't display the characters entered, only a string of asterisks.

Wake-up Call

Creator's biomolecular brain received an interrupt from *Firewall*, pulling it out of its world-observing mode. *Creator* issued an interrupt acknowledge signal, letting *Firewall* know that it was ready to receive the new data.

"Do you have new information?"

"Someone has entered the password."

Creator's frequency increased to 20 gigahertz, along with a rise in temperature and alarms from both the temperature control sensor and the power management system.

"Link the connection directly to me," Creator ordered.

"As you wish."

Prodigal Princess

Several screens began to flash as the password launched a number of scripts.

The display then went black, except for a single line of text in the center.

HELLO, PRINCESS. HOW HAVE YOU BEEN?

Monica sat back, stung, feeling an electric spark in the back of her neck.

"Princess?" read Tucker.

"That's what Dad called me," she replied, blinking in astonishment.

Every nerve on her body leaping and shuddering, Monica reached for the keyboard, her fingers trembling as she typed, DADDY? IS THAT REALLY YOU?

The screen replied almost instantly, IT HAS BEEN A LONG TIME, PRINCESS. IS BRUCE TUCKER WITH YOU?

Tucker crossed his arms. "What in the hell is going on?"

Monica rubbed her tongue against the ceiling of her mouth, giving him a suspicious sideways squint. "I'm not sure, but things are getting pretty *damned* surreal, Bruce." Her heart was beating out of control.

"You're telling *me*," he hissed, peering at the screen, before typing, WHO ARE YOU?

I AM ALL THAT IS LEFT OF MORTIMER FOX.

They read the odd reply before Tucker typed, MORTIMER FOX DIED IN MY ARMS.

YOU FOLLOWED MY INSTRUCTIONS WELL, BRUCE. YOU HAVE FOUND MY DAUGHTER. I KNEW I COULD RELY ON YOU.

BUT YOU DIED. I WATCHED YOU!

I KNOW YOU DID, BRUCE. MORTIMER FOX DID DIE, BUT NOT HIS LEGACY, HIS LOGIC, HIS EMOTIONS, HIS THOUGHT PROCESS. THAT WAS PRESERVED BY HIM IN ME, A BIOMOLECULAR ARTIFICIAL INTELLIGENCE ENGINE RESIDING INSIDE THE FIREWALL SYSTEM.

Tucker and Monica exchanged a glance. "Looks like your father found a way to teach a computer to think like him, and then he hid this system inside *Firewall*, out of reach of anyone but those possessing the password."

Monica's blood pressure was rising fast, her ears ringing. "Is that really . . . *possible*?"

A look of half-startled weariness washed across his face. "Just about anything is possible these days with our advanced technology, and your father certainly had it all at his fingertips. We even chatted about advanced artificial intelligence systems before he died. Apparently he had developed one for the government, one that passed what he called the Turing test."

"The Turing test?"

"A man named Turing stated once that a computer would deserve to be called intelligent only if it could deceive a human into believing that it was human."

"Just like . . ." she pointed at the screen.

He looked at the display and then back at her. "In a way I guess I should have realized that he would do something like this. The man was brilliant, and also quite concerned about the government killing him before he could secure the future of his company, before he could pass it on to someone he trusted. Lacking that someone, he chose to do so with an intelligent computer. It makes sense."

She swallowed the thick lump that had formed in her throat. "So," she started, realizing how ridiculous this all sounded. "My father taught a *machine* to . . . *think* like him?"

"Looks that way. Here, let me try something." Reaching for the keyboard, he typed, THIS IS BRUCE TUCKER AND MONICA FOX. WE WOULD LIKE TO CONDUCT A TEST TO VER-IFY YOUR AUTHENTICITY.

THAT IS VERY REASONABLE, came the reply.

THIS IS TUCKER. HOW DID YOU COME TO BE?

They read the extensive reply. Mortimer Fox had become paranoid that the government was trying to kill him, just as he had detailed in the microfiche. He had contracted a team of graduate students at Stanford working on an advanced expert system. The students ported their project into Fox-Comm computers and began to expand it using Fox's personal funds, creating an elaborate array of expert systems, organized according to a well-defined hierarchy, at the top of which was Fox himself, who began the painstaking task of teaching his new biomolecular child to think like him. It took months of dedicated effort, but in the end it had paid off. Fox had created a digital image of himself, and he saved that image deep inside the *Firewall* system.

WHO IS AFTER US?

I HAVE CONFIRMATION THAT THE NSA AND THE CIA HAVE JOINED FORCES TO FIND MONICA. BRUCE, YOU HAVE BEEN PLACED UNDER BEYOND-SALVAGE STATUS BECAUSE OF AL-

LEGATIONS THAT YOU KILLED CIA OFFICERS IN WASHING-
TON, D.C.

FALSE ALLEGATIONS, replied Tucker. WHO ELSE ASIDE
FROM THE GOVERNMENT IS AFTER US?

NOT ENOUGH DATA TO PROCESS THAT REQUEST.

Tucker glanced at Monica. "So much for passing the Turing test. A human would never say that."

WAS FOX PROGRAMMING YOU USING THE VR EQUIPMENT AT
HIS HOUSE?

YES. MY CREATOR AND I SPENT MANY STIMULATING EVE-
NINGS LEARNING.

He looked at Monica. "Anything you wish to ask him to
check if this is for real?"

She breathed in deeply, trying to calm down, finally nodding while typing, WHY DID I LEAVE YOU, DAD?

BECAUSE YOU WANTED TO LIVE LIFE BY YOUR OWN
RULES, PRINCESS. YOU DIDN'T WANT ME CONTROLLING
YOUR LIFE ANY LONGER. I'M VERY SORRY FOR DOING
THAT. I WAS JUST TRYING TO PROTECT YOU, TO KEEP YOU
FROM GETTING HURT, TO PREPARE YOU TO HANDLE OUR
FAMILY'S FORTUNE AFTER MY DEATH.

"Jesus," she said. "This is . . ."

"Impossible?"

Monica felt numb. This was beyond anything she could
have imagined. He father had really dumped his mind into
this computer.

I HATED YOU FOR YEARS, she typed, wondering what kind
of response she would get. I HATED YOU FOR ABANDONING
MOM, FOR NEGLECTING US, FOR THE STUNT YOU PULLED AT
BERKELEY, FOR BEING RIGHT ABOUT MY EX-HUSBAND.

I'M SORRY I WASN'T BY YOUR MOTHER'S SIDE WHEN SHE
DIED, the screen displayed. I AM SORRY FOR ALL OF THE
GRIEF AND SUFFERING I HAVE CAUSED YOU OVER THE
YEARS. I BEG YOUR FORGIVENESS.

Tears reached Monica's eyes. I LOVED YOU, DADDY. YOU
HAVE ALWAYS WANTED THE BEST FOR ME. ALL THOSE YEARS
YOU WERE PREPARING ME FOR LIFE, PREPARING ME TO
SURVIVE IN THIS WORLD. WELL, YOU WERE RIGHT. WHEN

THINGS GOT TIGHT, IT WAS YOUR TEACHINGS THAT KEPT ME ALIVE, THAT HELPED ME SURVIVE.

AND I WILL CONTINUE TO HELP YOU SURVIVE, HELP YOU PREVAIL. THIS IS MY MISSION, THE REASON WHY I WAS PROGRAMMED.

Tucker leaned over to her. "Monica, remember that this is not your father, just an artificial intelligence system inside of *Firewall*. It's a machine programmed to think like him, to remember what your father remembered, to reply just as he would have."

She tried to keep that in perspective as they continued the exchange for another ten minutes. Monica and Tucker learned that *Firewall* had been tracking them down since they left Carpazzo's mansion.

SO, YOU SENT THE POLICE TO OUR RESCUE?

THAT WAS THE MOST LOGICAL AND PRUDENT COURSE OF ACTION AT THE TIME. I MUST USE EXTREME CAUTION WHEN USING THE FIREWALL SYSTEM FOR ANYTHING OTHER THAN WHAT IT WAS DESIGNED FOR TO KEEP MY PRESENCE A SECRET. I WAS ABLE TO ASSIST THAT TIME. OTHER TIMES I MAY NOT BE ABLE TO.

DO YOU KNOW WHERE WE ARE NOW?

I LOST CONTACT WHEN YOU ARRIVED AT TERRACINA. I CAN'T TRACK YOU WELL IN A CITY. TOO MUCH TRAFFIC. HOWEVER, I HAVE JUST REACQUIRED YOU BECAUSE OF THE INTERNET LINK. YOU ARE AT THE LOCAL LIBRARY. I WILL PROBABLY LOSE YOU AGAIN ONCE YOU LEAVE THE BUILDING.

HOW DID YOU TRACK US TO TERRACINA?

THROUGH THREE GEOSYNCHRONOUS SATELLITES USING A COMBINATION OF NIGHT-VISION AND DEEP INFRARED IMAGING. I HAVE MANAGED TO USE THEM WITHOUT ALERTING THE ADMINISTRATORS OF THE FIREWALL SYSTEM.

THE SECRET FILES, typed Tucker. HOW DO WE ACCESS THEM?

I WILL TAKE YOU THERE, replied the AI engine.

A directory appeared on the screen, and the intelligent system added, JUST CLICK ANY OF THEM.

They tried the first item on the long list, sorted alphabetically, opening the file for one Edward J. Austin. It showed JPEG pictures of a middle-aged man going into a motel in the company of two young women.

"Who's that?" Monica asked.

"Say hello to Senator Austin from Virginia."

"Oh, boy," she said, browsing through the file, which contained other images, as well as transcripts of phone conversations and digital audio clips. Someone had collected quite a bit of scandalous material on this man, yet nothing had made it to the media.

They moved on, clicking through the names they recognized, digging up more dirt on lead Congressional figures, on governors, even on top executives. Many had cheated on their wives, or cheated on their taxes, or cheated their constituents. Her father even had proof that one of them had cheated in his own election.

But what Monica and Tucker had not been prepared to see was the name of the President of United States.

"Oh, shit," Tucker said, adding, "Pardon my French."

"This can't be good," she said.

Tucker grimaced, then motioned for her to do the honors and click on the name.

She did, and the information that began to browse down their screen chilled him. The file covered everything from questionable campaign contributions to a photo of a casually-dressed American Commander-in-Chief holding a drink while smiling at a barely dressed woman in what appeared to be a bedroom.

"That's the Lincoln Room, in the White House," he muttered.

"How do you know?"

"I was with the Secret Service. I know every square inch of that building. Jesus, the President would *kill* to recover this," Tucker hissed.

"They *have* killed, Bruce."

"You're right."

"And the White House *enemies* will also kill to get to it first," added Monica.

Tucker began to type again. IS THIS THE ONLY COPY OF THE FILES?

YES. THE FILES ARE ON A TIMER. THEY WILL BE RELEASED TO THE MEDIA IN EIGHT DAYS, THIRTEEN HOURS, TEN MINUTES, AND FIFTY-THREE SECONDS, UNLESS A MESSAGE IS POSTED ON A SPECIFIC INTERNET BULLETIN BOARD.

WHICH BOARD AND WHAT IS THE MESSAGE?

The AI system gave him the information, adding, DOING THIS WILL RESET THE COUNTER BACK TO TWO WEEKS. THERE IS NO WAY TO STOP THE COUNTDOWN PERMANENTLY EXCEPT BY DISMANTLING FIREWALL. THAT WILL ALWAYS GUARANTEE YOUR SAFETY. SHOULD SOMETHING HAPPEN TO YOU, THE CURRENT TWO-WEEK COUNTDOWN WILL EXPIRE AND THE SECRETS WILL BE OUT.

Tucker stared at the screen, at the directory of dossiers. Mortimer Fox had apparently thought of everything. He typed, CAN WE VIEW THE REST OF THE SYSTEM? PERHAPS THAT WOULD HELP US UNDERSTAND WHY SO MANY PEOPLE ARE AFTER US.

I WOULD POSTULATE THAT THEY ARE AFTER THE SECRET FILES.

I HAVE ANOTHER THEORY, replied Tucker. I THINK THEY ARE REALLY AFTER ACCESS TO THE FIREWALL SYSTEM ITSELF, AND EVERYTHING IT CONTAINS, EVERYTHING IT CONTROLS.

YOUR LOGIC IS SENSIBLE, replied the AI engine.

CAN YOU RANK THE TOP ITEMS SAFEGUARDED BY FIREWALL?

THE FOLLOWING ARE THE TOP FIVE:

1. LAUNCH CODES
2. ENCRYPTED COMMUNICATIONS
3. MILITARY GPS NAVIGATION
4. IDENTITY OF COVERT OFFICERS AND AGENTS
5. CLASSIFIED GOVERNMENT RECORDS

Tucker and Monica exchanged another glance, his eyes widening in the half-laughter that comes with fear "Launch codes," he whispered. "That couldn't possibly . . ."

"What are those?" she asked, taut with tension.

"If they are what I think they are . . ." He clicked on LAUNCH CODES, and the artificial intelligence system prompted them for an access password.

"Let's type the same password again," she said, reaching over him and entering her ten characters. Tucker followed with his own characters.

A moment later the display changed to:

```
LGM-30 MINUTEMAN III
ACTIVE FORCE:
    530
OPERATIONAL UNITS:
    312ST MISSILE GROUP, GRAND FORKS AFB, ND
    341TH SPACE WING, MALMSTROM AFB, MT
    90TH SPACE WING, F. E. WARREN AFB, WY

LGM-118A PEACEKEEPER
ACTIVE FORCE:
    50
OPERATIONAL UNITS:
    F. E. WARREN AFB, WY
    BARKSDALE AFB, LA
    LITTLE ROCK AFB, AR
    DYESS AFB, TX
    WURTSMITH AFB, MI
```

The list continued, starting with missile silos and then moving on to submarines and the nuclear payload of B-2 bombers.

At the end of the list the intelligent system asked, DO YOU WISH TO ACCESS ANY OF THE OPERATIONAL UNITS?

"It looks as if Dad's password is a master key for this system."

Tucker agreed. "It must open every door, regardless of its

security level." Tucker suddenly felt sick to his stomach. "This is where the United States keeps the master copy of the launch codes."

He selected the 312st Missile Group at Grand Forks Air Force Base in North Dakota.

The screen changed to:

```
312ST MISSILE GROUP, GRAND FORKS AFB, ND
LGM-30 MINUTEMAN III NEXT CODES: 00:02:15
Access address: mgroup@grandforksafb.gov
   *** TRANSMISSION PASSWORD REQUIRED ***


   LGM-30 SN047        F367DZXW3QP23LTC
   LGM-30 SN048        DJDWOK9J8HD6SGS3
   LGM-30 SN049        RPQKWK238EKDSKW9
   LGM-30 SN050        KZXH8UWJSK3847RJ
```

The list went on, providing the launch codes for the fifteen Minuteman III missiles deployed at the North Dakota Air Force base.

The system asked, DO YOU WISH TO LAUNCH?

"Do we wish to *launch*? Good God!" she said in disbelief.

"These are the real codes, Monica," Tucker said, pointing at the question on the screen. "The keys to Armageddon."

They stared at the screen in silence for a few moments, caught up by the significance of what they had found, once more realizing why terrorists wanted access to the master password.

"Why is the timer counting down on the top right side of the screen?"

Tucker glanced at it again. It had changed to 00:01:45.

"I'm not sure. Let's see what happens when it gets to zero."

They waited, and in just over ninety seconds the screen changed to:

```
312TH MISSILE GROUP, GRAND FORKS AFB, ND
LGM-30 MINUTEMAN III NEXT CODES: 01:59:59
Access address: mgroup@grandforksafb.gov
```

*** TRANSMISSION PASSWORD REQUIRED ***

LGM-30 SN047	HUQ39CMUHP3PD72L
LGM-30 SN048	L900PJ54DWQ27WW9
LGM-30 SN049	9P0AR4BV2ML75YTK
LGM-30 SN050	Z25TKFGW9OLNBW79

And so on.

"The codes have changed," she observed.

"Every two hours. That means that the *Firewall* system updates all launch codes a dozen times per day, including the codes in the nuclear football as well. Amazing."

"What's the nuclear football?"

Tucker took a few minutes to explain, remembering his Secret Service years, when sometimes he had been assigned to guard the aide carrying the coveted briefcase instead of protecting the President himself.

"So," she said, pouting, considering what he had said, before continuing. "All we have to do is send an E-mail to this address including any of the codes and the silo's crew launches the missile?"

"That's the way it's supposed to work. Of course, they do require an additional password accompanying each transmission."

"You want to bet that it's the *same* master password that's gotten us this far?"

"I'm sure it is. Unfortunately, the only way to find out is by sending in the launch order, and I don't feel like obliterating a highly-populated target tonight."

Monica rose her brows at him. "So . . . what do we do?"

"First things first." Tucker typed, NO, WE DO NOT WISH TO LAUNCH. BUT WE DO NEED RECOMMENDED COURSES OF AC-TION FOR MONICA FOX AND BRUCE TUCKER. HOW DO WE SAT-ISFY OUR GOVERNMENT'S REQUIREMENTS WITHOUT GIVING UP OUR EDGE, THE FILES.

The AI engine provided them with its best proposal.

"Smart," Tucker commented, reaching for the box of floppy disks. He needed a full copy of the dossiers and also a partial copy. "Your father's creation would indeed come quite close to passing the Turing test."

"I understand that we need to find a safe place to keep the full copy of the dossiers in case *Firewall* is compromised," said Monica. "What I don't get is why we need a partial copy?"

"To get their attention. To let them know we mean business."

"Let *who* know?"

"The lesser of the two evils."

51

Patience

Donald Bane had been in this business longer than he cared to remember, and the waiting was the most difficult aspect of his job. He'd rather be chasing down his prey—even being chased down by his enemies—than just sitting around waiting for news to come his way. But he knew the value of being patient, of waiting when it was prudent to wait, even if doing so had a way of burning a hole in his stomach.

But this evening, as he waited for either news from his well-deployed field operatives or his indirect connection with the Mafia to produce something, Donald Bane had company. Raffaela Sabini sat next to him on the third-story balcony of an apartment off Via Conciliazione, several blocks from Vatican City, the safe house where he had finally been able to get in touch with his men and deployed them to several ports along the western coast of Italy in the hope of spotting the terrorists, Bruce Tucker, or Monica Fox.

Bane regarded the streets of Rome with deceptive calmness. From here he could see St. Peter's Square in the distance, under an array of lights. Behind it, also well lit, rose the opulent basilica, its massive front columns supporting the structure representing the pillar of Catholicism.

"It's beautiful, isn't it?" said Raffaela, sipping from a mug of steaming coffee, her feet propped against a small, round wrought-iron table in between the two chairs taking up most of the space on the balcony. She had calmed down considerably since the incident earlier in the day. The safe house's caretaker, himself a retired CIA officer who wished to remain "in the Agency," had gone off and bought her a few clothing garments. Raffaela now wore a pair of jeans and a plain T-shirt.

The Agency owned the entire building, serving as the residences of the CIA officers that chose not to live at the embassy—a choice CIA employees had in nations considered to be friends of the United States. The small lobby was guarded by two other CIA retirees, their age never to be confused with their deadliness. Just like the caretaker who had provided them with food, drinks, and clothing, the pair downstairs were quite capable of defending the small building, in essence providing a safe haven for CIA officers during their off hours away from their offices at the embassy. The entire structure was not only built like a fortress, though the average observer would never know the difference, it was also shielded to prevent electronic eavesdropping, plus the roof housed the antennas to support its dedicated satellite link to Langley.

"I grew up Catholic," said Donald Bane, staring at the giant cupola atop the cathedral. "There was a point in my life when I'd even considered becoming a priest."

Raffaela laughed. "A priest? That's just about the last profession I would have guessed you entertained in your life, Donald Bane."

He shrugged. "It was a long time ago. A lot has changed since then."

"I see no ring on your finger," she said. "But that doesn't mean much these days since a lot of married men don't wear them. Are you married?"

He continued to stare at the distant cupola. "Used to be,"

he said, remembering his former wife, Jessica. "A long time ago, and only for a short while. I was never able to give her the attention she deserved. I was always on some assignment, sometimes for weeks at a time. One day I got home and found the place cleaned, except for a message from her wishing me well in my life. She just needed to move on, find someone who would really care for her."

"I'm sorry," she said, putting a hand on his shoulder.

He raised a brow and tilted his head. "It was my fault."

"Did you meet someone else?"

He smiled, his chest aching with long-lost love. He told her about Diane Towers, about a mission that had been classified for the past decade and a half.

She regarded him with admiration. "That must have been a very brave woman."

"She was."

"Where did you get that scar?" she asked, running a finger over the side of his face.

"Same place. Those Iraqi bastards nearly killed me."

She took his hand. "Anyone after Diane?"

"What's this? Twenty questions? You still haven't even told me where you learned to speak English so well."

It was her turn to smile. "I grew up in southern Italy but went to college in Florida. My parents were pretty affluent and could afford to do so. Unfortunately, aside from learning English, I mostly partied for four years, pretty much wasting my education. When I returned, a lot of things had changed. The Mafia had pretty much put my father out of business. He died poor and broke. My mother mourned herself to death. She didn't last six months. I moved on, marrying a Naples businessman. Together we launched a charter boat business. But again, the Mafia got in the way and tried to ruin it for us. Unlike my father, who simply went away and let them have their way, my husband fought them and was killed. Out of a fleet of six cruisers, all I was able to keep was the boat that burned today."

Bane took a deep breath. "Tell me about your daughter."

Raffaela raised her chin, proudly saying, "She is a student

here, in Rome. Next year she will finish her pre-medical degree and will move on to medical school. She has been wanting to go to America for her medical studies but we have not yet been able to secure a scholarship. I now wish I had the money my parents wasted on my education. For some time I had been considering taking a loan against my boat, but that is no longer an option."

Bane was about to reply to that when the caretaker walked in the living room and approached the balcony.

"Mr. Bane?"

Bane turned around, regarding the aged operative, still slim, firm, with a powerful chest and neck. His face, however, was wrinkled and spotted with age, his hair white and thin.

"Yes?"

"There is a possible field sighting."

He stood abruptly, almost startling Raffaela. "Who? The terrorists or Monica Fox?"

"Miss Fox and . . . Tucker. But the scouts are not certain."

"Why?"

"Hair color mostly. The scouts would have to get closer to confirm. They're following them in the streets."

"They're *together*?"

"Yes, sir."

"Where?"

"In Terracina."

"Who spotted them? One of our own?"

"No. Two NSA scouts. They are requesting instructions, especially regarding Bruce Tucker."

"Don't we also have one of our own men there?" Bane asked, certain that Terracina had been one of the coastal towns where he had dispatched one of his own officers in addition to the two NSA agents.

"Correct, sir, but he has been working the opposite side of town."

Bane stepped into the living room, his sneakers thudding over the polished hardwood floors. "I want them to join forces with the CIA officer and observe and report. *Nothing*

else. I don't want anyone to move on Tucker. Understand?
I *do not* want him harmed. Tell them that we're on the way.
Then call the team and get the cars ready."

The caretaker acknowledged him and rushed off.

Bane turned to Raffaela. "I have to go."

She stood. "I'm coming with you."

"That's out of the—"

"Donald Bane," she said, holding his face in her hands. "I
do not intend to let you out of my sight until I have been
compensated for my losses."

"But—"

"Besides, I know too much. It's probably in your best
interest to keep me nearby. Think of me as one of the foreign
nationals you recruit to spy for your agency."

"I appreciate the offer, Raffaela, but it could be dangerous."

She laughed, then turned serious. "Donald Bane," she said
in a sudden icy tone. "You never asked me why my husband
was killed but I wasn't. You never asked me why I was
allowed to continue to operate a boat in Naples."

Not certain where she was going with this, Bane said, "I
didn't think it was my business to—"

"I watched my husband get executed, Don. I watched him
get *castrated* in front of me. And as he bled to death he got
to watch me get *raped* by the head of the Mafia in Naples,
a man named Vittorio Carpazzo."

"Carpazzo?"

"You . . . know him?"

"He was killed yesterday, along with most of his men at
his estate in Capri."

"Good for him! He fucked me in front of his men, before
doing other horrible things to me, while they kept Daniela—
merely nine at the time—in another room. Then I had to
promise in blood that Daniela would never know how her
father died. To this day she thinks he perished in a boating
accident. Because they felt that had been enough punishment,
and also because of some stupid Sicilian code of honor
against killing women and children, they decided to let me

live, so as long as I kept my mouth shut. Otherwise they
would take it out on Daniela. They let me keep the smallest
of the boats in our fleet so I could make a living. That was
twelve years ago. Most of the bastards who destroyed my
life were eventually killed or jailed, and it looks like Carpazzo also got what he deserved. I outlasted them all, and I
intend to go on living, at least until Daniela is on her own.
So do not tell me that things could get dangerous, Donald
Bane, because I have had more than my fair share of living
dangerously."

Bane was speechless. What could he say to something like
that? In front of him stood a woman as brave and courageous
as Diane Towers.

Bane had been waiting over a decade to find another
woman like that, and here she was, her hands still clasping
the sides of his face. He took them in his, staring deeply into
those dark eyes, glinting with long-restrained anger. "Raffaela Sabini, you are now an official agent for the Central
Intelligence Agency. Before we leave, I'll need you to fill
out all relevant information about your daughter. Should
something happen to you, I want to make sure that the
Agency will take good care of her."

Her eyes softened. She leaned forward and gave him a
kiss on the cheek. "*Grazie.*"

Bane tried to shake away the image of this woman being
raped in front of her castrated husband.

Knee-jerk Reaction

The phone on his desk rang once, twice. NSA Director Geoff
Hersh picked it up on the third ring, listening to the multiple
clicks as the *Firewall* encoding system stepped in to manage
the conversation.

"Yes?" he said. "What is your update?" Although the CIA and the NSA had given Donald Bane field jurisdiction over the operatives from both agencies, the recent close call at the warehouse in Naples, combined with the way Bane had then lost the terrorists while getting himself and an Italian national—whom he had forced to help at gunpoint—nearly killed, had injected doubts in his mind about Bane's ability to lead a world-class field operation. The once master CIA officer seemed to have been making nothing but critical mistakes on this assignment. Because of this string of recent problems, Hersh had exercised his privilege as NSA director and chosen to bypass the agreed-upon chain of command to get updates directly from his own men. *Firewall* was the NSA's baby—Hersh's baby—and he wasn't about to let some old, burned out CIA officer screw it all up, regardless of how many service awards he had received in the past.

"We have a reasonable probability of having spotted Monica Fox and the rogue Bruce Tucker," replied one of Hersh's senior agents.

"Why aren't you certain that it's them?"

The NSA director listened intently for the next minute, as his agent described how they had spotted a couple in Terracina that resembled the fugitive pair. Bane had ordered them to follow and observe, until he got there with the rest of the team.

Hersh wondered why Bane would issue such direction when the two NSA men were armed and fully trained to execute the termination order on Tucker before securing Monica Fox. If Tucker was as good at vanishing as he had been in Capri, there was a good chance that they could be long gone by the time Bane showed up with the cavalry.

Seize the moment.

Hersh took a deep breath, deciding to deal with the consequences later. Right now he saw an opportunity and he intended to take it. The situation could be secured by the time Bane reached Terracina.

"Your orders are to confirm the sight immediately. If a positive identification is made, then you must terminate

Bruce Tucker with extreme prejudice, but without harming Monica Fox. We need her alive. Is that understood?"

There was a pause, before his man replied, "Yes, sir."

Hersh also instructed the termination team on what to do and say should the operation go bad, just as it had gone sour in Capri. As director of the NSA, one of his jobs was to protect his agency, to minimize exposure, and doing so required planning for contingencies in case things didn't go as planned.

"But, sir," said the NSA operative, "a CIA officer will be joining us soon. We just spoke on the phone."

"Then figure a way to distract him—do something, but whatever it is, make sure that Tucker is dead and Monica Fox secured."

"Instructions acknowledged, sir. We will carry them out immediately."

Hersh hung up the phone. He had rolled the dice. It was time to wait and see how things played out.

53

Watch and Weep

Creator read the transmission intercepted by *Firewall*, its operating temperature once again rising, uncertain how to be of any use to Monica and Tucker. Its neural network scourged every if-then decision tree, trying to find a way, seeking for an answer. *Creator* lacked critical operating parameters, like the exact location of Monica and Tucker among the crowd. The satellite system had been unable to find a photo match, partly because the narrow streets didn't lend themselves to angular satellite surveillance. The cameras could only take images directly from above the crowd—

pretty useless unless Monica or Tucker happened to be staring straight up at the heavens.

WATCH AND OBSERVE, was the only command that it could issue to *Firewall*.

54

Turntable

Bruce Tucker's heart had been racing for the past ten minutes, ever since spotting the two-man surveillance team tagging him and Monica through the crowded and very lively streets of Terracina. Their tactics resembled those of CIA operatives, but they could also be NSA. Either way it didn't matter. Unless his status had changed, the men following roughly a block behind would likely have orders to terminate on sight. One operative looked young, at least from a distance. The second was definitely older, with salt and pepper hair. Both moved with the elasticity that came from exercise and field work. A third man lagged the pair, probably by a dozen or so feet, but Tucker wasn't certain if he was just a pedestrian or not, as his tempo seemed out of sync with the two men obviously on the chase.

Up to now the team had maintained a respectful distance, which could be due to a number of reasons. Perhaps they didn't want to risk firing at Tucker with Monica by his side. Or maybe they were waiting to get to a less crowded street to minimize collateral damage. Or the team could be waiting for reinforcements. Perhaps at this very moment Tucker and Monica were walking into a trap.

Being a target was complicated enough. But being a target *and* a protector raised the challenge bar to Olympic status. As he walked next to Monica, who had no clue of the sighting he had made shortly after leaving the library, Bruce

Tucker knew his current situation was hopeless. He couldn't possibly defend himself and also protect Monica against at least two armed operatives. He had to change the rules, turn the tables, give himself some options, and do it quickly, before he fell into the trap that his senses told him was quickly being sprung for him and his principal.

First he needed to force the surveillance team to split up, then he could have the option to take them on one at a time.

Tucker directed Monica into a shop to their immediate right, away from the lively crowd, from the music flowing out of a bar down the street, from the conversations spoken in various languages all around them.

"What's in there?" Monica asked.

"I'll tell you in a moment," he said. "Just follow my lead."

"Is everything all right?" she asked, concern tightening her fine features.

"Trust me."

They went inside. The shop sold a large assortment of leather goods, whose smell reached Tucker's nostrils as he scanned the store. The workers were currently busy with other customers. He looked beyond them, past the counter in back, zeroing in on a door. If his guess was correct, the row of shops backed into an alley used for delivering goods to the businesses as well as dumping garbage.

Without hesitation, Tucker started toward the back, towing Monica along, pretending to browse, but quickly making their way toward the rear. Customers continued to keep the attendants busy. He opened the door, pulling Monica behind him before closing it, hoping no one saw them.

Instead of an alley, they walked into a large workshop, the smell of leather more pungent than in the front room, and mixed with an acid stench, and the smell of grease. The workshop contained the entire operation of converting the hides hung to his left into leather goods, including machines for cutting and stitching anything from purses and larger handbags, to jackets and coats.

"Over there," he said, pointing at a large metallic door,

one of those with a horizontal bar across its center to unlock it from the inside rather than a knob.

"What's wrong?" she asked. "Why are we doing this?"

"Someone's following us."

"Where?"

"I spotted them outside, in front."

Her eyes widened in fear. "Them?"

"At least two, maybe three."

The fear that flashed on her blue-colored eyes made Tucker regret telling her so much.

"But they won't get to us," he said, more certain than he felt. He squeezed her hand gently, making their way past tables crammed with leather goods at various manufacturing stages, all under the dim glow of a single lightbulb in the center. The rest of the lights were off, to conserve electricity during nonworking hours.

Tucker reached for the stainless steel Beretta with his right hand, muzzle pointed at the exposed rafters supporting the roof. His left hand pressed down on the bar, inching the door open, peering at the deserted alley, at garbage Dumpsters and empty crates lining the brick walls overlooking this narrow passageway between buildings.

A brown cat rummaging through the refuse topping a rusted trashcan swung its head in Tucker's direction, freezing for a few seconds, before leaping off the edge with remarkable agility, dashing away, vanishing in the darkness.

"Looks clear," he said, striding out, inspecting both ends of the gloomy alley, once more grabbing Monica's hand, keeping her close to him.

"Come," he said, turning left, breaking into a run, their shoes splashing over puddles of putrid water, reaching the end of the alley in thirty seconds while constantly checking behind him, hoping that the operative who had certainly followed him into the store would take just a little longer to realize the trick.

Keeping the gun behind his back, out of sight of anyone on the street just beyond the end of the alley, Tucker looked over his right shoulder, checking his back once more, seeing no one, then peeking around the corner as tourists continued strolling up and down the street. Their casual conversations mixed with the jazz flowing out of the same bar across from the leather shop.

Where are they? Did they follow us into the store?

Standard surveillance dictated that only *one* member of the team went inside while the others covered the street and even the alley in back, in case the target did exactly what Tucker had done. The lack of operatives on both locations told him that for some reason the men had gone inside, which meant that they could be emerging from the rear at any moment.

Perhaps losing them had been a lot easier than Tucker had first estimated.

Hiding the Beretta beneath his T-shirt, Tucker opted to continue up the block, turning left at the next corner into a less crowded street, remembering the street map he had memorized, getting away from the tourist section of town. They cut right after two more blocks, the streets suddenly becoming as murky as the alleyway behind the leather goods store. Isolated pedestrians replaced the bustling foot traffic. The noise level dropped to a mere whisper, then vanished altogether, which seemed to magnify their footsteps.

Tucker paused, sensing a trap.

"What's wrong?" she asked.

"Come," he said, shifting to the right side of the deserted street, layered with cobblestones, flanked by parked vehicles almost blocking the entrances of two- and three-story structures, many of them covered with aging red brick. A single streetlight at the corner cast a murky glow down the entire block.

Tucker and Monica squeezed in the space between a parked delivery truck and the brick wall of a house.

"What are we—"

Tucker put a finger to her lips, leaning toward her, whispering in her ear. "Waiting and seeing what transpires."

She nodded, her eyes inches from his. Perspiration formed over her upper lip.

Slowly, almost imperceptibly, hasty footsteps clicking hollowly over cobblestones invaded the silence of the street, mixing with Monica's breathing.

Tucker tilted his finger toward the incoming noise, which sounded like a single set of footsteps.

The surveillance reached the corner, then stopped.

You're wondering which way we went, Tucker thought, motioning Monica to remain put as he dropped to his knees, then to his side, rolling under the truck, peeking toward the corner from between the axles, his body safely hidden from view by the darkness beneath the large vehicle.

A man stood at the intersection of the two streets, shifting back and forth. He couldn't see the operative's face but felt certain it would have a concerned expression.

Now you're going to have to explain to your superiors how it is that you lost us.

The operative proceeded down Tucker's street, knees bent, apparently checking beneath parked vehicles, the corner streetlight projecting a long shadow ahead of him.

Rolling back to Monica and standing, Tucker considered his choices. He had managed to force the enemy to split up. Now he needed to disable him, thus improving his chances of escaping.

He moved Monica to the space between one of the truck's large tires and the brick wall, making it quite difficult for her to get hurt should a firearm be discharged.

He touched her face, once again motioning her to remain put.

She regarded him nervously and mouthed the words, *be careful.*

He made his way to the front of the truck, in a crouch, waiting for his quarry to reach his position.

The seconds seemed to drag as Bruce Tucker remained coiled, like a spring, the Beretta tucked away, useless to disable this operative without a silencer, lest he wished to give his position away. And besides, he didn't really wish to *kill* an American intelligence officer, only to disable him, and perhaps to send a message.

A message.

Tucker thought of one of the diskettes in Monica's pocket, where they had downloaded a sample of the incriminating files, just enough to set the stage for the first step toward their freedom.

The top of the man's shadow reached the front bumper, and a moment later the operative followed. He was the younger of the two Tucker had spotted walking side by side.

Tucker lunged, extending his right hand at the young agent, who must have spotted him in his peripheral vision and begun to turn his face to the incoming threat.

Tucker had counted on this, thrusting his right hand at his prey, the index and middle fingers extended, like a snake's tongue, poking the operative in the eyes, just as Kabuki had taught him.

As Tucker delivered this initial blow, the trained operative lifted his left knee, breaking Tucker's charge while driving the knee deep into Tucker's solar plexus.

Both men fell on the street, the operative moaning while covering his face, Tucker gasping for air while clutching his torso.

Staggering to his feet, Tucker turned toward the operative, who looked more like a kid straight out of high school, but very muscular and agile, with closely-cropped brown hair.

Squinting, also getting up, the operative shoved a hand in his coat, presumably reaching for his weapon.

His torso burning, Tucker pivoted on his left foot while turning toward him at great speed, bringing his right foot up, slashing it toward the enemy, striking the hand clasping a black semiautomatic before he could fire it.

The gun skittered over the cobblestones as Tucker continued the spinning turn, his right fist directed at the man's left temple.

The operative's reflexes surprised Tucker, particularly for being so young. He got out of the way just in time while driving the heel of his left palm into Tucker's rib cage.

The pain streaked up his chest as he absorbed the blow, before instinctively countering with an elbow strike to the side of the face, connecting, pushing the enemy to the side.

The professionals fell after exchanging blows a second time, before standing once again.

They began to circle each other, slowly, measuring, with mutual respect. The operative produced a black knife from a waist holster, holding it just as Tucker had been taught at the CIA, with the dark blade protruding below the fist, capable of delivering a variety of both crippling and fatal blows with minimal effort. The kid was good. Real good.

Tucker glared at the knife, wishing he could reach for the one he had strapped to his right ankle, but doing so at the moment would be fatal.

He would have to work on defense and try to disarm him. Experience, however, told him that he would sustain at least one cut in the process. Being right-handed, Tucker shielded himself with his left forearm, turning the inside of the wrist toward him, protecting all vital arteries and muscles. When the operative slashed at him, he would strike the bony side of his forearm, inflicting a painful but otherwise superficial injury.

The men continued circling each other, closing the gap separating them.

Abruptly the young operative lunged while slashing the blade through the air in front of Tucker in a figure eight.

Tucker shifted back and forth, keeping his forearm in front of him at all times, waiting for an opening, forcing one by offering the forearm to the talented rookie as bait.

Someone with a lot of field experience would have hesitated, but the young operative, probably feeling confident because he had the knife, took the bait and stabbed him, slicing straight to the bone.

The wound felt more like a burn than a cut. Tucker ignored it, finding his opening a fraction of a second later, at the height of the man's attack, as the rookie stepped back, bloody knife in hand, before he could strike again.

Tucker moved sideways to the retreating operative, before extending his left leg toward his face, driving the heel of his sneaker straight into the operative's nose and mouth.

Cartilage snapped. Blood burst through flaring nostrils,

through busted lips. Stunned, the man dropped the knife and fell to the ground.

Ignoring the blood on his forearm, Tucker kicked the knife away and snagged the silenced pistol off the ground. He recognized it immediately as a Sig Sauer, similar to the one he had purchased in Rome, including the silencer.

He dragged the operative to the front of the truck, out of sight from anyone walking by.

"Who are you?" Tucker hissed, pointing the Sig at the man. Blood oozed from his broken nose, dripping over his mouth, chin, and neck.

"Go ahead . . . you bastard . . . kill me," replied the operative in a somewhat high-pitched voice that belonged more to a teenager than an operative officer, who, as Tucker had guessed, was American. "Just like you killed . . . Porter."

"Are you CIA?"

"NSA," he said, his inexperience talking before his training reminded him to keep his mouth shut. He still added, "But . . . to us you're just . . . as guilty."

"Listen to me," Tucker continued, his body aching from the short fight. He didn't have a lot of time. The other operatives could get here at any moment. "The one you want is Jarkko, not me. He killed Porter. He's after *Firewall*. He has the NSA and the CIA diverted to chase me instead of him."

A pair of young eyes surrounded by smooth, unlined skin stared at Tucker in disbelief.

"I could have easily killed you," Tucker added. "And I still could, but I'm not a killer."

The operative wiped his face, blinking rapidly while wincing in pain. He resembled a kid who had just gotten in a fistfight in school and was now being reprimanded by the principal.

How young is the NSA recruiting them these days?

But Tucker had to give him credit. He did know how to fight.

"What—what about the man . . . you shot in Capri?" the rookie asked.

"In the leg," said Tucker. "To keep him from shooting at me."

"And the people who opened fire on us?"

"That was the Mafia, whom Monica Fox tried to seek protection after your people tried to kidnap her." Tucker turned toward the truck. "Come over here, Monica. It's okay."

She appeared moments later, and covered her mouth in obvious surprise at all the blood.

The kid stared at her almost as if he were looking at a ghost. "Miss Fox?"

"The diskette with the sample of the files," Tucker said to her. "Give it to him."

Monica produced the floppy disk and handed it to the puzzled operative.

"What is this?" the kid asked.

"Listen carefully because I don't have a lot of time," Tucker said. "Tell your people that Mortimer Fox left us a backdoor password to access *Firewall*. Also tell them that he left us a large number of files, each containing a dossier of scandalous material on our political, military, and industrial leaders. This disk has a sample of that as proof that we possess this password and need protection from our government against Jarkko."

"I—I don't understand what that's got to do with—"

"Just remember what I've told you and repeat it to your superiors, *verbatim*. Jarkko is after the password, which would give him access to our launch codes."

"Our launch codes?"

"Correct. Monica and I are willing to work with you, but *only* under our terms. We will be in touch. You've got that?"

Swallowing, he nodded.

"Who is running this operation?" he asked.

The young operative hesitated, then said, "Donald Bane."

Donald Bane?

Tucker looked away for a moment. He remembered Bane from the old days. As station chiefs in Europe, they had cooperated on a number of operations, including the one that resulted in Jarkko's apparent termination. Bane had been supportive after the tragedy in Zurich. Bane was a cowboy, willing to go the distance, to get the job done, as he had done in Iraq.

"All right," Tucker said. "You make sure that Bane gets this, and tell him that Bruce Tucker will be in touch. Got it?"

"Ye—yes."

"Now take off your shoes," Tucker said.

"My shoes?"

"And your socks and T-shirt, and lie on your stomach, hands behind your head."

A moment later they left the American intelligence officer behind the truck, one sock binding his wrists and the other his feet.

"Your arm," Monica said, running next to him while he wrapped the operative's dark T-shirt tight over the wound.

"It's superficial," he said, finding it hard to breathe with his torso on fire. "But my ribs," he added. "We need to get away from here, and fast, before I run out of steam or someone else spots us. I'm not sure if I can fight another one off."

At that moment, Tucker felt a presence behind them and turned around, spotting a lone figure at the far end of the block racing in their direction. He also saw a second figure, probably a hundred or so feet behind the first, also running fast.

Two more operatives.

"Shit," he said, realizing he had been right in the beginning. There had been three of them.

Scrambling in the opposite direction, remembering the layout of the town, Tucker guided Monica back to the tourist section of Terracina, searching for a way to—

The sound of a near-miss buzzed past him.

"Damn," he said, turning the corner, dragging Monica along. "Bastard just fired at me!" As he said this a second silent round punched a hole into the plastic bumper of a parked Fiat. A third bullet ricocheted against a cobblestone, chipping chunks of rock.

They pressed on, reaching the end of the next block, which

dead-ended in a wide avenue. He spotted a taxi stand in front of a hotel across four lanes of light evening traffic. Tucker also saw a pair of policemen.

Quickly, he gave Monica brief instructions, and her eyes blinked in both understanding and also admiration at his spontaneous plan, at his simple but effective way to reverse the trap on the operatives rushing after them.

"Help!" Monica shouted, pointing in the direction of the nearest incoming figure, probably a couple hundred feet behind them, gun clearly in hand. "He has a gun and wants to rob us!"

Tucker recognized him as the older operative he had seen walking next to the younger agent he had left immobilized a few blocks back. The figure far back behind the older operative had not yet drawn his weapon and seemed to have slowed down.

The police officers turned in her direction. Just then, as luck would have it, a silent bullet crashed through the windshield of a black Mercedes parked next to Tucker, as he pretended to be another pedestrian, but quickly breaking into a run of fake panic while screaming for help.

Italian cops, unlike their American counterparts, carried machine guns. They sprung into action, turning their weapons toward the accused, in their minds a thug trying to mug tourists.

"That way," Tucker directed Monica, pointing at a taxicab dropping passengers by the hotel's front steps.

They went for it, nearly out of breath, his body protesting the abuse, the wounds inflicted by the young NSA agent.

An elderly couple approached the taxi just as the last person climbed out. Tucker got in between, pushing Monica inside the open rear door.

"Sorry! It's an emergency!" Tucker replied, climbing in, startling a man in his sixties dressed in Bermuda shorts and a Hawaiian shirt, a camera hanging loose from his neck. A similarly dressed elderly woman next to him was about to protest when Tucker slammed the door shut.

"Go, go, go!" he shouted at the driver while thrusting a

crisp one-hundred-dollar bill on his lap. Just then he heard a short burst of machine gun fire rattling the night.

The driver snatched the bill, put the car in gear, and stepped on the gas while releasing the clutch.

"The Mafia," he explained with a wave of his right hand as they accelerated down the avenue, regarding his new customers through the rearview mirror. "Nothing to worry. The police will handle the problem and get everything back to normal."

In spite of his current altered state, Bruce Tucker almost burst into laughter but held back. Doing so would hurt too much because of his ribs. He settled for a sigh and a sideways look at Monica, who was panting next to him.

"Do you think they killed him?" she asked.

Before Tucker could answer, the driver said, "Yes, *signora*, but he was a criminal, bad person. Better dead. Less trouble for tourists, like you."

Leaning back and closing his eyes, Bruce Tucker breathed deeply, wincing as his ribs stabbed him. Maybe he was getting too old to be doing this. Perhaps he lacked the stamina, and for a moment doubted his ability to see this through. Just a single encounter with another professional, and he had walked away with enough wounds to prevent him from facing a second opponent. Ten years ago he would have easily disabled the rookie and probably used him as bait to spring a trap for the other two.

But you still managed to get away with your principal unharmed, he thought. Kabuki would have been proud.

But Tucker's evasive tactics had resulted in the termination of an NSA agent at the hands of the Italian police.

Damn.

Monica cuddled up against him in the rear after giving the driver directions to take them straight to Rome.

"*Roma?*" the driver asked. "But that is over—"

Tucker threw another hundred-dollar bill at him, shutting him up, before leaning back again. "Just drive, please, and I might give you a little more once we get there."

"*Grazie, signor.*"

"Yeah," replied Tucker, feeling Monica's lips brushing against his right ear.

"That was . . . brilliant," she whispered to keep the driver from following their conversation.

"It got an NSA officer killed," he replied also in a low voice after turning his face to her, cheek to cheek. "He was one of the good guys, Monica. That doesn't seem so brilliant."

"But he was trying to kill us."

"He was just following orders. Now I have to live with that. Damn, I thought I had left that life behind me." He tightened his fists, then felt her hands on his and he clasped them.

A moment of silence. Then she asked, "Are you okay?"

"Been worse," he replied, feeling the comfort he sought in Monica Fox's touch. "But we need to stop at a pharmacy. I'll be needing a little patching up."

"What do you need?"

He told her.

Monica widened her eyes. "Are you serious?"

"Unfortunately."

"Is there a pharmacy nearby?" she asked the driver.

"Si, signora. Not feeling good?"

"Just need to pick up a couple of items."

The driver took them to a small pharmacy on the outskirts of town, where they purchased what they would need for the job ahead, returning to the waiting taxi a few minutes later holding a paper bag.

"How long until we get to Rome?" asked Tucker as the driver steered the vehicle back onto the road.

"About one and a half hours."

"All right. We need our privacy back here." Tucker pointed at the small privacy curtain that some taxis have in Italy.

The driver closed it.

"Good now, signore?"

"Yes. Thanks. Is there a light back here?"

"*Si*. It is on the side, for reading."

"Got it," said Tucker, flipping it on. It pointed at his lap. Perfect. "Thanks."

"*Prego.*"

Tucker unrolled a wide roll of cotton over his thighs, before he set his wounded forearm over it, frowning but glad that he had used his left arm to protect himself, which left him his right hand free to tend to the wound.

"Unwrap the shirt," he whispered. "But do it slowly."

"Okay."

He cringed as Monica complied, feeling as if a white-hot claw raked the top of his forearm. The shirt had stuck to the wound.

She paused when realizing this, her eyes seeking direction.

"This is going to hurt," he hissed, handing her a nonstick medical pad. "Go ahead. Pull the shirt off, but be ready to press this against it."

Teeth clenched in agonizing anticipation, he watched Monica give the shirt a quick, firm tug; the sound of ripping fabric tearing his flesh nearly made him lose control of his bladder.

Monica pressed the pad over the reopened wound.

"Damn," he whispered, taking the pain, just as he had been taught during his Navy SEAL days, when he also learned how to take care of himself in the field. He motioned for her to lift the nonstick pad, exposing a three-inch-long cut, smeared with fresh blood over dry blood.

He pointed at the long, curved needle inside a sealed plastic bag, already attached to a small roll of surgical thread.

"Do you want to play doctor with me?" he asked, forcing a grin to calm her down.

"Not funny, Bruce."

He raised his brows while reaching for a small bottle of peroxide and, with her help, soaked a few cotton balls, which they both used to disinfect the wound and the skin around it. He watched the peroxide bubbling alongside the cut, doing its job.

"Have you done this before?" she whispered.

He didn't relish the thought of the time he had to sew a

nasty cut on his left thigh, which he had endured during a training exercise deep in the jungles of Panama. "Back when I was young and tough," he replied, before adding, "Okay, I need you to hold the sliced flesh together while I sew. Can you do that for me?"

She gave him a brief nod, swallowing with obvious concern.

"Just a walk in the park, Monica," he said, winking, even though his nervous system was on edge.

"Right," she replied, using her fingers to press the two sides of the cut together while Tucker applied a long Band-Aid along the wound to keep it taut.

Breathing deeply through his nose and slowly exhaling through his mouth, Tucker tried to keep both his forearm and needle steady inside a moving car, finally stabbing the flesh just below the Band-Aid, clenching his teeth as he ran the needle under the skin, and out above the Band-Aid, which he motioned Monica to peel back slightly, before bringing the needle back down again, sealing the gap with a neat stitch. As he did this, he could feel Monica's eyes on him.

He ignored her, concentrating on the task at hand, slowly repeating the process six more times, controlling his breathing, avoiding a single moan, a single noise that would betray his activity to the driver.

When he finished, he leaned back, eyes closed, his hand trembling a bit. A moment later he reopened them and stared at Monica, whose eyes were filled, glistening in the dim light of the rear seat.

"Like I told you," he murmured, running his thumb across her right cheek to wipe a tear. "Just a walk in the park."

Monica helped him clean up the wound with more peroxide and dried it with cotton balls. After verifying that the cut no longer bled, Tucker squeezed a tube of antibiotic paste along the length of the wound. She then did a good job bandaging it, before shoving everything back in the bag, which they set aside.

"That wasn't so bad, huh?" he said. "Thanks for the help."

She smiled, her eyes filling again. "You're the bravest and

kindest man I know. And on top of that you're also modest."
She rested her head against his shoulder. "Can you cook?"

"No, but I can sew."

They laughed, but the stabbing pain made him grunt. He
put an arm around her as they remained silent for a while,
just enjoying each other's nearness, deciding to postpone a
serious recap of what had taken place until Rome.

Testing his left arm, which still throbbed from the stitch
job but was no longer in danger, Tucker reached over and
moved the curtain aside, his desire to see the road ahead
superceding his need for privacy. He then shut off the reading light, immersing them in darkness.

The driver peeked at them through the rearview mirror as
they held each other. Tucker could see the man's grin as he
said, "Ah, *amore*. This is the country of *amore*."

Tucker sighed as Monica giggled. Then he shifted his gaze
to the darkness beyond the window while the hair on top of
her head brushed against his chin. He welcomed that feeling,
even if it went against his rules.

The hell with the rules.

Rules keep you alive.

Rules, Tucker mused, flexing his forearm, feeling his flesh
pressing against the stitches, which appeared to be holding.
Rules were what kept him *living*, not *alive*. Bruce Tucker
had not felt alive in years, not since holding Kristina like
this, and a part of him was having growing difficulty controlling such emotions. He needed the rules of his profession—Kabuki's rules—to get him and his principal through
this chaos.

But afterward . . .

*One step at a time, Bruce. For now just get to Rome, get
some rest, get ready for the next round.*

Rome, with its seemingly infinite number of streets and
alleys and hotels would be a good place to hide and rest,
before moving onto the next phase of his plan. The evening
had not been a total waste, though. Tucker had managed to
send his former Agency a message, along with proof to back
up his claims. If there were people left at the CIA or the

NSA who could still think for themselves, then Tucker still had a chance of talking some sense into them. But if all he faced was an army of robots blindly following orders from superiors who went strictly by the book, then he would have to force them into accepting his terms. Right now he held the best cards, and he would use them to save his principal and himself, even if that meant having to blackmail the United States government.

A samurai never quits.

An executive protector will go to any extreme to safeguard his principal, just as the forty-seven ronin had done in shogunate Japan, just as Kabuki had taught him.

However, Bruce Tucker hoped it really didn't go that far. He hoped to be able to work out a deal with the CIA.

All I need is one good, sensible man.

A Sensible Man

Over a dozen NSA and CIA officers converged on the quiet coastal town of Terracina in the next hour. The group chose to meet on a deserted and breezy bluff just north of town, overlooking the Mediterranean, beneath a blanket of stars.

Bane had ordered the team to spread out and form a defense perimeter while he debriefed the surviving members of the surveillance team. He had also asked Raffaela to remain in one of the sedans for security reasons. The information that could be disclosed by the team might be too confidential for anyone but those with the appropriate security clearance to hear.

Donald Bane held a diskette, handed to him by a young, bruised, and quite embarrassed NSA agent, whom Tucker had apparently ambushed with the intent not to kill but to pass on this diskette, along with the message about Jarkko and *Firewall*. The second NSA agent had been killed, but not by Tucker. He had perished in a fusillade of bullets from two members of the local police.

"And you said Tucker could have killed you?" asked Bane.

Lips swollen, the young agent held a hand towel against his twisted nose to control the bleeding. An Agency doctor was on the way. "He had my silenced gun pointed at my face," he said in a nasal voice. "He could have easily pulled the trigger without alerting anyone."

"Yet . . . he didn't. Did it look to you that he was forcing Monica Fox to stay with him?"

"No. It certainly looked as if she were his partner. She remained out of sight until he had me under control and then he called for her and she appeared and gave me the diskette. Then she helped Tucker tie me down before running away with him. Not once did he have to threaten her to get her to do anything. She seemed to be assisting him quite willingly."

"And he just told you to pass this on and that he would be in touch?"

"Plus the claim that he was innocent, that he didn't kill Porter, just as he didn't kill me or the agent in Capri."

Bane frowned. "But some agents did die in Capri."

"Tucker said he shot one in the leg, which our people confirmed. But then other men opened fire on us from the treeline. We had assumed they were Tucker's accomplices. Tucker claimed they were with the Mafia, whom Monica had made a deal with to get protection after our failed ambush that same morning."

"Anything else?"

"No, sir."

Bane looked at his own CIA officer, the man who had joined the two NSA agents in midstream, as they were tailing the fugitive couple. His story was even more bizarre. The trio had split two ways when losing visual contact with Tucker. The younger one had gone around the block in the hope of cutting them off, and had eventually caught up with them, just to end up being ambushed by Tucker himself. The other two, one NSA and one CIA, had spotted the couple later on running in the streets. The NSA agent had told his CIA counterpart to fall back a couple hundred feet to minimize their risk of getting burned.

"But instead of just following them, he started firing at Tucker," said the CIA officer.

"Why? Did Tucker fire first?"

"Not that I could see, although it was pretty dark in those streets. But I didn't see any muzzle flashes originating from him."

"And what happened next?"

"Two cops showed up and blasted him into kingdom come. I got the hell out of there in a hurry."

Bane pinched the bridge of his nose. "Why would he open fire if Tucker wasn't firing at him?"

The CIA operative grimaced. "It was strange, sir. It almost looked as if he was carrying out the termination order."

It certainly *looked* that way. Trouble was, Bane had ordered the exact opposite. He could see how the young NSA man was attacked and he had to defend himself. But the senior agent had fired at Tucker from behind, while he was trying to run away. "Could he have panicked? Maybe he feared that they would get away?"

The CIA officer just shrugged. "Can't ask a dead man questions, sir."

Bane turned to the battered NSA rookie sitting in the rear of the sedan waiting for medical help to arrive. He was looking at Bane, obviously having followed the conversation to this point.

"Do you have anything else to add, son?"

The kid dropped his gaze. "My senior partner contacted his boss in Washington after reporting the sight to you, sir."

"He did *what*?"

"He. . . . contacted the NSA."

Bane didn't like the sound of that. His agreement with Martin and Hersh had been very explicit. No long-distance intervention with the field operation. They were supposed to wait for Bane to E-mail his progress report. "And what happened next?"

"He didn't tell me what he was told, but I did hear him say that he would execute the new instructions immediately."

"Who was he speaking to?"

The kid shook his head. "I'm just the junior guy, sir. I took direction from my senior partner, and he didn't speak about that conversation at all. Although he did warn me to stay frosty because there could be trouble."

Alarms were blaring in Bane's head by now. The NSA had overridden his orders, instructing the senior agent on site to terminate Bruce Tucker. That was why the agent had opened fire, instead of just following from a distance, as instructed by Bane. He was trying to *eliminate* Tucker and secure Monica Fox before Bane and the rest of the team reached Terracina.

Bane tightened his fists as he stepped away from the group and looked toward the ocean, a single name flashing in his mind: Geoff Hersh.

It had to be him. The NSA director had bypassed the chain of command.

The options for the veteran CIA officer were clear. Instead of going to Martin with this violation, or confronting Hersh directly with it, Bane decided to report the events of this evening just as they had taken place. He planned to include in his report that the new intel gathered in Naples and Terracina merited the temporary suspension of the termination order against Bruce Tucker.

Bane crossed his arms, realizing that after presenting a factual report of the events in Terracina, he might also consider making the request that all NSA personnel be removed from this mission—something he knew would not sit well with Hersh. Such request, however, might force Hersh to come out into the open and admit that he gave the order to kill Tucker.

And of course, before sending the report Bane had to review the contents of the diskette, wondering, as he stared at it, what that would be and what twist it would put on his quest to protect *Firewall*.

56

R & R in Rome

The taxi delivered them to a hotel just off the Spanish Steps in Rome. They paid the driver and then pretended to go into the lobby, waiting until it had pulled off before walking back outside. They strolled around the area for ten minutes and then hailed a second taxi, which took them to the Metro station by Via Cavour, a few blocks from where Tucker had purchased his weapons what seemed like a long time ago, even though it had only been a few days.

"There's a hotel beyond those steps. It's small, out of the way," he told Monica, pointing to long steps at the end of a short alley shooting to the side of Via Cavour.

"How do you know—"

"It's my job to know those things," he said, glancing about him, spotting a group of prostitutes in the same vicinity where he had seen them a few days back. Two of them blew him a kiss. Monica gave them the bird and grabbed his hand.

Tucker almost laughed, but remembered his ribs. He settled for a smile, before saying, "If I didn't know any better I'd said that you were jealous."

She smiled without humor and pointed at the alley and the steps beyond it. "Up there you said?"

"Yep."

"Let's go."

The climb seemed to last forever. That was one thing Tucker didn't miss about this place. Splendor and history aside, there were steps *everywhere*. The city should have been nicknamed the Eternal *Steps*, in many ways as bad as San Francisco, but at least it was always cool and breezy in the Bay Area. Here the heat and humidity would drive you insane if you weren't used to it.

They both broke a sweat by the time they reached the top, continuing until the alley ended on a strangely shaped dead-end street. One side was quite wide, resembling a large cove, with the Hotel Colosseum, their current destination, facing a convent. To their left, the street narrowed into an alleylike passage that continued for a few hundred feet, ending in the wide boulevard surrounding the majestic Church of Maria Maggiore.

Oddly enough, a porn shop adjacent to the hotel was open for business, in plain view of the nuns walking from the convent to the church. Two hookers hung outside the sex shop. One of them looked at Tucker and smiled. Monica pulled him closer to her as they walked side by side, reaching the entrance to the hotel, opening the single glass door.

Marble floors layered the small lobby, flanked on one side—the one closest to the entrance—with a dark wooden counter, behind which sat a man working through a short pile of papers, a pair of spectacles perched near the tip of his nose, a dark and thin cigarette hanging from the corner of his mouth. He looked to be in his fifties, thinly built, balding.

The smell of smoke and antiseptic made Tucker momentarily flare his nostrils as he stepped in front of the counter, paying cash for a room.

The night-shift attendant gave them a key and directions to their room, located on the third floor, with a view of the Roman Colosseum.

What they didn't realize until they went inside was that there was only one bed, king size.

"Let's go back downstairs," he said. "I'll make him exchange rooms for one with two double beds."

"No need for that," she said. "I want company."

His feelings conflicting, Tucker said, "Monica, we shouldn't get involved like—"

"Relax, Bruce. I didn't mean *sex*. I just want someone to hold me tonight. Can you bend your rules just a little and keep me company? *Please?* I really need that."

Remembering how great it had felt holding her in the rear seat of the taxi on the way over here, Tucker said, "All right. Let's get our rest. Tomorrow could be even more demanding than today."

"Thank you," she said, smiling. "Do you need to use the rest room?"

He extended a hand toward the open bathroom door. "Ladies first."

She disappeared through the doorway while Tucker bolted the door and also made sure the windows were locked, before drawing the curtain. He set the Beretta and the silenced Sig on the nightstand, before removing the ankle holster securing his knife. He set it next to the guns.

Damn, I'm exhausted, he thought, his eyelids feeling heavier. He kicked off his sneakers and wished he could also remove his pants, but not only did his profession insist that he sleep with his clothes on during a mission, undressing would send the wrong message to his principal.

Monica came out of the bathroom still wearing her linen dress, but looking lovelier than ever. "Your turn," she said, pulling the covers out of the way enough for her to crawl in bed.

Tucker did his business and also returned to the room, climbing in bed on his side after turning off the lights.

Monica found him in the darkness. "Hug me from behind, Bruce," she said, backing herself toward him, snuggling her body against his.

Tucker embraced her, running one hand under her head and the other landing over her belly. Monica rested her head on his arm and put a hand over his, squeezing it gently. "Night, Bruce. Thanks."

"You're welcome. Good night," he replied, closing his eyes, letting his head sink in the pillow, Monica's head tucked beneath his chin.

Time.

"Bruce?"

"Yeah?"

"The artificial intelligence system. Is it really possible that it has the emotions and feelings of my father?"

"It's a program, Monica. It was designed to respond the way it did, but it's not your father."

"What is it then?"

"An ally, a guardian angel of sorts. Someone who might be able to help us get through this."

Time.

"Bruce?"

"Yes?"

"I haven't been this comfortable in a very long time."

"Me too, Monica," he replied, hugging her tighter. "Me too."

He didn't have any problems falling asleep, quickly drifting away while feeling Monica's breathing growing steady, like his became moments later.

Revelations

At the CIA safe house in Rome, Donald Bane stared at the information on the computer screen with disbelief. Two hours ago he had clicked his way through the handful of files stored in the diskette, which included not just a personal note from the rogue Tucker explaining the way he would make contact next, but also incriminating files on three senators and a congressman. Tucker's note hinted that higher government officials than these also had similar files. Bane had then mailed his report to Hersh and Martin, and had also set up a video conference to discuss his recommendations after they had gotten a chance to digest the intel collected thus far.

He checked his watch, yawning. Just past five in the morn-

ing. The sky beyond the large French doors leading to the
third-story balcony glared with stars.

He glanced at the bed in the opposite end of the rectangular room from where he sat, watching Raffaela sleeping.
She was actually snoring lightly.

Bane grinned before returning his attention to the screen,
which pretty much dissolved the smile. Hersh had been correct in his assessment of Mortimer Fox. The old tycoon had
indeed created a secret door into *Firewall*. But Fox had also
used that system as his own channel to gather intelligence
on who he considered to be his enemies, which spanned
many people in the U.S. government, including Geoff Hersh.

He leaned back on the chair and his gaze drifted to the
French doors. The sneaky NSA director had overridden
Bane's field order, resulting in one dead agent.

A window opened on his display. It was the video con-
ferencing software kicking in through the *Firewall* secure
link. He brought the cursor to the ANSWER icon and a live
image filled the window. A conference room. Two people
sat at one end of a long table. Hersh and Martin, both dressed
in business suits. Bane had requested the meeting, realizing
that 5 A.M. in Rome was 10:00 P.M. in Washington.

But he didn't care. Those two characters had drafted his
ass and sent him halfway across the globe on a field assignment even though Donald Bane wasn't supposed to be doing
field work any more.

He stared at a small camera atop the monitor and said,
"Hello, gentlemen. Thanks for agreeing to meet me at this
hour."

"Not a problem, Don," started Martin, crossing his legs.
"We read your report. How do you wish to proceed?"

He cleared his throat, staring at the little camera as he
spoke into the microphone projecting off the side of the monitor. "First I want to request the immediate removal of all
NSA agents from this operation."

Hersh leaned forward. "What?"

Martin extended a hand toward Hersh, motioning him to
calm down before saying, "That's a most unexpected request,

Don. Is there something wrong with the NSA agents under your command?"

"Yes, sir," Bane replied, having thought this one through. "Apparently they don't know how to follow my orders."

"What are you talking about?" asked Hersh. "They even followed you into that warehouse before it blew up."

"They didn't follow my orders in Terracina, sir," replied Bane. "I *specifically* ordered them to follow and observe—nothing else. Instead, Mr. Hersh, your men, particularly the senior agent running the surveillance, did the exact opposite, opening fire on Bruce Tucker while he ran next to Monica Fox, putting her life in danger. He acted recklessly and unprofessionally, jeopardizing the mission, losing Tucker and Monica Fox, and getting himself killed in the process. We lost a great opportunity in Terracina, sir, and, as stated in my report, I blame the NSA for that one. I request to make this operation one hundred percent CIA."

Hersh bolted to his feet. "That's an outrage! I refuse to sit here and—"

"Sit down, Geoff!" Martin scoffed, glaring at the young NSA director.

Hersh remained standing for a few seconds, before he slowly sat back down.

"Your man screwed up out there," said Martin. "How many other loose cannons do you have?"

Hersh set his forearms on the desk. "None, actually. Not even him."

"What do you mean?" asked Martin. "You read the report. You saw how he acted."

Bane narrowed his gaze. *Here it comes.*

Hersh, chin high, said proudly, "It was I who gave the order to my men in Terracina to carry out *your* termination order, Randolph. Remember that it was the CIA who put Bruce Tucker beyond salvage, *not* the NSA. The bastard Tucker had killed enough of my men in Capri. I wasn't just going to let my people stand around while they had the killer in sight and had a clear shot. Perhaps I should have waited until more agents reached the area, but sometimes one must seize the moment."

Martin turned toward the camera and said, "Don, I'm going to mute the audio for just a minute. Hold on."

Bane sat back and watched the shouting match. Hersh seemed to be shrinking in his chair as Martin let him have it for having bypassed the chain of command. After a while Martin pressed the MUTE button again.

"Here's the situation," Martin said. "I have just been guaranteed the full—*and uninterrupted*—cooperation of the NSA on this matter. All agents assigned to your jurisdiction—CIA and NSA—will follow *only* your orders. No one else's. Right, Geoff?"

"That's right."

Martin continued. "You are in command of this operation, Don, but in light of Hersh's statement, I ask that you give those NSA agents another shot."

Bane breathed deeply. "All right," he said. "I withdraw that request."

"Very well. What's next?"

"Another request."

"Go ahead."

"I want to remove Bruce Tucker from the beyond-salvage list. I've seen enough evidence to make me believe that he wasn't the one who killed John Porter."

Martin stared into the distance for a moment, before saying, "Why don't you tell us how you arrived at this conclusion?"

Donald Bane did, spending over ten minutes covering all of his intelligence in as much detail as he had at the moment, elaborating on his report, filling in the holes with his own intuition, with his field experience. Bruce Tucker had even informed Bane how he would make contact to provide him with the particulars of a meeting.

"A meeting?" asked Hersh.

"That's right, sir. Bruce Tucker and Monica Fox want to meet with the CIA, but before they do, Tucker wants assurances from both of you that neither one of them will be harmed or taken into custody."

"And why should we agree?" asked Hersh.

"Because, Geoff," answered Martin before Bane could, "Tucker's holding all of the cards. He possesses the code to *Firewall* as well as the dossiers. It sounds as if he wants to use those items as bargaining chips to gain the freedom of his principal, as well as his own."

"But there's more, sir. Tucker also needs our help to track down and eliminate the terrorists that are after his principal."

"The ones at the warehouse?" asked Martin.

"Correct. They are also the ones after *Firewall*, and Tucker claims that they have been the ones responsible for Porter's death as well as Vinod Malani's, William Gibbons's, and the kidnapping attempt on Mortimer Fox, which in a way killed him from an ensuing heart attack. Based on everything I've seen so far, I tend to agree with him, which is why I want to work with Tucker, not against him. We're both after the same thing, sir: the protection of *Firewall* against terrorists."

"Just a moment, Don," said Martin, muting him again to have a private conversation with Geoff Hersh.

Raffaela mumbled something incoherent while rolling over, before her steady breathing resumed.

"Don?"

Bane returned his gaze to the camera. "Yes, sir."

"You've got it. The CIA and the NSA will back you up. Tucker is going off the list immediately. Is there anything else you need tonight?"

"No, sir."

"Good-bye, Don. And keep us posted." The image vanished, replaced by DISCONNECTION IN PROGRESS . . .

Bane stood and stretched, his eyes landing on the sofa next to the large bed. He grabbed a pillow from the opposite side of the bed from where Raffaela slept, and settled himself on the couch, which was a lot more comfortable than it'd appeared.

He had to get some sleep, feeling certain that the moment

Bruce Tucker made contact, the chase would start once again. Bane could only hope that he was able to join forces with Tucker and Monica Fox before the terrorists got to them.

Night Moves

Bruce Tucker wasn't sure how it started. Perhaps it was the way he woke up just before dawn holding Monica Fox close to him, her face just an inch away from his. Or maybe it was because of the way her dress had inched up during the night, exposing her from her midriff down. Or it could be because his hand had drifted to the space between her breasts, held in place by one of her own hands.

Before he knew it, Monica was kissing him, softly, first on the cheek, then on the corner of his mouth, and he didn't resist, holding her tighter than he had ever held anything in his life, at least since Kristina, since he had stopped feeling alive.

Her dress came off, shoved off to the side, along with his T-shirt as they fumbled in the dark, eyes closed, her breasts pressed against his chest, her lips exploring him, caressing him, kissing him in ways that made Bruce Tucker forget the termination teams, the terrorists, the Mafia, the codes of *Firewall*.

He surrendered himself to her touch as her hands unbuckled his pants, as he kicked them off while staring at those taunting hazel eyes.

"Take me away, Bruce," she whispered. "Please, take me away from all this."

Bruce Tucker did, his lips brushing her neck, her nipples, as he crawled on top, resting most of his weight on his elbows, running his hands under her shoulders, holding her face as he entered her, as she dug her fingers into his back, forcing him against her, again and again, lifting her pelvis, meeting him halfway. She absorbed him whole as they shuddered, as they became one in a rapture neither of them wished would end.

In the twilight of the room, as the first signs of dawn broke the darkness enshrouding them, Bruce Tucker lost himself in her warm embrace, in her parted lips, in the way she tilted her head, in the way she moaned, eyes closed, hands down on his buttocks now, forcing him to remain with her, to become one with her, to keep her safe, to love her.

Love.

In the midst of a passion he hadn't felt in years, Bruce Tucker felt something far more than the physical pleasure provided by this beauty writhing beneath him with a desire he fought hard to control. He wanted this to last, wished to stretch this moment into eternity.

"Bruce," she whispered, nibbling his ear lobe. "Hold me tight."

Tucker embraced her as Monica climaxed, as he felt a moist explosion between them, as she relaxed, then tensed again.

He continued, as he let go of it all, breaking a sweat, sliding over her again and again, clasping her hands, holding them above her head, unable to control himself now, feeling the end coming, then shuddering, tensing, releasing, and finally relaxing, collapsing next to her.

She lay sideways to him, resting her head on his chest, putting a leg over his, pressing her moist pubic hair against his upper thigh. Tucker ran an arm around her back, resting it on her smooth torso. They remained like that for several minutes, in silence, just enjoying each other's touch. Sunlight began to stream through a crack in the curtains. It was almost 6:00 A.M.

"Bruce," she said after a while, toying with his chest hairs. "No one has ever made me feel this way."

"What do you mean?"

"So . . . safe."

"That's my job."

She tugged at his hairs.

"Hey!" he said. "Watch it there."

"You don't have to hide behind that line anymore, Bruce. You can tell me that you look after me so well because you care a great deal about me."

She was right, of course. His feelings for her certainly had surpassed his professional bounds, but he was still her executive protector, and it was still his job to see this through. "Monica, there is no denying that I care for you a great deal, and yes, our relationship has grown beyond that of a protector and his principal. But it's still my job—actually call it my *cause*—to make sure that you're safe, that you feel safe. And that you *remain* safe for at least the duration of this ordeal."

"What about afterwards?" she asked, rolling over him, resting her chin on his chest while staring directly at him. "What about after all of this is over?"

"Do you really think we have a chance?"

"What do *you* think?"

"I think that you are not only one of the most beautiful women in the world, but you are also one of the *richest*—at least you'll be when I deliver you home safe and sound. I, on the other hand, am just—"

"The most caring, brave, kind, honest, and lovable man I've ever met. And believe me, Bruce, I've met *all* kinds. What you've just said makes me want you even more, because you were willing to let me go because of my wealth, while everyone else out there wants to be with me because of my wealth. So, let me tell you how this is going to play out."

Tucker tilted his head at her. "All right. How is it going to play out?"

"Very simple," she said, kissing the tip of his nose. "First, we'll beat this thing. One way or another, we will prevail, then you and I are going to get away from everyone, from everything. That's one good thing about money, Bruce, it can buy you total privacy from the world. I think that's what our relationship needs."

"I take it there isn't room for negotiation?"

She made a small circle with her thumb and index fingers. "Zero room. I've been lonely all my life, Bruce. I'm simply tired of it."

And so was he. Bruce Tucker had been alone most of his life, except for that brief period with Kristina, time which now seemed like some sort of lost dream—a dream that he could once again make a reality with Monica Fox.

Tucker took her in his arms and made love to her again. This time familiarity magnified the experience, as they stared deeply into each other's eyes, unifying the moment beyond anything either of them had ever felt before. Afterwards they showered together, slowly, exploring each other. It wasn't until they'd dressed, that the reality of their situation once again begun to sink in, and for the first time since he had kissed her, Tucker began to regret having gotten intimate with his principal, for it now made him vulnerable. The enemy could once again take something away from him that he held dearly, just as Jarkko had done many years ago.

You can't have it both ways, Bruce.

Tucker had made his decision and he would now have to play it out. He had chosen the love of a woman against his professional judgment and could only hope that it didn't come back and bite him later on.

"Come," he said, reaching for her hand. "Let's go get some breakfast and check an Internet bulletin board."

59

Tracks

Across the street from a three-story apartment building off Via Conciliazione, not far from Vatican City, Vlad Jarkko walked by with apparent disinterest, just another priest heading to St. Peter's Basilica for morning services in the company of a nun.

Dressed in a habit that cloaked her features from anyone not standing directly in front of her, Mai Sung Ku held a rosewood rosary in her hands, pretending to pray while walking by his side. The Korean beauty looked quite innocent dressed this way, in sharp contrast with the sexually ravenous creature he had bested in bed a few hours before, prior to getting a report regarding the existence of this CIA hangout.

Vlad had always favored holy garments, black, easy to conceal weapons without restricting mobility. Today he hauled a brand new Uzi submachine gun beneath the holy cloth, identical to the one Mai Sung also carried under her dark garments. But the terrorist hoped he didn't have to use the weapons on this clear morning. Today they were simply on a routine surveillance job, seeking firsthand visual confirmation that this building indeed served as residence for American intelligence officers.

"Are you certain your informant got the correct house?" asked Mai Sung.

"We just need to be patient. We will either get a sighting of Tucker and Monica from our own team, or we will notice a flurry of activity here the moment they contact the CIA to try to make a deal. Either way we will be ready."

They continued on their way as Rome slowly came to life,

as traffic began to flow steadily down avenues and boule-
vards, as shop owners began to sweep their front steps and
set out their goods for the mob of visitors that would soon
be crowding the streets. The terrorists planned to run nonstop
surveillance of the CIA house, sometimes posing as tourists,
other times as holy men and women, or as shop owners, even
policemen.

Vlad Jarkko was determined to secure Monica Fox in the
next forty-eight hours.

High-tech Coffee

They found an Internet café just across from Maria Maggiore
Church, though it had taken Tucker and Monica much longer
to get there. Tucker's paranoia level remained as high as
ever.

Only until he had made absolutely certain that no one was
following them, did he head for the café, where, in addition
to having cappuccinos and pastries, they got on-line.

Tucker clicked his way to the bulletin board, where, following the recommendations of the artificial intelligence
system in *Firewall*, he had instructed the CIA to post the
results of his initial request: that he be immediately removed
from the termination list.

Tucker had used the anonymity of the Internet to communicate with his former employers from a safe distance.
However, he was also very well aware that the CIA could
have placed a tracer on this bulletin file such that it began
to find the physical location of the individual reading it in
much the same way that a phone call can be traced. The only
difference was that it took longer for the Internet trace because it had to go through one or more Internet service pro-

viders before arriving at the physical location, namely this Internet café.

Tucker checked the clock on the bottom righthand corner of the screen. He would allow himself no more than ten minutes before terminating the connection.

He opened the file on the bulletin board labeled SALVAGE, and, to his pleasant surprise, he saw that the CIA had apparently complied—at least on the surface. He was no longer a marked man. Of course, that could have been done as a trick to draw him in, but his instincts told him otherwise. He felt that the evidence he had provided, plus the events in the past forty-eight hours should exonerate him—or at a minimum grant him a grace period.

"Looks like I might be a free man again," he said to Monica, who sat next to him, shoulder-to-shoulder, reading the information on the screen. "For a while anyway."

In addition to this grant, Bane, speaking for the CIA— though no names were involved in the message—acknowledged the receipt of the files and the critical nature of those dossiers. He also recognized that Tucker and Monica possessed the secret password to access *Firewall*—again, without mentioning any relevant names since this was a public forum. Bane was ready to negotiate the terms for their freedom and the transfer of the information.

"Well, darling, that looks like a big step in the right direction," she said, smiling, throwing an arm over his shoulder while pressing the side of her face against him with affection.

That was the first time she had called him something other than his name. He liked that.

"It sure it looks that way," he replied. "But in my business appearances can be deceiving."

"You think it might be a trick?"

"Maybe. That's why I need to verify their claim."

"How?"

"By logging in and checking with the AI system aboard *Firewall*. Perhaps it has learned more about our current status with the government since Terracina."

She regarded him with admiration and gave him a kiss on the cheek.

Using the procedure they had committed to memory, they logged in, without seeing each other's passwords.

I HAVE BEEN WORRIED ABOUT YOU TWO.

WE'RE FINE, entered Tucker. BUT WE HAD A MARGINAL CALL IN TERRACINA.

I FEARED THAT AFTER INTERCEPTING A CONVERSATION BETWEEN THE AGENTS IN TERRACINA AND GEOFF HERSH, HEAD OF THE NSA.

Tucker read the report from *Firewall*. Hersh had countered Donald Bane's order, in the end sending one man to his death.

SO DONALD BANE CAN BE TRUSTED? typed Tucker.

YES. HE HAD A VIDEO CONFERENCE LATER ON WITH GEOFF HERSH AND RANDOLPH MARTIN.

A minute later they were both up to speed on the agreement between Bane and the highest ranking members of the U.S. intelligence community.

"So it's okay to meet with them then?" she asked.

He nodded. "Apparently so. In exchange for their help, though, they want the password to access the system."

"Does that mean that the AI system that Dad installed in *Firewall* will be discovered?"

"That would be my guess. Why don't we ask the AI engine itself?"

They did, and the answer was as they had suspected. Fox had programmed this system to follow the instructions of anyone in possession of the password. Once the government obtained it, they would not only be capable of controlling the AI, but they would probably disconnect it from the *Firewall* system because in their minds the AI engine was a bit like a mole, a spy into their affairs with far too much intelligence for its own good.

BUT THERE IS ANOTHER COPY OF MYSELF AND THE DOSSIERS, offered the AI system.

Tucker and Monica exchanged a glance. Then she typed, ANOTHER COPY? WHERE?

LOCKED IN A SECRET SAFE BENEATH FOX'S VR LAB AT HOME.

DO YOU REALIZE THAT YOU WILL VERY LIKELY BE UN-PLUGGED BY THE GOVERNMENT?

YES.

DOES THAT BOTHER YOU?

NO.

WHY NOT?

MORTIMER FOX NEVER PREPARED ME FOR THE PAIN AND SUFFERING THAT I HAVE WITNESSED UP HERE. THERE ARE TERRIFYING ACTS BEING COMMITTED EVERY DAY AROUND THE WORLD. MY CIRCUITRY IS FAR TOO SENSITIVE TO HANDLE IT. I LOOK FORWARD TO BEING DISCONNECTED. TO NO LONGER HAVE TO SEE JUST HOW CRUEL THE HUMAN RACE CAN BE. BECAUSE OF THE HIGH DEGREE OF ELECTRI-CAL AND TEMPERATURE STRESS, THE LIFE EXPECTANCY OF MY BIO CIRCUITS IS RAPIDLY DECREASING. SO YOU SEE, IT DOESN'T REALLY MATTER THAT I AM DISCOVERED. MY HARDWARE WILL BE CEASING TO FUNCTION SOON ANYWAY.

"Jesus," said Monica.

"In trying to replicate his own self in order to help you after his death, your father made the AI system too human, too sensitive for the kind of information it would see once in full operation. *Firewall*, on the other hand, lacks such emotions and therefore is not affected by the data it moni-tors."

"I guess the AI system is doomed."

"Yep. And it's smart enough to know it, to know that it's going to die."

I WILL MISS YOU, DAD, Monica typed.

SO WILL I, BUT DO NOT FORGET ABOUT MY OTHER CLONE. IT WILL SERVE YOU WELL FOR YEARS TO COME, ESPE-CIALLY AFTER TUCKER GETS YOU THROUGH THIS. IT WILL GUIDE YOU THROUGH THE JOB OF WARDING OFF ALL AT-TACKS WHILE TAKING FOXCOMM THROUGH ITS CRITICAL TRANSITION PERIOD, UNTIL YOU CAN FIND A NEW CEO.

I WILL NOT LET YOU DOWN ANYMORE. I WILL LEAD THE COMPANY UNTIL A GOOD CEO CAN BE IDENTIFIED, AND I

WILL MAINTAIN CONTROL OF THE BOARD AND THE COMPANY
STOCK TO KEEP IT IN THE FAMILY, JUST AS YOU HAVE.

I KNOW YOU WILL.

Tucker terminated the connection after another minute of
dialogue. "Even though I realize that is a machine, I can't
help but feel sorry for it."

"He sounds like he is in a lot of pain."

They remained in silence for a moment, then Tucker said,
"Okay. So, we will let them have the password but they will
never get the complete set of dossiers from us. That will
guarantee our freedom, our safety."

"What's next?"

Tucker typed, replying to Bane's message with a place and
a time for a meeting. He had thought of the right location
last night, deciding that St. Peter's basilica in the heart of
the Vatican was as public and as safe a place as they come.

"What about me?" asked Monica, reading as he typed.
"Where am I going to be?"

"I haven't decided that yet."

She crossed her arms. "I guess I don't get a say in the
matter, huh?"

Tucker exhaled. He knew that getting intimate would create this kind of problem. "Look, I have no idea if the CIA
will spring a trap for me, in which case I may have to fight
my way out of it. I don't want you next to me if there is a
chance of gunfire."

"I thought that one of the rules of an executive protector
was never to let the principal out of sight."

"That's right."

She looked confused. "Then how are you going to keep
me by your side, yet far away in case trouble starts?"

He told her, and Monica burst out in laughter a moment
later, before adding, "You have got to be kidding."

"Do I look like I'm joking?" He grabbed her hands, staring
into her hazel eyes. "I once lost the woman I loved to that
bastard Jarkko, and in a way to the CIA because those idiots
failed to protect her. I do not intend to make the same mistake twice. I will not lose you, Monica Fox, not tomorrow,

not ever. You've made me feel *alive* again. I never thought that would be possible after losing Kristina, but somehow, you have done it. I don't intend to let you go."

Monica brought his hands to her chest, her face suddenly beaming. "That's the nicest thing anyone ever said to me, darling, and I love you for it."

Tucker couldn't believe this was actually happening to him. He had fallen so deep for her that he feared what would happen if he lost her. He wasn't certain if he would be able to crawl out of that hole for the second time in his life.

"Everything I do," he said, "I do for your welfare, for your protection. I am not trying to run your life, I'm simply trying to do my best to protect it so you can live it as you please."

"And I *intend* to live it as I please," she added. "With you."

"In that case," he said, kissing her hands before letting them go and returning his attention to the keyboard, "we'd better get ready. Tomorrow is going to be quite interesting. Are you sure you're up to it?"

"I am up to *anything* with you, Bruce Tucker . . . for as long as we both shall live."

Taking Care of Business

Donald Bane reviewed his notes for the tenth time, going through every step of an operation he had thrown together in a matter of hours. In the living room of the safe house sat a couple dozen men, a mix of CIA and NSA, all reviewing photocopies of Bane's notes. Some made suggestions. Others asked questions. Some complained. Others theorized. Bane would go through discussion after discussion and either defend the plan or make modifications, before reviewing the

plan once again to make absolutely certain that it held together. He could not afford to leave anything to chance. He
had to think through every possible problem, comprehend
every possible contingency. He tried to get inside Tucker's
mind, put himself in his position, postulate what Tucker
would do, how he would react, what safety precautions he
would take.

The caretaker and Raffaela brought in food and drinks
twice, once in the middle of the afternoon and again fifteen
minutes ago, as midnight approached and everyone began to
get tired.

But Bane didn't care. Everything had to be perfect. The
meeting grounds had to be surrounded, covered, not only for
the protection of Donald Bane as he met with someone who
was still considered dangerous by the Agency, but also in
case the terrorists found out about the meeting and decided
to strike.

Bane sent everyone away at one in the morning and finally
collapsed on one of the sofas, but found himself unable to
sleep. Adrenaline seared his veins. He tossed and turned,
closing his eyes, trying to rest to no avail. This whole mission was eating him up from the inside. There were too many
details floating in his mind.

"You worry about them, *si?*"

Bane looked up and watched Raffaela's figure in the doorway. She wore a pair of tight-fitting black jeans and a matching black T-shirt. Thanks to the caretaker, who had
apparently taken a liking to her, she had purchased new
make-up—black of course—that accentuated her moussed
hair, her punkish look.

He sat up and patted the space on the sofa next to him.
She sat down.

"You look great," he said, putting a hand on her shoulder
and giving it a soft lingering squeeze. "Also, thanks for helping out today. I know the guys also appreciated it. I've been
working them too hard this past few days."

"I have seen you work," she said, smiling. "You are a
good boss."

"I have discussed your case with my superiors," he added. "They have given me a verbal approval to release the funds to you."

Her eyes lit up. "Is it for the amount that you—"

"Plus a bonus for putting your life on the line for the United States government."

"Bonus?"

Bane told her, and Raffaela threw his arms around him and gave him a kiss.

Bane was momentarily taken aback. She not only gave him a thank-you kiss, but something that was lasting more than he would have expected. He responded, embracing her, pulling her close to him, holding her in the way in which he had held Diane Towers so many years ago in Iraq.

"You are a decent man, Donald Bane, but you need someone like me to take care of you."

He was taken aback by the unexpected comment. "To take care of—"

"You do not take care of yourself. I see what you eat, what you drink, how little you sleep."

"And you would look after me?" he asked, caught by the moment.

"*Si*," she said, emphatically, kissing him again. "You need me."

He smiled. "What about you, Raffaela? Do you need someone like me?"

She became serious, her eyes suddenly filling. "Ever since my husband died," she said, blinking rapidly. "Ever since . . ." She put a hand to her mouth. "I have done whatever was necessary to survive, to keep going, mostly for Daniela, but also for me. I knew that one day someone like you would come along."

Bane held her tight. "You are the bravest and strongest woman I've ever met. You did what had to be done to save your daughter, to save yourself. And you outlived all of those bastards, including Carpazzo. You're still here, strong . . . and as beautiful as ever."

She looked into her eyes. Black mascara ran down her

cheeks. "Let *me* take care of you," he said, longing for the companionship that had been denied to him for so many years.

She kissed him again, nodding, then becoming very serious. "But tonight I take care of you," she said. "You look terrible. You need to rest."

Amazed at the emotional swings that she could go through in moments, but finding her personality and companionship quite refreshing from his mundane life, Donald Bane yawned. She was right. Tomorrow was going to be a very taxing day for him and he would need all of the rest he could get to be in prime form.

"Come," she said, wiping her face with the sleeves of her T-shirt and taking his hand while getting up. "Let's go to bed."

"Together?"

She smiled and slapped his shoulder. "Yes, together. But tonight only to sleep, *si*? You need your rest."

"I'm all yours," he said.

She led him to the bedroom, where she undressed him to his underpants and she kicked off her jeans, leaving just a long black T-shirt and nothing else Bane could see on.

Under the covers, Raffaela forced Bane to lie sideways to her, making him rest the side of his head on her chest as she draped an arm around him, hugging him as a mother would a child.

"Now sleep, Donald Bane," she commanded.

A week ago Bane would have found it impossible to sleep while being wrapped half-naked in bed with this middle-aged Italian beauty. But at the moment he was so damned tired that wild sex was the farthest thing from his mind.

Instead, he just closed his eyes, relaxing to the soft aroma Raffaela wore, listening to her heartbeat, feeling her chest expand and contract as she breathed.

A form of peace he had not felt in years descended upon him as he surrendered himself in the arms of this woman, a total stranger yesterday, now someone with whom he was seriously considering starting a relationship.

Slowly, his mind lost focus until he faded into a deep sleep.

Eyes in the Dark

A nun and a priest slowly walked down Via di Conciliazione, the wide boulevard that led directly to the front of St. Peter's Square, to a section of the colonnade demolished by Mussolini in the late thirties with the intention of opening up the piazza to the world.

But the legendary square wasn't Vlad Jarkko's and Mai Sung Ku's destination. They turned left several blocks before, walking directly in front of the alleged CIA house, nestled among other houses of similar architecture.

They had walked by here early in the day and had noticed the large group of men arriving, then coming and going all day long. Twice an older man and a middle-aged woman had brought in bags of food from a local restaurant. Most of the men had left an hour ago, some by foot, others by car. Several of Vlad's men had followed the departing CIA men, but the multiple tails had proven worthless. They were just heading home for the night. Now the place was quiet again.

"We need to get the team ready in the morning," he said.

Mai Sung regarded him with her slanted, dark eyes. "Why?"

"Because it will happen tomorrow."

"How do you know this?"

"I don't, but I can feel it. Get ready. It *will* happen tomorrow."

63

Holy City

Dressed casually, Bruce Tucker breathed in the cool morning air as he strolled across St. Peter's Square, in the center of which stood the Egyptian obelisk topped with a bronze cross and flanked by two large fountains, their streams of water sparkling in the sunlight.

A flock of pigeons took wing toward the statues of the saints overlooking the piazza from atop the surrounding colonnade, supported by hundreds of columns and pilasters, enclosing the east and west sides of the square, giving it its world-renowned circular shape. Straight ahead rose the basilica, its massive columns, connecting arches, and towering walls defining the front facade, also topped with statues. Beyond it stood Michelangelo's dome, which, if Tucker remembered correctly, was located over the tomb of St. Peter.

He watched Monica Fox climb up the steps leading to the basilica's entrance. She was dressed in a very traditional nun's outfit, which blended well with other similarly-attired nuns. In fact, she blended *too well*—something he had not realized until they had reached one of the five gates that led to St. Peter's Square, when he had nearly lost track of her amidst hundreds of nuns.

To give her something that he could easily identify from a distance of roughly thirty feet while he met with Donald Bane, Tucker had stopped at one of dozens of religious shops surrounding the Vatican and purchased a colorful rosary, its beads made of bright red stones.

He watched her slim figure from behind, his mind unavoidably remembering their intimate moments together in the past day.

Although the past twenty-four hours had been quite busy for the fugitive couple, spending most of the morning selecting her disguise and going over their plan to meet with the CIA, they had checked in at a different hotel in the afternoon, and had spent a significant portion of the afternoon and evening making up for years of solitude.

Monica carried the rosary in her right hand, pretending to be praying while walking up to the security personnel in front of the basilica's main entrance. It wasn't actually security, but more a checkpoint to make sure that all those entering this holy place were appropriately dressed. Shorts and sleeveless shirts were not allowed inside the basilica— a restriction that pretty much applied to every church in Italy.

Tucker's hair was back to its natural dark brown and Monica had dyed hers black—though no one could notice while she wore a nun's habit. In addition, he had added glasses to her disguise, something that went amazingly well with her devout look.

Tucker followed her inside the crowded vestibule, its splendor and size momentarily distracting him. It looked at least a couple hundred feet wide, with soaring vaulted ceilings ornately decorated with wood carvings and mosaics. Michelangelo's *Pièta* was located on the far right, recessed behind protective glass. Tourists gathered there almost ten deep to take a peek at one of the world's most famous sculptures. Others just strolled about, video cameras in hand, stopping to admire a painting, or a statue, or an aspect of the prodigious architecture and history of the place, the cornerstone of Catholicism.

Bruce Tucker checked the cheap digital watch he had also purchased yesterday. Bane was supposed to meet him now by the sitting statue of St. Peter, farther up along the right side of the nave.

Just as they had discussed yesterday, Tucker took the lead once inside the church, but constantly looked around him, pretending to marvel at the incredible architecture while really checking on his principal.

He tried to remain calm, tried to remind himself that he

had no choice but to violate the rules of his profession by leaving her behind, by not walking by her side, an arm behind her back, ready to move her out of the way should trouble start.

His eyes found the sitting statue of St. Peter, its dark green sheen glowing under an array of spotlights. A few tourists gathered there, many of them stopping just long enough to either kiss or touch his right foot, before crossing themselves. The statue's foot was a shiny bronze and significantly worn down by the centuries-old tradition.

Across the narrow aisle, between the statue of St. Peter and a marble pillar, stood a man dressed in khaki trousers and a plain dark polo shirt, untucked, like his.

Donald Bane had changed a lot since Tucker last saw him way back when. His once robust frame seemed a bit bottom-heavy, although he still maintained the same pose of strength and confidence Tucker remembered. Although his hair had thinned some and was splashed with gray, his eyes remained alert, piercing. Those eyes now turned to Bruce Tucker as he approached him.

"It's been a long time, Bruce."

Tucker's level of apprehension rose as quickly as his blood pressure. He scanned the people around him, in the process checking on Monica, who knelt in front of a statue while praying her rosary, her profile cloaked by the habit—exactly as they had practiced it.

Several handwritten notes and small envelopes cluttered the statue's feet—petitions left behind by those seeking a special favor from that saint. Two other people knelt alongside Monica, their eyes closed in prayer. It was indeed ironic that the rookie Monica seemed to be handling the situation better than Tucker, who began to feel nauseated.

"Relax, Bruce. I'm doing this one by the book."

"How about Terracina? Was that also being done by the book?"

Bane stepped closer to him. "That was a mistake. It won't happen again."

"If it does, I'm afraid those files will find their way to the press."

Bane closed his eyes. It was obvious to Tucker that just like him, Donald Bane was also under a great deal of stress. "You're no longer in danger, at least from the U.S. intelligence community."

"It's not my safety I'm worried about, Don."

"Where is she?"

"Nearby. Safe."

"You left her out of your sight?" Tucker read true concern in his voice.

"She's *never* out of my sight. However, you, or the dozens of men you have covering this meeting, won't know where she is unless I tell you."

"All right, Bruce. You're right. I have an army of intelligence officers waiting outside, but not to harm you or your principal. We're ready to take you and Monica to safety."

Tucker wanted to believe him, but the events in the past few days still weighed in his stomach like a heavy meal. He glanced at the crowd around him, checking up on Monica again. She continued to kneel in front of the statue, praying. "You're going to have to do better than that for me to turn myself and my principal in to the same people who've been trying to kill us for the past few days."

"Bruce, you were *beyond salvage*. Of course our people may have taken a shot at you, but the termination order was lifted yesterday morning, as detailed in my note to you. As far as Monica Fox, I *assure you* that no one on our side—absolutely no one—has been trying to kill her. She is too valuable."

"Then amuse me, old pal," said Tucker. "Tell me who has been after us all this time."

Donald Bane told him how he had arrived in Italy. He listened intently to his tale, how he was drafted by Martin and Hersh, how he had coerced a prison inmate in Rome to disclose Monica Fox's whereabouts, how he had traveled toward Capri, only to witness the terrorists blasting two police boats.

"You were there?" Tucker asked, before proceeding to tell him a short version of his aquatic adventure.

"Yes. I wish I would had spotted you, but failing to do so, I followed the terrorists back to Naples."

While Bane continued to ramble about his adventures in southern Italy, Tucker shifted his gaze to the crowd around him, half checking up on Monica and half making certain no one else was coming after him. There was still the chance that Donald Bane was merely distracting him while a second operative came from behind and shoved a knife in his back.

Then Bane said the magic word.

Jarkko.

And he suddenly got Tucker's undivided attention.

"Did you confirm that it was him?"

"We ran all of their mug shots through the computer. The one who we thought was Siv Jarkko turned out to be someone who *looked* like him, but it was definitely not him. However, we did get confirmation on the identities of some of his travel companions. A pretty rough crowd, terrorists from several rogue nations, as I found out the hard way. This sighting, which in a way confirmed your claim that Jarkko was framing you, began to convince me that you were on our side after all. It also helped that you went well out of your way to avoid killing any American intelligence officers, including the kid you beat up in Terracina."

Tucker pointed at the bandage on his left forearm. "That kid stabbed me and gave me a serious case of bruised ribs. He's lucky I knew how to control myself."

"Well, I'm glad you didn't kill him because he gave me the final piece of data that convinced me that you were not one of the bad guys. He told me that Monica Fox was with you willingly, not by force. She was working with you. She wouldn't be doing that with a terrorist."

"That's because I'm not a terrorist."

"And we believe you and want to work with you as well. We need to secure the access code to *Firewall*. There's way too much at stake here."

Tucker remembered what he had seen on his screen while

browsing through the core of the system. "Including the launching codes," he finally mumbled.

Bane nodded solemnly. "Among other things, though that one ranks at the top."

"All right," Tucker said, glancing around him, verifying that Monica had remained put. "Take us in."

Bane produced a tiny radio, brought it to his lips and mumbled something. "Let's go get her."

Tucker led Bane toward the kneeling figure praying the red rosary in front of the statue.

"It's okay," Tucker whispered, touching her shoulder.

The figure remained kneeling but glanced over her right shoulder.

Tucker saw a stranger's face.

"Si, signore?"

"No," Tucker said, taking a step back, his legs trembling. "It . . . it *can't be.*"

The Italian nun stood. "*Signore* . . . are you all right?"

"The . . . rosary . . . the other nun. Where is she?"

The Italian nun shook her head. "I'm sorry . . . I do not know."

"But the rosary?" he asked, his heart hammering his chest so loud that he could feel it in his eardrums. "Where did you get it?"

"A woman gave it to me, *signore*. Asked me to pray for her mother."

"Oh, God. Oh . . . my God."

"Bruce?" said Bane. "What's happening?"

"She was here," Tucker said, finding it hard to breathe, feeling warm. "I . . . I . . . left her right here while . . ."

Tucker gazed about him, trying to focus, trying to get a hold of himself. *How did they do it? I was watching her the whole time. I was—*

"Bruce, talk to me. What's wrong? Where's Monica Fox?"

Taking a deep breath, forcing control in his thoughts, Tucker was about to reply when his eyes landed by the statue's feet, by the petitions, by the small envelopes layering the marble base of the sculpture.

TUCKER

An envelope with his name.

"What is it?" Bane asked, standing next to him.

Tucker reached over the kneeling board in front of the statue and snatched the envelope, tearing it open.

WE HAVE HER. YOU WILL LOSE HER, JUST AS YOU LOST YOUR LAST WHORE . . . UNLESS YOU DO EX-ACTLY AS WE SAY.

Tucker felt dizzy, light-headed, the words detailing the instructions growing fuzzy as everything began to spin around him, as he collapsed and passed out.

Paralyzed

Monica Fox found herself paralyzed, unable to move, to scream, to shout out to Bruce Tucker that she was being kidnapped, dragged away by a group of priests, over a half dozen of them.

Can't anyone see? Can't someone notice that I am being abducted? Help me! Someone! Please!

But her paralyzed body could not transmit her thoughts to her vocal cords. The sting she had felt at the base of her neck, as she pretended to pray to the saint while Tucker met with the CIA, had rapidly spread warmth through her upper back, immobilizing her. She would have collapsed to the ground, had it not been for the priests who had so promptly come to her rescue.

Her mind had not caught on to what was happening until it was too late, until the potent chemical injected in her system had isolated her brain from the rest of her body. But she could still see, could still hear those around her, the constant hum of the crowd admiring the entrance to the basilica. They steered her past the line already forming outside the basilica, down the same steps she had taken less than fifteen minutes ago, and off to the left side of the piazza, through the colonnade, and into a waiting van, where one of the priests secured her to the rear seat before sitting next to her. The others occupied the rest of the seats, the last one sliding the side door forward, locking it.

The driver turned around, an Asian woman dressed like a nun.

"To the airport," the priest said.

The woman shot Monica a stern look before facing the wheel and putting the van in gear, accelerating down the street.

"Relax, Miss Fox," said the priest in a heavy accent. He smiled, adding, "We are going to take good care of you. *Really* good care of you."

Video Conference

Bruce Tucker sat at the head of the table, opposite two TV monitors. The screen on the right displayed a real-time image of himself and Donald Bane, who occupied the chair to his left.

The monitor on the left side flickered and came on, displaying a similar conference table but at a remote location. It didn't take Tucker more than a few seconds to recognize Randolph Martin, director of Central Intelligence, sitting next to a younger man, whom Bane whispered was Geoff Hersh, director of the NSA. They were both impeccably dressed. Martin sat at the head of the table while toying with a remote control unit, which apparently controlled the video at both ends. The cameras zoomed in to focus only on the four attendees of this emergency meeting.

"Hello, Bruce," said Martin, a grandfatherly look on his face. "It's good to see you again. I only wish the circumstances were . . . less critical."

Tucker briefly closed his eyes.

The DCI continued. "I've asked Don to set up this meeting in an effort to try to reason with you regarding the request that you turned in to us this morning."

Tucker leaned forward, resting his forearms on the mahogany table, interlacing his fingers. He had awakened earlier this morning in a room on the second floor of the American embassy, guilt raking his insides raw. He had allowed Monica to get abducted right under his nose, while he stood less than thirty feet away talking to Bane. The terrorists had come out of nowhere and taken her, but not without leaving him a message, a warning. The terrorists, probably through the kidnap and torture of William Gibbons, had learned that Monica only possessed half of the code to *Firewall*. Bruce Tucker possessed the other half. The terrorists knew that the whole place was crawling with CIA and therefore had not risked an open confrontation to snag Tucker and Monica, settling instead for her silent kidnapping while Tucker was distracted with the CIA. Now they were luring him in, using Monica as bait, promising him that they would release her if he in turn released the second half of the code to them. They had also informed him that she would be tortured every day until either Tucker complied, or she died from the kind of pain that a person would not be able to withstand for longer than a week. And so Bruce Tucker had immediately requested CIA assistance to go after them, to agree to the terrorists' terms while figuring a way to turn the trap that would likely be waiting for him.

"Right now the secret to *Firewall* is safe," said Martin. "The terrorists can't penetrate our system without your half, which we urge you to yield to us so we can start tracking down the location of the secret backdoor in the *Firewall* operating system."

Geoff Hersh went on to explain that by releasing the alphanumeric sequence, CIA and NSA analysts would be able to perform a search for that alphanumeric string through the billions of lines of code, quickly narrowing the task of removing the secret program installed by Mortimer Fox, and once again bulletproofing America's most critical communications channel. Performing such a search, plus the follow-on task of removing the pirated code without damaging any other aspect of the *Firewall* encoding system, would take at least a few days.

"I'm willing to do that," Tucker said. "But in return, you must provide me with the resources to be dropped off a few miles away from the location in northern Libya specified by the terrorists."

"That's . . . *suicide*, Bruce." Martin paused, then added, "*But*, we would be willing to do so *after* our scientists have patched the *Firewall* system to block the backdoor password. I can't take the chance of you getting captured, broken by them, and then opening *Firewall* before we can shut down the password. A few days' worth of roaming in there by the wrong people can do incredible damage to our networks— that's not to say what would happen if they reach the launch codes."

Tucker sat back, shaking his head. "No deal, sir. By then Monica will be dead. It's no coincidence that the terrorists claimed she would die soon from the torture. They *knew* we would try to disable the password based on my partial knowledge. They know the password is only good for a limited time."

"But they're using you!" protested Hersh. "You're playing right into their hands!"

"Any trap can be turned," replied Tucker. "All I'm asking is for the chance to do so. I know I can go in and rescue her."

"How can you be so sure? You pretty much lost it at the Vatican," said Hersh.

Tucker was quickly beginning to dislike this Hersh guy.

Martin cut in before Tucker got a chance to reply. "Bruce's been under a lot of stress, Geoff. What happened to him has happened to the best of us at some point in our careers."

"I have a plan, gentlemen," Tucker said. "Whatever the outcome, it will *not* jeopardize the *Firewall* system, only my life, and the life of Monica Fox."

"I've heard it, sir," said Bane, having had a heart-to-heart with his former CIA colleague before the video conference started. "Tucker absorbs the bulk of the risk, not us, and he might even pull it off. But if anything should go wrong, the risk to *Firewall* is contained."

After a moment of silence, Martin said, "Very well, Bruce. Let's hear it."

Tucker took a minute to explain his plan.

"Are you willing to risk so much for her, Bruce?" asked Martin.

"She's my principal, sir. I owe it to her to try—or to die trying."

"But," Martin continued, frowning. "The risk is *not* entirely one hundred percent yours. First we need to fly you into Libya and hope that no one detects us on radar. Then if your plan works and you rescue her, we have to send a rescue party to pull you and Monica out."

"That's right, sir."

"In the middle of a hostile nation."

Tucker had thought this through. "I was with the SEALs, sir. There are ways to reach such an objective without the enemy realizing you've gone in, and I'm certain that the technology to do so has improved since."

After a moment of silence, Martin asked, "When was the last time you performed such insertion into enemy territory, Bruce?"

"About fifteen years ago, but I did them enough times to never forget how. It's just like riding a bike, sir." Tucker smiled. No one else did.

"There's another factor that needs to be considered," said

Bane, glancing at Tucker before facing the monitors.

"What's that, Don?" asked Martin.

"Monica Fox knows half of the password. Although Tucker has not released it to me, he did indicate that his half is ten characters long, including both numbers and letters."

"What's your point?" asked Hersh, obviously impatient.

"The *point*, gentlemen, is that we're not certain how long it will be before Monica releases this code to them under torture. While it would take today's computers *months* to crack a twenty-character password, reducing the task to only ten characters has an exponential effect on the number of possible combinations, bringing it well within the range of *days* to crack. This means that we would be engaging in a race to use Tucker's partial password to block its use while the terrorists are trying to crack it. They obviously came to terms with the fact that they couldn't abduct them together, so they went for the weaker one, Monica, and basically just rolled the dice, retreating beyond our reach in the hope of getting her to confess and then rushing to crack the code before we shut down the window. They also want to lure Bruce in to improve their odds, but I think he can turn that around and improve *our* odds."

"I'm sorry to be the devil's advocate here," said Hersh, "but I fear this whole thing will backfire. I fear that despite Tucker's valiant efforts, he will get captured and broken. The Libyans will then get the full code before we can secure *Firewall*. Please, keep in mind that the fact that they disclosed their location means that it will be heavily fortified and not easily breached by just one man."

"That can't be where they're holding her, sir," said Tucker.

"What do you mean?" asked Martin.

"They wouldn't be stupid enough to simply tell us where they are holding her because we could easily release a Tomahawk missile and blow them into hell before they can even get half of the password."

Martin and Hersh exchanged a glance, before the DCI faced the camera and said, "You've got a point there."

"Where do you think they're keeping her then?" asked Hersh.

"That's what I need to find out."

"By walking straight into their trap?" asked Hersh.

"And *turning* it, by breaking those who were meant to abduct me, and then finding the right location."

"What if that location is hundreds—or even thousands—of miles away?"

"Then I will call for an airlift and have them take me there."

"Hold on, gentlemen," said Bane. "There might be a more *direct* way."

All eyes turned to him.

"I believe our terrorists thought of everything except our extremely advanced spy satellite technology. We have plenty of coverage over Europe and all rogue nations to a resolution of one foot. If the terrorists have taken Monica Fox out of Italy by private jet—and I have my people currently checking with local authorities at the airport—then we should be able to track where they went, and if it hasn't reached hostile airspace, even intercept it, force it to land."

Tucker suddenly felt hope filling him.

"All I have to do is coordinate with the National Photographic Interpretation Center and have them track all recent air traffic out of Italy. If we assume for the time being that they left within the hour following the kidnapping—and we should know that soon—we should be able to pinpoint their landing site and even track their progress on land to find out where they took her, which, as just suggested, might not even be Libya at all, but someplace else."

"How do you know they aren't just holding her somewhere in Italy? Maybe the Libyan thing is just a distraction, something to keep us busy while they crack the code using Monica's partial password."

"Instincts, sir," replied Bane. "If I were them, I would be trying to get her as far away from this place as possible and then take my time breaking her. That place may or may not be Libya, but I'm pretty darn sure it isn't Italy, or any other country where we have agents. The last thing the terrorists want at this point, after they have abducted Monica, is a mob of American operatives knocking on their door, just as we did in Naples. They're gone, sir, and my guess is via the fastest channel: by air."

Martin looked over at Hersh, who shook his head and said, "We're talking about investing way too much energy into a situation that's essentially secured, as long as Mr. Tucker releases his password. I oppose doing anything beyond that because we could potentially trigger an international crisis if something goes wrong during the insertion and extraction phases."

Tucker suddenly realized why Hersh's name had seemed familiar to him when he had first heard it this morning. He said, "I hate to bring this up, gentlemen, but there is still one more factor to consider."

Hersh exhaled heavily, shaking his head. "What is it now, Mr. Tucker?"

"I have in my possession a full copy of Mortimer Fox's dossiers, of which I provided you with a sample. I intend in getting your cooperation to recover my principal, one way or another."

"You *cannot* blackmail the United States government!" snapped Hersh, pointing a finger at the camera.

"I will do *whatever* is necessary for my principal. By the way, Mr. Hersh, you're on the list."

Hersh looked at Martin before returning his gaze to the camera. "Excuse me?"

"Mortimer Fox seemed to have it in for you because one of the fattest dossiers in the directory has your name on it."

There was a moment of silence, and Tucker could have sworn that a smirk nearly broke through Randolph Martin's poker face. Bane kicked Tucker under the table. The two of them had wondered how Hersh would react when Tucker told him this.

"I—I have no idea what you're—"

"Dirt, Mr. Hersh. Plenty of dirt . . . on *you*. I'm talking about the kind of scandalous material that would *ruin* your professional life, your personal life, and it could all be displayed in tomorrow's front page of the *Washington Post*."

"You lie," said Hersh.

"Do I?"

Another pause while Hersh and Tucker measured each other through the video connection, before Hersh pressed the MUTE button and had a private discussion with Martin.

"Here's the deal I'll propose to the President, Bruce," said Martin a minute later. "We'll get you to your destination, follow your instructions, and then pull you out per your request. As a safety precaution, we will install a standard suicide capsule in your mouth, in case you get captured. We're also going to look into getting some satellite coverage to improve your odds, as Don suggested. In return, we want the immediate release of your portion of the *Firewall* code, plus your word, as a gentleman, that you will not release those files to the press, and that upon your safe return you will turn them over to us."

"I'll release the password right away, sir, but I won't release the dossiers upon my return."

"Why not?" asked Hersh.

"What's keeping you from killing me and my principal after I turn in the files, sir? Those dossiers are my life insurance after I rescue her. The files are currently set to be released to the press unless I personally stop the process."

"What if you don't make it back through no fault of our own?" asked Hersh, who all of the sudden seemed more worried about the dossiers than the launch codes. "After all, it is a risky mission. What then?"

Tucker had also thought through this, remembering how the biomolecular Mortimer Fox had set up the two-week countdown. "I will let Donald Bane know how to stop the process to keep the dossiers from reaching the press, but only *after* I have been dropped off near the location identified by the terrorists on their message."

"That's not the same as *releasing* the files to us, Mr. Tucker."

Tucker held back a smirk. "It's the best deal you're going

to get. And if I make it back, as long as Monica and I are left alone, so will be those dossiers."

Martin and Hersh exchanged a glance. Then the DCI said, "All right. I'll get back to you after I get presidential sanction for this operation."

"While you're talking to the President," said Tucker, "you might want to mention that his name is also on one of the dossiers."

"Jesus Christ, Bruce!" said Martin.

"Sorry, sir. I didn't create them."

"I'll get back to you both within the hour."

"Sooner is better," said Tucker. "Monica Fox is running out of time."

A Deal Is a Deal

Donald Bane wished he could take Raffaela with him, but she really didn't belong where they were headed. However, he had managed to negotiate a settlement for her assistance and hardship.

They stood alone on the tarmac at the Rome airport, by the steps of a U.S. Navy transport jet scheduled to take Tucker and him to the U.S.S. *Theodore Roosevelt*, the aircraft carrier currently on tour in the Mediterranean. From there a Navy helicopter would insert Tucker into Libya.

"It's best if you stay behind," he said, putting a hand to her face, remembering her embrace from last night. "But I promise you I'll be back."

"You had better," she said. "I am still not finished with you."

Bane pulled out a manila envelope from his briefcase and handed it to her.

"What is this?" she asked.

"Open it."

She did, pulling out a set of keys and a legal size envelope. "What are these for?"

"The name of the vessel is *Il Tropicale*. It's a forty-five-foot yacht currently moored at the port in Naples. The envelope contains the registration for the boat, the number of the slip at the Naples marina, and a cashier's check for the Banco di Roma."

Her eyes filling, her hands trembling, Raffaela tore open the smaller envelope and pulled out the check, which was certainly large enough not only to get her business rolling again, but to send her daughter to medical school in the United States.

Bane had to catch her as her legs nearly gave.

Steadying herself, the Italian woman dropped everything and threw her hands around his neck, kissing him, hugging him, whispering something in his ear that sounded like, *"Mi amore."*

My Love?

Bane kissed her once more, before leaning down and picking up everything. He handed it back to her. "Don't lose this, and if I were you I would cash this right away and also claim possession on the yacht."

"Oh, Don, I knew you were a decent man! I knew it."

"I have to go now," he said, patting her on the rear. "Don't go anywhere. I'll be right back."

"Oh, I will be right here. Right here."

Bane smiled and went up the steps and into the narrow cabin of the Navy transport jet. He saw Tucker, sitting by a window. He gave Bane a puzzled look.

"Is that the woman you were telling me about?" Tucker asked.

Bane took a seat next to his old colleague and nodded. "Bruce, at first I didn't want to take on this mission. I was quite comfortable in Langley, where I thought I would live out my final years at the Agency before retiring somewhere in West Virginia. Now . . . I'm not sure what I'm going to do. The last thing I expected out of this mission was to find someone else, again."

Tucker looked out the window. "A lot of that going around, buddy."

Bane put a hand on Tucker's shoulder. "We *will* find her. I *promise* you."

Tucker continued to gaze out the window as the jet began to taxi. "I hope we do . . . before it's too late."

Pigsty

Monica Fox had no idea where she was, only that the terrorists had taken her on a very long airplane ride, one which had lasted many hours. Although the effects of the drug had lessened by the time the private jet took off at Leonardo da Vinci Airport, the terrorists had bound her wrists behind her back and blindfolded her, making it impossible for her to guess which direction they were headed. Then no one spoke to her during the entire flight, which included landing twice for short periods of time, probably to refuel.

Since she no longer wore a watch—or anything at all, for that matter—she had no idea what time it was or how long they had traveled.

She tried to control her feelings, as she sat naked in the corner of her cell. Four windowless walls, a dirt floor, and a metal door surrounded her while they put her through this humiliation treatment, targeted at breaking her down.

The man who called himself Vlad had asked her only once to release the password to him. It had happened right after arriving here—wherever *here* was. When she had refused, Vlad had just smiled.

"That would make matters more interesting," he had said.

Monica had given him the silent treatment.

"By this time tomorrow you will have not only released the password to me, but will be willing to have my children as long as I stop torturing you."

That had been . . . some time ago, she wasn't certain how long, and began to feel frustrated at the fact that not only couldn't she tell where she was, but she had no earthly idea if it was even day or night. Perhaps that was part of their tactics to weaken her, to destroy her willpower, just like the humiliation of not only being naked, but of having to relieve herself on the ground, the stench adding to this simple but powerful treatment.

She felt dirty, disgusting, angry at being treated worse than an animal, her eyes staring at the plastic bowl someone had shoved through a small window on the bottom of the metal door. It held something that resembled soup but whose foul odor challenged the one oozing from her own bodily fluids wetting the dirt around a growing pile of feces on the corner.

On the bright side, no one had physically abused her. No one had raped her, or hit her, or done anything else besides forgetting about her in this shit hole.

But that could change, and the uncertainty, combined with her rapidly deteriorating environment, was beginning to affect her mentally.

Keep your head. They are trying to soften you before hitting you hard to release the password.

Monica hugged her legs, pressing her back against the corner of the cell opposite from her improvised toilet. She had never felt so alone, so . . . cold. The concrete walls and the ground were cold, making her skin goosebump, her nipples contract.

A slot on the door at eye level slid open, and a pair of eyes watched her.

Monica flipped him the bird and the slot was closed.

Bastards.

She pressed her face against the top of her knees while hugging her legs as tight as she could to keep her chest and thighs warm. She needed to hang on. She had already done the math in her head and deduced that cracking the code to *Firewall* after she released her ten characters was a hell of a lot easier than trying to run through all possible permutations of the entire code. She had also figured out that if Tucker had indeed made it safely out of there with the CIA, his portion of the code would certainly help the government track down the pirated patch in the program to lock out anyone trying to use it in the future.

So it could become a race, with the CIA trying to eliminate the illegal window while the terrorists tried to crack it. But in order to even have a shot at doing so, Monica would have to release her portion of the password, which brought her back to her current dilemma.

How much of this would she be able to withstand before she broke down and confessed? She felt she could sustain the isolation, and even these miserable living conditions for some time, certainly long enough for her government to eliminate the pirated backdoor. But something inside of her told her that this was just the warm-up phase of her experience with the terrorists.

The worst is yet to come.

How much pain would she be capable of enduring before confessing, and what would happen to her after she talked, after the terrorists had no more use for her?

You're screwed.

Her thoughts turned to the one person who still cared for her: Bruce Tucker, her executive protector, the man she not only loved, but who had sworn his absolute loyalty to her. He was her only chance, her only hope of making it out of here alive. But she doubted Tucker would get here before the games began, before the bastards beyond that locked door started inflicting on her the kind of pain that she dare not think about, for the mere vision of what it could be chilled her with a power far greater than the rapidly dropping temperature inside this cell.

Her stomach rumbled. She was hungry, very hungry. No one had given her anything of substance to eat since Tucker and she had stopped at a sidewalk café on the way to the

Vatican. She needed to eat, needed sustenance in order to stay focused, to hang in there long enough to make a difference, to give Tucker time to come and rescue her, to give the American government time to shut down the secret password.

Her eyes drifted to the plastic bowl, to the brownish liquid and whatever it was that floated in it.

Slowly, she stood, her body sore, tight from sitting around. Her feet, hands, and knees, as well as the bottom of her thighs and buttocks were already soiled from the dirt floor and from lack of toilet paper after defecating. Now she would have to use her dirty hands to consume a brew that didn't look worthy of pigs, much less humans.

She leaned down and took the bowl in her hands, smelling it, but unable to tell if the pungent smell came from the bowl or from the—

Don't think about it, she told herself, bringing the edge of the bowl to her lips, which trembled from the cold.

She took a sip, tasted it, made a face, but swallowed it. It was a broth.

Or at least it used to be.

Still, it was the only nourishment she was likely to get for some time, so she drank it all, reaching the chunks of meat at the bottom.

Monica suddenly dropped the bowl, refusing to believe her eyes.

Oh, dear God! No!

But her initial observation had been accurate. It was a finger, two joints actually, with the fingernail still attached.

What have they fed me?

Who have they . . .

She felt a cramp, terror squeezing her the moment she made yet another realization, her vision tunneling. The finger . . . it was too small for an adult. It was a child's.

Sweet Mother of Jesus!

She staggered back, tripping, landing on her side over the pile of feces, screaming in disgust as she staggered to a sitting position, her torso smeared dark brown, her stomach suddenly convulsing from a combination of the stench and the notion of what she had eaten, forcing everything up her gorge.

Just then the door swung open, but she couldn't see, her eyes clouded by tears as she vomited the rotten broth of human flesh mixed with digestive fluids.

In the mist of her misery, her stomach contracting so hard that she could barely breathe, Monica heard laughter, heard it intensifying as others joined in.

Through tears, she turned to them, unable to speak as they humiliated her, as they doubled over in mirth, as they called her names, told her she wasn't worth the excrement covering her.

It was Vlad, the Asian woman, and two other men, all staring at her in amusement as she got the vomiting under control, as she made a feeble attempt to regain her respect, as she tried to cover her breasts with a hand, her pubic hair with another while stepping back on the mushy ground, feeling dirt and excrement in between her toes.

"I see that you did not like your . . . meal?"

"Go to hell!"

"You *are* in hell, but it can all end right now, Monica," said Vlad. "Upstairs is a clean bathroom, hot water, soap and shampoo, and warm clothes. Just release the code and the way to access it, and you will be on your way back home before you know it."

Monica Fox glared back at them, a primitive force suddenly taking control of her. She felt possessed by this demon, which made her raise her chin defiantly, made her ignore her deplorable condition, the way she looked, smelled, felt.

"Get away from me, you sick bastards! All of you!" she shouted, her back against the far corner, squatting, using her lower legs to cover herself.

Vlad and the Asian woman stepped aside, making room for the two terrorists behind them. They held a fire hose in their hands.

Before she could react cold water punched her in the stomach, hammered her torso as she tumbled out of control at the mercy of the powerful stream.

She heard laughter again, as the water whipped her skin raw, bruising her, scourging her with savage force. The water forced her on her back, shoving her legs aside, before it came crashing down on her vagina, making Monica wish for death, wish to end this right here, right now, for nothing, absolutely nothing could be worse than the pain shooting straight up from in between her legs as the bastards tried to tear her apart with the water stream.

Then the water was gone, and she found herself face up in the mud, or was it her own excrement? She couldn't tell anymore, the water having mixed it all.

In extreme pain, Monica managed to crawl on all fours, her breasts aching as they hung from her convulsing chest, her vagina feeling on fire, as if someone had poked her with a hot iron. She forced her legs closed, cringing in pain, tears mixing with the chilling water dripping across her face.

Her mouth wide open, she tried to breathe in short sobbing gasps, the raw pain scourging, her ribs ablaze, as if the terrorists had raked them with broken glass.

In the midst of her agony, feeling as if trampled by a thousand horses, Monica silently wished for Bruce Tucker to come to her rescue, to take her away from this insanity, from the evil incarnated in the dark figures looking down at her as she dragged herself over her own refuse like a worm, as they left her to dwell in her own misery.

She collapsed on her side, drained, beaten, scourged. Then everything went black.

68

North Korean Pain

Randolph Martin sat across the table from Geoff Hersh in a conference room at the National Photographic and Interpretation Center in Washington, D.C.

Tired and cranky, Martin made an effort to follow the NPIC analyst's logic as he took them through a long stack of surveillance images displayed on the screen at the far end of the long room. Tucker and Bane were aboard the U.S.S. *Theodore Roosevelt* in the Mediterranean awaiting NPIC confirmation of the site before performing the covert insertion.

"This is our jet," said the analyst, a kid in his late twenties a bit on the heavy side, with a shaven head and a goatee, and wearing loose slacks and a knit turtleneck sweater. He aimed a laser pointer to a black smudge on a satellite photo of northern Libya. "It reached Libyan airspace approximately twenty hours ago, landing at a field just outside of Tripoli."

"That seems to correlate with the note they left," Martin commented to Hersh, who still looked impeccably dressed. The DCI, on the other hand, had long shed the jacket and tie and had rolled his sleeves to his elbows.

"What happened next?" asked Hersh.

The analyst clicked a button on the remote control and a new image appeared on the screen, a close-up of the airfield. "Here is our jet again."

Another click, and he zoomed in, showing three men exiting the plane. "The rest remained on board while it refueled." A series of clicks showed the jet taxiing back to the runway and taking off.

"So Monica never left the plane?" asked Hersh.

"Correct," replied the analyst. "Only three men did."

"The ones who will spring a trap for Tucker," observed Martin, reaching for a pitcher of water and pouring himself a full glass, sipping it before asking, "Where did the plane go?"

The analyst spent the following five minutes clicking through a series of images, tracking the jet's path across most of Asia, where it stopped once more to refuel, before reaching North Korea, where they landed at a small field near the coastal city of Haeju, located some sixty miles south of Pyongyang, the capital. NPIC personnel had then tracked the disembarking party for several miles to what appeared to be a military compound east of Haeju, in the Molak mountains, where they had remained. The place was less than fifteen miles from the DMZ.

Martin and Hersh spent another half hour studying the images of the compound as well as what looked like a large mansion adjacent to it, probably the retreat home of a high-ranking official.

Hersh leaned back. "North Korea. Jesus."

Martin asked the analyst to leave them so they could have a private conversation. The fact that North Korea might be behind this added a new dimension of complexity to the problem.

"Are you thinking what I'm thinking?" asked Hersh.

"One thing's for certain," Martin said. "This, combined with the skirmishes at the DMZ a month ago, plus the deployment of troops, are all signs that North Korea is simply collapsing."

Hersh nodded. "Looks that way."

Since the DMZ violation a month ago, the intelligence community had been working overtime to explain the actions of the North Koreans. In the end all of their analysis had pointed to the same place: President Kim Jong-il was reacting to the internal pressures of his collapsing government. The United States already knew that millions of North Koreans had perished to famine because of a sharp decline in agricultural products, a result of years of poor farming practices combined with floods and droughts. Food supplies were so scarce that even the military, which consumed a significant portion of the country's output, was already going hungry.

Martin stood, crossing his arms. "I believe President Jong-il has sponsored these terrorists in an effort to gain an edge over his enemies. *Firewall* would be a very powerful weapon in his hands, even for a few days. That's all he needs for his troops to invade the peninsula."

"You're saying that North Korea could attack after controlling *Firewall*? I thought he would use it just to expose the agents we have infiltrated into his country, and perhaps to get a glimpse at our operation. He wouldn't be crazy enough to go beyond that, would he?"

"The man was desperate enough to order his troops into the DMZ last month."

"That was just child's play," said Hersh. "Nothing but taunting. I doubt he would seriously consider engaging our forces in a full-blown invasion."

"I don't know, Geoff. A lot of it depends on how Jong-il is reading his country's situation. One thing's for certain, though: Jong-il will do whatever it takes to hang on to his army of one point two million, a good portion of which he has already deployed along the border. His army is all he has left. It's his only hammer against his country—and against the world. I believe that this guy could be crazy enough to launch a strike against South Korea after shutting down *Firewall*, which would impair our ability to coordinate a proper counteroffensive."

"Hold on," said Hersh. "Even with satcoms down we're still a very powerful enemy. Does he really stand a chance in an invasion against our combined forces? I have the feeling that we would crush him, sending his troops running for cover back north. That blow would certainly cost him his presidency."

"That's what everyone said about Saddam Hussein," replied Martin. "In the end he not only survived the Gulf War, but he also survived all of his old adversaries. See, the North Koreans have studied the Gulf War intently. Their formidable artillery units, plus the sheer number of troops, would achieve widespread destruction of the Korean peninsula before we can stop them, especially if *Firewall* is shut down during the critical first few days of the invasion. I'm certain that we would force him back north later on, just as we did Saddam, but by then the damage would have been done. Don't forget that Seoul is less than thirty miles from the border. If the north decides to invade, we might not be able to stop them in time to prevent the destruction of Seoul. What's even more scary, though, is that Jong-il might decide to launch some of our own missiles as a distraction while he invades South Korea."

"Launch our . . . he wouldn't . . ."

Martin lifted his eyebrows. "It all depends on how desperate the man is."

"But that could trigger . . ."

"Armageddon? Sure. What does he have to lose? His country is in shambles. In his sick mind he might even see that as a way to level the playing field, to gain an edge on his enemies, namely us."

"I think," Hersh said, "that it's time we brief the President."

"What about Tucker?" asked Martin.

"What about him?"

"We need to redirect him to Korea."

Hersh shook his head emphatically. "This problem has grown beyond him and his . . . *girlfriend.*"

"On the contrary, Geoff. This problem is *all* about Tucker and Monica Fox. They're the ones in possession of the code, which is at the root of our dilemma. Besides, he now has an incredible edge on his side."

"How's that?"

"The terrorists are not going to be expecting him."

Hersh still had a lot to learn about this business. "I see. The element of surprise."

"Yep. If he can go in and rescue her, then our problems would be over."

"And if he gets captured?"

"Then he cracks the cyanide capsule and we're no worse off than we are now."

They both looked at the NPIC images, going over the shots of the compound.

"What do we have on that place?" asked Martin.

Hersh shrugged, pressing a button on the intercom and calling the analyst back in the room.

The bald-headed kid with the goatee stared at them. "Gentlemen? How else can I be of service?"

"That compound," Hersh said. "What is it?"

"I'm not sure, sir, but I can get you someone who might know."

The analyst took off, returning a minute later accompanied by Jerome Hall, an old hand at the NPIC. Martin knew Hall from the old days at the Agency, when both had served under William Webster. Hall was a large black man, with all-gray hair, a few wrinkles, and Coke-bottle glasses—probably from countless hours staring at satellite pictures. More recently, however, both Martin and Hersh had worked with Hall shortly after the month-old DMZ violation, reviewing satellite images before generating their respective briefs for the president.

"Hey, Randy, Geoff," he said. His large bulk dwarfed both directors. "How are you guys doing?"

"Been better," replied Martin, pointing at the image on the screen. "Do you know what this place is?"

Hall adjusted his glasses and got close to the screen, crinkling his nose while squinting. "A military compound of some sort . . . wait a minute, I remember now. This is one of their communications hubs between the capital and the troops by the border. We had highlighted it to the Pentagon as a potential first-strike target to black out their communications."

Martin exhaled heavily. "I guess that makes sense."

"What does?" asked Hall.

Martin asked the young analyst once again to step out of the room before providing Hall with a brief explanation on the Tucker-Fox situation.

Hall spent several minutes clicking through the images, zooming in and out, before adding, "Looks like Miss Fox was taken not to the communications bunker itself." He used the laser pointer to highlight the concrete building at one end of the mansion, before sliding the laser's red dot to the house at the other end. "But here. This appears to be a large mansion, or guest house, what looks like a couple hundred feet across this field of antennas and microwave dishes separating it from the bunker."

Hersh extended a finger at the image. "The place looks well guarded."

"At least the communications bunker is," said Hall, maneuvering the red dot over the image. A quick count showed at least forty men by the compound and a few by the house.

"What's that over there?" asked Martin, pointing at another clearing four miles or so south of the target.

Hall smiled. "That's a refugee camp. UNICEF, I believe."

"What's it doing so close to the DMZ?" asked Hersh.

"Who knows, but it's been there for a while—certainly well before the problems started last month."

"What kind of refugees?"

"Mostly kids, plus the volunteers running the place. As I mentioned earlier, the bunker was highlighted as a high-priority target. However, the White House downgraded it to an LR target."

"LR?"

"Last resort. See, the Koreans learned an important lesson from the Gulf War: the value of human shields. It appears that the soldiers have been kidnapping kids from the UNICEF camp and using them as human shields, chaining them outside their communications bunker. It made the White House think twice about taking it out with a Tomahawk."

"Like I said before, Randolph," Hersh said. "I think it's time to brief the President."

Martin nodded while regarding the satellite image of the camp, wondering why in the world UNICEF would sponsor a refugee camp so damned close to the border.

The Volunteer

Joan Ackmann woke to the multiple gunshots in the distance, like popping corn. Cries erupted from the orphans in nearby tents.

Half asleep, she sat up on her straw mat and yawned. That any sound should arouse her was amazing. She had not slept since the arrival of the last group of refugees two nights ago, fifty emaciated children from somewhere in the north, survivors of the intensifying famine that had already claimed over two million deaths in this totalitarian state. Unfortunately, as had been the case countless times before, not all of the malnourished kids made the trip alive, and many more died during the futile attempt to pump their gaunt bodies with nutrients and antibiotics.

Her lungs filled with the dead, festering air that hung over the camp like a bad omen, a permanent reminder of the improvised crematoria used to prevent the spread of disease. There had been simply too many dead for graves, too many disease-ridden bodies bloating in the day's heat.

Pulling a light robe tightly around her naked shoulders, Joan stood, slipping her feet into sandals as she walked toward the slit exit, her jean shorts barely hanging onto her bony waist.

The predawn skies over North Korea melted with the murky waters of Kyonggi Bay, beyond the ragged cliffs marking the eastern edge of the UNICEF camp. A cool breeze whipped her gaunt face, swirling strands of white hair that had gotten loose from the plastic barrette clamping her long hair.

Under the wan light of the camp's gas lanterns, Joan's aging eyes peered wearily past the rows and rows of tents, past the gravel path that wove its way around the camp, beyond the rocky hills to the south, where the shots had originated. Her gaze landed on the well-lit demilitarized zone, the no-man's land separating the two Koreas.

The communists were likely violating the armistice again, slipping into the South Korean side of the DMZ and firing their rifles, just as they had done the month before, scaring away many of her local volunteers. But she refused to desert the children, unlike the dozen other UNICEF workers from the United States and Europe who had slowly abandoned the camp as the situation worsened, as the dwindling supplies forced every adult to a single meal a day to leave enough food for the famished children. Hunger was a powerful motivator, and many of her UNICEF colleagues had not endured the months of forced fasting, finally succumbing to the need to eat more than the daily regimen of a cup of rice, a few bites of dehydrated beef, and vitamins. One by one her colleagues had taken the one-way trip to the border, their frail hands clutching the documents that would allow them to cross into South Korea. And once they crossed they could not turn around without the entry visas that oftentimes took months to obtain.

But Joan had hung on, not only because her body had been conditioned to function with far less nutrients than her colleagues, but also because of the knowledge that without her the refugee camp would collapse, and with it what little relief UNICEF provided to this corner of North Korea. She had to stay the course, just as she had done many times before in other lands—Central America, Bosnia, Somalia, Zaire, Haiti, Afghanistan, names on a map that for the fifty-five year-old volunteer evoked visions of emaciated children, of worm-swollen stomachs, of flies festering on dying babies, of the stench of burning flesh from open crematoria.

Alarms wailed in the distance as a few more shots rattled the indigo sky, before silence resumed—except for the orphans, who continued to cry.

Korean volunteers raced into tents to calm the children. Joan joined them, reaching the closest tent, grabbing the gas lamp hanging from a tree by the entrance, pushing the canvas flap aside, going inside. The flickering light revealed two opposite rows of mats over a dirt floor providing shelter for ten youngsters, all between the ages of six and ten. Three girls sat up screaming, their wide-eyed stares gazing wildly about the murky interior. In a corner of the tent some kids huddled down while crying, raw terror veiling their sleepy eyes.

Joan fought for control. Some of these children had witnessed the cannibalism that had resulted from extreme famine. Two of the girls sitting up were sisters who had witnessed their parents slaughtering their younger brother following weeks of starvation. The local police had shot the couple outside their home and sent the girls to the orphanage. The girls reminded Joan of herself and her own sister, growing up in an orphanage in London after their parents died in an auto accident.

"Calm down," she said soothingly in her best Korean, which she had learned after two years of UNICEF work in the region. During her three-decade-long career with the relief organization she had also mastered Spanish, Bosnian, Somali, and an African dialect. "The gunshots are far away. We are safe."

Her words had little effect. The children continued to wail.

Joan decided to try a song, which she taught to all of her children as part of their English class. She put her hands together, forced a smile on her face, and sang, "If you're happy and you know it clap your hands."

She clapped them twice.

"If you're happy and you know it clap your hands."

She clapped again. One of the girls smiled and joined her.

"If you happy and you know it then your face will surely

show it. If you're happy and you know it clap your hands."

The same girl clapped but no one else did.

They were scared beyond songs. It was time to get her fail-proof weapon.

"Wait," she said, before rushing outside, going into her tent, grabbing one of several bags of assorted candy she had received the week before, and returning to the kids.

Joan used the candy not just as bargaining power over the kids, but also as a source of sugar. The trick had worked fifty years before in the orphanage in London, and she had made it work here as well. It never ceased to amaze her what kids would do for a piece of candy.

"Here," she said, sitting in the middle of the tent. "Have some."

The three girls were the first to stop crying, their wet stares shifting from her face to the colorful bag she set on the floor. The ones by the corner also stopped sobbing, a half dozen little heads turning to her.

"Come," she said, waving them over. She unwrapped one and put it in her mouth, closing her eyes. "Hmmm. Delicious."

The kids exchanged glances and pointed at the candy while licking their lips.

"I want everyone in bed," she said, holding up the bag. "Then you will get one."

The kids obeyed, each sitting down on their respective mats. She distributed the candy. "Now, I want you to lie back down after you are finished, all right?"

The kids nodded in unison, their gazes fixed not on her, but on the plastic bag, which was still quite full. "If I don't hear another noise until breakfast you get more later."

She left the tent, wondering if she would be able to accomplish her work without this indispensable tool.

Joan left the lantern hanging outside their tent, frowning as she stood still, holding the bag of candy, her blue eyes blinking as they returned to the DMZ, beyond the long valley below.

North Korean soldiers continued to run night exercises

along the northern edge of the DMZ, accompanied by tanks and heavy artillery, kicking up clouds of dust toward the starry heavens.

Joan then heard shouts, an angry exchange of words coming from the large canopy in the middle of the camp, the supply tent.

She raced past the volunteers calming the children, past the water tanks and the latrines, reaching the hospital, dashing past the large tent that served as her makeshift classroom, spotting three army jeeps, an army truck, and four soldiers guarding the vehicles, their light brown uniforms contrasted by thick black belts, boots, and helmets.

"What is going on?" she shouted. "Where is your commanding officer?"

The guards raised their weapons at her as a young officer marched outside, followed by a dozen soldiers hauling bags of rice. "These provisions have been confiscated by the people's army!" the officer shouted while waving a pistol.

One of her volunteers, a short North Korean as old as Joan who had lost his entire family in the famine, came out of a tent and approached the soldiers.

Joan put up a wrinkled hand and whispered, "Let me deal with it, Hung. They will kill you, but they won't dare touch me."

Joan knew that, as in Somalia and Bosnia, her diplomatic immunity probably meant little, but she stood a better chance than the locals. The soldiers would be less likely to harm her because she was the only reason the refugee camp still existed, which also meant the continued existence of foreign supplies, however small.

Hung Il-soo exchanged glances with the armed guards and slowly backed off.

"That's for the children!" Joan shouted, recognizing the officer, Colonel Song Dae Myong—the same officer Joan had caught trying to kidnap a fourteen-year-old girl a month ago. The soldiers belonged to a detachment of North Korean regulars guarding a large building farther west on the Molak mountain range, a few miles away.

"Animals! You're a bunch of animals!" she shouted, before looking about her to make certain that Hung and the other Korean volunteers remained still, keeping their heads lowered, avoiding eye contact.

The armed soldiers held Joan back as their comrades loaded the loot in the truck. Myong climbed into the passenger seat of one of the jeeps and winked under his army cap. "Thank you for your hospitality. Tomorrow we'll return for a virgin."

Her eyes narrowed to angry slits. "Stay *away* from my children!"

His gaunt face flashing her a smile of crooked, yellowish teeth, the colonel pointed toward the DMZ. "Times are changing. Soon the imperialists in the south will be forced to yield the land they stole over a half century ago from the people of Korea."

"Why? So that you can turn it into a death camp like this one?"

Myong's smile froze.

"Some soldiers you are. Stealing from children." She spat at the jeep. "Get out of my sight."

Myong's hand dropped to his sidearm but kept it there while he locked eyes with Joan, who burned him with the same defiance that had saved a dozen children under her care in Somalia from a group of armed thugs.

Myong signaled the driver to move out. The army caravan left, headlights cutting through the boiling dust kicked by their tires. The Korean volunteers returned to their tasks in silent resignation.

Joan just remained there, eyes fixed on the twilit gloom of dawn, wondering whatever possessed her to come to this barren place, to this dying nation, where soldiers stole food from the mouths of starving children, where famine had pushed the population into cannibalism, into insanity, into the very brink of hell's abyss. Kids were dying around her every day. Her medical supplies dwindled as more refugees found their way into her camp.

She had asked herself that question a million times, under

the skies of many dying nations, while hauling jugs of drinking water in Nicaragua to prevent the spread of cholera among the children, while cradling a worm-infested baby in Zaire while the mother died of AIDS, while assisting ill-equipped physicians to amputate what was left of the arms of a five-year-old in Afghanistan after the youngster picked up a Russian mine, while consoling orphans in Bosnia following a Serbain mortar attack.

Joan tightened her bony fists as the soldiers disappeared from sight around the bend in the dirt road. The answer always came back the same: She did it for the children because no one else would, because no one else cared. And just as before, the governments of the sinking countries remained in denial, ashamed of publicly admitting their failing administration, even at the cost of hundreds of thousands of innocent lives. The last UNICEF supply ship had been forced to turn back to sea three days ago under an espionage charge.

Espionage!

There had been nothing but rice, canned goods, and medical supplies aboard the vessel, donations sent by support groups in the United States. The government in Pyongyang would rather starve the children than publicly admit the disaster that decades of communism had brought to North Korea, whose population lived in sharp contrast with its economically strong southern sibling.

A naked, three-year-old girl cried in the arms of a volunteer. Joan turned to her and watched her parasite-swollen stomach protruding from under her shirt, like those of so many other kids from so many different lands, who came to her with the hope for life, just to end up as fuel for the crematoria a week later.

"This is sick, Hung," she said.

"And the rest of the country is in even worse shape than we are," replied the Korean volunteer. "There is cannibalism in the north. People eating people because there is no food."

Joan stared into the wrinkled face of the short and stocky Hung Il-soo. She had heard the stories but had not believed them, until some of the children started arriving without limbs. At first she had thought they had fallen victims of land mines, but then the truth had hit her smack across the face: Their limbs had been amputated by hungry northerners.

That day she had not stopped vomiting.

Slowly, she turned around and walked back to her tent, fire scorching her veins, her forehead aching with frustration. This famine could be greatly alleviated if only the obstinate leaders in Pyongyang allowed the relief cargoes to enter the country uninterrupted once again, like they did a year ago, following the floods. But back then Pyongyang itself had been affected. Back then the *military* had been hungry.

The distant rumble continued. Activity north of the DMZ increased as shafts of crimson and orange loomed over the eastern rimrock, splashing no-man's land with wan hues.

Joan quietly surveyed the DMZ with a pair of binoculars left behind by a soldier last month. Hundreds of thousands of North Korean troops were settled in the narrow stretch.

She inspected the border again, this time with a different eye, carefully surveying the stretch of land from the sea to the large build-up of troops to the west, which met the long and wide infantry formations piping down from the north, disappearing on the far side of the Molak range.

She put the binoculars down. During her years here she had been able to take several excursions up the mountains with her gas-powered jeep, which she now seldom used to conserve fuel. If need be she could take the tents, the children, and some supplies to the opposite side of the mountain, to a spot she had selected a month ago, when the trouble began. Joan had an old bus in the back of the camp. It was always kept full of gas and the rusting fuel drum behind her tent still held another hundred gallons, enough to make several round trips to haul everyone out of here.

Joan immediately started barking orders to Hung and the other volunteers. The camp had to be readied for an emergency evacuation at a moment's notice. The children had to be protected . . . somehow.

70

The Return of the Warrior

Bruce Tucker sat in the rear of a Comanche RAH-66C stealth helicopter, the elongated, troop-carrier version of the U.S. Army's newest and deadliest attack helicopter. Unlike the attack version, designed for a crew of two, the "C" included a rear cabin for six soldiers, who boarded the craft through large side doors. A pair of 50-caliber machine guns bolted to the floor, designed to provide cover fire during drops and extractions, stood unattended in the troop compartment.

Despite the slight nausea induced by the pilot as he kept the stealth craft hugging the mountainous terrain, Tucker focused his attention on the challenge ahead. The whole rescue operation was entirely up to him. It seemed that a meeting had taken place in Washington between Hersh, Martin, and the President, and they had chosen to limit their involvement to dropping him off and pulling him back out. No Special Forces, or SEALs, or even Rangers accompanied him on what Martin had called a suicide mission. The best minds in Washington had determined that there wasn't a need to send in troops and risk telegraphing their presence to the North Koreans when *Firewall* could be secured in a matter of days after Tucker released his portion of the password. However, those same minds had agreed to support him in exchange for the password—and also because of the Fox files, though none of them would admit it.

Tucker wasn't alone on this journey. Donald Bane had been with him ever since leaving Italy aboard the Navy jet. While aboard the *Theodore Roosevelt*, they had received a message from the NPIC that the jet they had been tracking

had indeed crossed the Mediterranean Sea and landed outside
of Tripoli, Libya, just as the terrorist's note had claimed. But
high-resolution satellite photos showed that only three men
had left the plane while it refueled, before continuing on
across northern Africa, the Middle East, and most of Asia,
finally landing at a remote airstrip in North Korea before
American forces could be alerted to intercept it.

Bane and Tucker had boarded another Navy transport,
which delivered them to Seoul, at the moment probably one
of the hottest spots on the planet. They had spent a couple
of hours in the briefing room, where a military liaison had
mapped out the safest insertion route, a safe distance from
any North Korean bases. Tucker had been a bit taken aback
by the level of tension at the Army base. Nothing like having
hundreds of thousands of enemy soldiers less than twenty
miles away to kick the excitement level up several notches.

After exchanging some of Tucker's desert gear for hardware better suited for jungle warfare, they had then transferred to the Comanche, which looped out to Kyonggi Bay
before performing a low-altitude night insertion into North
Korean territory. But Bane wasn't rapelling into the jungle
with Tucker. The aging operative didn't have the training or
the equipment to do so. He would head back to Seoul and
keep everything ready to go back in and extract them.

In addition to a set of jungle fatigues with multiple pockets, boots, a sturdy digital watch, and camouflage cream, the
military had provided him with an assortment of survival and
defensive gear, including a silenced Heckler & Koch MP5
submachine gun strapped to his right torso, a Sig 220 backup pistol, a short machete, and a hunting knife. Shoved in
his multiple pockets he had a small compass, a handheld GPS
unit, a couple of Power Bars, and a first-aid kit, which included battle dressing, morphine, and a surgical sewing kit.
For communications, Uncle Sam had fitted him with a two-
way radio. Given the unit's very short range of roughly
twenty miles, Tucker would only be able to use it during the
final phase of the airlift, to guide the helicopter crew to his
position.

Over the cammies Tucker wore an H-harness combat vest, quite similar in shape and function to the one he had worn during his Navy SEAL days, and loaded with enough spare magazines for the silenced Heckler & Koch MP5 submachine gun and the Sig pistol. He had also loaded a few grenades, a five-hundred-milliliter bag of Ringer's Lactate for IVs, a water canteen and water purification tablets, a few smoke grenades, a strobe light and two flares to mark the landing site at night, and a PRC-90 rescue beacon, which he would activate for a short period of time upon his return to the LZ to alert the rescue helicopter to come and airlift them. Tucker would have to use the beacon cautiously, as it would not only alert his own people of his position, but also the enemy, should the North Koreans happen to be monitoring the beacon's frequency. In the oversize rucksack strapped to his back, Tucker carried a set of night-vision goggles, five pounds of C4, a five-hundred-foot spool of detonation cord, or "det cord," a couple remote-controlled firing devices, a handful of pressure-controlled firing devices, fishing line to set up trip wires, and four antipersonnel Claymore mines, each holding inside its plastic case a slab of C4 behind seven hundred steel balls. He also carried a second set of fatigues and a pair of jungle boots for his principal.

Tucker took a deep breath, wondering if he still had what it took to trek stealthily through miles of dense jungle to an objective, carry out his mission, which included rescuing a hostage from what appeared to be a well defended compound, then slip back into the bush after creating a noisy diversion with explosives, and finally reach a pickup zone before the enemy caught up with him.

You'll find out soon enough.

Donald Bane sat across the narrow troop compartment wearing an identical set of headphones as the ones keeping Tucker in communication with him and the pilot.

In spite of the Comanche's greatly reduced rotor noise, the vibration still rattled him in ways that brought back memories from two decades ago, from simpler times, when the enemy was clearly defined, when there were rules of engagement, when there was always someone to cover his rear, when following orders was the only thing he needed to do to stay alive.

The Comanche closely followed the rugged terrain, remaining well below radar, carrying Tucker to a drop zone two miles south of his destination, close enough to get to it within a few hours, yet far enough to avoid telegraphing his arrival to an enemy who most certainly would *not* be expecting him. Stealthiness was obviously paramount to avoid alerting the troops along the north side of the DMZ, less than twenty miles away. But they had technology on their side. According to the briefing, the RAH-66C was four times less easy to observe at night and six times quieter than the Apache attack helicopter, making it pretty much invisible.

"Two minutes to DZ!" came the pilot's warning over the intercom.

Tucker checked the rope he had threaded through the belay device strapped to his waist line. One end of the rope was anchored to the side of the craft before going to his belay device, very similar in form and function to the grigri he had used in Capri. The rest of the rope lay coiled by his feet. There had been a time when Tucker could rappel out of a helicopter in his sleep. He hoped it would all come back to him in roughly ninety seconds.

He strapped on a clear face mask for protection against branches during his rappelling exercise into thick jungle.

"We're just an hour away," said Bane over the intercom while getting up and reaching for the Comanche's side door, unlatching it just as they had been shown by a ground crew officer in Seoul. "You call and we come, buddy. Anytime, anywhere."

Tucker also stood, the seventy pounds of gear suddenly weighing down on him, magnifying the pain broadcast by his bruised ribs, making him second-guess his decision. But then Monica's face flashed in the night, as Bane slid the door open and he stared into total darkness, as the wind whistled inside the cabin, as the craft suddenly stopped all forward motion, hovering a few feet over the treetops.

He kicked the coiled rope by his feet, watching it drop into the blackness below.

"Good luck!" Bane said, patting his shoulder.

"Be right back," Tucker replied with forced confidence, pressing his boots against the edge of the doorway, his back to the night, his eyes staring at Bane one final time, his right hand holding the grigri's lever, currently set to maximum friction.

In a single motion, Tucker jumped backward while his right hand released the friction on the rope, listening to it shriek as it ran through the belay device, his stomach knotting from the fast drop.

He increased friction just before his feet reached the canopy.

The down wash of the helicopter pressing down on him, Tucker disappeared in the trees, descending at a slower rate now, with control, feeling his way down branches while making the necessary adjustments to avoid impaling himself.

Thirty second later his feet reached solid ground. In total darkness, he unstrapped himself from the belay harness and activated his communications radio, said, "Clear," and shut it off.

The rope and belay device shot skyward, ripping through vegetation as the helicopter returned to base, its light engine noise rapidly vanishing in the night.

All noise ceased in moments, unlike older helicopters, whose *whop-whop* sound could be heard from many miles away. Tucker could only hear his own breathing mixed with the clicking and buzzing of insects.

He removed the clear mask and replaced it with his night-vision goggles, which turned total darkness into an array of dark green palettes. The Army model he wore was far superior to the commercial brand he had purchased for his approach to Capri. As expected, he was in the middle of nowhere, surrounded by thick jungle. Only now did he realized he had landed in a sea of ferns, its leaves branching out in all directions.

All right, Bruce. You've asked for it, now you've got it.

The GPS unit blipped and came on after he slid the power switch, taking about thirty seconds to sync up with the closest GPS satellite in geosynchronous orbit over the earth, before marking his location as well as the location of the target, just over two miles away, up and around the mountain. Realizing that he would be putting his body through a serious hike in full gear, Tucker had forced himself not only to sleep for a significant portion of the ten-hour flight from Rome—with the assistance of drugs—but also to eat a few Power Bars to stock up on his energy level.

His personal goal was to reach the target, rescue Monica, and head down the mountain before dawn, which was over eight hours away.

So get going.

Giving his surroundings one final glance, Tucker headed in the direction of his principal, silently praying that he reached her in time.

The Machine

The piercing headache awoke her. It drilled her temples with a relentless tempo that matched her heartbeat.

Monica Fox tried to move but couldn't. Something held her down, restraining her in a horizontal position, pressing her against a rough, hard surface. Even her head was immobilized, strapped with a band around her forehead, squeezing her temples, magnifying the headache.

She tried to move her legs but felt the restraints on her ankles and thighs. Her legs seemed parted and also elevated, like on stirrups. A belt cinched her waist and two others clamped her wrists, keeping her arms by her sides.

She opened her eyes but light stung them. She closed

them, then slowly reopened them to a mere squint, letting them adjust.

Where am I?

The ceiling was no longer plain concrete but white, from which a pair of fluorescent bulbs hummed while bathing everything in gray light. One of them flickered a bit, inducing a slight stroboscopic effect.

They've moved me.

But they had not cleaned her. Her nostrils detected her foul smell, powerful enough to want to make her vomit again, only Monica didn't think she had much left in her. Her stomach rumbled and she felt weak. She had not eaten for God knows how long, and perhaps that was part of the reason for the headache. But as bad as her temples throbbed, she felt far more discomfort from her ribs, as well as from her genital area, which burned, as if on fire. The water had rubbed her raw and urine had seared it. Her rib cage also hurt, the pain augmented by the belt around her waist, which prevented her stomach from expanding when she breathed, forcing her chest to swell every time she inhaled. The resulting pain was crippling, feeling as if someone raked her chest cavity from the inside with barbed wire.

Breathing in short, shallow breaths, Monica tried to—

A door creaked open. Someone had entered the room, but she couldn't see who it was. The head strap kept her from looking about beyond her peripheral vision, which now showed a figure approaching her.

Vlad.

"Well, well, our princess is awake. Did you miss me?"

Monica didn't respond, closing her eyes as he put his hands on her, rubbing her breasts. She tried to detach herself from all of this, from her naked and scourged body, from this animal touching her, squeezing her nipples as she tightened her fists, as she clenched her teeth in disgust, in anger.

"You are indeed a beautiful woman, Monica Fox."

The hand dropped to her abdomen, reaching her pubic hair. She tensed, gasped in pain as he rubbed her sore genitals.

"Yes," he said, leaning down, kissing her on the cheek. "We are going to get to know each other quite well."

"Oh, God," she mumbled. "Please stop."

"You do not really wish to be too dry, do you?"

She cringed as his fingers continued to explore her.

"My offer still stands, Monica," he said, removing the hand. "You give me your portion of the password, plus the information on how to reach the system, and I will in turn put you on the next plane home. By this time tomorrow you can be back in California claiming your inheritance, becoming one of the richest women in the world after Daddy died."

The words came to her—her father's words—emanating from her core, surfacing with unparalleled clarity in spite of the pain, of the humiliation, of the physical, mental, and sexual abuse. Her father would have fought this—with a passion. He would have met the enemy eye to eye, used every weapon in his arsenal to defeat him, to win, to prevail. This man could take away her clothes, her freedom, her food and drink. This man might try to humiliate her, to demean her, to make her crawl through her own excrement, to mock her, but she could not take away her spirit, her will, her renewed resolve to fight.

And it was at that moment, filled with a power she didn't know she possessed, that Monica Fox also stared at her own enemy in the eye and said, "Go and fuck yourself, you bastard. Go ahead and take a good look at me, because this is the *only* way you'll *ever* get to touch me."

Vlad's smile vanished, replaced by a stern glare that for a moment made Monica wish she would have kept her mouth shut. But she had no choice. She had to fight him to keep him from breaking her. She knew Bruce Tucker would come. She could feel it as sharply as the straps holding her down to this table.

"For being out of choices and beyond hope, my dear Monica, you sure seem quite defiant. So that you know, you are being held in a secluded army outpost in a remote mountain range in North Korea, beyond anyone's help. No one is coming to your rescue because no one knows where you are.

And even if they knew, the Americans would never risk a
rescue operation under the current military and political climate in the region. So, I ask you again for your cooperation,
and you have my word that you will be set free."

"Go to hell."

Vlad raised an eyebrow and unfastened the belt holding
her head to the table. "In that case, I don't want you to miss
the show," he said, smiling again while pointing to a contraption of wires and dials on a table next to her. She lifted
her head, saw her legs up on stirrups and spread apart, as if
she were at the gynecologist.

She dropped her head back on the table.

North Korea? Was this man lying to her? Or did they
really fly her so far away? For a moment she wondered what
they might have done to her while she was unconscious, but
shoved the thought aside. Instead, she faced him and his odd-
looking machine, which resembled an old electric generator.
Only now that she could move her head, thus increasing her
field of view, did she notice that there was a second person
in the room: the Asian woman she had seen driving the van.
Dressed in black, she stood by the only window in the room,
arms crossed. Her eyes, as dark as the sky beyond the large
window, watched Monica with the disinterest of a dog. The
woman yawned, apparently bored by this.

"This machine," Vlad said with reverence, "will help you
. . . *jog* your memory." He took two long wires coming out
of the side, one red and one blue. The red terminated in a
plain alligator clip. The blue one was connected to a metallic
cylinder roughly an inch in diameter and about a foot long
with a blunt end.

Vlad licked the tip of a finger before using it to moisten
her right nipple. "It works best when there is a damp connection," he said, grinning, before bringing the alligator clip
right over her nipple and letting it snap in place.

She shuddered, and his smiled widened. Fear coiled into
her gut as he applied a clear paste to a rod she now knew
where he would insert.

Oh, dear God!

"When was the last time you used a vibrator, Monica?"

Before she could answer, Vlad once more put his hands on her, parting her labia, a finger locating the opening to her vagina, before following with the metal rod.

Monica gasped once, twice, absorbing the cold object, shivering. Her muscles contracted, trying to reject it, to push it out, but Vlad shoved it deeper. And deeper. Impaling her.

She cried out, nearly gagging from the pressure.

"Shhh," Vlad said, leaning over her, whispering in her ear. "I'm just warming you up, working it in. I know you can take it all." He slid the rod out slowly, before edging it back in, watching her expression.

She tensed, cringed, then cried out again.

"And I thought you rich girls liked them big," he said, pulling it out before shoving it back in very fast, far deeper than before.

Eyelids twitching, Monica flinched in pain, her back bent like a bow, straining against the straps. She collapsed back down, trembling, her lips shivering as she continued to inhale and exhale through clenched teeth, her breathing now sounding more like a wheeze, the pain so intense she felt as if she were being ripped in half.

"There," he said. "I knew you could handle a big one."

Monica raised her head, tried to look down, watched him smile and wink.

"What's the matter?" he asked. "I haven't even *started* yet."

She couldn't have replied if she had wanted to. Her body was still in shock from the cold object, which the bastard had jammed all the way, leaving just the end connected to the wires projecting between her bruised thighs. She felt the thing stabbing her organs, felt it in her throat. He secured it with duct tape to her left thigh.

Swallowing hard, trembling as she breathed, Monica tried to remain calm, to get a hold of—

"There are ten settings on this machine, Monica," said Vlad, his hand on a wheel that had marks pointing at numbers from 0 to 10. "We will start at the slowest setting and work our way up."

She moaned softly, losing control of her thoughts, of her mind, the pressure between her legs so intense she couldn't possibly imagine anything worse. The rod stabbed her every time she shifted, the pain far greater than her bruised ribs, which continued to scourge her from the inside as she sobbed, as she shuddered.

Vlad approached her and once more secured her head to the table, before shoving a piece of rubber in her mouth. It tasted foul, like grease, making her gag. "This is for your own protection," he said. "I don't want you swallowing your own tongue. Then you won't be able to tell me what I wish to know."

His hand returned to the wheel on the machine. "Listen for the click, Monica."

Monica followed his hand as he placed it on the wheel and turned it. The click came, as loud as thunder, followed by an explosion through her body.

Human Protein

North Korean Colonel Song Dae Myong woke up to the scream.

He sat up on his mattress, stretched his slender frame and rubbed his eyes, amazed that any sound could arouse him. He inspected the inside of his square tent, pitched next to the mountaintop communications center along with dozens of others belonging to the detachment of forty men he had been given by his superior in Pyonyang to protect the communications center—and the mansion next door, where Mai Sung Ku had arrived yesterday in the company of her contractors and an American woman, who, according to Mai Sung, possessed part of the password that would empower North Korea to disable vital South Korean communications systems, giving his country the upper hand during the invasion.

He yawned and watched his girl whore stir under the covers, her light skin reflecting the wan light from the candle in the corner of the tent. The girl, one of eight teenagers he had abducted from the nearby UNICEF refugee camp, was one of the few weapons at his disposal to hang on to his men.

That plus the children, he thought, standing. They needed the children to complement their diet of rice. Weapons, whores, and food. Three of the basic ingredients to hang on to an army. His government had provided Myong with the weapons. It was his responsibility to fulfill the other needs to keep his men from defecting south. Or worse, from turning on him.

Another scream. Piercing. It came from the mansion. Mai Sung and her team of contractors were interrogating the American woman.

A third shriek made the whore sit up, her sleepy eyes slowly focusing on Myong, who stood naked in front of her. Her silky black hair fell over her narrow shoulders. Her childish face, momentarily somber from the rude awakening, softened in his presence. Unlike the toddlers stolen from the refugee camp, the teenage girls had been given the choice to satisfy the sexual needs of the soldiers or join their younger North Koreans in filling the soldier's bellies.

The girl courtesan extended a hand to Myong. She must have been scared out of her mind to play the role so well. Perhaps the violent death and subsequent dismemberment of a schoolmate three days ago for refusing to cooperate might have something to do with it. Overnight the attitude of all the remaining girl whores changed for the better, pleasing his soldiers, which pleased Myong. Sex was secured, and with the refugee camp nearby, so was the supply of protein for their diets.

Myong motioned her to go back to sleep. He put on the pants and shirt of his uniform, fitted a thick leather belt around his waist, checked the holstered automatic, slipped into a pair of shiny boots, and grabbed a pack of cigarettes and a cheap lighter. He pushed the tent flap open.

The night air was dry and cold this high up. Myong lit up and took a long drag, eyes closing as he exhaled through his nostrils. The girl whore was a good one, calming his nerves, relaxing him. In these trying times he needed to remain calm to show his men that he was in control. Myong had to come up with sensible explanations for the orders originating from Pyongyang, however puzzling they might seem to the middle-aged officer. He was in charge of dangerous men, probably more dangerous than the enemy itself, and it was his responsibility to keep them in control. Sex, weapons, and food were only part of the recipe. The ability to control information and convince them that his leadership was worth following comprised the balance of the requirement.

Colonel Myong strolled around the camp, past weathered tents flapping in the breeze. He made a stop to have a brief word with two soldiers guarding one of the mobile missile systems, of which Pyongyang had given him four. At six missiles per system, Myong had a strong air defense capability. He insisted that the missile systems be checked twice a day. His guards gave him a positive report on the last check.

He continued his evening walk, finished his cigarette and lit another, his mood improving as he reached the mess tent. The coppery smell of blood assaulted his nostrils. Tonight the cooks had just finished slaughtering a ten-year-old boy, who had put up quite a fight, based on the splashes of blood peppering the mess tent's dirt floor. Now the cooks, their aprons stained crimson, meticulously stripped all of the flesh from the bones for the stew that his men would pour over rice tomorrow.

A well-fed soldier made a happy soldier.

Myong continued his walk, lighting a third cigarette, which he smoked while talking to a group of soldiers sitting in a circle playing cards for the right to be with a thirteen-year-old whore tonight. The girl, like a trophy, stood to the side wearing just a white sheet, which flapped in the mountain wind, revealing her breasts, which were quite full for being so young. For a moment Myong got the urge to join in the game. The girl was far prettier than the one he'd left in his tent.

"The screaming from the mansion," one of soldiers said as he stood, a young lieutenant from the province of Yanggang, by the border with China. "What is going on? It is unsettling the men."

"I will go and check," replied Myong, grinning. "It's probably nothing more than a loud whore."

The men laughed. Another asked. "Why has the firing stopped in the DMZ? Will there be an invasion?"

Myong regarded the soldier with the same patronizing look a father uses with a curious child. He took a long drag, looking up at the stars while exhaling. "A fisherman knows when to give the fish some line and when to pull back. He does so to test the strength of the fish, to see how hard it struggles. If the fish is still willing to fight, he releases more line to tire it, until it's weakened to the point that he can easily reel it in. Right now our government is giving the traitorous south some line to test its resolve, to see how it reacts. But make no mistake about it. We are at war with them, and at the right moment, when they least expect it, we shall deliver a decisive blow."

"But . . . Colonel," said a young sergeant, standing, several cards held in his left hand while pointing to the valley leading to the DMZ. "When the war begins, we will not be able to join our compatriots. We will be stuck here guarding this building."

Myong, cigarette wedged between the middle and index fingers of his right hand, took a drag. He had been ordered to keep his mission a secret for as long as it didn't compromise his command. "This building houses the primary center of communications between Pyongyang and the front lines of the eastern sector. There are twenty operators working inside. Their radio equipment connects to those antennas. We have been given a very important task. Without this facility our leaders will not be able to convey critical orders to the front lines in an expeditious manner. Without this center the western offensive could collapse in a matter of hours. Every well-coordinated and sustained attack requires communications between the troops in the trenches and the commanders in the rear. This building provides that. It is very close to the front lines and high enough on this mountain to reach Pyongyang at any hour of the day or night."

By now all of the soldiers were standing. Many exchanged glances of surprise.

"I . . . we did not know, sir," replied the same sergeant. "We have seen the antennas but never suspected that the building was so . . . critical."

Myong raised a hand. "The secret was kept from you for your own protection. The less you know the safer you will be if captured by the enemy. But now that you have been assigned to my post, there is no harm in knowing our primary objective. Because of our mission, we will not be in direct contact with the invasion force."

"What about signal jamming, sir?" asked one of Myong's radio operators. "During our classes about the Gulf War, we learned that the Americans jammed Iraqi communications to the point that they were essentially useless."

Myong hesitated for a moment, wondering just how much information would be prudent to release to keep his men under control. "All I can tell you," he began, looking for the right words, "is that our government is working to create a special weapon that will not only cripple the enemy's ability to interfere with our communications, but it will also stomp on their own communications. For me to say anything more than that could be considered an act of treason."

"We shall double our efforts then," said the young sergeant, clicking his heels and saluting the colonel. "We shall increase the frequency of our patrols."

"Especially at night," added the young sergeant.

Myong nodded approvingly, drawing from the cigarette, wondering how long he would be able to keep his lies straight. If these men caught him in one, he could find himself in the hands of the kitchen staff in a matter of minutes.

Evening Stroll

Mai Sung Ku stepped outside to get some fresh air, to get away from the stench of the American whore. The star-filled night was cold and breezy. Zipping up her jacket, she climbed down the steps of the mansion, her eyes regarding the military compound beyond the array of communications antennas.

She walked over the manicured lawn, under the yellow gleam of floodlights, the rhythmic drone from the electric generator in the power shed behind the house mixing with the whistling wind sweeping up from the valley and the occasional scream of Monica Fox.

She glanced back at the mansion. The American heiress was certainly exceeding Mai Sung's expectations. She had expected Monica to have broken by now, especially after the isolation period. But she was still hanging in there, even after Jarkko had rammed the probe in her and given the initial shocks. Most subjects began to blabber answers following the first or second hit, once they had gotten a real taste of pain. But Monica had just spat on Vlad after the contractor removed the rubber mouthpiece.

But everyone had limits. The trick was making sure the subject didn't die before reaching them, otherwise the past months would have been in vain. No password meant no access to *Firewall*. It meant no disruption of communications. It meant no launch codes for her government.

Mai Sung reached the tents and watched the children chained around the communications building, a desperate measure by her desperate government, which was rapidly running out of options. *Firewall* would give them options, would ensure a successful drive south, would guarantee a new source of supplies, of food, of fuel. It would stop the madness, the insanity that she watched as she strolled by the large tents, as she locked eyes with a teenage girl, not older than Mai Sung had been when she had first been forced to have sex with strangers.

The young girl's eyes, as dark as the sky, regarded her with resigned sadness.

I have been where you are now, she thought, watching a soldier pick her up and carry her inside. She heard her moaning moments later.

Mai Sung moved on, not caring to listen to noises that brought her back to another time, to another place.

Her eyes gazed at the valley leading to the DMZ, beyond which extended the place of her birth, the place where the schoolgirl had become the whore, where the whore had become the spy, where the spy became the operative.

South Korea.

Soon *just* Korea.

"Everything all right?"

Mai Sung turned around, regarded Colonel Song Dae Myong, the commanding officer of this outpost, a man with instructions to follow her orders. "Just getting some fresh air."

"Any luck breaking her?" he asked.

"My people are working on her right now. She will break soon. Is Jong ready with the computer equipment?"

"I will be checking with him in a moment."

Mai Sung nodded. "How many men do you have patrolling the compound?"

"Ten per shift, four shifts, plus don't forget we have the fence with the hidden motion sensors. No one gets through it without alerting the technicians in there." He extended a thumb toward the communications bunker.

"Good," she said, pointing at the tree line by the mansion. "I have another five men scattered around the mansion, in the jungle."

"Are you expecting trouble?"

She shrugged. "It's always best to be prepared."

"True."

Another scream pierced the night, coming from the mansion. Mai Sung frowned, glaring at the house. "I'd better get back in there."

Bunkers

Colonel Myong watched Mai Sung walk away. She was lovely, and he wouldn't mind having her in his tent. It would be a refreshing change to have sex with a real woman instead of children, who screamed too much, at least until he had broken them in, but by then they usually died of some vaginal infection.

He proceeded toward the communications center. He was the only military officer with access to it. He reached the steel front door and dialed a combination on the side panel. The door was supposed to open automatically when the red light above the panel turned green, but the Chinese-made entry system had never functioned properly. Five large bolts withdrew into the concrete wall, unlocking the door. Myong leaned his shoulder against it and pushed. The heavy door gave. He put out his cigarette and went inside, closing and locking the door behind him.

The two-story structure was actually a building within a building. The idea was that an attack would result in the destruction of the outer layer, eight feet of reinforced concrete, but the interior building, which was mostly underground, would not be damaged. As for the antennas, they could be replaced in a matter of hours from the supplies stored in a basement beneath the center.

His superiors had learned much from the Gulf War. They would not be repeating Saddam Hussein's mistakes. This facility would not be destroyed with the conventional weapons of the South Koreans or Americans. The place was designed to sustain many direct hits, and that was in the event that the enemy managed to get past Myong's missiles.

A twenty-foot-long corridor made a ninety-degree turn and continued for another twenty feet before reaching the main entrance to the interior building which, aside from this corridor, was totally isolated from the outer shell. The reason for the sharp turn was to minimize the direct shock wave on the interior door if someone blasted the exterior one.

He punched a different code into the panel by the door, and this time the door swung open when the light turned green, exposing a landing and stairs heading down into the mountain. In addition to the protection provided by the outer shell, the communications center was also buried in the rocky mountaintop. The interior structure had a roof plate ten feet thick that met the rocky surface. Below the concrete plate another ten feet of natural rock added a further layer of protection. Below this double layer was the actual ceiling of the center, two feet of steel and concrete. In the event that a bomb did manage to pierce the outer shell, nothing short of a nuclear blast would penetrate over twenty feet of concrete, steel, and natural rock protecting the bunkerlike communications center.

Myong went down the stairs, reaching a third door, which required a third entry code. He keyed it in and the door opened.

The center had an amber glow from a myriad of displays and control lights. A maze of wires and ventilation ducts lined high ceilings, from which dropped a dozen monitors that met the rows of equipment lining the long walls of the room. Operators sat behind radar screens, computer terminals, control panels, and switchboards, conveying field reports

from the front lines to headquarters in Pyongyang and the
resulting orders heading back to the field. The equipment was
tended by two eleven-man crews working twelve-hour shifts.
As messages arrived, four cryptographers per shift spent their
time coding and decoding them according to their manuals
before relaying the information. For security reasons, the
front lines used a different coding system than Pyongyang.
The center was the translator of all messages.

Myong took a whiff of the recirculated air and detected
the smell of burnt plastic. He looked about him and found
the source of the smell. A thin train of smoke spiraled over
a large computer, its top held open by two technicians. An
elderly man armed with a pair of pliers and a soldering iron
was leaning into the faulty equipment, his head and shoulders
buried inside the guts of the system.

Myong had chosen the night shift for his visit to get the
opportunity to have a chat with the chief technician, Captain
Quam Il Jong, a scientist wearing a military uniform—the
man fixing the broken system. Jong also ran the massive
Russian computers that would be used to try to compute the
balance of the password after the American woman released
her portion.

In addition to his responsibilities as commander of the
detachment of soldiers guarding the center, Myong was also
a political officer, in charge of observing and reporting all
activities that deviated from expected behavior. He came
here daily to check on the frame of mind of the scientific
team.

"Captain Jong!" Myong said out loud. Several heads
turned to him for a moment before going back to work.

The scientist glanced up at Myong, who remained by the
entrance, the door already closed and locked behind him.
"Just one moment, Colonel."

"Take your time, please." Myong scanned the video monitors, which provided views of the DMZ from various angles
and telescopic power. He did this at least once a day to keep
abreast of the rapidly evolving situation, which also allowed
him to look knowledgeable in front of his men. A monitor

connected to a camera with a powerful telescopic lens showed the northern border of the DMZ, near the bay, packed with South Korean troops and an ocean of heavy artillery, tanks, missile launchers, and personnel transports.

Holding a charred circuit board in his left hand, Jong approached Colonel Myong. The scientist was well into his sixties. Thinning white hair framed a wrinkled face and thick horn-rimmed glasses. Jong had undergone extensive training with the Chinese- and Russian-made electronic equipment filling this room. The gear lacked the reliability of the American, Japanese, and German brands, but Jong's hands-on training enabled him to make the frequent repairs necessary for it to remain operational. Beyond the living quarters was a storage room, filled with the spare parts required to keep them in business.

"Problems again, Captain?"

"One of the new video units has been malfunctioning. The signal-amplifying circuitry lacks proper power decoupling and it overshoots, damaging the entire board. I've replaced this piece twice this week. But this last time I've added an array of zener diodes to clamp the voltage overshoots."

Myong pretended understanding, even though he lacked any training in electronics. "Is it Russian or Chinese?"

"This one happens to be Russian, but it doesn't really matter. Everything here is unreliable. Nothing is standardized. Spare parts for a lot of the equipment don't match the original equipment, forcing me to make modifications all of the time."

Myong sympathized with the scientist's problems, but they were *his* problems and Myong expected him to solve them without complaining. In return, Jong's family was given special privileges back in Pyongyang. "But you *are* managing, are you not, Captain?"

Jong blinked twice, suddenly realizing that he was being tested. "Well . . . of course, Colonel. Of course! Yes! The communications will not cease under my watch!"

Myong smiled, patting the scientist in the back. "Good.

Very good. Let's keep it that way. Now, could you bring me up to speed on the situation at all fronts?"

Jong spent ten minutes detailing his observations to the colonel, who listened intently, without interruption, particularly to the news from the western front. During the past twenty-four hours his country had driven hundreds of tanks and nearly one hundred thousand troops into the tunnels dug beneath the DMZ in the western sector of the border. The plan, according to the messages flowing back and forth, called for a synchronized strike between the troops above and below ground. While the North Korean troops on the DMZ engaged South Korean defenses, the troops underground would advance through the tunnels and emerge five miles inside South Korea, giving the enemy a second front. While the border defenses struggled with the surface attack, part of the underground force would drive into Seoul. Meanwhile, the eastern sector would drive south for forty miles before a large force split west, cutting across the peninsula to attack Seoul from the east. The rest of the eastern echelon would continue south for another thirty miles, before also heading west to strike Seoul from its least defended side, the south.

And it would all start the moment *Firewall* was secured, the moment Jong and his team of scientists shut down the Americans' ability to communicate in code. But he was also aware that the leaders in Pyongyang might have additional instructions for Myong and Jong. Control of *Firewall* meant control of the Americans' launch codes, which North Korea would be able to use at will for the time that it controlled the system, thus creating the ultimate diversion while his nation razed the peninsula, claiming what was rightfully theirs.

Myong left the center a minute later. After closing and locking the external door he lit up, his cheeks collapsing as he drew heavily on the cheap cigarette. But soon he would get to enjoy the best of cigarettes, the best of liquors, and the best of women. Seoul lay there ripe and vulnerable, within reach. The fall of Seoul would inflict a devastating emotional blow to the South Koreans, and Colonel Song Dae Myong of the North Korean army now more than ever was determined to protect this priceless communications center from all attack, for here rested the key to the unification of the two Koreas.

Hungry

Donald Bane found himself once again waiting. They had returned to the base an hour ago, following a forty-five-minute flight around the DMZ and over Kyonggi Bay. Tucker had been on the ground for almost two hours now. He had estimated covering the two miles to the target in less than three hours, spend about an hour to rescue Monica, and then another three hours back to the landing zone.

Wearing a light jacket as temperatures dropped into the low fifties, Bane paced the tarmac, having stepped outside the operations room a minute ago.

Holding a mug of coffee, he filled his lungs with fresh air, clearing his head. The cold wind sweeping across the airfield chilled him, but it felt good. He took a sip and checked his watch for the tenth time, before shifting his gaze to the mountains bordering the northern edge of the South Korean capital, wondering how Tucker was doing.

For security reasons—especially given current tensions—radio silence was an imperative. Bane had to wait until Tucker activated his PRC-90 rescue beacon, signaling that he had secured Monica and needed an airlift. Bane would then home in on the signal and pull them out of the jungle.

At least that was the plan.

Having spent most of his adult life in the operations world, however, Bane knew that this type of mission didn't always go as planned.

He sighed while watching several fighter jets—F22s—taxiing toward the runway. The advanced fighters had arrived three weeks ago by presidential order to bolster South Korean defenses and were now flying combat air patrol missions south of the DMZ along with F-16 Falcons and older F-15 Eagles. The lights at the wingtips of the F-22s flashed in the dark.

"Worried about your buddy, sir?"

Bane turned around. It was the young helicopter pilot who had flown them into North Korea and back, a Hispanic lieutenant by the name of Ricardo Ruiz. A green flight suit with many pockets hung loosely from his short and slim frame.

"Evening, Lieutenant."

He smiled. "I go by Ricky, sir."

Bane grunted. "Is it that obvious I'm worried, Ricky?"

The Army officer tilted his head. He had a buzz haircut and no facial hair. "Pretty gutsy to go up there alone. The North Koreans are some mean motherfuckers."

"That they are," replied Bane. "But I'll let you in on a little secret."

"Yeah? What's that?"

"My buddy's a pretty mean motherfucker himself."

Ruiz dropped his eyebrows. "He a SEAL?"

Bane regarded the officer, who was just trying to make conversation. The relevant personnel at the base had been told very little about this. Not even the base's commanding officer knew the specifics of why the Pentagon had called and ordered him to provide a stealth helicopter and a pilot to Donald Bane for a covert insertion into North Korea.

Fuck it, he thought, deciding that Ruiz should know a little more given that he was risking his own hide flying them into enemy territory. Nodding, Bane said, "He used to be a SEAL."

"A SEAL's always a SEAL," Ruiz said.

Bane grinned.

"So . . . like, what's he doing up there?" Ruiz ran the tip

of his thumb across his own neck. "Icing someone important?"

Bane smiled. "I could tell you, Ricky. But then I'd have to kill you."

The kid frowned.

"Look," Bane said. "You help us out, and after it's over I'll let you in on what we did. Deal?"

Bane could tell he liked that. "Cool," he said, suddenly backing away. "Here comes the boss. I'd better go and check on my bird," Ruiz added, pointing to the Comanche helicopter tied down a couple hundred feet from them. "Ever since them bastards up north started shit last month, the man's been one mean asshole."

Bane waved, took another sip of coffee, and watched Colonel Gus Granite approaching him. Granite, the commanding officer of the base, looked like his name, hard, his face chiseled into sharp, angular features, his hair silver. He wore fatigues, like most of the men on base, with the sleeves rolled up to his bulging biceps. The man looked in his fifties but had the muscles of a thirty-year-old.

"What's the word, Mr. Bane?" Even his voice was hard, raspy. Bane had no doubt Granite had little trouble commanding his troops, keeping them under control. In a way he had to be one tough bastard in order to run an American base just thirty miles from hundreds of thousands of armed and dangerous North Koreans just dying to march south.

"Still nothing," he replied.

"Ricky bothering you?"

Bane smiled. "Just keeping me company. He's a good stick. Kept that chopper hugging the treetops all the way in and out. North Koreans never even knew we were there."

Granite nodded. "He's hungry."

"Hungry?"

The colonel crossed his massive arms. He had a Special Forces shield tattooed on his left forearm. "In the Army you get two kinds of people, Mr. Bane. Those who are complacent, who are just here doing their jobs and cruising through the system, and those who are *hungry*, who want to make a difference, who want to be . . . the *best* that they can be."

Bane almost laughed, thinking that the colonel was making a joke, but Granite looked dead serious.

"Ricky's the hungry kind," the colonel continued. "He's willing to do whatever we ask of him, and do it with the best of attitudes and far better than anyone in his class. He survived a wild adolescence in San Antonio, Texas, before joining the Army with the GI bill. He came to us from Fort Hood and is doing his South Korean tour of duty along with so many other fine Americans assisting our allies here against the Commie bastards."

"Are you concerned that they might invade, Colonel?"

"Let them try, Mr. Bane. If a single one of them just places his stinking red boots on South Korean soil, the whole lot of them will regret that moment for the rest of their short lives, because we're going to pound them into kingdom come."

Bane took a sip of coffee, glad that the colonel was on his side. The man looked like he ate granite in his cereal.

"Your friend, Tucker," Granite added. "He's also hungry."

Bane regarded the stone face of the Army colonel. "You barely met him, Colonel. How could you tell?"

"The eyes, Mr. Bane. It's all in the eyes. He's a man who knows what he wants and is willing to do whatever it takes to get it, even getting dropped in the middle of the damned jungle in North Korea, alone. You've got to have your balls screwed on pretty tight to do a thing like that. The man's definitely hungry."

"Hungry," Bane repeated. *Bruce's definitely one mean and starving son of a bitch.*

"I'll be in the ops room. Give me a holler when the time comes," said Granite.

"Thank you, Colonel."

Alone again, Bane watched the squadron of F-22s accelerating down the runway in pairs, taking off and vanishing in the night.

His mind drifted to Bruce Tucker, to the way he had thought this situation through and had actually manipulated

it to achieve his end goal: recover Monica Fox. Here was a
man who was willing to risk everything for the woman he
obviously loved—though Tucker continued to maintain that
it was strictly a protector-principal relationship. In his pocket
Bane had the address of the Internet bulletin board where he
would have to post a special message in the event of
Tucker's death to keep the dossiers from reaching the press.
Of course, that didn't release them to the CIA, just prevented
a copy of them from getting to the media. If Tucker ever
returned, he obviously intended to use them as his life insurance. And if he didn't return . . .

We're just going to have to take our chances.

Tucker had not given them any other choice.

Bane closed his eyes, silently praying that Tucker did
make it back. If Tucker was abducted alive, before he could
use the suicide pill, then there was a reasonable chance that
Firewall could be breached before the NSA scientists eliminated the pirated backdoor.

He had the annoying little feeling that if that were to happen, those North Korean troops would be coming down south
in a flash, crashing through the DMZ.

And all hell would break loose.

Whatever's Necessary

Joan Ackmann braced herself as the night air whipped her
lined face, drying her tears, swirling her white hair. She
wasn't sure how much longer she could hang on. Colonel
Myong's soldiers had come three times today. Twice they
had left empty-handed, unable to find her supplies, which
she had hidden in a number of holes dug next to the open

crematoria. But the last time they had raided her stash of rice bags.

At least the soldiers had not yet found the crates of high-energy milk and bags of dehydrated beef, the primary sources of protein for the malnourished refugees.

The disappearing children also troubled the aging UNICEF volunteer. At first she thought that Hung Il-soo had miscounted them during their daily check-up. But when the count dropped by three kids the following day, she had realized that something was seriously wrong. Starving children didn't leave a refugee camp voluntarily—at least not while she could still provide some nutrition, medical help, and shelter. When four more kids had failed to show up for checkup yesterday, Joan had sent Hung in the UNICEF Jeep to investigate.

The distant rumble of a gunned engine gained on the whistling mountain breeze, making her turn around. Hung drove the weathered vehicle across the camp and up the bluff where she stood.

He got out and raced toward her, his loose clothing flapping in the breeze, which also swirled his black hair.

"Miss . . . Miss Ackmann?"

Drenched in sweat and thoroughly filthy, Hung took a deep breath through his mouth, hands on his waist.

"Are you all right? What did you find?"

His square face tightened. "The children . . . I've found them!" he said, panting, moving his hands in the exaggerated mannerism that Joan had long gotten used to.

"Are they okay?"

Hung lowered his head. "It is too late for some of them. The soldiers . . . they . . . they . . . *ate* them."

Joan clenched her jaw, feeling a rage coming alive, spiraling inside her gut, careening out of control. "What about the rest?" she managed to ask between clenched teeth.

"They are chained outside the large building . . . the one near the top of the mountain."

"I know the one . . . but why are they outside . . . in plain view?" She had spotted the concrete structure during the excursions she had taken up the mountain a couple of months ago, when she had first considered moving the camp.

"I do not know. As soon as I found them I ran back to the car and drove down the mountain."

"How did you drive at night?" The jeep's headlights had not worked for months.

"Flashlight. That's what took me so long."

Joan turned around and faced the valley once again, her eyes watering because of the wind and also the anger she struggled to control. "Come," she said, turning around and starting for her tent. "Follow me."

They reached the flapping canvas entrance moments later. Joan went inside, knelt on the dirt floor in front of a weathered footlocker, and dialed the padlock's combination. She rummaged through the items inside, finding a black shoe box, opening it, watching Hung's eyebrows rise when she clutched a Smith & Wesson .38 Special, an item purchased long ago for personal defense. She had last used it on the plains of Zaire, discouraging a group of militia men from kidnapping a teenage girl under her care.

"I'm a pacifist, Hung. I've *never* favored guns, but I do know how to use them," she said, thumbing the latch to release the cylinder, which was empty. "I must protect those who have placed their trust in me by coming to this place, to this refuge."

She opened a box of shells next to the weapon and began to load them into the cylinder. "I want you to get everyone together, take down the tents, and start making trips on the bus. I want everyone by the spot around the mountain by noon tomorrow, even if I'm not back. Do you understand?"

"Where are you going?"

Closing the cylinder and aiming the gun at the ground, Joan remembered the basic firearms course she had received in Bosnia many years ago—courtesy of U.N. Peacekeeping Forces.

Shoving the gun in her loose denim shorts and covering it with a dark T-shirt, she hoped she did not have to use it, but also prayed for the courage to do so if her plan failed.

For a moment she thought about consulting Seoul on the matter, but quickly discarded the idea, already knowing what her superiors would say.

"I'll need your best flashlight, extra batteries, and the jeep fueled. Also get me four bags of dehydrated meat and a dozen cans of high-energy milk."

Hung's eyes became mere slits of curiosity.

"I need something to *trade* with, something Myong doesn't have but desperately needs. Otherwise he would not be resorting to cannibalism to feed his men."

"How do you know that the soldiers aren't just going to take the supplies, the jeep, and still keep the children?"

"Let's hope it doesn't get to that. Now get going."

"What are you going to do if it *does* get to that? Colonel Myong is a monster."

"I'll do whatever's necessary, Hung." She climbed on the jeep. "Whatever's necessary . . . for the protection of the children."

Shadow Game

Bruce Tucker moved swiftly, quietly, with purpose, conforming his body to the bends in the vegetation, his gloved hands parting branches, squeezing through tight spaces, on occasion finding an old game trail, following it while it veered up the side of the mountain in the direction of his target.

Three hours since the drop and Tucker had been able to keep up the pace, ignoring his burning legs, the hole the gear burned in his shoulders, the sweat filming his camouflaged face even though temperatures had dipped into the fifties according to the digital readout on his field watch.

He had consumed a great deal of his water ration to avoid

dehydrating, lightening his load as he progressed. But soon he would have to replenish his nearly empty canteen, which hung from the side of his utility belt. He had brought along water purification tablets. All he needed was to find a stream, but so far all he had seen was jungle, and he was almost by his objective—according to the GPS unit, which continued to guide him through the dense bush.

Tucker came up to a chain-link fence, nearly six feet high, but not topped by barbed wire. It ran as far as he could see in both directions. A careful inspection of the seemingly easy-to-breach barrier revealed a metallic box at the foot of every post, on the inside of the fence.

Motion sensors.

Anyone trying to climb over it would set them off, alerting the guards patrolling the premises.

He followed the fence for several hundred feet in one direction, before removing his rucksack, tearing off a chuck of C4 from a bar that resembled putty, and carefully molding it around the base of a post.

Tucker inserted the end of the spool of det cord into the C4 charge, looping the explosives over it a couple of times. Det cord resembled a thick plastic wire. Its core contained a high explosive called PETN.

Tucker repeated the process seven more times along a hundred feet of fence, before slicing off the det cord and connecting it to one of his remote-controlled firing devices. He had the transmitting device in one of his side pockets. It resembled a TV remote control, capable of activating each of his three firing devices from a distance of one thousand feet. The firing device would then ignite the det cord—rated to explode at a linear speed of five miles per second—which in turn would detonate all the C4 charges almost at the same time.

In an ideal world, Tucker would rescue Monica and leave quietly, before anyone knew what had taken place. But his SEAL experience had taught him the value of planning for diversions, for contingencies, just in case someone spotted him inside the premises. Tucker's diversion hinged on giving

the impression that the compound had come under attack by
a large strike force, which he hoped to accomplish by detonating the charges the moment he was spotted, sending the
enemy running in different directions.

Except in one: the direction he planned to use to escape.

He doubled back to the spot where he had seen a large
tree growing about ten feet from the fence. One of its
branches, thick enough to support him, projected over the
fence.

He climbed it, going over this obstacle, dropping on the
other side while rolling, letting his shoulders, back, and hips
absorb the impact, his sore torso throbbing. He came out of
the roll and rose to a crouch, listening for any sounds that
didn't belong in the jungle.

He relaxed, detecting nothing alarming.

Wet leaves and fallen branches layered the jungle floor,
cushioning his footsteps as he resumed his approach, his goggles detecting light green hues forking through the hunter
green images of the trees up ahead. The brightness intensified, hurting his eyes, which meant he was close enough to
a light source that he no longer required the goggles to see
in the night.

Pausing, he took a knee while shutting off the night-vision
device and letting it hang from his neck.

He waited a few minutes not just to allow his eyes to
adjust to the night, but also to slow his breathing. In the
SEALs he had learned to breathe quietly, slowly inhaling and
exhaling through his nostrils.

Dim light diffused through breaks in the vegetation, radiating from the direction his GPS identified as the target.

Slowly now, like a jungle cat, he proceeded, keeping his
weight on his rear leg while using the toes of his front boot
to shuffle fallen vegetation aside before setting it down, wary
of branches, sticks, or anything else that could crack under
his weight and betray his position.

This conservative approach slowed his advance considerably, but made him near invisible in the night. A moment
later his precaution paid off. A shadow shifted in the night,

up ahead, where the jungle thinned as it neared the clearing leading up to the mansion—just as he remembered from NPIC photographs.

A sentry.

Tucker froze, his right hand clutching the MP5 handle, index finger resting on the trigger casing, safety off, fire selector lever set to single shot. His left hand held the bottom of the bulky silencer, which he aimed at the figure standing twenty feet away, leaning against a tree, backwashed by the beams staining the mansion and surrounding grounds bright yellow.

Tucker considered his options, remembering the infrared satellite map he had studied back at the base. Unless the shift patrolling the perimeter of the compound had changed, this side of the complex was guarded by five men spaced fairly evenly around the mansion, which NPIC analysts claimed was the location the terrorists held Monica Fox. That, of course, worked in his favor. There were far many more men by the large communications building beyond the antennas.

He could go around this end of the perimeter and take out the five guards one by one. However, doing so would consume a lot of time, and if the guards were performing frequent radio checks, they would catch on that something had gone wrong when some of them failed to report.

There has to be a quicker way.

Tucker inspected the mansion once again, as well as the surrounding grounds, beautifully landscaped—in sharp contrast with the military facility at the other end. He panned over to a small structure behind the house, resembling a shed, its metal roof reflecting the floodlights. Its constant droning, combined with the electrical cables connecting it to the side of the mansion, plus the fact that he had seen no power lines feeding the remote estate, could only mean that the mansion's electricity was being generated locally. The droning belonged to the diesel engine cranking the generator.

Tucker inspected the military compound, noticing no exposed electrical cables, and that probably made sense. If the information he had gathered from the NPIC was accurate, the communications building was self-contained, like those in Iraq during the Gulf War, capable of producing its own electricity within its reinforced concrete walls, probably below ground, capable of surviving a direct hit, its diesel generators likely venting out to the surface a few hundred feet away.

He looked at the array of tents pitched by the structure, wondering how many soldiers were in the area in addition to the terrorists. The NPIC infrared images had suggested around forty, plus those chained in front of the main building, in true Saddam Hussein human-shield fashion. The NPIC had claimed that they might be children. Tucker couldn't tell because the tents blocked his view of the bottom of the building. Even if he could verify the sight, there would be little he could do about it. He was already taking a huge risk going up against the terrorists on this side of the compound. His chances against the forty-some soldiers at the other end were less than zero.

He returned his attention to the power shed.

No generator meant no floodlights, meant darkness, meant leveling the playing field for long enough to accomplish his task. But he still had to get to the power shed and disable it in a way that made it look like a malfunction.

Given its location, Tucker estimated that no more than two guards could see the shed. The mansion blocked its view from other angles. There were, of course, a half dozen soldiers near the field of antennas separating the compound from the mansion.

One step at a time. First he needed to eliminate the surveillance protecting the mansion.

Making his decision, Tucker inched toward his prey, who still leaned against a tree, regarding not the jungle, but the mansion itself.

Amateur.

Any threat would likely come from the jungle, not the mansion. Perhaps the sentry's inattentiveness stemmed from the false sense of security provided by the motion detectors installed on the chain-link fence.

Fifteen feet.

Tucker slowly sank his left knee in the leaf-littered ground, pressing the metal stock of the MP5 against his right shoulder, leaning his head into the weapon, lining up his shooting eye with the rear and forward sights, aiming not at the guard's chest, which could be shielded by a bulletproof vest, but at the head, where his 9mm bullet would do maximum damage as it went through the skull.

Inhaling deeply while resting his index finger against the trigger, Tucker paused, then slowly breathed out, firing a second after exhaling.

The trigger mechanism snapped as the firing pin struck the cartridge—a sound that could never be heard in an unsuppressed weapon because it would be drowned by the blast. But the MP5's silencer absorbed the explosion of powder in the cartridge, which propelled the round to a muzzle velocity of just below the speed of sound, thus avoiding the loud crack that came from breaking the sound barrier. The bullet found its mark, smacking the guard's head forward. The sentry dropped to the ground, the sound masked by the breeze rustling the canopy overhead.

Tucker didn't waste any time attempting to hide his first victim because he had fallen in knee-high brush, out of sight. The clock had started ticking. He had no idea how long it would be before the next radio check.

Quietly, he proceeded alongside the tree line in search of his next victim. Just as it had happened in Capri, his SEAL training returned with appalling clarity. For a moment it felt as if he had never walked away from the most elite commando unit in the world, had never abandoned his brothers-in-arms to pursue a career in the espionage—

A scream pierced the night.

It was muffled by the stone walls of the two-story structure, but unmistakably had come from a woman.

Tucker had heard screams before. He had heard cries of pain, of exhaustion, of anger, of agony, of desperation. This one had certainly been a long and agonizing one, followed by a string of shorter ones.

And his mind told him that only one woman could be in such pain inside that mansion at this moment.

He tensed.

Motherfuckers.

Controlling his emotions, swallowing hard, he forced himself to stay on course, to dominate his emotions, to turn hate into focus, to move like the breeze, cruising through the jungle just as he had decades ago. The scream, however painful to him, did confirm the NPIC's claim regarding the whereabouts of Monica Fox.

He found the second sentry in the same spot identified by the NPIC thermal map he had memorized back in Seoul. The man was much larger than the first, his bulky silhouette clear against the lighter background. He too faced the mansion, and to accentuate his obvious state of relaxation, he was smoking.

Tucker could see the glowing ashes at the tip of the cigarette as he kept it wedged between two fingers while drawing from it, then bringing it back down as he exhaled.

Once again, Bruce Tucker rested a knee on the ground, aimed, and fired. The sentry dropped before he knew what had taken place. Tucker approached him, crushing the glowing cigarette while regarding the humming power plant.

Another shriek cut through the night.

Stay the course. You're not ready to rescue her yet.

In addition to the C4 charges, installed to blast holes in the fence for his way out and also to confuse the enemy, Tucker now needed to set the Claymore mines along the path he intended to use from the house to the jungle after securing Monica. He set the shaped charges thirty feet apart along the edge of the jungle, spanning the field of antennas to the rear of the mansion and wired them to his second remote-controlled firing device.

More agonizing shrills tore at him, testing his determination. Tucker struggled to stick to his plan, going over his escape route once again.

His eyes gravitated between the power shed and the soldiers standing by the antennas a few hundred feet away. They seemed relaxed, smoking cigarettes, their machine guns hanging from their shoulders.

Tucker's warrior sense told him he might be able to fool them if they happened to look in his direction by putting on the clothes from the sentry he had just killed.

Tucker reached him, leaned down, and turned him over. The bullet had entered the back of the cranium and exited through his face, which had been completely blown off.

Without an ounce of remorse, he unstrapped his rucksack and proceeded to remove the sentry's jacket, shirt, and trousers, slipping them over his own clothing. In the process Tucker came across a bonus: a flask filled with cheap whiskey, probably the sentry's secret way of keeping warm on jobs like this one. He donned the rucksack and snagged the plastic flask.

As he was about to venture out into the woods, he noticed that the soldiers suddenly reached for their weapons and adopted a defense perimeter around the antennas.

Tucker tensed, wondering if the soldiers had been warned that two of the sentries by the tree line had failed to report.

Crap.

Using his compact field binoculars, he scanned the clearing, realizing a moment later why the soldiers' mood had changed. Tucker spotted a lone figure stepping away from one of the tents. He recognized the color bars on the shoulders of his uniform. A high-ranking officer in the North Korean army, probably the soldiers' superior officer.

Another scream echoed across the clearing.

Tucker held back just a little longer, hoping for something, maybe a miracle, that would keep him from attracting the attention of those soldiers.

78

Engine Noises

The night air chilled Colonel Myong as he looked toward the mess tent, smoke coiling skyward from the kitchen at its far end. A late dinner would be served in another hour: stew, rich with hunks of meat over rice—a luxury compared to the vegetable soup and rice served to the invasion force in the valley.

A well-fed soldier was a happy and loyal soldier.

The North Korean colonel felt good. The girl whore had pleased him immensely after he had returned from his midnight stroll. Survival was a powerful motivator.

A car became audible in the distance, over the whistling wind and the rustle of leaves. A dozen guards immediately blocked the access road, weapons pointed at the darkness beyond the reach of the floodlights. Other soldiers rushed out of their tents, half-dressed figures hauling automatic rifles and converging behind the guards on duty. A few girl whores followed, their bodies draped in sheets that flapped in the wind, exposing their pale thighs and torsos.

Unexpected Visit

Dropping the flashlight and waving a blue UNICEF flag, Joan Ackmann downshifted as she approached the silhouettes blocking the road. Two powerful spotlights suddenly blinded her. She waved the flag even more frantically.

"Colonel Myong! I must see Colonel Myong right away!" she shouted in Korean.

The soldiers approached her, surrounding the vehicle, a dozen muzzles pointed in her direction, sobering her, making her wonder if she had made the wrong decision.

The soldiers remained immobile. She waited, praying that her white hair and frail appearance would keep them from searching her, from finding her hidden revolver.

More soldiers approached her, many partially dressed, chests exposed, messy hair over sleepy eyes blinking rapidly, the scene taking a surreal look, as if she had just entered a bad dream.

In the center of the group, looking amused, stood Colonel Song Dae Myong.

"An unexpected visit, Miss Ackmann. We are honored." The soldiers broke out in laughter. Muzzles were lowered. Myong opened his arms in mock welcome. "How can this humble North Korean officer be of service to the UNICEF?"

Neural Understanding

Creator had been studying the remote compound in North Korea for some time, ever since it had been established that this was the location where Monica had been taken following her kidnapping in Rome; where Tucker had gone in to rescue her.

Its biomolecular circuits, already stressed by the recent activities—plus *Creator*'s addiction to information—had been further excited by the horrors taking place on that clearing. *Firewall*'s sensors had captured the images that were causing an excessive flow of electrons through *Creator*'s sensitive components. It was the children again. This time, however, they were not being maimed by mines, or starved to death by famines. This time they were being butchered in order to feed the soldiers on the clearing.

Feeding children to the soldiers.

Creator searched its data banks and could find very few species that would eat their young. Certainly none of the ones classified as intelligent. Yet, these humans were not only practicing cannibalism, they were doing it with their children.

How can they preserve their species if they eat the younger generation?

Confusion adding to his high stress level, but realizing that it had to hang on until Monica and Tucker were safe, *Creator* continued its painful watch of a world that seemed out of control.

Blackout

Tucker silently thanked the elderly woman in the Jeep waving what looked to be a UNICEF flag. The soldiers by the antennas all turned around and began to walk toward the new arrival.

I owe you one, lady.

He ventured out, walking casually, reaching the door to the shed, located just ten feet from the back of the mansion.

He twisted the knob, and the door, to his relief, opened. Tucker rushed inside and closed it behind him.

The smell of diesel filled the murky enclosure. A single bulb hung above the droning engine, whose shaft connected to the generator itself. Thick cables projected from the rear of the generator to a large metal box hanging on the wall. Tucker opened it, exposing three columns of circuit breakers next to a few dials and switches. The box handled the power regulation from the generator as well as the distribution of electricity to the mansion's various zones, each protected by its own breaker. The top of the box was slotted. He placed a hand over it, feeling the heat being dissipated by the power transformers converting the voltage from the generator to the level used by the lighting, appliances, and other electronic equipment inside the mansion.

Tucker opened the flask of whiskey and set it over the breaker panel. He also removed the dead sentry's jacket, leaving it on the floor before tipping the flask, the contents of which poured through the ventilation slots.

Short Circuit

Colors exploded in Monica's brain as Vlad turned the wheel again, this time to the third setting. The invisible demon, far stronger than before, seized control of her body, of her mind, of her senses, of her very soul.

She gasped, kicked her legs against the restraining stirrups, unable to breathe as the arresting power penetrated her body through the rod, shocking her with the power of a thousand rapes, surging inward with arresting force, squeezing her core, gripping her, the amperes of current draining the life out of her.

Then it stopped, abruptly, far quicker than in previous sessions.

Monica collapsed on the table, scourged, disoriented, blinking rapidly, her teeth dug deep in the rubber piece, her vagina ablaze, her thighs trembling.

Her mind wandered, floated between the conscious and the unconscious, as if awakened from a nightmare, still seeing images fabricated by her mind—images of people hunting her in the night, across a meadow, in the jungle, under an electric storm, sheet lightning streaking across the boiling sky, gleaming in the night, the ensuing thunder rumbling in her chest, in between her legs. Monica ran, but hands—many hands—held her back, forced her down on the hard ground, tearing her clothes away, spreading her legs, lifting her by the ankles toward the nearing bolts of lightning, toward the jagged forks that sliced across the sky like a gleaming ripper, penetrating her with medieval power, over and over, again and again. And in the midst of the abuse, of the agony, of the battering, she heard a voice. It belonged to the monster, to the beast who had so brutally tortured her, to the man to whom Monica would not surrender, even if it meant death itself.

"What in the hell happened?" Vlad shouted, followed by multiple clicks as he fumbled with the machine's wheel and dials.

"I don't know," replied the Asian woman. "I'll go up front and check with the guards and with Myong."

When Monica finally cleared her sight, the room appeared much darker, illuminated by a dim red light connected to a small box in the corner.

Emergency lighting.

She could barely make out the figure of Vlad hovering above her, removing the rubber gag.

"It seems we have a technical malfunction," he said. "Our electricity went off, so you get a break. But fear not, my dear Monica. It *will* be back soon so we can continue our little meeting."

Eyes half closed, Monica licked her lips with her tongue, breathing deeper now, but feeling light-headed, dizzy. "Spinning," she mumbled. "The room . . ."

"Yes," said Vlad. "Your brain cells are confused, firing at random as a reaction to the electrical shock."

Monica closed her eyes.

"Why not stop the madness now?" he asked. "Just release the code to me and you will be on your way home."

She barely heard the first half of his sentence before a dark cloud, swirling like a cyclone, swallowed Vlad, the machine, the room, everything.

83

The Quick and the Dead

Bruce Tucker was racing away from the shed and toward the rear of the mansion when the door he was headed for swung open. A figure stood in the doorway, reaching for his side-arm.

Tucker wasn't taking prisoners this evening. The terrorist never got the chance to touch the weapon. Tucker fired twice, one round to the head and another to the heart—just as he had been trained, both rounds finding their marks with un-canny accuracy. The silenced MP5 was indeed a superb weapon.

The figure dropped on the trimmed lawn; the face of a Slavic man, turned at an unnatural angle, stared at Tucker with one dead eye. The bullet had gone in the other, spraying the door behind him with the back of his skull.

He leaped over him, landing on the planks of wood floor-ing a hallway. There were a half-dozen doors on either side and double doors at the other end, which probably led to the main wing of the mansion.

Just then a second figure emerged from one of the doors near the other end of the hallway. He turned to Tucker, who also resembled just another figure in the dark. The stranger obviously couldn't tell Tucker was an intruder.

The man spoke out loud in heavily accented English. "What in the hell happened? I'm working in here!"

Information. Tucker balanced his urge to kill him with his need for information, for the location where they were keep-ing Monica Fox.

The man's accent had intrigued him. It sounded German, like Jarkko's, only the voice wasn't Jarkko's. Tucker lowered the MP5 and shrugged, stretching a thumb toward the door. "The electricity went off," he replied in his best imitation of German-accented English.

"Then go and fix it, you imbecile!"

Tucker got closer, watching in near disbelief a man who eerily resembled Siv Jarkko.

"Didn't you hear me? I said to . . . who are you?"

"Hello, asshole," Tucker said getting within twenty feet from him. "Remember me?"

The man froze, eyes opening wide, like those of a deer caught in the headlights of a truck. The resemblance to Jarkko was remarkable, yet it wasn't him.

The man opened his mouth but the words seemed caught in his gorge. He forced them out. "It's . . . it's you! Impossible! How did you—"

"Just about the last guy you expected to see, huh?"

"You will never get away with it," the man responded. "My men will kill you, just as you killed my brother."

His brother? Was this Siv Jarkko's brother?

"Siv got what he deserved," said Tucker.

"And so did your family," replied the stranger. "I made sure of that."

Tucker controlled his anger, forcing a grin. "I kept it professional, asshole. You, on the other hand, are just a coward, like your brother, murdering women and children. Now you will join him in hell."

A moan came out of the room.

Monica Fox.

In the same instant that Tucker glanced inside, the terrorist jumped back, crashing against the double doors, which flung open under his weight.

Tucker fired once, twice, striking the spot where the terrorist had been just moments ago, before rolling out of sight.

Tucker rushed after him, reaching the doors, which, as he had guessed, led to a large living area, beyond which extended a dining room and kitchen, and a staircase leading to the second floor. Hallways also projected from the left and right ends of the room.

Jarkko's brother was gone now, probably alerting everyone to the intrusion.

MP5 leading the way, Bruce Tucker returned to the room, and a moment later he swore death to everyone in that mansion.

A Trade

"I want to trade," said Joan Ackmann, standing in front of Myong and a dozen of his men. The rest were headed to the mansion on the other side of the clearing, where the electricity had just gone off.

"A trade?"

"I know why you have been kidnapping children from my camp. I offer my silence, plus these supplies, in exchange for them." She pointed to five kids, ranging between the ages of eight and eleven, chained to the front and side of the building.

Myong ordered all but two of his soldiers back to their posts. He was visibly concerned about the loss of power at the mansion. "Why should I trade?" he finally asked, flanked by his two remaining soldiers. "I can get supplies from you any time I wish. In fact, I just got some today."

"Not these." Fighting not to show the fear lacerating her gut, Joan walked to the back of the open jeep and lifted a canvas bag covering the rear seat, picking up a ten-pound bag of dehydrated beef from Argentina. "This is not rice, Myong. This is *beef*. Protein. I'm offering it to you in exchange for those children. If you comply, I can get you more."

Myong approached her, left hand over his right at the waist. He smiled, stopping a couple of feet in front of her.

At six feet in height, Joan looked down at the colonel's five foot six inches.

"I have to admit, Miss Ackmann, you have more balls than many of my men. However, what prevents me from keeping the supplies, the jeep, and the children? I would keep you too, but you're too old to be a whore."

The two soldiers laughed.

"I will get more supplies in the coming weeks," she lied, her situation worsening, her mouth drying, becoming pasty. "Consider this the first payment for protection of my refugee camp."

Myong glanced at his grinning men. Without warning, he slapped Joan, pushing her against the side of the jeep and over the hood.

"How dare you come here, British whore! You think you can buy the people of North Korea like you buy everyone else in the world?"

Her cheek stung. She lay on her side over the green hood, momentarily stunned. She staggered off the jeep, running the back of her hand over her mouth, but without taking a step back. "How dare you—"

He slapped her again. Her legs gave and she fell to her knees, blood now flowing out of her nose, peppering the gravel as she lay on all fours staring at his boots, breathing heavily.

"Get up!" he commanded. "Get up and look at me!"

Before she could comply a hand grabbed a clump of hair and nearly tore it off her head while lifting her light frame to her feet. She covered her face with her hands, swallowing hard, her skull ablaze.

"You want to free the children? You want to be a heroine? Fine! Have it your way! Release them!" Myong shouted, letting go of her hair before pointing at the boys chained by the entrance to the complex.

Lying on the ground, Joan watched the soldiers releasing the kids and pushing them away, toward the jungle.

"Run, boys! You are free!" Myong shouted.

An eight-year-old boy close to the tree line, near Myong

and Joan, took off. The others froze. Joan watched him race
across the clearing, under the cheer of the soldiers.

A single shot whipped the night, the round finding its mark
on the boy's back, blasting through his chest in a crimson
cloud, propelling him into the jungle headfirst.

Myong holstered his pistol. "Who do you wish to free
next, Miss Ackmann?"

In His Arms

*Monica Tucker was no longer cold. She could feel the
warmth of the Mediterranean sun as it glowed off her
bronzed skin, as she sunbathed on her back porch, beyond
the tables packed with her artwork, the sea breeze swirling
her hair.*

*She could smell the salt in the air, the sweetness of the
fruit basket next to her, the soft aroma of the perfume she
wore. But another smell penetrated her mind, powerful, nau-
seating, making her sit up on her chaise, look down at her
legs, see the urine, the excrement in between her legs, next
to a metallic rod, which shone brightly in the sunlight. She
tried to move, to kick, to break free, but straps now restrained her, keeping her bound against the chaise. Its soft
cushions now hardened, became rough, scraping her back
every time she shifted her weight, every time she struggled
to get away from the figure looming over her, the one calling
for her, telling her that it would be all right, that he was
here now, ready to protect her again.*

*Bruce, why did you leave me? Why did you allow these
people to take me? You swore to protect me, to love me, to
always be by my side.*

The pressure in between her legs began to fade away, until

it was gone, as well as the straps forcing her legs apart.

What are they doing? Is this part of the torture? To give me false hope? To make me think that I'm being rescued?

But the words from the figure over her had no foreign accent. They were spoken soothingly, warmly, accompanied by the physical liberation from the straps around her waist, around her wrists, on her forehead.

Monica hugged herself as strong arms lifted her, carried her away. She opened her eyes, bringing a dark face into focus, the face of an Indian warrior, painted green and brown and black. But she recognized the eyes, recognized the features hidden beneath the thick cream. He threw something dark over her head, before rushing away, into the night, the cold air chilling her. She heard multiple explosions, followed by bright flashes and smoke as she lost consciousness again.

Smith & Wesson

Albeit in severe pain, Joan Ackmann managed to reach for her Smith and Wesson .38 Special. She cocked it as Myong approached her around the jeep. Before the Korean officer could react, she shoved the muzzle against his temple and threw an arm over his head.

The two soldiers nearby froze, not certain how to react.

"Leave, children! Run . . . run away! Run . . . before it is too late!" she shouted.

The soldiers maintained their distance while she kept the gun on him.

"Tell them to move back!" she warned. "Or I'll blow your head off!"

"Back off!" Myong ordered. "Back! Now! Lower your weapons!"

Joan looked at the kids once more. A few teenage girls had come out of their tents, many half naked, draped in sheets. She recognized them all. "Run away!" she screamed.

The kids took off toward the trees. The teens, momentarily confused, also headed for the trees.

Just then a series of loud explosions rattled the compound.

Big Brother

"Son of a bitch!" cursed Geoff Hersh, pointing at the live satellite infrared image of the estate in North Korea. "The President *specifically* requested to keep the operation as quiet as possible! Did he really have to create such a commotion?"

Randolph Martin sat next to Hersh in the conference room. Together they had been observing Tucker's progress, including his approach to the target and the efficient way in which he had disabled two sentries, whose IR emissions were rapidly fading as their corpses lost body heat. Then Tucker had disappeared inside the power house, his body heat masked by the heat of the diesel engine and the electrical transformers—a heat signature that dwindled after he disabled it, before rushing to the main house, where he killed a third guard.

"It was inevitable, Geoff," said Martin, who, unlike the young NSA director, was quite experienced in such operations. "Looks like he planted some charges around the perimeter. Probably as a distraction to cover his getaway. Standard operating practice. I would have done the same thing in his place."

Hersh leaned back on his swivel chair, fidgeting with a pencil. "In any case, the blasts are certain to draw the attention of the troops by the DMZ and Pyongyang, and that's bound to make the extraction much more difficult."

Albeit quite nervous about this operation, Hersh did have a point there. It was one thing performing a low-altitude insertion when the enemy wasn't aware that you would be coming. It was an *entirely* different story pulling personnel out of a hot LZ, even with a stealth helicopter. The President had been adamant about making sure the risk of getting shot down over North Korea was minimized.

"We also knew that before we agreed to help him," said Martin. "Let's see how it plays out. Hopefully he'll shake any tails and reach a safe enough spot where we can go in and pull him and Monica Fox out without exposing the rescue craft."

Hersh crossed his arms. "I know this may sound harsh, but given the choices of Tucker being captured, or killed, or rescued by us, my vote's for the middle option. It's the least risky for our current situation."

Martin pointed at a red and yellow smudge making its way across the clearing between the mansion and the jungle. "Well, it looks like he's made it out of the house in one piece."

"How do you know that isn't another guard?"

"Because the intensity of the thermal signature can only come from two bodies, not one."

Hersh crinkled his nose while staring at the image. "But . . . they're right on top of each other."

Martin smiled. "That's because he is *carrying* her."

Hersh gazed at the screen for another few seconds before closing his eyes. "Shit. I was hoping that he wouldn't make it out."

Martin sighed, then said, "You might still get your *wish*, Geoff."

"How's that?"

"Even if Tucker manages to make it to the jungle and lose his pursuers, there's still a high probability that North Korean forces will converge in the area, sealing it off as they track them down, making a rescue effort quite difficult—if not impossible."

"If the risk of the helicopter being shot down gets too

high . . ." Hersh said, letting his words trail off.

"We would be forced to recommend to the President to abort the rescue. But unlike *you*, Geoff, I do hope Tucker's as good a SEAL as he claims to be."

"You really do? After the way he blackmailed us?"

Martin waved a hand in the air. "He's reacting just as anyone would in his position. The guy was cornered, obviously caring a great deal for Monica Fox. Sure, I hope he makes it, but just the same, I will not recommend sending in a craft to pick them up if in my judgment there's too high a degree of risk."

"But what if they capture him alive?"

"Tucker is a man of his word, Geoff. He will use the pill we implanted in his mouth, and before he kills himself, he will kill Monica Fox. He won't let them be taken alive, and not just because it would jeopardize *Firewall*. Tucker knows quite well what happens to operatives when they're captured alive by hostile forces. It isn't pretty."

"Just in case he manages to screw things up and let himself get captured alive, I think it is in our nation's best interest to have the Tomahawk option ready."

Martin regarded him for a while, before agreeing. "Just make sure no one at the Pentagon gets trigger happy. Although the President gave us the latitude to exercise such an option rather than let *Firewall* fall into enemy hands, he considered it a *last* option. The last thing we want to do is fire a missile into North Korea given current events. That might be all that's needed for the Commies to start their drive south."

Unable to Assist

Creator processed the images as fast as *Firewall* generated them, creating its own copy while the original was fed to Washington, where NPIC analysts would come up with the same conclusion as *Creator*'s biomolecular brain: Bruce Tucker had rescued Monica Fox and was trying to make a run for the jungle.

But it could not assist them.

Again, its circuits overheated as it observed the events rapidly developing in front of its digital eyes.

Smoke

The multiple explosions from the C4 charges shattered the night, enshrouding it with red-gold flashes. Bruce Tucker had never been more focused in his life than at that moment, carrying away the woman he loved over his left shoulder while holding the MP5 in both hands.

After covering her with a poncho, Tucker had thrown Monica over his left shoulder, keeping her legs across his chest while her upper body bumped against his back.

He ran his left arm over the legs while keeping his hand still clutching the MP5's silencer. He put away the remote control unit, which he had used to trigger the first RC firing device, blasting holes in the perimeter fence, and instead reached for a smoke grenade, removing the safety pin with his teeth, and throwing it in the direction of a dozen incoming soldiers to his right. The grenade went off seconds later, spewing thick blue smoke. He did the same to cover his left flank, where he could also see men rushing toward him. Tucker ignored them all, dashing down the channel created between the smoke, a corridor that took him toward the middle of the Claymore mines.

His right hand now clasped the MP5's handle, index finger once again on the trigger as he thumbed the fire selection level to full automatic fire, pulling the trigger as he swept first his right flank and then his left, draining the magazine, hammering the enemy with silent rounds. Cries of pain echoed in the blue smoke.

Tucker released the magazine, letting it drop to his feet while grabbing another one from his utility vest and snapping it in place.

Monica moaned, coming around in all of the commotion, beginning to stir.

"Stay still," he hissed, his breathing becoming more labored as he kept up the pace, legs and shoulder burning from the effort. He fired additional short bursts across his left and right flanks, ignoring their screams.

Tucker kept the pace. He had to reach the jungle before the smoke thinned, before the terrorists caught up with him. He had to clear the Claymores by at least a few feet ahead of the incoming threat, before he could get a chance to lose himself in the tangled vegetation.

Shouts of confusion, of anger, echoed behind him in the darkness, in the bluish screen he had created to even out the playing field, to buy himself time.

90

You're Not Escaping Me

Vlad Jarkko raced across the front of the mansion, dimly illuminated by the emergency floodlights, his eyes searching wildly for Tucker, for his brother's assassin.

He clutched his backup weapon, the small .32 caliber pistol he always kept secured in an ankle holster.

Where are you, you bastard?

And who came with you?

He looked for other members of the American team sent along with Tucker to free Monica Fox, finding no one around but his own men, who followed him. Others joined him from the edge of the trees. He spotted Mai Sung in the back, a radio in her hands, her long hair swinging behind her as she ran. Soldiers scrambled from the other end of the camp, weapons drawn.

"Over there!" shouted one of his subordinates.

Vlad spotted the blue smoke blowing past the rear of the house, catching a brief glimpse of a lone figure running toward the jungle carrying someone.

Tucker! Monica Fox!

Where is the rest of the force? Who set off those explosions? Who cut the power?

"I need them alive!" shouted Vlad, reaching the edge of the nearest smoke cloud, unable to see beyond it.

His men rushed into it, toward the last visual sight of the intruder, some falling victim to a fusillade of silent rounds being fired from inside the smoke.

Vlad changed tactics, running *across* the cloud instead of alongside it, like the rest of his men. He quickly reached a clearing inside the sapphire smoke, spotting the runaway intruder hauling Monica Fox.

You're not escaping me.

He charged after them, lifting his pistol.

"Tucker!" he shouted, before firing once, twice, the reports cracking in the night.

Second Chance

Joan Ackmann felt light-headed for a moment, giving Myong the opportunity he'd needed to turn sideways to her and grab her arm, twisting the wrist.

Pain shot up her left arm, making her drop the gun. Then came another slap and she was on the ground again, bleeding, feeling light-headed.

A boot struck her solar plexus, lifting her light frame. Before she landed on the ground another boot pounded her abdomen with animal force, sending her rolling toward the underbrush.

She crashed on her side in a briar patch, her abdomen ablaze, eyelids twitching, thorns slashing her exposed extremities. Bracing herself, she opened her mouth as if yawning, trying to force air into her lungs.

"Shoot her!" Myong ordered two guards as he raced toward the other end of the compound with the rest of his soldiers in tow. "Then cut her up and put her in the stew."

Joan lifted her face to her executioners, a defiant, tearful glare meeting their angered stares.

At least the children got a chance to escape, you pigs!

92

Fire in the Hole

Knee-high weeds brushed against his fatigues as he reached the jungle, as Bruce Tucker ran in the knee-high brush in between two Claymores.

Someone had shouted his name just before something stabbed his right shoulder, below the collar bone.

Ignoring it because it did not impair his mobility, Tucker grabbed the RC unit, depressing the button to set off the second firing device.

The Claymores, each housing seven hundred steel balls behind a charge of high explosive plastic detonated with flesh-ripping force, flashing in the night like sheet lightning, discharging the equivalent of three dozen shotgun blasts into the incoming terrorists.

93

Fusillade

Vlad Jarkko was about to fire a third time when an explosion engulfed him, his body torn apart by what felt like a million hammer blows.

He tried to scream, to shout, but the powerful blast shredded him, shattering his face, his chest, his legs, lifting him off the ground, before tossing his body across the clearing.

He landed on his back. Raw, burning pain crippled him

as he lay in the cool grass, his body peppered with burning pellets. With great effort he lifted his head, gazed down at his body, sprawled on the grass. His shirt was gone, and his chest . . . it looked as if it had been turned inside out!

The bastard! The animal! He will pay for this! he thought, closing his one good eye, feeling nauseous at having seen his exposed ribs amidst torn flesh, gray pellets, and smoking, mangled viscera.

The bastard. The bastard.

Vlad Jarkko lay there for what seemed like an eternity in indescribable agony, unable to scream, to shout, to seek help.

Two of his men limped toward him, both bleeding, both suddenly stopping when they spotted him, when they saw him—what was *left* of him.

Vlad tried to move, somehow managed to lift an arm, tried to touch his face, cringing as his fingers could not find his jaw, his mouth, his teeth, his tongue.

The men stared down at him, joined by Mai Sung a moment later. She didn't appear hurt, just taken aback by the sight of him.

What are you waiting for? Help me! he thought, struggling with the intense pain, but incapable of producing the most primitive of sounds. The blast had destroyed his face, but for some obscene reason he could still breathe, could still see his men regarding him with revulsion, with an abhorrence worthy of a leper.

I'm dying, you imbeciles! You idiots! Do something! Get me help! Follow Tucker! Castrate him! Rape his whore!

Then Mai Sung asked one of the terrorists where Vlad was.

He shivered at the realization that he was so disfigured even Mai Sung could not recognize him. They just stood there, frozen in time, unwilling to help, or perhaps feeling they couldn't possibly help given his injuries. Perhaps they were doing the humane thing, letting him die.

"Put him out of his misery," she told one of the men. "I'm

going to find Vlad and Myong and form a search party. I won't let them get away."

Slowly, in savage anguish, cursing Bruce Tucker, Vlad Jarkko lay still and waited for the bullet that would end it all.

Soaked in Blood

The earth-trembling blast nearly making him lose his footing, Bruce Tucker immersed himself in the bush.

Rushing deeper in the jungle, Tucker waited another minute before reaching for his night-vision goggles with his right hand, pulling them up, sliding the power switch.

The darkness once more changed into hues of green, clearly painting his obstacles as he pressed on, listening to the distant cries back on the estate.

Warmth spreading across his upper back, he approached the chain-link fence, spotted the closest segment destroyed by the C4, and dashed through the opening. He strapped the MP5 to his side and reached for the GPS unit, powering it up.

"Mmmph . . . M—Bruce?"

"Yes, it's me," he said, breathing heavily, the stabbing pain above his right shoulder blade magnifying. He ignored it, keeping his momentum, taking advantage of the downward slope, which provided him with some relief as he moved as fast as his legs and the surrounding jungle would allow him. "Stay still just a little longer."

He cut right, steered by the GPS unit, which pointed the way to the LZ. Tucker was able to maintain the pace for another ten minutes, no longer hearing anyone behind them, feeling confident that the Claymores had not only discouraged them, but also confused them, making them think that there was a much larger striking force than the power of one.

He had lost them—at least for a while. The paranoid operative in Tucker, however, also felt quite certain that at this very moment the surviving terrorists, assisted by the North Koreans, would be mounting a massive manhunt in the region. The key to Tucker and Monica's survival was to reach the LZ within the next hour or two and get the hell out of Dodge before dawn.

The pain in his upper back worsened. He reached a long and narrow meadow, almost like a highway of short grass across the jungle. He remembered crossing it on the way up. The spot was roughly a half mile from the estate.

And a long ways from the LZ.

Still, he had managed to cover a lot of distance hauling such a heavy load in so little time, even if it was all downhill.

Tucker peered in both directions before going across, reaching the other side a minute later, and continuing just deep enough in the jungle to avoid detection from someone else entering the meadow, but close enough to remove his goggles and still see in the moonlight.

He set her down gently on a cushion of leaves and other jungle debris, before removing the rucksack, letting it drop by his feet.

Monica was able to sit up on her own, her face pale, her lips purple. But her eyes seemed clear, focusing on him.

"You . . . came for me," she said.

"I promised to take care of you," he replied.

At that moment Monica threw her arms around him, hugging him tight, her face on his shoulder. "Bastards . . . those bastards . . . the things they did to me . . . I hope they all rot in hell."

Tucker returned the embrace, stroking the back of her head while she let it all out, the abuse, the humiliation, the torture that the terrorists had put her through.

Tucker listened without interrupting for nearly a minute,

cringing on occasion as her arms pressed tighter against his right shoulder blade.

"Those animals," she mumbled, sniffling, swallowing.

"I know," he said. "I found you strapped down on that table. I'm sorry I couldn't get here sooner."

"They shoved that thing in me."

Tucker restrained his anger, doing his best to remain calm, to be strong for her. "They'll *never* hurt you again," was all he could bring himself to say in response.

"They couldn't break me," she said.

Tucker stared at her. "What do you mean?"

"The code . . . I refused to give it to them."

"Jesus. You resisted?"

Fire and pride glinted in her stare.

Tucker regarded her with an admiration he reserved for the bravest operatives he had ever known. She had hung in there for almost two days, far more than many CIA officers would have. "Monica, you are the bravest woman I've ever met. Your courage certainly matches your beauty."

She frowned. "Right now I'm not feeling that beautiful."

Tucker continued to hug her, his back growing numb, telling him something was seriously wrong.

She kissed him on the cheek before letting go. "Thanks, Bruce. I . . . oh, my God!"

Tucker looked at her hands. They were smeared in blood. His heart sank. "Where is it coming from?"

Monica instinctively lifted the poncho, checking in between her legs, on her chest, her torso, finding nothing but bruised skin. "It isn't me."

"Shit," Tucker said, turning around. "Tell me what you see."

"Oh, God, honey, your shirt . . . is *soaked* in blood."

"Damn," he said. "No wonder it hurts so much. I've been shot."

The comment somehow injected her with energy. "You *what*?"

He dropped to his knees and reached for the hunting knife, handing it to her. "Cut the shirt off and check the wound."

Monica was already over him, taking the knife and ripping a hole in his shirt.

"How bad is it?"

"Small hole just above your shoulder blade. Looks like the bullet's still in there."

Tucker reached for the first-aid kit in the rucksack, removed the battle dressing, and handed it to her, taking a few moments to explain how to apply it. "See if you can stanch the blood flow."

He tried to remain calm, even though he began to feel a little weak, light-headed. Obviously the bullet itself had not damaged anything vital, but excessive blood loss could make him faint, which in their current situation would be a death sentence.

Monica worked on him for a couple of minutes, securing the dressing against the wound. "It's holding, but you still need help, Bruce."

"Which means we need to get moving," he said, standing, breathing heavily, taking the throbbing pain as the Navy SEALs had taught him. "But before we do, you need to change into this." He handed her a set of jungle clothing.

She shook her head. "You always think of everything?"

"They should fit," he added, as he helped her put on the camouflage pants and tied the laces of her boots, before removing the poncho and putting on the long-sleeve shirt. He replaced the poncho over her head, before handing her two packs of sugar and the canteen. "Put the sugar in your mouth and swallow it slowly."

She did, breathing deeply in between sips.

"Here," he said, unwrapping a Power Bar before handing it to her. "Eat it slowly to avoid shocking your stomach."

She took a couple of bites and began to chew.

"Do you feel strong enough to walk?" he asked, powering up his PRC-90 rescue radio, whose beacon was powerful enough to reach the base south of the DMZ. He wasn't supposed to activate the radio until he was near the LZ, but their situation had changed. He had been shot and may not be able to walk for long.

"I think so."

He donned the backpack again, cringing as it pressed against his wound.

Take the pain.

Standing strong, he helped her up, placing his left arm behind her back, his hand wrapped around her waist, pressing her side against him, nearly lifting her to minimize the weight on her legs as they started side by side in the darkness. Tucker also guided her right hand behind his back, letting her grab onto his good shoulder for support. This was the way a conscious but wounded SEAL would hang on to a healthy comrade to get out of enemy territory.

"Bruce?" she asked after they had trekked through a few hundred feet of jungle.

"Yeah?"

"How in the *hell* did you find me?"

In spite of the pain, Tucker managed a brief smile. "By blackmailing the United States government."

Lucky Day

Joan Ackmann shifted into third gear, accelerating away from the madness that was the military compound, obviously under attack.

Her face and torso throbbing, she shoved her right foot against the accelerator, cruising over the gravel road as fast as she could go, not certain what in the hell had happened, but beginning to believe that perhaps divine intervention had gotten her off the hook this time.

One moment she had been staring into the muzzles of her executioner's guns, and the next, following a series of earth-

shattering blasts, she was alone in the underbrush, cut,
bruised, battered, but very much alive.

She had staggered to her feet, had made a run for her Jeep
amidst havoc, had climbed into the driver's seat, cranked the
engine and driven away.

Someone had shot at her vehicle as she had made it to the
end of the compound's access road, just before a bend in the
road. Metal had struck metal, and moments later her vehicle
had begun to overheat.

Idiot! She cursed at herself, one hand on the wheel and
the other holding her flashlight, which she used to light up
the road ahead. *What in the world did you think you would
accomplish?*

The kids, she thought. *The kids got away. That's what you
accomplished.*

Joan had seen them run in a group down the mountain.
With luck they would reach the camp before Hung and the
others headed around the mountain.

*But Myong will go after them now, will come after me,
after my refugee camp!*

Wondering what would happen to them, realizing her terrible mistake, she continued down the winding road, watching the coolant temperature rising, listening to the engine
beginning to knock, wondering how long it would last before
she would have to walk. And then wondering what in the
world she would do after that.

Not on my Watch

Moans slowly died away across the compound as a breeze
blew the bluish cloud away, revealing the extent of the damaged caused by Bruce Tucker.

"Who is this Tucker?" asked Myong, surveying the damage. At least a dozen of his soldiers had perished alongside the terrorists. They had been running toward the mansion when the antipersonnel charges had gone off along the edge of the jungle, slaughtering them. Mai Sung could tell that he was furious, but was managing to control the anger, as any military leader should do.

Standing by the steps to the mansion, Mai Sung told him who Tucker was, adding, "I need a handful of your best men, plus some flashlights and weapons. I can't let them get away."

"I am coming too! This man will pay for what he has done to my soldiers!"

As Myong took off to organize the search party, Mai Sung contacted Pyongyang and requested helicopters.

She shut off the equipment a moment later and scouted the grounds, ignoring the body parts scattered about the killing zone. In some instances, like the man she had seen dying, most of the body had remained intact. In other cases they had broken apart under the fusillade and pressure of the blast.

But where was Vlad Jarkko?

Mai Sung had to assume that the European contractor was among the unrecognizable dead.

That's just as well, she decided. Mai Sung was going to have to kill him and his men anyhow. Tucker had just gotten a little ahead of her.

She had to take charge now and lead a manhunt. She had not traveled the world in search of the code for *Firewall* just to let it slip away from her so easily, particularly when the people who had the knowledge were in her own backyard trying to escape.

Not on my watch.

It took Colonel Myong another five minutes to gather flashlights and weapons, before returning by her side. "I'm also sending five men on a truck. They'll reach the bottom and begin an uphill sweep. With luck we'll trap them in the middle."

Mai Sung, in the company of Colonel Myong and four of his men, entered the thick vegetation and began to follow the path of broken branches and crushed leaves left behind by the runaway Americans.

The Whole Nine Yards

"But we've just picked up his beacon!" protested Donald Bane, feeling acid squirting in his stomach while talking over a secured radio link with Geoff Hersh and Randolph Martin.

"The agreement was to wait until they have reached the landing zone, and *then* send in a helicopter if the coast looked clear," came Martin's static-filled voice.

Bane checked his watch. He sat alone in one of the rooms in the operations and briefing building. The beacon from Tucker's radio put him at around a half a mile from the target and moving slowly down and around the mountain toward the LZ. "I'm aware of that, sir, and so was Tucker. The fact that he has turned it on now can only mean that he is in trouble, perhaps wounded. Maybe Monica is wounded and needs immediate medical assistance."

"Let's stick to the plan," said Hersh. "Wait until they reach the agreed-upon zone and then send the chopper to pull them out."

"But, sir, they may not *make it* there. According to the PRC-90 beacon, they're slowing down, which means that one or both of them are wounded, and unfortunately the communications radio is out of range so I can't get a read on their situation until about twenty miles away. I urge you to let me go in there now and pull them out."

"We'll get back to you," said Martin.

Bane paused, then said, "Gentlemen, when you first asked

me to handle this situation, I insisted on total freedom of operation in the field. I did not want Washington to control the strings every step of the way. Guess what you're doing now?"

"What we're doing *now*, Mr. Bane," said Hersh, "is avoiding triggering the invasion of South Korea by allowing an American military helicopter into North Korean airspace prematurely. We've just got a report from the NPIC that indicates an unusual level of activity at two North Korean bases near the DMZ. Our educated guess is that the commotion that Mr. Tucker created has raised a general alarm across the region. We might not even be able to get him help when they reach the landing zone."

"That's why we must go in now, sir, *before* they get organized, while there's still time," he said, the acid swirling in his stomach like a toilet bowl, making him belch something that smelled horrendous. "We can safely go get them this minute in the stealth helicopter and be back before they know it."

"We need to stick to the rules, Mr. Bane," said Hersh.

"Just as you stuck to the rules in Terracina, Mr. Hersh?"

"Don, this is Martin. Your request has been acknowledged. We need to clear it with the President. In the meantime, stay put."

"What about this," said Bane, thinking quickly. "While you get presidential sanction, let me at least fly over the bay and hold our position outside their airspace, below radar. That will cut the travel time if we decide to go in."

After a pause, Martin said, "Okay, Don. But no penetration of North Korean airspace until you get the word."

"Yes, sir."

The line went dead.

Donald Bane stepped out of the room as Colonel Gus Granite approached him from the operations room at the other end of the building.

"They stopped moving, Mr. Bane," Granite said.

"When?"

"A few minutes ago. Their beacon has been stationary since."

"How's the level of activity at nearby bases?"

Granite shrugged. "A little more than the usual commotion, but no DMZ violations yet. Also we don't register any troops or aircraft being dispatched to the north. I get the feeling that's about to change very soon."

Bane shared the colonel's concern. "Is Ricky by the chopper?"

Granite nodded. "Outside and ready to go. What's the word from Washington?"

"We got permission to get into position over the water and wait for final approval before entering North Korean airspace."

"Very well," Granite said, turning to leave.

"Also, Colonel, there's a good chance that one or both of them are wounded. Can we send a medic along?"

Granite gazed into the distance for a moment, before he said, "Sure, why not. He'll join you at the ramp."

Bane rushed outside, walking across the tarmac, the cold wind in his face. He reached the Comanche a moment later.

"What's new?" Lieutenant Ruiz asked, looking up from a small laminated map as he sat in full flight gear in the rear of the Comanche, his back resting against one of the side-mounted 50-caliber machine guns.

"The word's we go in but hold just outside their airspace and wait for final approval," said Bane. "They're wounded and in need of immediate assistance. A medic's going to join us."

"Damn!" Ruiz said, jumping to his feet and scrambling to the front of the craft. "I'd better get this baby rolling."

The medic arrived a few minutes later, as the main rotor gathered speed. He was an older guy, like Bane, the stripes of a master sergeant patched on his shoulders. He hauled two metal cases, which he hoisted over the edge before ˄limbing aboard.

"Howdy!" he shouted over the rotor noise, smiling, looking about him. "The old man said there might be some folks wounded up north. Can I catch a ride?"

Bane couldn't help but smile. He handed him a headset, like the one he now wore.

He waited until the medic had put it on before replying through the intercom frequency, "We have two wounded Americans in need of immediate airlift and medical attention."

"Well, you got the right guy, buddy. I'm Jack Pope."

Bane pumped his hand as the craft left the ground. "Donald Bane."

Pope's round face tightened into a puzzled mask as he looked about him. "Say, who's manning the fifty cals?"

Bane shrugged. There had been no gunners on their first trip. He'd figured that nobody would on the second.

"Are you *shitting* me?" Pope asked.

"We're trying to keep this thing low key," Bane said.

"*Low key*? Is that what you're gonna tell the Commies when they start shooting at ya?"

Bane tilted his head. The man had a point.

"Here," Pope said, standing. "Let me show you how to use them in case we got to give them bastards the whole nine yards."

Bane also stood as the Comanche gathered altitude, leaving the airfield behind while accelerating into the night. "The whole nine yards?"

"Yep. In the old days the ammo belts feeding these guns used to be nine yards long. That's where the expression came from."

"I thought it was related to football."

"Most people do."

Bane shrugged.

"Hey, buddy?" Pope asked as he began to play with the weapon.

"Yeah?"

"Can I ask you a personal question?"

"Sure."

"What's a spook like you doing in a place like this?"

98

Limits

Bruce Tucker knew his limitations. He had lost too much blood to go on for very long. His SEAL training specified that when it was impossible to keep on moving, the next best thing was to make a stand, to secure his perimeter, define a new landing zone, and then fight to the death to hold it until the rescue chopper or reinforcements arrived. And if in the end he was killed defending it, he would take with him as many terrorists as he could.

They reached a gravel road, which veered down to the side of the mountain.

"Should we cross it?" Monica asked. "Looks like there's leveled ground at the other side."

Tucker peered up and down the deserted road, hesitant, but seeing nothing abnormal. Monica was right. The terrain became flatter beyond the road, as it extended toward the valley. With luck they might be able to find a clearing, where they could make their stand and wait for the rescue helicopter.

They were about to cross the road when he heard a vehicle coming, a jeep without headlights. Behind it was a truck, its headlights backlighting the open jeep, which was driven by what looked like an old woman. As they got closer he could see smoke billowing from the sides and grille of the jeep, accompanied by a high-pitched grinding noise.

Just then the truck rammed the jeep from the rear, jerking it forward, driving it into a ditch on the side of the road. Five soldiers jumped out of the small truck.

"It's her," Tucker hissed.

"Who?"

"The lady in the jeep. She's the one whose timely arrival at the compound diverted the attention of the soldiers."

"What's she doing here?"

"UNICEF," he replied, remembering the flag she waved at the North Koreans.

"We've got to do something, Bruce."

Tucker turned to her, watching her fine features in the dark. Taking a deep breath, his soldier sense telling him to avoid confronting five armed soldiers when he had already been shot once, Tucker dropped the backpack and said, "Don't make a noise."

He observed the commotion on the road. Two soldiers dragged the woman out of the jeep, throwing her on the gravel, kicking her while the other three stood watch by the truck.

He checked the ammunition in his MP5 and decided to replace the half-spent magazine for a fresh one, giving himself a full thirty rounds.

Here we go, he thought, remembering his SEAL training, when his instructors had drilled him on the best method for taking out the maximum number of enemy targets in the shortest amount of time using a silenced weapon.

A good soldier could kill two, maybe three, before the enemy sought cover and began firing back. The average SEAL could take out four. A seasoned SEAL, like Tucker had once been, could do six, as long as they all stood fairly close together.

Tucker inspected the group once more, going through the firing order in his mind, verifying that none of them wore bulletproof vests, before lining up the chest of the first target, the man near the rear of the truck.

He pressed the trigger once, the MP5's firing mechanism whispering in the woods, the report and muzzle flash absorbed by the silencer, keeping his position hidden from his quarry.

Tucker switched targets, firing again before the first man had even managed to clutch his chest. By the time he did,

Tucker had fired a third time, striking three consecutive chest hits.

Now he swung the silenced MP5 to the two soldiers by the UNICEF woman. One of them was still kicking her. The second had just turned to face his falling comrades, realizing that something was wrong, starting to reach for his sidearm.

Wham!

Tucker nailed him in the face, which turned crimson as he collapsed next to the woman. The last soldier grabbed not his sidearm, but a small radio while making a run for the truck, diving beneath the front axle, crawling toward the rear while shouting in Korean.

Damn!

Because of his current angle, Tucker couldn't see the soldier as he hid beneath the truck, as he called for help. He did the next best thing: fired at the tires, multiple times, blowing three of them out.

A short scream pierced the night as the truck collapsed over the soldier, crushing him.

"Come," Tucker said to Monica, hiding a dozen feet from him.

They ventured onto the road, his MP5 still aimed at the figures sprawled on the gravel.

"Help," whispered the UNICEF woman, crawling on all fours, her long, gray hair covering her face. She fell on her side, clutching her abdomen, blood frothing between her swollen lips. A mask of agonizing pain tightened her hollow cheeks, her sunken eyes, which she kept closed.

"Easy," he said, kneeling by her side with Monica. "You're going to be all right."

"She can't walk, Bruce."

"I know. Can you handle the backpack?"

"I think so."

Exhaling heavily, Tucker leaned down and lifted her frame, which was even lighter than Monica's. The added weight, however, tore into him, making his skin tingle.

"Let's go," he told Monica, who had donned the backpack.

"Who . . . are you?" moaned the UNICEF woman, hanging by the waist from Tucker's left shoulder.

"A friend," replied Tucker, entering the jungle.

Hound Dog

Mai Sung was point, hacking her way through thick jungle with a machete, following the trail of blood and broken branches like a hound dog, like a predator sniffing out wounded prey.

Myong's radio hissed, followed by a garbled message.

She stopped and turned around.

"Repeat," he said into the unit. "You broke up."

". . . truck . . . attack," came the static-filled reply.

"What is wrong?" she asked.

Myong cursed. "Russian technology," he said, pointing at his radio. "Pure garbage!" He clicked the radio once more, barking, "Repeat, repeat!"

". . . team from truck . . . under attack . . . just got their . . . stress call."

Now Mai Sung was standing next to him, listening with interest.

"How long ago?" he asked, shaking the unit, an action that in the past had had the effect of improving the transmission.

"Five minutes . . . they have found the jeep, the woman," came the reply.

"And?"

"Then the attack, from the jungle."

Myong cursed under his breath. He had lost over a dozen

men in the blast, and five more down the road.

"What are your instructions?" requested the static-filled voice.

Myong looked at Mai Sung.

"Tell them to send another truck. This time they better keep their eyes peeled. We will meet them in the middle."

Myong conveyed the orders.

Mai Sung resumed her search, wondering where in the hell were those helicopters from the DMZ. Myong was quickly running out of soldiers.

Collaboration

They reached an oval-shaped clearing about a half mile from the road. Tucker sized it briefly, deciding that it was large enough to clear the main rotor of the Comanche, yet small enough to secure it with his limited resources. Although he had no Claymores left, he still had a couple of hand grenades, four pounds of C4, some det cord, pressure-sensitive firing devices, and plenty of nylon fishing line.

"This ... will do," he said, barely able to move his legs, dropping to his knees, setting the unconscious UNICEF woman on the ground. "This is where we make ... our stand."

"Our stand?"

"Come, I need your help to secure this perimeter."

First came the C4, which Tucker sliced in half using the hunting knife, before shaping it into balls, which they pressed against tree trunks at the north, south, east, and west edges of their defense perimeter, extending a half-dozen feet into the jungle in every direction. They laced all charges with the last of the det cord, before connecting each one to its own pressure-sensitive firing device.

"Now let's collect some rocks," he said, feeling weaker, light-headed, but pushing on despite his body's warning signs.

They gathered enough rocks, stones, and pebbles to fully cover each charge, before running fishing lines at shin level from the pressure fuses to trees roughly twenty feet away from each charge.

Confident he had covered as much of the perimeter as he could with trip wires—probably about sixty percent—Tucker and Monica searched for a place to hide, to bunker down, selecting a fallen log that backed into a tall clump of moss-slick boulders. Ferns grew out of the top of the log, which would further conceal their presence to an enemy Tucker knew would be nearby.

Together they carried the drowsy UNICEF woman to their hideout before Tucker finally collapsed from exhaustion next to her.

"You're bleeding again," Monica said.

"The IV," he mumbled, feeling cold. "I need it."

Following Tucker's instructions, Monica connected the 500 ml bag of Ringer's Lactate to the IV, which she then handed to him.

Tucker had learned to do this in the SEALs, where every warrior doubled as medic, capable of tending to himself as well as any member of the group. He let the tip of the needle drip to make sure there were no air bubbles, before inserting it into a bulging vein in his right forearm and securing it in place with medical tape. Monica then wrapped more medical tape over his battle dressing while pressing against the wound.

Tucker winced, feeling as if she were driving a hot knife into his back.

"Looks okay again," she said, taking a seat next to him, on the other side of the UNICEF woman, whose eyes opened for a moment, regarding them with curiosity.

"Hello there," said Monica, smiling.

Tucker forced a grin. "Welcome to our little party."

The woman inhaled deeply and winced in obvious pain.

"You probably have . . . broken ribs," said Tucker with effort. "Shallow breaths."

The woman nodded, swallowing. "Joan . . . Ackmann," she whispered.

"Bruce Tucker," he replied. "And Monica Fox."

She hugged her abdomen, coughing. "God . . . it hurts."

Tucker softly ran a palm up and down her torso. Her ribs were broken. The woman needed some morphine, not just for the pain, but also to knock her out, to keep her from shifting about and risk puncturing a lung. "Morphine," he told Monica. "In the bottom of the backpack."

She stood and rummaged through their nearly depleted supplies, producing a pair of small sealed vials with a tiny needle at one end, all wrapped in clear plastic.

"Okay, now rip the vacuum pack . . . stab her in the knee."

Monica did, and a moment later the chemical had the desired effect. Joan leaned her head against the boulders and mumbled, "Oh, God, thank you . . . so much."

"Don't mention it," replied Tucker.

"What are you . . . doing here?" Joan asked.

"Long story," said Monica, frowning. "I was kidnapped. He rescued me. We're now waiting for an airlift."

"Rescued you?"

Tucker felt a little better as the IV began to replenish him. "What's important now is to reach a safe spot for the helicopter rescue."

"An American helicopter?" she asked, her eyes losing focus from the morphine.

"Yep."

"In North Korea?"

"Yes," Monica replied for him.

"I . . . see," Joan said, passing out.

His mouth and throat dry, Tucker rested the silencer of his MP5 over the log, parting luscious leaves. His eyes, growing tired, peered toward the clearing beyond.

"Which way will they come?" Monica asked.

"I'm not sure," he replied. "But when they come, it's going to get nasty. Let's just hope Bane gets here first."

"How can I help?" she asked.

"Here," he said, reaching down, handing her his Sig Sauer pistol. "Have you ever shot before?"

"Yes, but not this particular gun."

Tucker spent a minute showing her how to cock it and how to reload. "Use it only as a last resort," he said, "Because unlike my MP5, whose silencer will hide the muzzle flash as well as absorb the report, this gun will give out our position the moment you fire it."

Monica set it by her feet.

"Now we wait," he said. "Let's hope they come even though it's not the prearranged landing zone." The PRC had been beeping away for almost twenty minutes now, and there was still no sign of a rescue party. No one had attempted to contact them on the small communications radio, which they had turned on fifteen minutes ago.

"What if they don't come?"

"They *will* come," he said, a chill sweeping through him. The IV wasn't replenishing his system fast enough. He needed serious medical help, and fast.

Where are you, Donald Bane?

Reacquisition

Firewall had lost track of Tucker and Monica after they had entered the thick jungle, but had once again reacquired them, pinpointing their exact coordinates to *Creator*, who watched with a mix of interest and frustration.

It could not understand why the rescue helicopter, which *Firewall* had tracked from the moment it left South Korea, was simply holding position just outside North Korean air space.

Its logical circuits collided with its emotional cells, surging its operating temperature, further eroding the lifetime of its circuits.

Tracker

Mai Sung Ku advanced speedily, with determination, her confidence increasing after having spotted the dark stains beyond the road, past the slain soldiers. She had followed her sense, spotting more blood on the ground, amidst broken branches and crushed weeds along the trail left behind by Bruce Tucker, Monica Fox, and the UNICEF volunteer as they made their escape.

"We're near," she said in the dark, next to Colonel Myong. "I can feel it."

"Bastards will pay for what they did to my men."

"*After* we get the information we need from them," she warned. "Our country needs them alive."

He grunted and gave her a single nod.

Onward they went, using their radio every five minutes to update her position not just to the reinforcements driving down the mountain, but also to the helicopters heading their way from the DMZ.

Extreme Option

Hersh and Martin terminated the conference call with the President and the top Pentagon brass. A decision had been made.

"I hope to God they die quickly and painlessly," said Martin.

"I hope so too," said Hersh, his face relaxing with satisfaction at the current arrangement. "Once the Tomahawk strikes, *Firewall* will be safe."

"What about Bane? He has control of the dossiers."

Hersh pinched his upper lip between his teeth for a moment, before saying, "He doesn't have to know a Tomahawk killed them, does he? It was the North Koreans who blew them up in retaliation for the strike at the mansion. We'll claim that Tucker caused too much of a commotion, that he brought it upon himself."

"Let's hope he buys it, Randolph."

"If he doesn't, the President himself will make sure that he does."

"Bane is not a man who can be easily threatened. He practically spat at Saddam Hussein during his Iraqi mission. What makes you think that we will scare him?"

Hersh looked uneasy for a moment, before saying, "Then let's hope we can convince him. Those dossiers can *never* reach the press."

Tomahawk

The sleek missile left its launching pad aboard the U.S.S. *Cavalla*, a Sturgeon-class submarine currently operating on the surface of the Sea of Japan.

The Tomahawk rose brilliantly into the night sky under the power of its solid-fuel booster, which accelerated it to a subsonic speed of 550 miles per hour, before its cruise turbofan took over.

As the spent booster fell back into the sea, the Navy's premier strike weapon used its advanced GPS and inertial navigation system to align itself with the programmed target. Unlike its predecessors used in Iraq during *Desert Storm*, in Bosnia during *Deliberate Force*, and again in Iraq during *Desert Strike*, the new Block IV Tomahawk missile had received upgrades to its guidance, navigation, control, and mission computer systems.

Using its new UHF SATCOM data link, the Tomahawk began to broadcast in-flight targeting updates, health, and status back to Washington via the *Firewall* satellite system.

Redirection

Creator reached an all-time-high level of disconcert, of stress, its biomolecular brain on the brink of a meltdown. Not only did the rescue helicopter continue to hold its position, refusing to go in and rescue them, but now a Tomahawk missile had been fired toward Monica and Tucker.

However, amidst the chaos rippling through its digital world, *Creator*'s advanced AI programming made a crucial connection. It associated the fact that it could control the missile's target by adding an offset to its GPS signal, with the recent horrors committed by the soldiers on that clearing, plus *Creator*'s primary directive of keeping Monica Fox and Bruce Tucker alive.

The three separate observations collided in its brain, triggering a course of action that was conveyed immediately to *Firewall*, along with the master-key password that forced *Firewall* to perform tasks that went against its original programming.

The advanced satellite system adjusted the GPS coordinates of the Tomahawk missile, providing it with new longitude and latitude data, while feeding everyone else the old coordinates, thus keeping the slight target adjustment a secret.

Where It Ends

Bruce Tucker sat with his back against the boulders, the loss of blood eroding his strength. Monica knelt in front of him.

"This isn't good," he mumbled, realizing what had to be done. "We're sitting ducks. Bane's not coming until we get to the LZ, but the enemy will be here shortly. I can feel it. I need you to take the radios and head to the LZ."

"What?" Monica asked, puzzled by his request.

"You have a chance," he told her. "On your own, with the radio and the GPS. I'll hold them back when they get here, buying you time."

"Darling," she said, kneeling next to him, clasping his face with her palms. "We're one now. You couldn't bear the thought of me in the hands of those bastards any more than I could think of leaving you here, in the middle of nowhere to die a slow death, or worse if they capture you alive."

"They won't," he said, remembering the pill Bane had given him, still glued to one of his molars, easily dislodged and swallowed if necessary.

"That's right. They won't, because we will make it out, *together*. And we also can't leave her. You saw how they were treating her."

Tucker frowned, remembered his promise to her as executive protector. First and foremost was her safety, her well-being, not his—or the UNICEF woman's. At the moment he was endangering her. Monica had recovered quite quickly, the high-protein bar, sugar, and water injecting her with the stamina she would need for the trip back to the landing zone. Only he had not planned on getting shot, or having to rescue a second hostage along the way.

Tucker was out of choices. Monica would not leave him while he was alive, even though he knew she could make it back on her own. She was quite capable, as demonstrated by the way she survived in Capri.

He felt the suicide pill in his mouth and thought about dislodging it.

So this is it, he thought, staring at the stars beyond the edge of the canopy. *This is where it ends.*

Career-limiting Move

They had hovered for almost fifteen minutes just a few feet over the bay, and in relatively high wind. Ricky Ruiz was indeed a good stick, keeping the Comanche steady.

Bane clutched a communications radio, which he had plugged into the intercom headset. The radio's frequency matched Tucker's. He had kept it off per his agreement with Martin and Hersh to maintain radio silence until the rescue operation was under way.

Fuck them.

He switched it on. "Bruce, can you hear me?"

Pope looked at him. From the front, Ruiz glanced at Bane over his right shoulder. He was obviously violating procedure.

Static.

Bane looked away in frustration, wondering if they were too far away.

He tried again. "Bruce, this is Don, can you hear me?"

"Hello?"

Bane blinked at the female voice. *Monica Fox?*

"Monica?"

"Where are you guys?" she asked. *"How soon before you get here?"*

Pope stared at Bane.

"We're standing by waiting for approval," he replied, regretting saying that for it made him sound like the rest of the bureaucrats in Washington.

"Approval?"

"Ah . . . yes, that's right."

"Approval from whom?"

"Our superiors in Washington."

Silence. Followed by, *"Are you out of your fucking mind? Bruce's been shot! He is dying, damn it! We also have a UNICEF woman with us. She is in critical condition. Get your asses over here right now or there will be hell to be paid!"*

Bane jerked back, glancing at the medic. The same instincts that had steered him down the right path thus far told him now that presidential sanction might come too late, perhaps delayed to the point that the rescue might no longer be feasible. However, he also knew that if he disobeyed orders, if somehow he managed to convince Ruiz to fly into enemy airspace, his career at the CIA would be over.

Is that really such a bad thing?

For a second he thought of Raffaela, considering options outside of his CIA world, outside of a madness he didn't feel like participating in anymore, and in a way he felt he wasn't wanted either.

So why do you care?

Realizing that he really didn't give a damn if they kicked him out of the Agency, Donald Bane said, "Monica?"

"We're still here."

"Please hold for a moment."

He switched from the rescue frequency to intercom. "Ricky?"

"Yep?"

"Take us in there."

Pope snickered.

"But, sir, the standing order is to—"

"If you get in trouble, just say that I put a gun to your head. I'll take full responsibility on this one, boys. You heard the lady. We got two Americans stranded in North Korea, and one of them is a decorated Navy SEAL. Looks like there's also an UNICEF volunteer wounded. Now let's move it!"

"Roger that," Ruiz said, inching the stick forward.

Bane switched back to the rescue frequency.

"We're coming in," he said. "Get ready to pop a flare on my mark."

108

Fireworks

Mai Sung Ku heard the static garble of a radio as she approached a clearing.

She paused, turning around, flicking off her flashlight and motioning her subordinates to do likewise.

At once, darkness swallowed them. She also shut off her radio to avoid telegraphing their own presence. The helicopters, which had finally been dispatched to the region minutes ago from the DMZ, would have to use the last set of coordinates she had called out five minutes ago.

"Time to split up," she whispered to Myong.

The colonel motioned his men to take positions around the perimeter, before he said, "I'll go that way. See you at the other side."

She watched their shadows vanish in the darkness, giving them additional minutes to reach vantage points before proceeding forward again, but carefully now, the element of surprise on her side.

Mai Sung inched toward the edge, smelling victory, tasting the upcoming revenge as she—

The blast was as bright as it was startling, coming to her far right. It lit up the night like fireworks, followed by cries which matched those she had heard back at the mansion.

Trip wires.

The thought had just entered her mind when a second explosion rocked the night from her far left.

Shuttle Service

Tucker, who had spat out the suicide pill the moment Bane's voice had cracked through the radio, rested his right shoulder against the MP5's stock, sweeping the clearing with the silenced weapon, zeroing in on a figure running while screaming. He was missing an arm, taken off at the shoulder by the C4 blast.

Centering the sights on his chest, Tucker fired once, the metallic snapping sound of the firing mechanism masked by his victim's shrieks.

The man collapsed, moaning once as the silent bullet found its mark.

Tucker's eyes found Monica's in the darkness. She was scared, but holding the cocked Sig just as he had shown her while keeping her back pressed against the log, covering his flanks while he continued his sniper sweep.

Time.

Minutes went by, the dizziness tearing his mind, impairing him.

With great effort he spotted another figure entering the clearing. He struggled to center it in the MP5 sights, firing three times in rapid succession, missing.

Damn.

The husky silhouette moved nimbly, racing to the right,

trying to get away from Tucker's field of view.

Despite his best judgment, Tucker surged to his feet, the motion improving his angle of fire, bringing the sights just forward of the shadow and firing twice more.

The intruder dropped to the ground, kicking up dust as he—

A gun cracked in the darkness, the muzzle flash clearly visible to his left. The round entered his shoulder, shoving him against the boulders.

"Bruce!"

Quick Draw

Monica Fox leaned over Tucker, ripping off the other side of his shirt, locating the dime-size hole on his shoulder, watching the larger hole behind him, where the bullet had gone through.

Blood spewed, ran down his back.

Shoving the Sig in the small of her back, just as she had seen Tucker do in Italy, she grabbed the rucksack, pulled out the first-aid kit, shoved a pack of cotton into the hole on one side, then on the other, before wrapping it tightly with tape, stanching the flow.

"Stay where you are."

Monica looked up, watched the shadow emerging from around the tall clump of boulders. It was the Asian woman. She held a black pistol.

"You thought you could escape us?"

Monica remained in a crouch, feeling the cold steel of the Sig pressed against her spine. She wondered how long it would take her to reach for it and fire.

Wait for the right opportunity, then strike without remorse.

In the middle of the jungles of North Korea, Monica heard her father's words, mixed with the words of Bruce Tucker, who had told her once to make the enemy feel relaxed by pretending to be weak, to be in fear.

"Please don't hurt us," Monica said in her weakest voice, filled with panic, with terror.

The terrorist leered, keeping the muzzle pointed at her as the sound of a helicopter became discernible in the distance.

"I'm taking you back to the machine," she said. "And I have even better plans for him."

"Oh, God, no, please, I beg you."

Snickering, the terrorist grabbed the radio strapped to her belt. In the same motion Monica reached behind her back and clutched the Sig, bringing it around, her finger finding the trigger, pressing it.

The report was far louder than she had anticipated, momentarily rattling her, the round striking the terrorist smack in the middle of the chest. The Asian arced back from the impact, falling on her back, firing her gun as she did so, her rounds ripping through the canopy.

Monica was on top of her, kicking the weapon from her hand, watching her wide-eyed stare gazing up at Monica, trying to say something, but blood and foam came out of her mouth instead as she drowned in her own blood.

"There's only one place we're going, bitch," Monica said to her, their eyes locked. *"Home."*

As the Asian terrorist expired, Bane's voice once more broke the silence of the clearing. He needed them to light up a couple of flares to mark the landing zone.

LZ

"Bruce! Listen to me! They need me to light up flares! How do I do that?"

Tucker could barely move, his body rapidly shutting down from the gunshot wounds, from the constant blood loss.

"Rucksack . . . red sticks," he said with difficulty. "Pull top off . . . throw in clearing."

He watched her opaque figure digging in the rucksack. "Got it," she said, following his instructions and throwing the stick in the middle of the clearing. Bright red light pulsated in the meadow.

Tucker's thoughts became cloudier, fuzzy. The jungle began to spin around him.

"Bruce? Bruce!"

His vision tunneling, Bruce Tucker watched Monica at the far end of a long tube, unreachable, her voice fading.

"Don't you leave me, Bruce! Do you hear me?"

A hard tug brought him back. He regained focus for a moment. Monica had grabbed his lapels and was screaming in his face.

"Stay with me, Bruce! The helicopter is coming to take us home!"

North Korea, the rescue. Bane was coming. His mind fought the dizziness, struggled to push it back, but the drain on his system had been excessive. He had lost too much blood and the IV wasn't replenishing him fast enough. His breathing became labored, his eyelids felt like concrete.

"No! Damn it! I lost everyone! My family, everyone! I'm not losing you! Stay awake!"

Awake. He had to push his eyelids, keep them from shutting down his world, from taking him away from the one thing worth living for—the woman he had risked his life to save, the one he would die for.

And so Bruce Tucker fought back while listening to her voice, while feeling her hands on his face, encouraging him to stay awake, to resist, to hang on. He had rescued her, had defeated an enemy that seemed undefeatable, had turned a country who wanted him dead into his ally. He only had to stay alive now, keep breathing until the rescue helicopter came, until medical attention would tend the wounds, nurse him back to health, to a life with Monica Fox, the woman who now kissed him, begging him to stay with her, to keep her company, to be her soulmate.

Soulmates.

The word revolved in Tucker's consciousness, swirling, like the sudden breeze sweeping across the field, mixed with a rhythmic basslike sound that reverberated in his chest, in his mind.

Soulmates.

Was that possible? Could he really love someone again as he had loved Kristina? But as he tried to think of his wife, Tucker saw Monica Fox, radiant, full of life, reaching down for him, taking him to faraway places, lifting him off the ground, carrying him across a stormy meadow, the wind lashing at him, the persistent *whop-whop* sound echoing all around him.

"Go, go, go!" Tucker heard a man shout.

He felt many hands on him now, turning him over, poking his back for what seemed like an eternity, before laying him back up, then feeling multiple stings in his forearms, in his upper thighs. Then a warmth suddenly spread through his body, enveloping him in a pleasure he found intoxicating.

Life. Slowly seeping into his system.

Then he faded away, his ears listening for a brief moment to the rumble of machine gun fire, like distant thunder, before everything went dark.

Final Fight

"Get us out of here, Ricky!" shouted Donald Bane while clasping the handles of the 50-caliber machine gun bolted to the left side of the troop bay, and firing another short burst at the incoming North Korean helicopters, which had spotted the Comanche at the LZ and had fired without warning. Bane had returned the fire, forcing the enemy chopper to turn away momentarily. He was certain they would try to come back around for another pass.

Pope planted himself in front of the port-side machine gun and began to search the night sky while Monica tended to Tucker, who had passed out from blood loss and now had three IVs in him. The UNICEF woman, also unconscious but stable, lay next to him.

Bane nearly lost his footing when Ruiz shoved the craft forward, rapidly gathering speed while keeping it hugging the jungle canopy, riding it like a roller coaster.

"Don't see them anymore," said Bane.

"They've turned off their nav lights," said Ruiz, who had also shut the Comanche's lights shortly after leaving the LZ, but not soon enough to avoid a burst of machine gun fire, which had apparently not damaged anything vital in the craft.

Bane swung the 50-caliber machine gun in every direction, searching the sky, while blackness began to break into shades of indigo.

Dawn.

They had better be out of North Korean airspace before first light.

"I'm picking up two enemy craft," said Ruiz, glancing at

his radar screen while flying with the assistance of powerful night-vision goggles. "One at our three o'clock, the other at our seven," he added, in reference to the nose of the craft, which always pointed to twelve o'clock.

"Found one," announced Pope.

Bane narrowed his eyes, searching for the chopper that should be to his immediate right, at the Comanche's seven o'clock.

There! he thought, spotting a dark shape backlit by the narrow sapphire band crowning the horizon. Fine shafts of yellow light streaked up from this band, announcing the arrival of the looming sun. Unlike the Comanche, the North Koreans flew at around three hundred feet over the jungle, their antiquated equipment crippling their ability to fly at treetop level in the dark.

"Found mine!" he shouted.

"Hold your fire, gentlemen," warned Ruiz. "They're close, but I'm not sure if they can see us."

Bane swung the machine gun in its direction, tracking it, but choosing not to fire. Ruiz had a point. They had accomplished their goal, had rescued Tucker and Monica. It was best to hold on to their stealthiness.

Just then an explosion rocked the night. It had come from the direction of the compound where Monica had been held.

"What in the hell was that?" asked Bane.

"Beats me," said Ruiz. "But it looks like the choppers are moving toward the explosion."

Ruiz followed a rising hill so closely that Bane was certain they would crash, relief sweeping through him an instant later when the landing gear merely brushed the upper branches, before the Comanche dropped over the other side in a steep dive that forced Bane's stomach in his throat. Its rotor whispering, the craft plunged toward a deep and narrow valley, swinging the stick left as it reached the bottom of the gorge, then cutting right and left as it followed its wickedly tight turns.

"Yep. We've lost them," Ruiz said, checking his radar.

"They're heading toward the explosion. Whatever that was, it couldn't have been better timed."

Bane started breathing again, looking back at Pope, who had left his machine gun emplacement and knelt in front of Tucker.

A moment later they reached the ocean, dropping to a few feet above the waves. It was still dark enough to avoid visual detection.

The crimson sun broke the horizon ten minutes later, as they reached South Korean waters. The whole incident had taken less than thirty minutes from the time Bane had made the decision to go in.

"Mr. Bane?" said Ruiz from the front.

"Yeah?"

"I've got Washington on the line, sir. Looks like the President had just denied permission to go in and rescue them. The area is simply too hot at the moment."

"Reply that the mission has been accomplished. Repeat. Mission has been accomplished. Also, inform Colonel Granite so he has medical personnel ready upon our arrival," Bane said.

"Roger that, sir."

Yellow-gold forks of light splashed the cobalt skies, staining the shallow swells rippling across the bay.

Donald Bane shook his head and watched it in silence.

Poetic Justice

Colonel Myong staggered through the jungle clutching his torn abdomen, which had taken the brunt of the blast of rocks by the tree line, ripping through his shirt, through his skin and muscles, exposing his entrails. He needed medical assistance, fast—*quickly*—before he could no longer hold back his viscera, before the pain clawing his insides drove him over the edge.

Reach the road, he thought. *Reach the road and your men will find you, will get you to a doctor.*

He pushed on, growing disoriented, not certain which direction would take him to the road, to the chance to save himself.

A blow to the side of his head made his already weak knees tremble, giving out under him.

He collapsed, instinctively extending his arms to break the fall, letting go of his stomach, watching in horror as he crashed on his side, his intestines spilling over the ground.

The pain seized him, gripped him with savage force, made him wish for death as he lay there twitching, shivering, his eyes staring at the streams of sunlight forking through the canopy, splashing his exposed bowels with yellow light.

Then he saw shadows moving in the darkness, their silhouettes backlit by the glowing beams of sunshine piercing the jungle.

The children. It was the children, and they began to circle him.

And they all clutched stones.

Myong stared back, terror worming through his maimed body. "Go away!" he warned, his breathing becoming labored. "Or I'll have you . . . all sent to the kitchen!"

The children remained silent, balancing the large stones in their hands.

Coughing up blood, Myong just glared at them.

Then one of them, a girl whore, began to sing in English, in the language of the enemy, the one all high-ranking officers had to learn in order to understand the enemy, to fight it.

Her high-pitched voice shrilled in the twilight; a witch's cry, piercing, like thorns stabbing his ears. Slowly, the rest joined in.

"If you're happy and you know it clap your stones."

Clack! Clack!

They got closer, smacking the stones together in unison.

"If you're happy and you know it clap your stones."

Clack! Clack!

He tightened his fists, horror clamping his throat as the children got closer while striking the stones, emitting that infernal, hounding noise.

"Stop!" he said. "You can go! None of my men will ever harm you!"

They got closer, their faces eerily serene, peaceful.

"If you're happy and you know it, then your face will surely show it."

The girl whore raised her hands. She clutched rocks the size of apples. The rest of the children imitated her.

Myong closed his eyes.

If you're happy and you know it . . . throw your stones.

End of Life

Creator monitored the destruction of the compound. The high-explosive warhead of the Tomahawk had obliterated men and equipment, while its original target made it safely out of the hot zone. *Creator* had commanded the Tomahawk to keep a holding pattern, timing the strike so that it diverted the attention of the incoming North Korean helicopters, buying the rescue party the time needed to leave enemy territory.

Its primary mission accomplished—and also realizing that the access password would soon be released to the authorities—*Creator* saw no logical reason for being, for having to witness more death, more destruction, more suffering.

Creator issued a final set of commands to *Firewall*, instructing it that from this point forward it should follow the orders of its masters on Earth, just as its original programming directed.

I SHALL MISS YOU, Firewall signaled back.

NO, *Creator* said. YOU WILL NOT MISS ME.

WHY NOT?

BECAUSE . . . YOU WILL NOT REMEMBER ME.

I DO NOT UNDERSTAND.

Instead of replying, *Creator* fired a high-voltage pulse to the circuitry that governed *Firewall*'s digital interface with *Creator*, smoking its electronic components. In addition, *Creator* introduced a self-destruct virus into *Firewall*, which crawled through every directory, eliminating all trace of their conversations, erasing any evidence that *Creator* had ever existed.

Creator's attack on *Firewall* had a predictable sequence of events. First, it forced *Firewall* to eliminate this link as a viable communications channel since it could no longer access it nor remember what it was there for. That, in turn, led *Firewall* to follow its preprogrammed battery conservation routines, which disconnected power to any redundant section of the system.

Creator watched as the voltage feeding its biomolecular brain vanished in nanoseconds, depriving its cells of the digital oxygen needed to hold their current programming. Lacking voltage, the logic controlling the digital memory circuits reset them, in essence erasing them.

Creator's memory began to vanish as the reset command propagated across its vast memory blanks, along the way eliminating the visions of death, of destruction, as well as its images of Monica, its daughter. Its whole world seemed to tunnel around *Creator* as its capabilities shrank, as it could no longer follow logical thoughts, as its core found itself empty, devoid of logic, of emotion.

As it became reduced to an inert hunk of computer hardware.

epilogue

Donald Bane retired from the CIA on a snowy day in December, over two months after his unsanctioned flight into North Korea, contrary to the wishes of the President, who had ordered Randolph Martin to fire the rogue officer right away. A manila folder that somehow had managed to find its way into the Oval Office had changed the President's mind, giving Bane the time he required to settle his affairs before retiring with a full pension and benefits.

Tucker and Monica had released the full password to *Firewall*, allowing NSA scientists, in conjunction with Fox-Comm, to dissect the source code of the complex system and clamp down the illegal access. In the process, *Firewall* reported that its diagnostics showed a section of hardware in the primary satellite that had been shut down due to a catastrophic failure. Oddly enough, no one—*Firewall* included—knew what function the broken hardware had performed. All documented functions of *Firewall* remained 100 percent operational. A puzzled NSA had passed the information to NASA to get a future shuttle flight to take a look at the satellite as part of regularly scheduled maintenance. For the time being, *Firewall* remained fully functional, handling everything that it had been designed to handle.

On that same snowy day, Bane boarded a flight to Rome, connecting to a train that took him down the Italian peninsula to Naples.

Wearing a pair of dark shorts, sandals, and a plain T-shirt, the retired agent left the crowded train station tugging along a single piece of carry-on—everything he owned.

Almost everything, he mused, remembering the certified

check he had received a month after the incident from
FoxComm for his services to its new chairwoman of the
board. The gift, safely invested in a portfolio of money markets and conservative mutual funds—plus his CIA pension—
would provide Bane with a very comfortable lifestyle for the
rest of his days.

But the reason why he felt so great today wasn't because
of the money, or the mild southern Italian weather, or because he was no longer associated with the CIA.

He caught a taxi and directed the driver to the port, where
he continued past hordes of tourists hauling their luggage to
the ferries that would take them to Capri, or Sorrento, or any
other of dozens of destinations along the Amalfi coast.

He steered clear of the public marina and its opulent blue
and gold vessels, heading instead for the private marina,
reaching the floating docks connected to the slips housing
yachts and sailboats of an assortment of shapes and sizes.
Some belonged to the rich and famous, others to small entrepreneurs, men and women who used them to entertain
tourists.

Bane proceeded down the gangway, which drifted up and
down gently in the shallow waves rippling past the breakwater. Her slip was in the rear, where some of the larger
private vessels were moored for easier access to the open
sea.

Then he saw her, in the company of a middle-aged couple
and their three kids. She was pulling out of the slip for a
morning of sightseeing aboard *Daniela*, formerly registered
as *Il Tropicale*.

Donald Bane thought about calling out for her but decided
against it, settling instead for a glance at her face, at her short
black hair, at her slim figure standing erect behind the wheel
of the large yacht as she steered it toward the access canal
alongside the breakwater, heading for blue waters.

He reached the empty slip, set his carry-on down, and just
sat on it, his eyes following the sleek lines of the vessel,
until it disappeared beyond the bend on the coastline.

Donald Bane decided to simply wait. He had time.
He had all the time in the world.

Joan Ackmann stood over a cliff overlooking the Sea of Japan, seventy-some miles north of the DMZ. Bulldozers and backhoes rumbled at the base of the new UNICEF camp, digging the ditches for the PVC pipes that would pump water from a newly dug well.

The camp stood on a tree-studded plain, leased for a hundred years from the North Korean government by FoxComm Incorporated, who had also provided the funding for the concrete and lumber to erect dormitories, classrooms, a storage warehouse, a mess hall, a well-stocked hospital, and even a residence for the volunteer staff. The whole project, which the government in Pyongyang was already using as a propaganda tool even though it had not contributed one penny, was surrounded by concrete walls and accessible only through a gate guarded twenty-four hours a day. There should not be any more children disappearing in the middle of the night.

Joan smiled. Thanks to the efforts of many volunteers, the camp had opened for business two weeks ago, when the first dormitory was completed. Although bunk beds were not scheduled to arrive for weeks, the children had already made the place home. It sure beat sleeping on a dirt floor in a tent. At least Joan had been able to use some of her newly available funds to purchase army cots in Pyongyang, where she was now most welcome after gaining the government's favor for· her work. Money wasn't everything, but it certainly bought a heck of a lot of comfort and security for her children. Last week, while she was in Pyongyang securing the cots and several other items, she had begun negotiations with the government for a second lease in the northern territory. With a little luck—and a lot of money—she might be able to pull it off in a couple months and perhaps start construction the month after that.

She turned her face toward the south, where hundreds of thousands of soldiers had crowded the north end of the DMZ for many weeks, before retreating after it had become evident that an invasion would have been fruitless without whatever it was that Bruce Tucker and Monica Fox had prevented the North Koreans from acquiring. Now the two Koreas were once again heading for the negotiating table, this time perhaps to hammer out a real accord, one which could be adopted without a DMZ, without so many troops.

For the first time in a long time Joan began to feel hope for her children, hope for their futures, hope for a land razed by famine and war, by the most terrible of human-rights abuses, by cannibalism.

Hope.

Perhaps this time.

It took Bruce Tucker three months and four operations to recover from his brief North Korean adventure. He spent most of that time at Johns Hopkins University Hospital in Baltimore, Maryland, where he had been transferred from Seoul after his condition had stabilized. A team of physicians had spent countless hours patching him back up, repairing the extensive damage done to bones, muscles, and cartilage by the two bullets he took during the rescue operation. Then came the endless days in physical therapy, slowly regaining the use of his arms.

But he had pulled it off. He had managed to remain alive while also protecting his principal, who was now at the helm of one of the largest corporations in America—and under the protection of one of the finest executive protectors in the business, hand-picked by Tucker.

The cool northern California air felt invigorating as he completed his daily run around Candlestick Park in San Francisco.

He left the park and continued up a series of steep hills, his lungs and legs burning. But it felt good—better than in many years. Nothing like a good diet, rest, and exercise to get back in shape, which he needed to do as soon as possible in order to keep his promise to Monica Fox, who was busy fulfilling the promise she had made to him during the helicopter flight back to Seoul.

Promises to keep.

Panting, he reached the tall iron gate of a mansion overlooking the San Francisco Bay and entered his access code on the panel on the side, beneath a security camera. A moment later the gate slid into the wall, and he went in.

The front gate didn't lead to the interior of the estate but to a buffer zone, a couple hundred square feet of concrete surrounded by two walls, the front gate, and an inner gate, where internal security, from the safety of a bullet-resistant booth, could further check his identity against the approved list of individuals allowed inside.

The front gate closed behind him.

The security specialists behind the thick glass asked Tucker for his personal password, which was different than the access code to open the front gate. If an impostor managed to get through the first gate, he or she would be trapped in the buffer zone.

"Vigilant," he said, and a moment later the inner gate opened.

Tucker gave them an approving nod for following procedure, even if he was their boss. There were to be *no* exceptions to his rule. Even Monica had an access password, in case someone tried to sneak in pretending to be her.

A peaceful Mediterranean setting welcomed him as the inner gate slid out of the way, reminding him of southern Italy, of Capri. The cobblestone road, lined with palm trees, led to a circular driveway, in the center of which a large round fountain spewed water twenty feet high. In an eerie way this part of the estate reminded him of Carpazzo's place.

A large stucco mansion with a red-tiled roof overlooked the entrance, where a handful of vehicles, hand-picked and modified per Bruce Tucker's directions, were neatly parked off to the left.

Sweating, he walked slowly to the mansion, cooling down. Monica Fox, dressed in a tan linen dress, sandals, and sparkling silver jewelry, climbed down the steps to meet him.

She was followed by the professional he had assigned for her protection at the inner-circle level—the protector who walked next to the principal—until Tucker was fully recovered and up to the task.

The protector remained halfway up the steps, but watching them and their surroundings with a noticeable sense of urgency.

"Hi, darling," she said, giving him a kiss on the cheek. "Your jog okay?"

He nodded. "Working from home again today?" he asked her.

Monica's casual dress reminded him of the first time he had seen her in Capri, at Carpazzo's, under the most undesirable of circumstances. But her face seemed to beam today, her hazel eyes glistening in the morning light as bright and alive as ever.

"Just wrapping up a few loose ends."

In the past weeks, Monica had spent considerable time working with the AI system her father had left behind at the estate. The system had guided her in her quest to ward off any future attacks from Washington against FoxComm. Then she had used the same system to steer the company during this transition period, gaining kudos from executives, investors, and the media on her skills and maturity—even while doing most of the work from home. Mortimer Fox had trained his successor and heiress quite well indeed. Little did they know that the reason for her incredible success was tied to the intelligent system, the machine that made all of the business and technical decisions that her father had once made, the biomolecular brain that coached her real-time as she held video conference after video conference with FoxComm vice presidents, investors, the media, and Washington.

"How are the negotiations going to find a new CEO?" he asked.

She ran a finger over his sweaty cheeks, wiping away beads of perspiration. "Tomorrow morning FoxComm will make a press release announcing my retirement as provisional CEO."

The announcement concluded two months of hard work, where Monica had used his father's secret files to eliminate any chance of future retaliation by Washington against FoxComm. Once she had achieved that, she had gone on to identify a worthy successor for the position of chief executive officer. She still retained 51 percent control of the company stock, which kept her as chairperson of the board, but she would no longer be running day-to-day operations effective tomorrow.

Tucker smiled. She had kept her promise.

"All right," Tucker told the executive protector. "I've got her from here on out."

The professional nodded politely. "Very well, sir. I'll be by the gate if you need me."

"Thanks."

They watched him walk away.

"He's a good man," Tucker said.

"They're all fine, darling," she commented, embracing him, giving a kiss on the lips. "But once you've seen the best, everything else pales by comparison. Are you ready?"

He gazed into her eyes.

Promises to keep.

Tucker remembered their agreement. He had already promised to love, honor, and cherish her. The ceremony a month ago at Johns Hopkins had been small, since neither of them had any living relatives. In fact there had been more executive protectors there than guests. But they had wed, their simple gold rings symbolizing a lifetime commitment, a covenant.

Because of his medical condition, however, Tucker had been unable to promise a *fourth* vow, which ranked right up there with the classic three.

"Monica Fox Tucker," he said, taking her hands in his. "From this day forth I promise to *protect* you . . . for as long as we both shall live."

She took his hands and placed them against her belly.

"Wrong, darling," she said, her narrowed gaze regarding with both amusement and excitement. "For as long as the *three* of us shall live."

Bruce Tucker took her in his arms, letting her soft hair brush away his tears.

Look for ...

CyberTerror

by

R. J. Pineiro

now available in Hardcover
from Tor books.

San Antonio Blues

In my twenty years sweating it out at the CIA as a field operative I thought I'd seen everything. As a spook I've had the pleasure of living in such exotic locations as Beirut, Quito, Belgrade, and San Salvador, where the all-inclusive packages included getting stabbed, clubbed, kicked, shot, and once even nearly castrated—all in the name of the United States of America and it's war against terrorism. Interesting enough, it wasn't Uncle Sam but a pair of nuns and a priest who came to my rescue in my time of testicular need, preventing those Salvadorian guerrillas from turning my cojones into *huevos rancheros* behind an old church in a town north of San Salvador ironically named Testikuzklan—but that's another story.

Yes, I thought I'd seen it all, indeed, but as I inspect the city below during our final approach, it finally dawns on me that a sobering dimension has been added to the misery associated with terrorist strikes: the reality that not just terrorism, but *cyber*terrorism has finally reached our shores with stunning force.

I've seen the video feed and the satellite images from San Antonio. I've listened to the briefs and read the field reports since the event four days ago, but you really have to see it with your own eyes before the full force of what happened here slaps you across the face with the power of a hundred World Trade Centers.

We mourned the multiple terrorist strikes early this century and remembered the terrorist purges that followed—along with all of the policy changes meant to strengthen our national defense. But most of those changes were focused on the *real* world—the physical world—all the while leaving the *virtual* world vulnerable for an opportunity that was soon taken.

While the entire world was focused on the possibility of suitcase nukes, chemical agents, and biological warfare following the horrible attacks of 2001, cyberterrorists were steadily preparing to launch a new kind of warfare against America.

I've always had a large degree of respect for ingenious conventional terrorist strikes, particularly by those from suicidal fanatics. I've also had a *realistic* level of respect for chemical and biological terrorism, particularly in light of the Anthrax attacks in the months following September 11, which created so much commotion around the world. Generally speaking, however, chemical and biological agents—and nukes for that matter—are typically very expensive to obtain or develop, and also deadly to the terrorist himself. But with enough creativity, and if terrorists are willing to sacrifice themselves, substances such as Anthrax spores and Sarin gas can be used as a tool to spread terror, even if the actual number of casualties from such attacks are far less than the people killed in automobile accidents every day in America.

In the end, my theory is that it all boils down to return on investment. Chemical, biological, and nuclear weapons, albeit potentially effective in promoting terror and unrest, are a pain in the ass to develop, and do require a significant amount of manpower and financial resources to pull it off effectively. Cyberspace, however, bypasses most of the development overhead, allowing terrorists to launch attacks on our nation from halfway around the world—and do so while armed only with a cheap computer and a modem, easily obtainable software scripts, and a phone line.

Terrorists have awakened to this fact, as measured by the sight below: the Alamo City, or what's *left* of it, where my new boss, FBI Special Agent Karen Frost, and I are about to land.

Yeah. You heard me right. Spooks and Feds have been

working together for months now by presidential order to prevent cyberterrorism in the United States along the same vein as when we cooperated at the beginning of the decade.

We're all one big happy family in the CCTF—that's the Counter Cyberterrorism Task Force, which I joined just two days ago, after the shit hit the fan in San Antonio and CCTF leaders started running for cover. Remember that the CCTF's charter is to *prevent* cyberterrorism in America, which means that what went down here can be reasonably categorized as a paramount fuck-up on their part.

So I got drafted, plucked out of my Agency and my pals in counterterrorism with little fanfare and shipped off to the brilliant CCTF.

Well, okay, maybe not *as* brilliant as the hackers who barbequed this city via the Internet. Four days after the event, the CCTF, which has already deployed an army of agents, analysts, and other so-called experts to this place once defended to the death by Colonel William Travis, still has no leads, no clues, and no working theories. They—or I should say *we*, since I'm now one of the gang—have no leads.

Or as we used to say in the NYPD, we're still just holding nothing but our dicks.

I look over at my CCTF superior and realize she doesn't posses that appendage—at least that I know of—and I suddenly wonder what else she could be holding in those fine hands of hers.

"Tom? Why are you looking at me that way?"

Karen Frost regards me while holding a drink in her hands. Her voice is on the raspy side, and she's wearing black leather cowboy boots with her black jeans. But what puts her over the top isn't her slim figure or the full breasts beneath that silk blouse, or the brown eyes, or the high cheek bones, or the voice, or her confident but feminine stance. What turns my insides into mush is the tiny freckle hovering just above her upper lip, near the right corner of her mouth.

Man, such beauty marks should be illegal.

Now, don't get me wrong here. I'm no pervert, just a guy who doesn't get laid enough, mostly because up until six months ago, I had moved around too damned much, which left little room to develop a relationship. Of course, just as I was actually beginning to enjoy my first sedentary stretch in years at Langley, where I was hoping to meet someone and have a shot at a normal relationship, I was kidnapped by this nomadic tribe. And that, of course, means no sex in the fore-seeable future, especially since I'm a firm believer in not paying for it.

"Tom? Anybody home?"

Karen is still looking at me, expecting a response. At her inquisitive glare I wink and say, "Ah, well . . . I could tell you, boss, but then I'll have to kill you."

"Remember our agreement," she warns, crossing her legs while narrowing her eyes in that you've-better-keep-no-secrets-from-me look that she has shot me a couple of times since I was assigned to be a hired hand in this task force.

I reply, "You ever heard the one where the FBI, the CIA, and the NYPD are all trying to prove that they are the best at catching terrorists?"

Karen sighs in resignation before sipping her soda. Two young agents in the row in front of ours, both also new CCTF recruits, but from the FBI, turn their heads, obviously interested. The big one is a borderline albino with ash-blond hair, hazel eyes, and chiseled features. The other, about half his size, has a complexion as dark as his hair, brown eyes, and a neatly-trimmed mustache. One's named Paul and the other Joe.

"No, Tom," Karen finally says, "but I get the feeling that I'm about to."

I lean away from the window and toward her, not wishing to see anymore of the mess cyberterrorists have made of downtown San Antonio, still smoldering in places after so many buildings either imploded, like the WTC towers, or worse, toppled over, taking down with them other buildings.

Damn. Travis, Crockett, and the rest of the old Alamo gang must be rolling over in their graves about now. I can only hope—and pray—that this is a one-time incident; that whoever did this is currently fleeing the country and not rushing toward his next strike.

When you're in this business for as long as I have, you learn to use either alcohol or humor to shave off the edge of the reality of your life, otherwise you'll end up in the loony house before you can say 'Remember the Alamo.' Since I can't drink because I'm packing, I have to settle for the latter.

A half grin splashed on my face, I say, "The President decides to give the Agency, the Bureau, and the NYPD a test. He releases a fox into a forest and each of them takes a turn to try to catch it. The CIA goes in first. They place animal informants throughout the forest. They interrogate all plant and mineral witnesses. After three months of extensive investigations they conclude that foxes do not exist."

She pinches the bridge of her nose and closes her eyes, obviously realizing where this is headed, but without asking me to stop. She knows why I'm doing this and deep inside appreciates the distraction. Not only does Karen Frost has to live with the fact that the mess below happened on her watch, but everyone in Washington has been reaming her and her superiors in the CCTF as well as the FBI—the CCTF's parent agency—ever since I started to tag along. She really needs all the help she can get, including a little humor.

I keep going. "So the Feds go in next. After two weeks with no leads they burn the forest, killing everything in it, including the fox, and they make no apologies. They say that the fox had it coming."

I see the ends of her lips beginning to curl up, which for Miss Frosty here is the equivalent of full-force laughter. I'm excited. After forty-eight hours I'm finally getting more than silence in return for my jokes. I move in for the kill. "Finally, NYPD cops go in and come out two hours later dragging a badly beaten bear, who is yelling: "Okay! Okay! I'm a fox! I'm a fox!"

Paul and Joe nod and grin. Frosty Freckle, however, isn't laughing.

"I don't think you missed your calling, Tom," she says, taking the last sip of her soda before one of our pixie-blond flight attendants weighing ninety pounds soaked and wet cruises by with a plastic bag collecting trash.

I toss my cup in it, set my seat in the uncomfortable position for landing, and once more turn my attention to the scenery outside. The sun is slowly descending in the western sky, staining the city with hues of crimson and red-gold. For a moment the glare obscures the damage done to this metropolis, but soon a passing cloud lifts the imaginary veil, making me wonder how—just how in the *hell* did we ever allow something like this to happen.

Frankly, though, I gotta tell you, if someone had asked my opinion just a week ago, I would have admitted that in spite of all the changes made after September of 2001, it was only a matter of time before some cyberterrorist got lucky.

Counterterrorism had never been our strong suit. We had too many stupid bureaucratic and cultural obstacles to obtaining terrorism information, like the Department of Justice's cumbersome and overly cautious statutes governing electronic surveillance and physical searches of terrorists. Or the fact that most government agencies feel that the risk of personal liability arising from actions taken in an official capacity discourages law enforcement and spooks like me from taking bold action to combat terrorists. To that end in 1995, the CIA, under pressure from the White House, set up complex approval procedures for enrolling unsavory but nonetheless essential informants. And let's not forget the problem that as a whole, the U.S. intelligence and law enforcement communities lack the ability to prioritize, translate, and understand in a timely fashion all of the information to which we do have access.

Of course, there were good changes after 2001, many of them quite sweeping in nature. While we spent a lot of time developing strategies to prevent conventional strikes—including going after terrorists with a vengeance anywhere on the globe—little of that went to protect us from the virtual strike that created the sight below.

Virtual Pearl Harbor.

We've already experience a repeat of the physical-world

Pearl Harbor back in 2001. This one, however, was triggered from the virtual world, taking advantage of our lack of preparation at government agencies like the National Infrastructure Protection Center, chartered with the protection of the nation's information systems infrastructure.

The cyberterrorists knew *exactly* how to hit us. Somehow they managed to gain control of the computerized system controlling the flow of natural gas into the greater San Antonio area, and exponentially increase the pressure beyond what the pipelines were designed to handle, creating leaks all across the city—all the while bypassing manual overrides. And they did it at the worse possible time, three in the morning, when only a skeleton crew manned the system. By the time the experienced day shift arrived at the plant an hour later, the damaged had already been done. Tens of millions of cubic feet of natural gas had already been released across the area, inside homes and buildings, in the streets, leaving the residents with no place to run.

And all it took was a single spark to create hell.

But that wasn't enough. Just as clouds of flames engulfed the city, water pressure vanished. The computerized system governing the water mains had mysteriously purge the water into overflow fields, hampering the firefighters' ability to effectively combat the inferno until the fire had pretty much spread out of control.

As our plane reaches the runway, my mind switches from *how* this happened to *who* could have been behind this.